cass freeman

decision trees

Bryan H. Kelly

cass freeman

decision trees

By Bryan H. Kelly

Foreward By Elva Hick Glover

Technical Editor Elinor Velasquez, Ph.D.

Freeman Press
Oakland, CA

CASS FREEMAN: DECISION TREES

Published by **Freeman Press**
Oakland, CA
freeman-press,com

ISBN: 979-8-9925667-0-3

Library of Congress Control Number: 2025902513

Cover Design by **Ulises Mendicutty**
Technical Editor: **Elinor Velasquez, Ph.D.**

This is a work of fiction. While this story may reference actual people, places, or events, these references are used fictitiously. The characters, events, and incidents depicted are the product of the author's imagination. Any resemblance to actual persons, living or dead, beyond those mentioned in a fictional context, is purely coincidental.

For permissions, inquiries, or bulk orders, contact:
freeman-press.com

Printed in the United States of America

First Edition

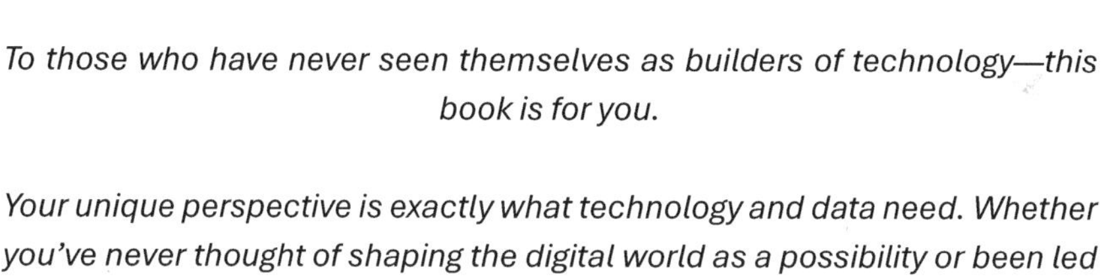

To those who have never seen themselves as builders of technology—this book is for you.

Your unique perspective is exactly what technology and data need. Whether you've never thought of shaping the digital world as a possibility or been led to believe it's not for you, know this: your creativity, your determination, and your unique way of seeing the world are the very qualities that will drive more inclusive, transformative solutions for a better tomorrow.

The causes you care about, the communities you love, and the change you envision are waiting for innovations only you can imagine. Let this moment be the spark that fuels your drive to learn, build, and create. The path to technology doesn't require a specific background—only the willingness to dream, grow, and build with all of who you are.

"I counted everything. I counted the steps to the road, the steps up to church, the number of dishes and silverware I washed... anything that could be counted, I did."

— Katherine Johnson,

Pioneering NASA mathematician in space exploration and computing

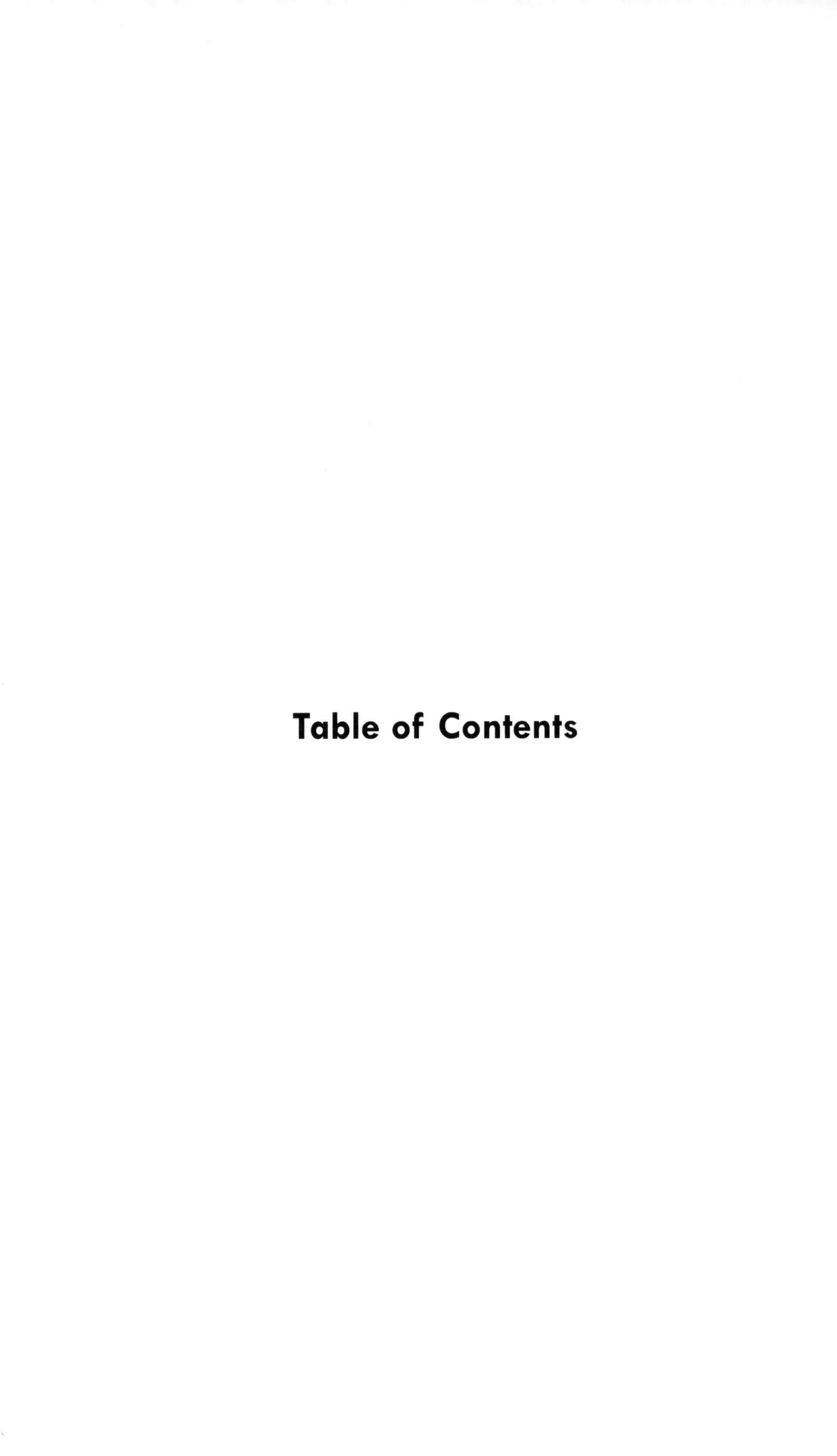

Table of Contents

Foreward

As I read Bryan Kelly's *Cass Freeman: Decision Trees,* I was reminded of the timeless words of Khalil Gibran in *The Prophet:*

"Your children are not your children.
They are the sons and daughters of life's longing for itself.
They come through you but not from you,
And though they are with you, yet they belong not to you.
You may give them your love but not your thoughts,
For they have their own thoughts."

These lines beautifully reflect the journey of young Cass Freeman, whose story reminds us that our greatest gift to the next generation is to nurture their curiosity and independence. Through determination and a spark of scientific discovery, Cass takes her first steps into a future shaped by her vision and power.

Growing up in Shadyside, Maryland, with my grandparents, it was my aunt who first introduced me to the wonder of numbers, teaching me to count to 100—a small milestone that set me on the path to a lifelong career. In mathematics, I found a quiet language that spoke to me, offering clarity and precision in a complex world. This early foundation helped me see that mathematics wasn't just numbers; it was a key to understanding the world and unlocking the mysteries of science.

This story fills me with hope. Bryan Kelly captures the magic of that first spark, when a young mind discovers that science, technology, engineering, and mathematics offer unique lenses through which to view and shape our world. He reflects the importance of mentorship, something I experienced firsthand during my 34-year career at NASA's Goddard Space Flight Center. Encouraged by a teacher who believed in my potential, I joined Goddard in 1960 as one of five Black female mathematicians. While others had arrived before me, I was the youngest of the group. During my time there, I worked on significant projects including the International Ultraviolet Explorer, contributing to discoveries that transformed our understanding of space.

When young readers see themselves in characters like Cass, they will recognize their own potential in any field of science and innovation. This book, like my journey, shows what unfolds when natural curiosity meets opportunity and determination. Mathematics, with its patterns and logic, provides the foundation that connects all STEM disciplines - whether you're coding algorithms, designing bridges, studying ecosystems, or exploring space. Whatever your personality, background, or circumstances, there is a place for you in these fields. Each perspective brings unique insights that enrich our collective understanding and drive innovation forward.

The tools of science and technology have evolved dramatically since my early days at NASA, from slide rules to supercomputers to cloud computing and AI, but the fundamental process remains unchanged: observe, question, analyze, discover. In Cass's world of decision trees and data science, I see echoes of the same analytical thinking that guided our early space exploration work, now applied to new frontiers.

In Cass Freeman's story, we see how analytical thinking combines with imagination to solve complex problems. Through her experiences, we're reminded that scientific pursuit, in all its forms, helps us better understand the world and our place in it. Bryan Kelly has crafted a narrative that honors both the rigor of scientific thinking and the quiet determination it takes to pursue one's path in science, technology, engineering, or mathematics.

Elva Hicks Glover
1995 Retired Mathematician, NASA Goddard Space Flight Center

Root Node

The root node is the foundation of a decision tree, the starting point from which every branch grows. It represents the central question or challenge that must be addressed. From this single node, the structure begins to form, and the flow of decisions takes shape. Like a seed, the root node contains the potential for countless outcomes, each determined by the paths and splits that follow. It's the origin, the anchor, and the core of all possibilities.

THURSDAY, JUNE 27

Cass, a lanky 16-year-old girl from Oakland, hunched over her laptop, her fingers tapping a staccato rhythm across the keys. Braids framed her face, and the glow from the screen reflected off her gold-rimmed glasses. Large gold hoops dangled from her ears, one adorned with a small targus piercing that caught the light. She wore a vintage Aaliyah T-shirt tucked into faded overall shorts, the straps loose on her frame. A flannel shirt was knotted around her waist, its worn fabric draping over her thighs. Her bare feet rested on the floor.

'Almost there,' she muttered, pausing to adjust a slide on her screen. Printouts and notes on asthma prevalence in West Oakland lay scattered around her. A scholarship letter from the Quintin Hale Foundation was pinned to the wall, its corners curling slightly.

On the top bunk near the window, Ayesha, a 17-year-old Indian high school senior from Mountain View, rested against several pillows, her long, thick braid draped over one shoulder. The bedside lamp cast a warm light across her deep brown skin. Dressed in a well-worn NASA hoodie and leggings, she balanced her laptop on her knees, fingers moving quickly over the keys. She glanced up. "Remember our first week? You spent half of day one wrestling with Python installs," she said, a faint smile shaping her words. "You looked ready to trash your computer when the environment wouldn't work."

Cass paused a slide on her screen, then pushed a loose strand of hair behind her ear. "I was sure I'd never get it done in time for the first lab," she replied. She reached toward the Quintin Hale packet pinned to the wall. "My grandparents were excited when the scholarship came through for this boot camp. Dad, too—though he kept mentioning they'd miss me at the restaurant."

Ayesha closed her laptop with a soft snap. "Well, that means he cares," she said.

Cass nodded at the notes on her desk. "He just wanted me working hostess shifts. But being here feels like I'm doing something bigger for everyone back home." She angled the laptop screen.

Ayesha powered down her own computer. "You'll turn into a spreadsheet if you don't rest," she said lightly. "We have a final presentation tomorrow. Let's not fall asleep halfway through."

Cass tapped a few keys. "I'm almost done verifying the node splits in our decision tree," she said. "We can't have random outliers skewing the correlation."

Ayesha looked toward the darkened window. "We've been at this for hours," she said, stepping down from the bunk. "I'll wait another day to see if my parents still think I should be some Kaggle 'Grandmaster.' You can wait another day to perfect everything."

Cass chuckled. "They really say 'Grandmaster'? Sounds like they're mixing data science with chess." She shook her head. "It's an odd title."

"Yeah, well, half the group here last year were junior coding experts. My parents expected I'd level up, too. But these skills take time," Ayesha said.

Cass eyed a line of code. "Should we swap the random forest model for logistic regression?"

Ayesha set her water bottle on the desk and pressed a few keys. "Logistic regression is easier to interpret, but our data has non-linear patterns. Random forests handle those better." The updated metrics appeared on the screen. "We'd lose some nuance from the tree-based splits. These categories need that complexity."

Cass reverted to the previous setting. "Thanks for catching that," she said.

Ayesha shrugged, then nodded at the slides Cass had prepared. "Ready to show me the rest?"

Cass clicked to the next slide, revealing bar graphs and heat maps highlighting high asthma rates in West Oakland. "I grew up there," she said, entering data on her laptop. "I used to think inhalers were normal for everybody. All my friends had them in their backpacks."

Ayesha watched the graph. "Seeing these stats is intense," she said, tapping the screen. "West Oakland's rates are nearly double the national average, and people don't realize how traffic pollution factors in."

Cass clicked to another slide. "Many trucks reroute through residential streets," she said, her tone sharpening.

Ayesha glanced at a separate chart. "It's bigger than just data," she remarked. "You're highlighting the neighborhood where your grandparents still live."

Cass brought up a map of pollution hotspots. "Mom's driving down from Oakland for tomorrow's presentation," she said, setting the keyboard aside. "She works at a clinic after her nursing shifts, and it's a long trip, but she insisted on coming."

"Real data, real experiences," Ayesha said. "It's not just a title or a project."

Cass shut her slide deck. "I'll ask Isaiah for a final check on the correlation table," she said, her fingers tapping lightly on the desk.

Ayesha grabbed a binder lying near the lamp. “Sure, I’ll bring him these references,” she said, sliding the binder under her arm. “Also, remember you added the KQED truck-ban article to the appendix. It proves how commercial traffic affects certain neighborhoods.”

Cass glanced at her phone. “Thanks for reminding me,” she said, typing out a quick text. “I’ll let him know.”

Ayesha stepped toward the door. “Finish up,” she said lightly. “But don’t pull an all-nighter. Better to show up alert.”

Cass gave a small nod. “I’ll stop soon,” she said, though her fingers continued to hover over the keyboard.

Ayesha slipped out, the door clicking shut. The lamp’s buzz matched the subdued hum of Cass’s laptop fan. Cass glanced at the last bullet points on the slides, reversing a minor tweak. Laughter and footsteps passed along the corridor.

Moments later, a low chime sounded on Cass’s computer. She increased the lamp’s brightness and squinted at a Discord window that had popped up.

TheFreemanBoys: “Cass, are you there? Mom and Dad have been arguing. Something about a collector calling the restaurant while Mom was at work.”

Cass typed quickly. “Archer, Carver, you two should be asleep. It’s late.”

TheFreemanBoys: “We’re serious! Something’s off! Dad even slammed a door!”

She checked her phone—no missed calls. Her fingers tapped once on the desktop. “I’m coming home after my presentation tomorrow,” she typed.

A beep sounded in the hallway, and the mini-fridge clicked on with a soft hum. The Discord indicators switched from Online to Offline. Cass stood, crossing to the closet. She grabbed a duffel bag from the shelf, the nylon scraping gently. She tossed it onto the lower bunk, the zipper rattling against the mattress.

While she was tossing a few clothes into the bag, the doorknob turned again. Ayesha walked in, a textbook under her arm. She paused at the sight of Cass’s duffel bag. “What happened?” she asked.

Cass spoke without looking up from the desk. “My brothers texted. Mom and Dad are arguing at home. Something about a collector. Archer and Carver sounded spooked.”

“Hey, hey, Cass. Hold on.” Ayesha locked eyes with her, her warm hands gently holding Cass’s cold fingers and guiding her to breathe. “Just breathe slowly, okay?

Let's think this through... think through the actual data with me."

Cass nodded.

"Okay, good... let's slow down. What exactly did they tell you? What information do you have, Cass?" Ayesha asked, her voice firm but soft.

Cass pointed to her laptop on the cluttered study desk. She wanted to explain but couldn't find the words. Ayesha flipped open the screen and scanned through the twins' chat.

"So, from the 'data' you got from your 'source,' we can gather two facts for now," Ayesha said, pacing her tone to emphasize each point. "One, your parents have been arguing. Two, they've been at the restaurant more, leaving your brothers home alone."

Cass stared at the dimly lit desk lamp; its glow shone brighter the longer she looked into it. She blinked, then covered her face with her hands, trying to block out the overwhelming thoughts swirling in her mind.

"Hey, I understand why you're upset, and it's okay to be afraid." Ayesha placed a hand on Cass's arm, her voice firm but soft. "I'm not trying to dismiss your feelings with logic here, but think about it—if it was really serious, wouldn't your parents, or someone at the restaurant, have called?"

Cass stared down at her phone. "I tried Aunt Zora. She didn't pick up."

"Listen," Ayesha said, sitting on the edge of the desk. "You've been away from home for almost six weeks. That's the longest you've been away, right? And tomorrow's this huge presentation we've been stressing about..." She paused, choosing her words carefully. "Sometimes when we're already on edge, our brain goes straight to worst-case scenarios. Like, your first instinct was to pack a bag and bolt."

Cass looked at the half-packed duffel and let out a shaky breath. "I guess I did kind of jump into panic mode."

"Totally normal reaction," Ayesha said. "But let's take a beat here. Mom's coming tomorrow for the presentation. You can talk to her then, figure out what's actually going on."

Cass paused briefly, then nodded. "You're right," she said. "I overreacted."

"That wasn't an overreaction, that was a full crashout in progress," Ayesha said with a slight grin. "You went from zero to packed bag in like, two minutes flat."

They spent the next hour adjusting references and confirming data sources. Cass focused on West Oakland's health issues, while Ayesha refined the technical sections. Occasionally, Cass glanced at her phone but found no new notifications. They both worked in near silence until Ayesha stepped away from the desk.

"That's enough," Ayesha said, stacking the last pages. "I'm going to bed."

Cass nudged the duffel aside with a foot and flicked off the main light. The streetlamp cast long, angular shadows across the room, stretching over the desk and up the walls.

The room quieted, the only sounds the soft rush of air through the vents and the distant murmur of campus life outside. Headlights from passing cars traced lines across the dorm wall. Cass pulled a red notebook from under her pillow, the university seal embossed on its cover. She clicked her pen and jotted down a few brief figures.

When she finished, she set the notebook aside. The phone on her desk remained silent. Outside, the distant noise of the dorm slowed, and the room stayed still. Cass lay back, her eyes closing as the gentle hum of the building filled the room.

THURSDAY, JUNE 27 | JOURNAL ENTRY

6: The weeks I've been at this camp, learning, grinding, pushing through. First week? Thought I was finna get humbled by Python. Now? I'm out here running decision trees like I was born for this. But, I miss home. I miss real food. I miss my people.

0: The convos I had with my parents today. No texts, no calls. They always busy, but I should've known something was up. I been so caught up in my own world, I didn't even peep the signs.

2: The number of times Ayesha told me to go to bed. Girl, I hear you, but we not finna embarrass ourselves in this presentation tomorrow. Plus, my brain won't shut up anyway.

12: The hours I spent making sure our final project was airtight. Bar graphs, heat maps, correlation tables—I got it all. Ain't no way I'ma let some sloppy analysis take us out. Data don't lie, and neither do I.

14: The slides in our deck. Every single one gotta hit. If Professor Avery don't look at this and see that I ate, I'ma be sick.

500: The data points I analyzed to get our model right. People out here playing chess—I'm playing with air quality statistics and asthma rates. We not the same.

73%: The accuracy of my predictive model. Could be better, but you know what? I was out here fighting for my life against dirty data. This is a W. The last 27%? That's just room to grow.

3: The seconds I actually let myself feel proud before my brothers hit me with that "Cass, you there?" text. Instant stomach drop.

1: The packed duffel bag sitting at the foot of my bed. I was ready to run home on sight. Didn't even think twice. Just threw in some sweats and my laptop like I was on a mission.

10: The deep breaths Ayesha made me take before she let go of my hands. "Think through the data." That's what she told me. Like I wasn't already running numbers in my head trying to make sense of this mess.

4: The ways I tried to convince myself everything was fine. If it was that bad, Mom or Dad would've called, right? But they didn't. Which means... either they don't know, or they do and don't want me to.

15: The times I checked my phone waiting for another text from Archer and Carver. They went ghost. That's what scared me the most.

7: The times I whispered just one more slide before I finally shut my laptop. Ayesha ain't let me pull an all-nighter, but I wasn't finna sleep easy anyway.

30: The minutes I laid in bed staring at the ceiling, trying to count my own thoughts like data points. If I had a scatter plot of my stress levels, the trend line would be ugly.

∞: The questions running laps in my head. What's happening at home? Why ain't nobody called? What am I finna walk into after this presentation? And the worst one—what if it's already too late?

FRIDAY, JUNE 28

The first streaks of morning light stretched across the lower bunk, nudging Cass awake. Around her, the dorm came to life—doors opening, showers running, footsteps moving hurriedly in the hall.

Her phone screen lit up as she reached for it, squinting at two messages sent in the early morning hours.

“Got called in early, doing a double today. Isn’t Lola going to be there?” her mother’s message read.

Below it, from her father: “Sorry, babygirl, not going to see you in action. I know you’ll do great. Can’t wait to have you back at the hostess stand.”

Cass rolled her eyes and set the phone face-down on her blanket. Across the room, Ayesha was still in her sleep shirt, sorting through hangers in the closet.

“What’s up?” Ayesha asked, pulling out a blouse.

“Mom got called in for another shift.” Cass’s fingers traced the edge of her phone case.

Ayesha turned from the closet. “After everything last night, too. Must be important for them to work today.”

“Isn’t it always?” Cass’s voice carried a practiced sarcasm.

She rolled her neck with an audible crack. “Whatever. Let’s get ready,” she said, pushing off the blanket.

Cass pulled a navy dress from the closet. The bathroom door clicked shut, then opened minutes later as a knock rattled their room.

“Cass, Ayesha, you ready?” Isaiah’s muffled voice carried through the wood.

“Just a minute!” Ayesha called back. “We girls have to look perfect!”

“Don’t believe the hype, y’all,” Isaiah shouted. “Just do you. Whatever makes you feel comfortable is what counts.”

Cass tapped her heel against the floor. “Yes, we are,” she said, adjusting the hem of her dress. “When it comes to style, both brains and beauty have to be on point.”

Ayesha opened the door. Isaiah stood in the hallway, practically bouncing on the balls of his feet.

“You look ready to conquer, Cass! Those shoes are killer,” he said, eyes widening.

Cass clicked her heel again. "Lola's idea. She swears shoes like these help with confidence."

In the hallway, they clustered together for a photo as other students streamed past. The scent of coffee and whiteboard cleaner lingered, mixing with the buzz of fluorescent lights overhead. Laptop bags bumped against hips, and dress shoes clicked against the linoleum.

Isaiah laughed and gave Cass a light nudge. "She might be right. There's a rumor about a prize for the best data project—maybe an exclusive event to meet top professionals. Time for the big show."

Ayesha adjusted her bag strap, checking the pen secured in its outer pocket. "I heard Marcus and Jin's wildfire prediction model is pretty solid," she said, "but our air quality data is going to knock it out of the park."

The scent of coffee and whiteboard cleaner hung in the air as students filled the hallway, their laptop bags bumping hips and dress shoes clicking against linoleum.

"Time to show them what we've got," she added, joining the flow of students.

Cass fell into step with Isaiah, who was muttering under his breath, rehearsing his section. "And as you can see from these confidence intervals..." he gestured to an imaginary screen, then stopped and shook his head. "No, that's not right."

They pushed through the dorm's side entrance into crisp morning air. The path ahead lay in shadow of tall redwoods, and Cass tugged on a light cardigan, smoothing its sleeves. She walked in step with Ayesha and Isaiah, inhaling the leafy scent carried by a mild breeze.

Soon, the conference center came into view, its glass facade reflecting the early sun. Through wide automatic doors came the aroma of strong coffee and the low murmur of practicing students. The air conditioner inside added a gentle hum to the background. They passed small groups rehearsing lines, the tap of keyboards sounding between hushed conversations.

A large display case near the auditorium entrance showcased a carefully curated collection of photographs and artifacts celebrating the contributions of women in STEM. At its center, a striking portrait of Katherine Johnson stood prominently, her poised expression radiating quiet brilliance. Below her image, bold text displayed one of her most famous quotes:

"I counted everything. I counted the steps to the road, the steps up to church, the number of dishes and silverware I washed...anything that could be counted, I did."

Surrounding her portrait, smaller photographs and documents highlighted the legacies of other pioneering women in science and mathematics, each frame telling a story of perseverance, innovation, and groundbreaking achievement.

Cass paused, reading the quote. She smoothed the edge of her dress, her fingers grazing the fabric before falling still.

"She's amazing," Cass said, her eyes on Johnson's image. "If she guided entire missions into space as a 'human computer', we can handle our data project."

Ayesha leaned in, adjusting the zipper on her bag. "She noticed every detail," Ayesha said. "That's what we do with data—counting every step."

Cass glanced between Ayesha and Isaiah. "Thank you," she said quietly. "Six weeks ago, I couldn't analyze a dataset. Now we're presenting on asthma stats. Feels unreal."

Ayesha gave a small nod. "We've come a long way."

Isaiah clasped his hands together. "Let's back each other up. If one of us slips, the others step in."

The digital display above the auditorium doors flashed 9:00 AM. Students streamed past them, laptop bags swinging, voices rising with last-minute questions. Cass studied her reflection in a nearby display case, then her lips curved into a smile.

A bright banner labeled DATA SCIENCE FOR SOCIAL GOOD: DATA IN ACTION pointed them to the correct auditorium. Cass slowed slightly, letting Isaiah and Ayesha flank her. She matched their pace.

"All set?" Ayesha asked, rolling her shoulders.

Isaiah tapped his closed laptop. "Data, slides, references—everything's ready."

Cass brushed her hand across the strap of her own bag. The digital clock above the auditorium read 8:55 AM, and a cool draft from the air conditioner brushed her wrist. She inhaled quietly, then exhaled in time with her steps.

"Let's do it," she said, lengthening her stride. "Data Science for Social Good, here we come."

*****

The auditorium stretched before Cass in neat, concentric rows of chairs, each seat angled toward the stage in gentle tiers. She entered with Ayesha and Isaiah, guided by the steady hum of conversation and the occasional hiss from laptops starting up. A quiet expectancy pervaded the space, intensifying when a chair squeaked or a stack of papers shifted. Overhead, the vaulted ceiling amplified the rustling of notes and the creak of folding seats. Vivid banners in blues, reds, and golds lined the walls, each marking milestones from past cohorts. Cass slowed briefly when she noticed Stanford's emblem among them, the distinctive tree logo giving the event an added sense of formality.

Near the entrance, long tables covered in white cloth displayed poster boards and flyers. Some showcased 3D models, others featured colorful infographics. Cass paused to read a few titles—projects on climate analytics and resource optimization—then continued after Isaiah, who moved confidently through the narrow aisle with one arm around his notes.

"We should run through our transitions again," Ayesha said, leaning closer, her voice quiet.

Cass set down her laptop on a small foldout table. "Sure, let's do it." Together, they went through each part of their presentation, keeping their voices low. Isaiah lightened the mood by joking about tricky Q&A moments, drawing small smiles from Cass and Ayesha.

The house lights dimmed. Conversations faded, broken only by the shuffle of people settling in. From Cass's position, the stage lights cast a glow across the polished floor, illuminating the microphone and podium. Above the curtains, Stanford's logo appeared under low lighting. Cass pressed her fingertips against her laptop, pausing as the room fell silent.

A slight stir near the front led her to spot Professor Avery—short silver hair catching the spotlight—as she stepped onstage. Applause spread across the auditorium, and Cass clapped along, watching the professor's composed stride. When the clapping receded, a tangible anticipation settled over the assembled rows of seats.

"Good morning," Professor Avery began, her voice carrying throughout the room. "Today, we celebrate a moment when data moves beyond mere information and becomes a driver for human progress." Cass sat upright in her seat, listening as Avery spoke about future possibilities shaped by data-driven innovations. "Imagine using data to detect disease outbreaks before they start," Avery said, "or optimizing resources to benefit entire communities. Data must be a force for sustainable solutions."

Onstage, the professor continued describing data's influence in environmental science, healthcare, and social justice. She cited a project that harnessed open-source data to mitigate flood risks in coastal towns. Cass tapped a key on her half-lit laptop, glancing at the stage as Avery spoke about the power of such tools when directed at real-world challenges.

"Each data point represents a story, a life, an outcome," Avery concluded. "Our role is to interpret and act on these narratives. With deliberate focus, we can uncover hidden patterns and direct those insights for the greater good." Applause spread through the auditorium. Cass pressed her palms together in applause as Isaiah joined in with an animated grin, while Ayesha offered an approving nod.

As the lights stayed low, the crowd stirred with renewed conversation. Ayesha's phone vibrated, drawing Cass's attention. "She made it," Ayesha remarked, showing her screen. "My mom found a seat in the back." Moments later, Ayesha greeted someone behind them—a maternal figure with similarly deep brown eyes—who pressed a quick kiss to Ayesha's cheek. Cass checked her own phone and read a text: "See you soon, Lola." She raised her eyebrows slightly, scanning the rows until she spotted Lola's wave, to which she responded with a brief grin.

They stood and moved toward the stage steps at the side. Their names were announced, and they proceeded onto the stage. Each footstep echoed on the wooden floor. Cass briefly spotted friendly faces among the audience, including Lola's encouraging smile, which seemed to keep her poised. At the podium, she adjusted the microphone, drew in a measured breath, and prepared to speak.

"Good afternoon, everyone," she said, introducing herself in a steady voice. "I'm Cass Freeman, here with Ayesha Patel and Isaiah Harris. Today, we'll be sharing our research on the impact of freeway pollution on asthma rates in Oakland."

Behind them, the first slide lit up, displaying a map with color-coded markers. Ayesha clicked forward as Cass continued. "Nearly twenty percent of children in Oakland have been diagnosed with asthma," she said, pointing to a chart. "Those numbers represent entire neighborhoods near Interstates 880 and 580, where pollutant exposure is part of daily life—leading to missed school days, missed work for caregivers, and crowded hospital waiting rooms."

Isaiah then explained the data layers they had combined, flipping through bar graphs and heat maps. Cass kept a hand on the podium, remaining still as the slides showed comparisons across states. "Here," Cass said, indicating a key statistic, "some Oakland zip codes face triple the national average in hospitalization rates. We also found a clear correlation between these hotspots and freeway proximity."

She moved to the next slide, where potential solutions appeared: tree planting, new emissions regulations, and broader use of home air purification units. Ayesha described the recommendations with an even tone, and Isaiah outlined how local decision-makers could adopt these measures. Their final slide displayed a statement of hope in bold letters. Cass cleared her throat and spoke once more.

“Thank you for listening,” she said, bowing her head in acknowledgment. “We hope this project inspires further investigation and prompt policy changes that prioritize public health.” Applause rose around them as they left the lectern. Under the stage lights, the entire scene seemed bright and clear. Professor Avery came forward, her expression reflecting approval.

“Excellent work,” the professor said, looking from Cass to Ayesha and Isaiah. “Your integrated approach—connecting environmental and health data—truly shows data science’s potential.” Cass gripped the remote, standing beside her teammates as applause filled the space. The audience’s response and the professor’s words together marked a fulfilling conclusion to all their preparation.

*****

After their presentation, the Q&A session turned into a lively mix of questions. One student asked about the geocoding techniques they’d used; another pressed for details on data validation. Pens scratched notepads as attendees absorbed the responses. Cass stood with Ayesha and Isaiah, noticing how people gravitated toward them with curiosity. The Head of the School of Computer and Data Science focused on geocoding methods, while a Professor of Mathematics and Statistics discussed validation approaches. Visiting professionals gave approving nods, senior lecturers praised their slide structure, and tutors offered tips, eager to see the analyses in real-world applications. Some handed over business cards; others wrote notes on the printed programs, excitement in each exchange.

“Can you believe it, Cass? We did it!” Isaiah said, his voice raised above the ambient chatter, lightly nudging her shoulder. Clusters of students navigated the hallway, relieved post-presentation.

“We really did,” Ayesha added, smiling at Cass. “You were brilliant up there. Could go pro, you know.”

Cass let out a small laugh, glancing between them. “Thanks, but I never could’ve done it alone.”

“Teamwork,” Isaiah quipped, sweeping his arm theatrically, drawing a grin from a student nearby.

“And caffeine,” Ayesha teased, miming a toast with an invisible mug. They shared a brief laugh, relief in each motion.

Cass glanced down the hallway, scanning the crowd for Lola. She spotted Lola waving from a distance and waved back, waiting as Lola threaded her way through.

“Hey, you were all fantastic,” Lola said, stepping up with an enthusiastic grin. She handed Cass a cup of milky tea and black pearls. “Especially you,” she joked, nudging Cass’s shoulder. She held out more cups. “I’m Lola—I got boba for everyone. Didn’t know your flavors, so I went with my usual favorite.”

“Thanks, Lola,” Cass replied, juggling her laptop bag and the cold drink. “This is Ayesha, my dorm buddy and co-adventurer, and Isaiah, our tech guru.”

Lola shook their hands. “Cass talks about you a lot. Feels like I already know your inside jokes.”

Isaiah laughed, sipping from his own cup. “If you’ve heard the story of us almost deleting our entire dataset, you know too much.”

Ayesha lifted her straw. “Thanks for the boba, Lola. Perfect way to celebrate.”

Lola’s demeanor softened as she turned to Cass. “Hey, about your text—are you okay? You mentioned Archer and Carver.”

Cass shifted the drink in her hand. “They texted me that Mom and Dad were arguing. I’ve been worried, but talking helps. Thanks for listening.”

“Sorry you have that on your mind,” Lola said, gently tapping her cup against Cass’s in support. “And your parents couldn’t be here. Let’s chat about it on the rideshare back, maybe find a fun distraction.”

Cass’s nod was brief. “Sounds good, thanks.”

A movement at the hall’s edge drew their eyes. Professor Avery approached, her short silver hair catching the overhead lights. Lines at her eyes deepened as she smiled.

“Cass, Ayesha, Isaiah,” Professor Avery greeted them. “That was outstanding. You didn’t just meet expectations, you exceeded them. Making complex ideas accessible is no small feat, and the way you combined EPA data with local health reports? That’s exceptional work.”

She met Professor Avery’s gaze. “Thank you, that means a lot.” Cass loosened her grip on her cup. “It’s been a steep learning curve, but the more I learn, the more there is to discover.”

Professor Avery nodded. “That’s how you keep growing. Once you think you know it all, you stop exploring.”

Professor Avery gestured towards a display case featuring a collection of photographs, with Katherine Johnson’s portrait prominently situated in the center. “I know you’re all familiar with Katherine Johnson and her groundbreaking contributions to NASA, but have you noticed the other remarkable women featured in this display?” she asked, pointing to a photograph of herself alongside another trailblazing Black woman. “The woman next to me in that picture is Elva Hicks Glover.”

Cass and Ayesha leaned in to take a closer look at the photograph, curiosity piqued by the unfamiliar face.

“I met Elva at the Delta Sigma Theta National Convention in Washington, D.C., back in 1990. She’s not only my sorority sister but also a trailblazer in her own right,” Professor Avery said. “She worked as a mathematician and programmer at NASA’s Goddard Space Flight Center in Maryland from 1960 to 1995, navigating the complexities of space science at a time when African Americans, especially women, were rarely recognized in STEM fields.”

Cass and Ayesha leaned in slightly.

“Elva used to say, ‘Persistence paves its own path.’ She didn’t just excel; she broke barriers with her intellect and determination,” Professor Avery continued.

“These women are testaments to resilience, intellect, and ambition. Many would call them ‘Hidden Figures,’ but I see you three as ‘Emerging Figures,’ the next generation to carry the torch forward,” she said, scanning their faces.

Cass glanced at the display case, then at Professor Avery. “I didn’t know you were a Delta.”

Professor Avery folded her arms. “Of course I am. Being a Delta means standing on the shoulders of women like Elva. Strong, brilliant, and unshakable.”

Cass adjusted her stance. “My aunt is an AKA.”

Professor Avery chuckled, shaking her head. “Oh, bless her heart. That explains why you’re so poised.” After a pause, she added, “But don’t let her fool you. I bet she had a Delta mentor somewhere along the way.”

Cass shook her head. “She’d never admit it.”

Professor Avery laughed. Cass turned back to the display case, studying the faces in the photographs beside Katherine Johnson and Elva Hicks Glover. Other photos filled the display, each accompanied by a small plaque with a name and title.

Professor Avery handed out sleek business cards, the embossed text catching the light. Cass ran her thumb over the raised lettering. Beside her, Ayesha and Isaiah studied their own cards.

"I look forward to staying in touch with each of you," Professor Avery said. She smiled as her gaze shifted between them. "Success is about making connections—and having the talent, humility, and drive to chase your goals with relentless focus. You three have those qualities in spades."

Cass lowered her eyes briefly. "Wish my parents had heard you say that, but maybe next time."

The professor gently touched Cass's shoulder. "I'd love to meet them. Meanwhile, be proud of what you've done and stay in touch." She moved off to speak with another group, leaving the three students in a thoughtful pause.

Isaiah broke the silence with a grin. "Should we book a worldwide data conference tour or take a nap first?"

Ayesha laughed, rolling her eyes. "A nap, please. But you juniors need to hit the books—SATs are right around the corner. I'm shooting for early decision, and Professor Avery's already agreed to write me a reference."

Cass groaned, turning the cup in her hand. "Ugh, you sound like my mom. But I guess she's right. One quick toast before we go? To all the data that brought us together."

"To the data," Ayesha agreed, lifting her cup.

Cass tapped her cup to Ayesha's. "And to you, may every admissions board see your brilliance."

Isaiah added his cup. "And to us juniors. We'll survive, right?" He glanced at Lola, who had been quietly sipping her boba. "What do you think, Cass? Ready for late nights and coding challenges?"

Cass looked up, a wry smile on her face. "Not yet. Give me a few days to sleep in first."

Lola raised her boba, grinning. "Well you can count me in. I'll bring the boba to inspire those late-night breakthroughs."

They all laughed, the sound carrying through the atrium as the conference wound down around them. Laptops snapped shut, and the shuffle of feet echoed off the polished floor as attendees filtered out into the late afternoon sunlight.

Cass drained the last of her tea and stood, shouldering her bag. “Alright, time to head back and grab our luggage before the dorms close for the summer.”

The group navigated through the thinning crowd, making their way back to the residence halls. The campus hummed with end-of-year energy as students hauled suitcases and said their goodbyes.

*****

Cass ran her fingers lightly over the edge of the door panel. “How’s the stereo in this thing?”

Lola’s eyes flicked toward her with a slow grin. “I thought you’d never ask.” She tapped the touchscreen, and a smooth beat filled the car. “This is my new drive-time bop—Thuy, Hair Down.”

Cass nodded to the rhythm as the music flowed through the speakers. “Solid choice.”

Lola drummed her fingers lightly on the steering wheel. “Right? Windows down, music up—best way to clear your head.” She slid her thumb over the volume control, nudging it up a few notches. The bass deepened, the vocals spilling into every corner of the car.

Cass rolled her window down slightly, the wind ruffling the ends of her hair. “I see the vision,” she said, shifting her shoulders in time with the beat.

Lola smirked and turned the dial up another notch. “Now you get it.” She tossed Cass a quick glance before tapping out a rhythm against the steering wheel. “You have to let the chorus hit, though. Non-negotiable.”

The chorus dropped, and Lola tilted her chin slightly, lips moving with the lyrics. The car glided through traffic, brake lights flickering against the windshield. A passing cyclist glanced over at the sound, nodding once before pedaling ahead.

Cass leaned back against the seat, the city lights reflecting off the glass as the song played on.

“I love your car,” she said. “If you hadn’t picked me up, I’d be on BART right now—Mom couldn’t make it. This is definitely an upgrade.”

Lola grinned, fastening her seatbelt. “It’s nice, right? There’s a certain freedom in having your own ride.” She pressed a button on the touchscreen, and the electric motor hummed softly. “Any idea when you’ll get your license?”

Cass drummed her fingertips lightly on her thigh. “I turn seventeen in February. Honestly, it’s not top priority. Plus, I have a best friend with a fancy Tesla,” she added, shooting Lola a playful grin.

Lola laughed and shifted into drive. “Fair point. This car’s just another guilt gift from my parents. Missed dinners and big events, then they give me something shiny. I guess that’s their version of family time.”

Cass’s expression changed slightly as she glanced at the window. “I guess parents not showing up is more common than I realized.”

They pulled into a line of Friday evening traffic. The dash clock read 5:23 PM, and rows of brake lights formed a slow-moving ribbon ahead, reflecting off tall buildings. A billboard for new condos flickered against the bright sky, while a pigeon pecked at crumbs on the curb. Inside the Tesla, the air conditioner whispered softly.

“Ever think about all the data these Teslas collect?” Cass asked, her voice subdued but steady. “Like routes, speed, every stop—stuff like that.”

Lola gave a short glance toward Cass. “Not really,” she admitted. “Now that you mention it, though, it’s unsettling. They probably track everything.”

“It’s interesting from a tech angle,” Cass said. “But imagine if they blocked certain routes or shut down if you went somewhere they didn’t approve.”

A small crease formed on Lola’s brow. “Let’s hope that stays in sci-fi. At least we’re not living in robot cocoons yet.” She tapped the touchscreen, shifting the conversation. “Anyway, it’s better than the alternative.”

Cass’s lips curved in a slight laugh, her gaze moving to the passing city blocks and suburban houses beyond. “I still wonder who sees all that data,” she continued, her tone thoughtful. “At boot camp, we learned how everything from apps to cars logs our moves. They call it telemetry—it basically tracks you.”

“Awesome,” Lola joked. “So there’s a huge spreadsheet of my late-night taco runs somewhere?”

Cass smirked when Lola mimed typing on an imaginary keyboard. “It’d show a big spike every Friday night,” she teased.

“Guilty,” Lola replied, a soft chuckle escaping. The traffic eased, and faint backyard barbecue smells mingled with distant honks. Soon, they found a calmer stretch of road.

“Anyway, thanks for letting me borrow your shoes,” Cass said, glancing at the velvet heels on her feet. “They were surprisingly comfortable.”

“Just another guilt gift,” Lola said with a small smile. “Keep them if you want. You’re stepping into something new, so they might fit.”

Cass nodded. “Thanks. And not just for the shoes—for being here. You in the audience...it meant a lot.”

“Of course.” Lola’s eyes flicked to the side mirror. “Professor Avery seemed pretty impressed with your work.”

“She helped a lot,” Cass agreed, watching a mall sale billboard pass overhead. “I wouldn’t have tackled data science like this without her support. The scholarship covered nearly everything, even a laptop and cloud subs. I felt out of place at first, but the team was amazing, and I caught on.”

“Sometimes the unexpected path is the best one, Ms. Data Wizard.” Lola signaled and changed lanes. “You looked confident up there. You even convinced me about machine learning.”

Cass let out a quiet laugh. “I never thought analyzing numbers could feel so personal. But it’s about the people behind the data.”

They drove in a comfortable silence for a minute, passing green lights and leaving the city’s tall buildings behind. Suburban streets appeared, lined with leafy trees. The sun dipped lower, painting the sky in orange and purple.

Lola nudged Cass’s elbow gently. “On a different note, did you see how Isaiah kept looking at you all day? He seemed pretty distracted.”

Cass flicked a strand of hair behind her ear. “He’s just being supportive,” she said evenly. “We worked together for a while, so it’s no big deal.”

“Sure,” Lola said, eyebrows raised. “Could be nothing. Could be something.”

Cass started to reply, but Lola turned onto a quiet street with tall redwoods swaying in the breeze. Fewer cars passed by now. A light draft slipped through Lola’s window, carrying eucalyptus scents.

Another turn, and they pulled up to a two-story house tucked off Claremont Avenue in Rockridge. Painted sky blue and gray, it had well-trimmed hedges and a freshly swept path. Worn steps rose to a door with slightly chipped paint. A mailbox leaned at an angle, as though observing the neighborhood.

“Thanks for the ride,” Cass said, stepping out. The late-day air carried hints of eucalyptus and faint car exhaust. “And everything else today,” she added. “It made a difference.”

Lola cracked her door open an inch, leaning out with a light grin. “Is tonight the night I finally get to see your place? I can say hi to Archer and Carver, maybe beat them at their own games?”

Cass shifted her bag strap, glancing briefly at the tilted mailbox and worn porch rail. “Not tonight,” she said, resting a hand on Lola’s door to shut it gently. “They’re probably busy with whatever. Next time, okay?”

Lola’s expression softened. “All right. Let me know if you need anything.”

“Will do.” Cass watched the Tesla’s headlights sweep across the driveway as Lola settled back in. “Thanks again,” she said quietly.

The car glided away, the electric hum fading. In the stillness, Cass approached the door, noticing a small paint chip on the handle. Light from the living room lamp fell onto the porch, and she stepped inside, the air carrying the subtle warmth of home.

*****

Cass stepped into the house, warm and still under the dim light of the entryway. A small thermometer on the wall read 79 degrees, and the air conditioner switch stayed off under the household rule of waiting until 81. The warm air sat heavy in the living room despite open windows, and Cass wiped the back of her hand across her forehead before flicking on the overhead light near the shoe rack. Two oscillating fans on the lower level whirred steadily, their rhythm steady but ineffective against the heat. A lone couch sat in the center of the room, a single pillow resting at one end, as though someone had used it recently. Cass set her duffel bag there and stood still for a moment.

A faint clinking noise came from the kitchen, like a utensil slipping in a drawer, while the soft hum of a streetlamp buzzed through an open window. “Archer? Carver,” she called into the quiet house. “I’m back. It’s Friday, so maybe we can watch one episode of Psych before bed.

“Then it’s lights out. We definitely don’t want to be up when Mom and Dad get home. Let’s just keep things easy tonight.” said archer

Archer and Carver appeared at their bedroom door. Archer wore faded pajamas, and Carver stood just behind him, leaning against the doorframe. Both blinked in the still air, their movements slow like the heat had drained them. Archer's hair clung slightly to his forehead, and Carver swiped his palm over his neck, his shirt sticking slightly to his back.

Archer looked toward Cass. "Hey," he said quietly. He stepped forward, wrapping his arms around her tightly. "We missed you." As they hugged, Cass noticed how much taller he had gotten, nearly matching her height now.

Cass hugged him back briefly before Carver joined, squeezing her on the other side. "We missed you, Cass," Carver said, his voice quiet but firm. He was catching up to her too—almost as tall as Archer now.

Cass nodded as they pulled away. "How's everything been?" Archer and Carver hesitated. She added quickly, "Camp was good. You guys had me worried last night."

"Camp was great," Cass replied quickly, before glancing at a small clock near the couch. It showed a time just past eight. "Mom and Dad'll probably be home late. No point staying up. Let's watch one show, then it's lights out."

Carver shrugged. "We've just been playing video games, trying not to set anything off. Things have been tense, but we're managing." He glanced at Archer, who shifted slightly and added, "Mom and Dad never argue, but it's like everyone's waiting for something to happen."

Cass nodded and moved toward the kitchen. A plate labeled 'blackened salmon' in her father's sharp handwriting sat in the fridge, sealed neatly with foil. "Did you tell Aunt Zora?" she asked, her voice steady, while she lifted the foil and caught the spicy, smoky aroma laced with cayenne. She lifted the foil, catching a spicy, smoky aroma laced with cayenne. She placed the salmon in the microwave and tapped the buttons until a low hum kicked on.

Carver hovered at the doorway, resting one hand on his forearm. "No," he replied to Cass's question. "But they've been talking about Miss Linda. Dad said she left the restaurant. Something about money."

Behind him, Archer added, "Mom keeps acting normal, but it seems bad. Dad mentioned overdue bills."

When the microwave beeped, Cass retrieved the salmon, steam curling into the still air. She cut the fillet into smaller pieces. "It's all we have right now," she said, placing two plates on the counter. "Eat it while it's warm. I'm going to check something."

She walked down the hall to a door marked with a small wooden sign reading "Booker," slightly askew. Inside, the office felt hotter than the rest of the house. The desk was strewn with envelopes, many stamped "Past Due." A makeshift calendar pinned to the wall listed overdue amounts. A distant fan hummed from another room. Cass replaced a letter on the desk and returned to the living room, a thin layer of sweat on her upper lip.

Archer and Carver sat on the couch with their plates. The overhead bulb glowed weakly, and Archer placed both plates to the side when Cass re-entered. From the TV, the opening notes of Psych played at low volume. Cass climbed the stairs briefly, then came back down changed into lighter clothes, settling on the couch's edge as the episode continued. The faint sounds of yard barbecues drifted in through the windows, mixing with the lingering spice of the salmon.

When the credits rolled, Cass stretched. "That's one," she said. "Time for bed. Mom and Dad'll be in late, so let's not wait up."

Archer switched off the TV, and Carver stacked the plates on a side table. Cass pushed the living room window open a little wider. The night stayed heavy and warm, the outside stillness broken only by the faint murmur of yard barbecues. She climbed the stairs again, each creak echoing in the stillness.

Upstairs, the house felt heavier as evening settled in. Cass's room had an overhead fan rotating slowly, stirring the warm air. She dropped her bag on a worn chair and loosened her shirt collar. A cardinal-red journal lay beside a small lamp on the desk, its cover reflecting the dim light. After changing into pajamas, she returned briefly to the living room. Archer and Carver were already preparing for bed, so she headed back to her room.

A mild hush took over the house, interrupted only by the fans and a distant passing car. Cass switched on a small lamp at her desk, the faint scent of blackened salmon still clinging to her shirt. She tapped her foot twice on the floor, the sound syncing with the slow, creaking rotation of the overhead fan. Finally, she sat at the desk, opened the journal to a blank page, and began writing. Distantly, a car engine idled, and a fan squeaked downstairs. She paused her pen for a moment, then continued, carefully recording each detail of this warm Friday night at home.

FRIDAY, JUNE 28 | JOURNAL ENTRY

2: The texts from my parents this morning. "Got called in early, doing a double today." "Sorry, babygirl, can't make it. I know you'll do great." Whole time I thought they'd be in the crowd, watching me present, and instead? I got hit with the "we proud of you, tho" texts.

1: The eye roll I hit after reading Dad's text. Not at him, but at this whole situation. Like, yeah, I get it. Grown folks got bills. But man, would it have killed them to show up? Just once?

100: The level of hype Isaiah was on. This boy was bouncing down the hallway like we just hit the finals. He kept saying we might win something, but I just wanted to not choke on stage.

9: The number of times I read Katherine Johnson's quote before walking into the auditorium. "I counted everything. I counted the steps to the road, the steps up to church, the number of dishes and silverware I washed… anything that could be counted, I did." Felt like she was talking straight to me.

5: The glances I caught from Isaiah. He was on something. I don't know if it was post-presentation adrenaline or something else, but bro was looking at me like he just figured something out.

3: The steps I took before I saw it. The couch. Dad's blanket bunched up, pillow with that slept-on look. So he never made it to bed. The arguing my brothers mentioned—it wasn't just a one-night thing.

42: The minutes I stared at my ceiling, listening. No voices. No movement. Just the sound of the fan clicking as it rotated. But it didn't feel peaceful. It felt like the house was holding its breath.

12: The messages from my friends I ignored. Everybody talking about what's next—where we're meeting, who's going on vacation, which scholarships we should apply for. My brain couldn't hold that right now. Not when I'm trying to figure out what's wrong here.

4: The times I reached for my phone to text Lola before putting it back down. She already knew something was up. I wasn't ready to explain it.

*****

Cass lay in bed when the low murmur of voices crept up the stairs, each word sharp as glass against the silence. She sat up, phone in hand, briefly glancing at its screen before lowering it. Her mother's raised voice carried up, distinct in the hush of the night.

"Booker, we can't keep ignoring this!" Maya said. "The restaurant is hemorrhaging money. We're barely staying afloat!"

"You think I don't know that?" Booker's reply cut through the stillness. "I pour my heart and soul into that place every day!"

Cass left her bed and moved toward the door, stepping lightly on the floorboards. A small clock on her nightstand showed it was past midnight. She paused, listening to the voices through the closed door.

"What about us?" Maya asked, quieter but still firm. "We can't keep sacrificing everything for a failing business."

"Failing?" Booker's voice wavered. "That restaurant is my dream, just like this house was yours. We shouldn't sacrifice one for the other."

Maya responded, voice echoing, "Dreams don't pay the bills, Booker! We have three kids, a mortgage—we can't pretend things are fine when they're not."

Booker's footsteps thudded across the floor. "You think I'm pretending? You think I don't lie awake every night wondering how we'll survive?"

"Stop yelling," Maya said, lowering her tone slightly. "The kids can hear us. Let me pick up more shifts, we cut back expenses, and find a way to manage."

"And what about Cass?" Booker asked. "What about her future? We can't let her give up everything because of my mistakes."

A brief lull followed. Cass opened her bedroom door a crack. In the dim light below, she saw Maya place both hands on Booker's shoulders. "You haven't failed," Maya said. "You've built something people care about. But we need to be smart about it."

Booker nodded. "I need time to think."

Maya's voice carried again, quieter now. "I wish we didn't have to do this so late. We need to check on the kids."

No further words reached Cass for several seconds. She eased back onto her bed, staring at the ceiling. The hallway fan whispered a slight breeze over the silence.

Moments later, two sets of footsteps approached on the upstairs landing. The knob on Cass's door turned, then Booker stepped inside, glancing in. "She's asleep," he said. "We should check on the twins."

Maya stood behind him, one hand at his elbow. "Yes," she said softly. "Then... are you coming to bed?"

"Not yet," Booker answered. "I have more work and might stay on the couch."

Maya murmured a short reply. They lingered for a moment, then moved away toward Archer and Carver's room. The door to Cass's room clicked shut, and the hallway grew still. Outside, a lone car rumbled past and faded into the distance. Cass lay on her side, motionless, until no sound remained. She rolled onto her back, eyes shifting to the clock's faint glow as the last bits of warmth and quiet night air pressed in. Eventually, her breathing slowed in time with the overhead fan, and the house settled into silence once more.

Initial Split

The initial split is the first dividing point, a moment of choice where pathways emerge. Each path represents a different possibility, a distinct future shaped by decisions made. This is where complexity begins, as the simple transforms into the multifaceted. The initial split is both a challenge and an opportunity, requiring a thoughtful understanding of the data and conditions at hand. It's the starting point of clarity in the midst of uncertainty, the pivot to new directions.

SATURDAY, JUNE 29

Morning light spread across the kitchen's worn linoleum floor. Cass walked in, noticing the smell of scrambled eggs and toast. Maya stood at the stove, an apron quickly tied over her scrubs, while Archer and Carver sat at the small dining table, flipping through comic books.

"I'm glad you're back, sweetie," Maya said, keeping her eyes on the pan. "I was looking forward to hearing about your presentation." Her voice, though calm, sounded slightly strained.

Cass placed her bag on a chair. "Morning," she replied. A glance at the counter revealed Booker's wallet and keys were gone. "Where's Dad?"

Maya's hand paused on the spatula. "He already left for the restaurant. He wants you at the hostess stand today."

Cass blinked. "But it's my first day home." She reached for an empty mug near the sink. "Couldn't I just—"

Archer and Carver glanced over, but Maya continued. "He's missed you working up front," she said, turning to the stove to stop the eggs from overcooking. "Having you saves labor costs. We don't have to schedule extra help."

Cass gripped the mug. "All right," she said quietly. She reached for the small carafe on the counter and poured a cup of her mother's signature coffee—Brazilian Cake Lady from Red Bay Coffee.

Maya slid scrambled eggs onto a plate. "I'm sorry we weren't there for your presentation," she said, placing the dish on the table. "I really wanted to meet Professor Avery. I'm sure she liked your work."

Cass offered a half-smile. "Yeah, she mentioned how thorough my analysis was. I wish you and Dad could've been there." She set the mug down.

"Of course she praised you," Maya said, switching off the stove. "You work hard. She saw that."

Archer nudged Carver, who silently flipped another page of his comic. Maya's gaze flicked to Cass, then back to the eggs.

"Is there any left?" Cass asked.

Maya nodded and put a plate in front of her. Archer took a slice of toast, and Carver searched for the butter knife. Cass picked up a fork.

"We'll drop the boys off at Aunt Zora's," Maya said, standing with her arms resting at her sides. “Then I’ll drive you to the restaurant. Your dad needs you there. We can’t spare anyone else.”

Carver leaned back in his chair. “She’s probably gonna make us do an art project or read a bunch of books.” He glanced at Archer, who smirked slightly and mouthed, ‘Told ya,’ toward Cass.

Archer smirked faintly, flipping his comic page. “Anything’s better than cleaning out her garage again.”

Maya shot them a look. “She’s helping us out, so I expect you both to be polite—no complaints when we get there.”

Cass looked at the coffee in her mug, her voice steady. “Mom, I’m sixteen now. Can we talk about me learning to drive? Lola’s already got a new Tesla.”

Maya set the spatula in the sink, her tone firm. “Lola’s family is in a whole different league. Her dad owns a construction company, and her mom’s a lawyer. We’re not them, Cass.”

The phone on the counter buzzed. Archer checked the screen. “Mom, it’s Hal,” he said.

Cass glanced toward the phone. “Why’s he calling on a Saturday morning? Everything okay?”

Maya stepped over and pressed a button to silence the ring. “Boys, ignore it,” she said, placing the phone facedown. “We’re running late as it is.”

Archer and Carver exchanged a quick look. Carver said nothing, and Archer made no comment.

Cass rested her fork on her plate, leaning slightly forward. “I’m not asking for a Tesla, Mom. I just want to learn how to drive. That’s it.”

Maya crossed her arms. “You think it’s just the car? It’s insurance, gas, maintenance—it all adds up. We’ve got enough bills as it is.” She gripped the edge of the counter, fingers pressing into the surface before she let go. “And we’re not exactly rolling in extra money, Cass. Even a parking ticket can set us back—Oakland doesn’t play.”

Cass pressed her palm flat on the table. “Mom, I get that we’re struggling, and I honestly don’t know why. Everyone around here is working 12 hours a day, and we’re still stuck. And all I’m asking is to learn how to drive. All my friends have cars. I’m the only one who doesn’t even have a license. People keep asking me about it—do you realize how embarrassing that is?”

Maya shook her head, turning off the stove with a click. “Cass, what you should understand is that I do not appreciate your attitude, entitlement, or disrespect. It’s not in the budget, and that’s just how things are right now.”

Cass nodded once, her lips drawing into a line. She glanced at her brothers, who stayed quiet. “Fine,” she said. She lifted her mug.

“Now what you can do is fix your face and appreciate what we have—our home, this neighborhood, your school, your luxury data science camp,” Maya said, her voice rising. “We can drive to your grandma’s house and see a whole bunch of folks really struggling, folks who would love to have your life.”

Maya checked the clock. “Finish up, everyone,” she said, addressing Archer and Carver. “We’re leaving soon. Aunt Zora’s waiting for you two, and Cass, your dad wants you at the restaurant.”

Cass took one last sip of coffee, stepping away from the table. Archer and Carver watched her briefly before returning to their comics. Maya gave Cass a brief nod, and Cass nodded back.

“Ten minutes,” Maya repeated, picking up utensils from the counter. “We’ll talk more later, Cass.”

Cass said nothing further. She left the kitchen, coffee in hand, aware that her father expected her up front that day. The earlier tension lingered, but there was no time to address it. They had to go.

*****

Cass stepped into the brick building, its arched windows catching the soft morning light. The neon sign above the entrance—“Booker’s Pages and Plates”—flickered faintly in the daylight. Inside, “We Got Our Own Thang” by Heavy D played quietly. Although the restaurant was mostly empty, the upbeat music gave the space an energy that suggested it was ready for the day’s customers.

Afternoon light poured through the tall windows, casting warm tones on the worn wooden floors and tables. Towering oak bookshelves lined the walls, their colorful spines creating a patchwork of hues. Between the books, framed photos and posters honored Black luminaries: James Baldwin, Zora Neale Hurston, and Ishmael Reed. The items’ presence seemed to ground the place in history.

Cass spotted Booker by an antique card catalog. She made her way through the room, where a few patrons sat on wooden benches, some reading as they waited for their meals. Potted ferns and spider plants in macramé hangers softened the restaurant's vintage feel.

Past the lunch hour, only the occasional chair scrape or utensil clink broke the stillness. Cass found her father at an empty table in the corner and walked over. "Hey, Dad," she said, hugging him. Booker Freeman, tall, with graying hair and deep brown eyes, returned the hug firmly, resting a hand on her shoulder before letting go.

"I missed you, Babygirl," he said in a quiet voice. "I hated missing your presentation."

Cass noticed tension in his posture. When he released her, it was only enough to meet her gaze. "I checked in on you last night," he said, "but you were out cold."

She nodded, a slight grin crossing her face. "Yeah, I was exhausted."

"How's today going?" she asked, noticing the dark circles under his eyes.

"Better now that you're back," Booker replied with a faint shrug. He glanced at the mostly empty tables. "We've had slow days, but I'm hoping things pick up."

Cass nodded, her gaze passing over a chalkboard by the wall and a cart of books waiting to be shelved. "They usually do," she said, although the stillness in the room gave a different impression.

"Cass! You're here!" Maria's voice called out as she walked in from the kitchen door. Cass turned and gave her a quick hug.

"I've missed you, Maria," Cass said, stepping back.

Nearby, Sarah, a server, lifted a hand in a brief wave before turning away. She busied herself wiping a table, avoiding further conversation.

"Hey, Sarah," Cass said in a friendly tone. Sarah only nodded and continued her task. From behind the kitchen window, Mike, the head chef, greeted Cass politely, wiping his hands on a towel before turning back to his work.

Cass looked around. "So...where's Linda?" she asked Maria.

Maria's smile faded slightly. "She was let go a few weeks ago. It's been tough. We had to cut hours, and your dad had to make some hard decisions," she explained. "Linda's found something else, luckily."

Cass blinked. "I didn't realize," she said quietly. "That's awful. I hope she's okay."

Maria nodded. “She’s fine, thankfully. A couple of the kitchen staff were let go, too. We’re all stretching ourselves thin.” Her gaze wandered to the few customers in the dining area.

Across the room, Sarah’s voice interrupted them. “I’m taking out the trash, then I’m on break,” she said, hoisting a half-full bag over her shoulder. The faint clink of glass suggested there was more than simple waste inside. She headed to the rear exit.

Cass watched Sarah go, frowning slightly. After the door closed, she turned back to Maria. “How’s everyone holding up?”

Maria sighed. “We’re trying, but it’s been rough.” A moment later, Mike’s voice came from the kitchen, asking about a missing catering slip. Maria shook her head. “I’ll go check the office for that.”

Cass stood quietly for a moment, glancing from Maria to where Sarah had exited. The half-full trash bag, the clink of glass—something seemed off, though she couldn’t pinpoint why.

During the quiet lull, Cass eventually joined her father at a table in the far corner. He was looking over a stack of bills, reading glasses perched on his nose. “Slow days? What’s going on?” She gestured at the empty tables. “This place used to be packed.”

Booker rolled his shoulders back, stretching slightly before rubbing the back of his neck. “It’s rough, Cass. Prices keep going up—eggs, oil, everything. Rent, too. I started out wanting to buy this place, but now I’m on a hamster wheel. Can’t seem to get ahead. The new folks are eating there now, and our older regulars… they just can’t afford to eat out. Some can’t even afford to live here anymore.” He shook his head. “We had to bump wages last year, then cut hours this year. Can’t win.”

The front door swung open, letting in a gust of warm air. A delivery driver stepped inside, adjusting a clipboard under his arm. “Got a drop-off for Booker’s.”

Booker turned. “Mike, can you take care of this?”

Mike stepped out from the kitchen, wiping his hands on a towel. “Yeah, I got it.” He took the clipboard, scanned the invoice, and nodded toward the back. “Load it up near the walk-in.” He handed the clipboard back and disappeared toward the storage area.

Booker watched Mike go. “Mike’s stepped up a lot lately. I don’t know what I’d do without him.”

A plate clattered in the kitchen, followed by a muffled curse. Booker glanced toward the pass-through window but didn't move.

He turned back to Cass. "Anyway... we did what we could, but we had to let some staff go. Linda too. That one stung. She's at that new Mexican place now—at least she landed quick." His gaze settled on the counter. "Last shift, she left her apron folded on the desk. Didn't even take her staff meal."

Cass pulled out her phone and typed a message. Her thumb hovered over the screen. Maria wiped down a counter that was already clean. Booker rubbed his temples, looking down at the stack of bills on the table.

During a lull, Cass joined her father at a table in the far corner. His reading glasses rested on top of the papers in front of him.

"Dad, can I ask you something?"

He looked up and nodded. "Sure."

"Do we track details like reservations or sales data?"

Booker set his glasses on the ledger. "Mike handles most of that. Why?"

"At camp, I picked up some ideas," Cass said, pulling up a visualization. "We can run A/B tests on promotions—try offering a 10% discount on dinner specials on Mondays and compare customer response to our usual pricing. If conversion rates increase by at least 15%, we keep it. If not, we iterate."

Booker raised an eyebrow. "How do we measure that?"

"I'll use our order data to track revenue per customer before and after the promo. I'll also analyze the repeat customer rate. If people who redeem discounts return within two weeks at a higher rate than non-discounted customers, we'll know it's working."

Booker scratched his head. "That's... a lot of math."

Cass smiled. "Think of it as a recipe—mixing the right ingredients to find what our customers love best."

Booker nodded. "Have at it. But I still need you out front. Use my computer, and be careful with it. I don't want to lose any records or pay for repairs," he added with a tired smile.

"Thanks, Dad," Cass said, returning the smile. "I'll be careful."

*****

Hours crept by, and the sky outside the narrow window had darkened. The wall clock read 10:57 PM, and the fluorescent lights maintained their stark glow over the small office. An old computer hummed softly, its fan adding a constant undercurrent in the otherwise hushed room.

Cass's fingers moved steadily across the keyboard. She paused to check a neat stack of handwritten notes before continuing. Outside, chairs scraped across the floor as the final staff completed closing duties. Cass glanced at the door, then refocused on her work.

The door hinges creaked, and Cass lifted her head.

Maya and Booker stood in the doorway. Maya held the doorknob lightly, while Booker's shoulders filled the remaining space under the low frame.

"Cassie, what are you doing here?" Maya's voice was edged with fatigue. Her gaze shifted across the office and settled on Cass.

Cass pulled off her headphones, looking toward them. "Just, um, going through the sales records," she said, glancing at the screen.

Booker stepped forward, his eyes taking in the laptop and the papers. "That's why you've been asking about passwords all day?"

Cass pressed her lips together. She knew she'd been cautious, but seeing the weariness in their faces, she decided to speak. "I overheard you arguing last night," she said, voice low. "It worried me. Archer and Carver called me at camp because they were scared."

Maya drew in a quiet breath, then placed a hand on Cass's arm. "Cassie, we're sorry. We didn't mean for them to hear any of that."

Booker exhaled, glancing around. "We were trying to spare you, too."

Cass set aside the keyboard. "How bad is it?" she asked, her tone calm.

"We're almost three months behind on rent," Booker admitted. "Last month, we couldn't cover the house and the restaurant bills. It's really tight."

"That's the problem, Booker," Maya cut in, her arms folding. "We haven't looked at the details closely enough."

Cass straightened. "So let's do that. Let me help with the numbers, Dad. I'm on summer break. I have time."

She opened a folder, hesitating as she gestured toward the documents. "I just got access to the restaurant's financials, so I haven't gone deep yet. But from a quick look, some figures don't add up. I might need help from my team from the boot camp, but I can figure it out."

Booker frowned. "Not sure I'm okay with a bunch of high schoolers seeing my finances." Maya stood nearby, arms crossed, glancing at the piled papers. "It's embarrassing," she murmured.

"Thanks for checking," Maya said, her eyes shifting to Booker. "But your dad has to handle this. It's his responsibility."

Booker looked at the table, resting his hand on it briefly. Cass's eyebrows drew together slightly, and she sat up. "Mom, Dad, you know those tests can be biased."

Maya turned toward Cass. "Cassie, enough. Standardized tests are what colleges look at for scholarships. Things aren't good financially, so you need to be serious."

"I agree," Booker added, a glance at his watch. "We've got to go. Zora has the twins."

Maya nodded. "I told her to have them stay over. We'll see them tomorrow for dinner at your parents' house," she said.

Booker stood and smoothed his shirt. Cass closed her folder, staying where she was until Booker spoke again in a gentler tone. "Come on," he said.

Maya lifted her bag and followed him out, saying she was tired and ready to head home. Booker waited, looking at Cass with a brief pause in his expression. "You riding with me?" he asked, voice a little softer. Cass nodded, picking up her folder before trailing behind him to the car.

The ride home was quiet, the engine's hum occasionally interrupted by the sound of tires on uneven pavement. Streetlights flashed by, illuminating Booker's features. Cass sat in the passenger seat, phone in hand.

At an intersection, the faint scent of burnt rubber lingered. Fresh skid marks looped in tight circles near a corner lot. A car rolled by slowly, Too $hort's bass-heavy track rattling the windows as it passed.

Cass: "Hey, everyone, I'm back from boot camp! I can't wait to share all about my summer. Sorry I missed you. I was at Dad's restaurant. Maybe next Tuesday?"

Replies appeared quickly—Jake, Alex, Sophia, and Nia welcomed her back. Cass glanced at the texts.

Alex: “Cass, your dad’s place is cool, but how about something trendy? A new spot just went viral. Interested?”
Cass: “Sure, let’s meet where you want. Just remember I’m not driving. :-)”

A sleek white Tesla passed them, briefly casting light across the car’s interior. Cass watched it recede into the distance as Booker continued down the road, both silent.

SATURDAY, JUNE 29 | JOURNAL ENTRY

3: The seconds it took for me to realize something was wrong. Not just off—wrong. Dad was already gone when I woke up. No text. No call. Just his blanket still on the couch, like he barely slept before leaving.

10: The deep breaths I took before walking into the restaurant. I thought maybe today would feel normal, that maybe I was overthinking. I wasn't.

30: The minutes I spent in the office, flipping through Dad's notes, receipts, and sales numbers. It's bad. I don't even know how bad yet, but the math ain't mathing.

2: The number of knocks on the door before it opened and Hal walked in. I didn't even know he was coming. The way Dad's face changed when he saw him—I knew it before they even said it.

3: The times Dad said "Hal, come on, just give me more time." Hal wasn't trying to hear it. Said he's been patient. That business is business.

6: The letters in the word EVICTION printed in bold red ink at the top of the paper. Six letters that made the whole restaurant feel smaller.

∞: The weight sitting in my chest. The realization that we don't have six weeks. We don't have a plan. We don't have the money. And if I don't figure something out, we won't have a restaurant.

SUNDAY, JUNE 30

*****

The dining table bore several steaming dishes: a large platter of roasted chicken at the center, bowls of mashed potatoes with gravy, buttery corn on the cob, and a bubbling macaroni casserole. In front of Cass sat a basket of fresh biscuits, while a tangy coleslaw added color to the spread.

A savory mix of aromas filled the dining room. Maya passed out plates and opened a nearby window, letting Oakland's early-evening air drift in along with the distant hum of traffic. Archer and Carver took seats beside Cass, exchanging quick glances at the food. Maya moved around the table, handing plates to Booker, then to Grandpa James and Grandma Lillian. Grandpa James, dressed neatly as always, leaned in to take in the scent of chicken and biscuits. Grandma Lillian placed a napkin on her lap, her silver bracelet catching the light.

"Here you go," Maya said, passing Cass the last plate. A quick look at her watch suggested it was getting late.

"How was that camp of yours?" Grandma Lillian asked, picking up a chicken wing.

Grandpa James tapped a finger on his water glass. "Six family dinners without you, Cass. Seemed longer." He glanced her way.

Cass bit into a biscuit. "I missed this. Camp was great. I learned a lot and met new people." Archer reached over her plate for the chicken, nearly tipping his water glass. Cass steadied it and offered him a piece. "Careful there," she said.

Booker passed over the macaroni casserole dish. Cass took it and slid the coleslaw bowl back to him. After setting the warm casserole in front of Archer and Carver, she scooped some onto each plate. "It's hot," she warned, steam rising from the dense center.

Aunt Zora described her latest sculpture project, her hands moving animatedly as she described it. "It's made entirely from salvaged metal," she said, her voice lifting with excitement. "The whole idea is to highlight social justice themes—turning discarded pieces into something meaningful and powerful. It's going to be displayed at the community center next month."

"Powerful?" Booker teased, raising an eyebrow as he reached for another biscuit. "Zora, you mean a pile of rusty car parts welded together, don't you?"

"Oh, you've got jokes now?" Aunt Zora shot back, narrowing her eyes with mock indignation. "Well, Booker, if we're telling jokes, maybe I should tell everyone about the time you got stuck in a kitchen window during your firefighting days."

Cass perked up instantly, her fork hovering over her plate. “Wait—what? Dad, is this true?”

Booker groaned, rubbing his forehead. “Zora, don’t you have any nice stories to tell?”

“Oh, I’ve got plenty of nice stories,” Aunt Zora said with a mischievous grin, leaning forward. “But this one is way better. Kids, listen up. Your dad here was a rookie firefighter back in the day, trying to impress everyone. There was a kitchen fire over on 42nd Street, and he decided to climb in through the window to save the day. Only problem? The window wasn’t exactly... accommodating.”

“You mean he got stuck?” Archer asked, his eyes wide with delight.

“Like a cork in a bottle,” Aunt Zora said, bursting into laughter. “One leg inside, one leg out, arms flailing. The whole crew was just standing there, watching, trying not to laugh. Finally, the captain yells, ‘Booker, if you can’t save the house, at least save yourself!’”

The table erupted into laughter. Carver nearly choked on his water, while Maya covered her face, shaking her head. “Booker,” she said, trying to catch her breath. “Please tell me this is exaggerated.”

“I plead the fifth,” Booker said, though his sheepish grin betrayed him. “That window was unusually narrow, and I wasn’t stuck. I was... reevaluating my strategy.”

“Reevaluating your strategy!” Aunt Zora echoed, cackling. “It took three firefighters and a crowbar to reevaluate that strategy.”

Cass was doubled over, wiping tears from her eyes. “Dad, you’ve got to be kidding me.”

Booker sighed and leaned back in his chair, shaking his head. “Go ahead, laugh it up. But just remember, I made it out of that window eventually, and the fire was put out.”

“Not by you!” Aunt Zora quipped, earning another round of laughter from the table.

The laughter finally began to settle, and a warm, easy silence filled the air. Booker took a sip of water, still shaking his head at Zora’s storytelling, while Grandma Lillian gently patted his arm in mock sympathy. Cass looked around the table, savoring the moment of lightheartedness.

“So, Booker,” Grandpa James said, leaning forward, his tone shifting slightly as the room quieted, “how’s the restaurant doing?”

Booker exhaled. “It’s been rough. Too many slow days, and I’ve used up more of our savings. We’re falling behind.”

Maya set the gravy boat down. “I’m picking up extra shifts at the hospital,” she said, “but it’s not enough.”

Archer gestured toward Cass. “She’s been on her computer all summer. She might have ideas.”

Cass paused, aware of everyone’s attention. The evening light through the window cast a mellow glow on the table. “I started looking at the data,” she said. “I don’t have full access yet, but I can do what analysts do—optimize the business with numbers. For example, we hardly sell sweet potato pie before two in the afternoon, so we might prepare less in the morning. And if half the people who order fried chicken get coleslaw, we could bundle them. Regression analysis might help us set prices, and social media promos could target slow hours.”

Booker’s brow rose. He rubbed his knee under the table. “That’s a lot of work. Are you sure you can handle it?”

Maya folded her arms. “She should be focusing on SAT prep, not just the restaurant. This is a busy year.”

Cass placed her hands on the table’s edge. “I’ll manage both. Maybe with clustering algorithms we’ll spot unusual menu combos. It won’t fix everything overnight, but it might help.”

Aunt Zora rested her fork on the plate and turned to Booker. “She’s grown up, Booker. Let her help.”

Grandma Lillian offered a small smile and clasped her hands in her lap. “Fresh perspectives can be a blessing,” she said quietly.

Booker tapped his knuckles on the table. “Every new idea costs money, and we never see results right away. That’s what worries me.”

Grandpa James laid his hand flat on the table. “Don’t dismiss Cass’s help. She’s learning valuable skills.”

Cass glanced between them. “Just give me a chance. Maybe we’ll spot something we’ve missed.”

They continued the meal, trading stories. Aunt Zora mentioned family history, and moments of laughter mixed with quieter stretches. After they finished eating, Cass and Booker moved to a corner of the living room while everyone else cleared plates. Booker sat in a worn leather chair, and Cass perched on the arm of a sofa. Framed photos along one wall showed Grandpa James in a union jacket, a church group portrait, and pictures of Booker, Maya, and the kids from earlier years.

Booker's gaze lingered on a photo of nine-year-old Cass, her smile wide and eyes bright as she stood proudly outside Booker's Pages and Plates. "Seems like yesterday," he said, tapping the chair's arm.

Cass rested a hand near his shoulder. "I remember how you talked about preserving that old bookstore atmosphere."

Booker nodded, recalling how the building once served as the Oakland Freedom Library, later became a community center for the Black Panther Party, and then was bought by a bookseller named Gerald. He described how Hal purchased the building so Booker could run a restaurant with books still lining the shelves.

"Gerald liked that I kept the books," Booker added. "He didn't want to lose the place's roots."

Maya came over, mentioning a buyout offer they had refused months ago. "They wanted the space but not the books," she said. Booker admitted it had been tempting, but he wanted the restaurant to stay true to its heritage.

Cass stood by his chair. "I'm ready to help. Let me get more data—maybe we'll find what's missing."

Aunt Zora appeared in the hallway, inviting everyone to the kitchen for sweet potato pie. Archer and Carver led the way, cracking jokes over who got the largest slice. Grandma Lillian sliced the pie, Grandpa James mentioned church announcements, and Maya described her last hospital shift. Booker lingered by the sink, taking a plate while rubbing his knee.

Once dessert ended, they moved back to the living room. Grandpa James settled in his favorite chair with a folded newspaper. Grandma Lillian reflected on the old neighborhood, and Maya guided Archer and Carver to rinse dishes. Booker leaned against the wall, drumming his fingers.

Eventually, it was time to leave. They exchanged goodnights with Grandma Lillian and Grandpa James. Aunt Zora teased Cass about missing out on hair-braiding and movie night, then waved goodbye. Outside on the porch, Archer challenged Carver to a race to the car. With an energetic count of three, both took off across the lawn.

Cass paused on the top step and glanced at a tall oak tree in the yard. The porch boards creaked underfoot as Maya reminded Archer to buckle his seatbelt. Cass slid into the back seat, where Archer grinned about winning the race, and Carver grumbled about the result. Booker lowered the window on the passenger side, letting in the night air.

They drove through streets lined with Victorian homes and modern storefronts. A new coffee shop with minimalist decor had replaced what used to be Mr. Kim's corner store, its sign still bearing faint outlines of the original lettering. Across the street, a Pilates studio filled the space where the old laundromat used to be.

Murals and a few groups of teens came into view under the streetlights, while faint music carried over from a nearby block. Archer brought up a new video game, Carver responded with a joke, and Maya hummed along to the quiet radio. Booker rested an elbow on the door, tapping his fingers. Cass watched the passing blocks under the warm glow of the streetlamps, the engine's hum continuing as they approached home.

SUNDAY, JUNE 30 | JOURNAL ENTRY

6: The deep breaths I took before walking into Grandma and Grandpa's house for Sunday dinner. The food smelled the same—mac and cheese bubbling, biscuits warm, fried chicken crisp—but the weight in my chest wouldn't lift.

10: The times I caught Grandma Lillian watching Dad too closely. She knew something was wrong before we even said a word. Grandparents always do.

3: The fake smiles Dad gave while Grandpa James asked how business was. "We're making it work," he said. The lie sat heavy between us, thick like the humidity outside.

5: The number of times Aunt Zora looked at me like she was waiting. She knows me too well. She knows when I'm holding something back.

20: The minutes I spent talking to her in the kitchen after dinner. She told me about her new art students, the way she's been reinventing her career instead of trying to fix things that don't wanna be fixed. She wasn't talking about art. She was talking about us.

8: The minutes it took for her words to sink in. What if the restaurant can't be saved? I don't wanna think like that, but the numbers don't lie.

12: The hugs from family before we left. Tighter than usual. Like they could feel something shifting, even if we didn't say it out loud.

4: The times I checked my phone for a message from Lola. She finally texted late: "Everything good?" I started to type something, then just sent "Yeah." Not a lie, but not the truth either.

11: The time on the clock when I finally got upstairs. My room felt smaller. Or maybe it's just me that feels different now.

100: The number of times I realized today how much I missed being here. Grandma fussing over my hair, Grandpa telling one of his long stories, Aunt Zora roasting everybody at the table. I didn't know how much I needed them until I was sitting there, letting it sink in.

∞: The questions circling my head. Do we fight? Do we cut our losses? What happens to us if the doors close? I keep trying to run the data, but there's no equation for what comes next.

Branch Conditions

Branch conditions are the rules that guide a decision tree, determining which direction each path takes. These conditions filter possibilities, separating and categorizing outcomes based on criteria that refine understanding. At every branch, decisions grow more specific, creating a structure where complexity is organized into clarity. The logic behind branch conditions is key—decisions can only be as good as the rules they follow. It's a process of filtering, refining, and moving closer to resolution.

MONDAY, JULY 1

Morning light filtered through the front windows of Booker's Pages and Plates, revealing faint dust motes in the still air. Outside, a few neighbors sipped coffee on their stoops, and an AC Transit bus rumbled past. Inside, a 90s R&B tune played from a small radio on the counter, and the hardwood floor gave a light creak whenever Cass shifted her stance.

She was arranging menus when a tall man entered. He walked past the tables without pausing, heading straight for the narrow corridor behind the kitchen.

"Hi, do you need a table?" Cass asked. "Or is this to-go?"

He didn't respond, his footsteps tapping steadily over the hardwood as he continued toward Booker's small office. Cass set aside the menus and followed, holding a pencil between her fingers. In the hallway, Booker stepped out of the office, his gaze shifting from Cass to the visitor.

"It's fine, Cass," Booker said quietly. "This is Hal, our landlord."

Hal's crisp shirt and polished shoes caught the overhead light. He turned to Booker, exhaling in a measured way.

"I've been patient," Hal said. "But you've been ducking payments and making only partial payments for months."

Booker spoke in a low voice that did not carry past the threshold. Cass rested one hand against the corridor wall, the aroma of cooking oil and fresh coffee mixing nearby. The R&B beat continued from the dining area.

"You had a good run," Hal went on, "but this arrangement isn't working anymore for me or for you. I need three months' rent in six weeks, or I'll have to evict you."

Booker's chair scraped inside the office. "Hal, please," he said, his voice a touch louder. "Just give me more time."

"You needed more time a while ago," Hal replied. "I'm sorry, but this is business."

Hal brushed past Cass in the narrow space, his shoes tapping along the corridor toward the dining area. Cass stepped into the office, where Booker leaned on the edge of his desk. A paper lay atop scattered receipts, bearing the words EVICTION NOTICE in bold, red letters. The radio's melody seeped into the small room, blending with the muted noise of traffic outside.

"He wants three months' rent in six weeks," Booker said, glancing at the notice. His voice sounded unsteady.

Cass stood near the desk, and the pencil slipped from her grasp, rolling a few inches across the hardwood. In the front, the R&B track continued at the same steady volume, unaffected by the conversation.

"I guess your mother was right about dreams. I'll deal with it," Booker said, setting the notice aside. He stepped into the hallway, and Cass walked with him. Their footfalls on the hardwood led them back to the front of the restaurant, where sunlight crossed empty tables. The music played on, maintaining its easy rhythm despite the tension in the air.

*****

A clock perched above a dusty bookshelf chimed softly at 2:00 PM, its notes blending with the soulful tune drifting in from the corridor. A musty smell lingered in the cramped book room, where Cass sat at a battered salvaged desk. Stacks of papers and data charts surrounded her laptop, and the overhead fan pushed warm, stale air with a low whir. Each time she moved her elbows, the wooden desk gave a faint squeak.

Through the thin walls, her father's voice carried—an abrupt complaint about cornbread being too dry, a comment on peas coming out too soft—followed by mumbled apologies. Cass glanced at her old phone, which buzzed on the desktop.

Cass: "Sorry, I can't meet up today. Something came up."
Isaiah: "No worries. Let me know if you need anything, Cass."

She began to type a request for restaurant help, then stopped and deleted it. Another alert popped up:

Lola: "Hey, girl! We're all heading to Walnut Creek. There's a new smoothie place. It's roasting here, but at least they blast AC! You in?"

Cass tapped a reply:

Cass: "Not today, Lola. Got stuff at the restaurant."

The ceiling fan rattled as her phone lit again:

Lola: "Cass, are you okay? You've been quiet since you got back from camp."

Cass paused, inhaling slowly, then typed:

Cass: "Just busy with family stuff. Talk later."

She set the phone aside, but more group-chat messages appeared:

Alex: “I’m here! Where is everyone?”
Sophia: “On my way! Stuck in traffic :(”
Nia: “Just parked. See you at the food court!”
Lola: “Guys, Cass can’t make it today :’(”
Sophia: “Maybe she’s busy with that data science stuff?”
Nia: “I miss her. It’s not the same without Cass.”
Lola: “I know. I’m worried about her.”
Alex: “Well, who’s ready for smoothies?”
Sophia: “Me! Heard the mango tango flavor’s in season!”
Nia: “Ooh, that sounds good. Save some for me!”

Cass turned her phone’s volume down. The door opened, and Booker entered. Flour smeared the front of his apron, and he wiped sweat from his brow with the back of his hand.

“We don’t have time for this,” he said, his voice brisk. “I sent a few people home to cut labor costs, but the front got busy sooner than I expected. We need you out there.”

Cass stood from the squeaking chair, sending loose papers sliding across the desk. Past the doorway, dishes clanked, and voices rose in the dining area.

Booker glanced around, then placed a hand on the doorknob. “Come on,” he said, urgency in his tone. “Customers are waiting.”

He stepped into the corridor, and Cass hurriedly gathered a few charts into a messy stack. The musty air pressed around her as she followed him. Passing the kitchen, she heard something sizzling and spotted a line cook rushing by with plates. At the dining room’s threshold, the mix of conversations grew louder, blending with faint background music. Clutching the charts under one arm, Cass stepped into the busy front area, where Booker was already greeting customers.

*****

Late evening shadows crept across Booker’s Pages and Plates. Under dimmed lights, a solitary customer hunched by the window, fork scraping against the last bites of fried catfish and collard greens. The sharp scent of vinegar from hot sauce mingled with industrial dish soap and cooking oil. Metal scraped metal as servers stacked the day’s dishes, their movements mechanical after hours on their feet.

Cass balanced a cleared tray against her hip, scanning tables still dotted with empty glasses and crumpled napkins. The floorboards creaked beneath her feet as she headed toward the back hallway. Voices leaked through the kitchen's swinging door—Mike and Sarah speaking in low tones. Their conversation cut off abruptly at the sight of her. Mike's hand moved quickly, sliding something into his apron pocket. The paper crinkled softly. Sarah's eyes darted between Mike and Cass before she offered a stiff nod.

They brushed past, their shoes squeaking against the freshly mopped floor. The heavy back door groaned on its hinges as they disappeared into the night. In their wake, the corridor fell silent except for the steady drip of a leaky pipe and distant clattering from the kitchen. The air felt heavier somehow.

The storeroom door protested as Cass pushed it open. A single bulb flickered to life overhead, casting harsh shadows in the cramped space. Her makeshift office filled one corner—a metal folding table precariously supporting her new laptop, a gift from the Hale Foundation scholarship, its screen casting a blue glow over scattered papers and receipts. The walls seemed to lean inward, decades of stored restaurant supplies leaving their mark in shelving scars and faded labels.

The chair squealed as she sat. Her laptop hummed awake, spreadsheets materializing with their neat rows of data—each number representing another plate served, another dollar earned or lost. A pen rolled toward the table's edge, its movement arrested by her quick grab. Her phone buzzed against the metal table, making her jump.

Professor Avery's name lit up the screen.

"Hello, Professor," Cass whispered, conscious of how sound carried through the old building's ductwork. The ventilation system rattled overhead, pushing stale air through rusted vents.

"Cass, I'm glad I caught you," Professor Avery replied. "I sent an email about our first mentoring session since the program ended, and I wanted to check if you'd seen it. Sometimes those messages get buried."

Cass nudged aside a small stack of receipts, noticing a row of lights switch off in the dining area through the narrow gap of the doorway. "I might've missed it," she admitted. "I've been juggling a lot here. Actually, I'm really sorry I haven't been more responsive. It's just... my father got some bad news about the restaurant, and I'm still trying to process it all."

There was a pause on the other end of the line. "I'm sorry to hear that, Cass. Is there anything I can do to help?"

Cass tapped a loose thread on her sleeve before responding. “I’ve been looking at the sales data and labor costs, trying to find patterns or ways to cut expenses. I’m worried I’m not ready to apply what I’ve learned in a real-world situation like this.”

Professor Avery’s voice softened. “Cass, I want to be clear: data science isn’t a quick fix. It’s a tool, and like any tool, it takes time and practice to use effectively. Real-world data is rarely clean. You won’t have a perfect dataset handed to you—you have to build structure out of the chaos. Think about it like this: before you analyze patterns, you have to understand the data pipeline. Where does the information come from? How reliable is it? What’s missing?”

Cass exhaled, opening a spreadsheet. “Right now, I’m just trying to consolidate everything into a usable format. Some of these records are handwritten, and some come from the POS system. I already found a bunch of missing values and duplicate transactions. And I haven’t even started looking at food costs yet—just sales and labor, and I can already tell there are gaps. I don’t even know if I can trust half of these numbers.”

“That’s your first task—data cleaning. Before you even think about analysis, you need to standardize formats, remove duplicates, and flag inconsistencies. Start small. Look for one or two key metrics in each area—like customer retention in sales or peak hours in labor. You don’t have to solve everything at once.”

Cass grabbed a pen and scribbled a note on the corner of a receipt. “Okay. That makes sense. I’ll run some basic descriptive stats first—see what stands out.”

Professor Avery remained steady. “Good. But how do you know these gaps actually matter?”

Cass adjusted the laptop screen. “What do you mean?”

“Just because something looks strange in the data doesn’t mean it’s significant,” Avery said. “What’s your benchmark? How do you know these fluctuations aren’t just normal business variation?”

Cass clicked open another sheet, scanning previous months’ numbers.

“If you don’t have a baseline, you’re working blind,” Avery added. “Compare your current data to last quarter’s. If the fluctuations are consistent, they might not be an issue. If they’re unusual, that’s where you start digging.”

Cass made a note:

✓ Define a baseline—compare fluctuations to last quarter’s data.

✓ Find historical norms before assuming something is wrong.

"You've already started with sales and labor," Professor Avery continued. "That's great. But to get the most complete picture, you'll need to look at all four: sales, labor, food costs, and marketing. And when it comes to food costs, be careful trying to line them up with daily sales. They're what we call a 'leading cost'—they often don't match up neatly with sales on a day-to-day basis. You'll need to look at trends over time."

Cass nodded, though Professor Avery couldn't see her. She clicked into a new tab in her spreadsheet and added a moving average column to smooth out the fluctuations.

"I'll start pulling together the data for all four," she said.

"Good," Professor Avery said warmly. "And for marketing? Focus on promotions that bring in returning customers. A good place to start is repeat customer rate. How many customers come back within 30 days? That's your churn metric."

Cass jotted another note.

She exhaled. "I don't know what I'll find, but at least this gives me a framework."

"Good," Avery said. "But don't just rely on tables. Try visualizing the data. Sometimes trends are hidden in the raw numbers but jump out in a plot."

Cass adjusted her glasses. "I know how to make a bar chart, but I don't have time for that yet."

"Just plot one thing—sales trends over time. If nothing stands out, fine. But if something does, you'll be glad you did."

Cass made a note:

✓ Run a simple time-series plot of daily sales.

Professor Avery chuckled. "That's how data science works. You don't start with answers—you start with questions. And remember, you're not alone. That's what the mentoring session on July 12 is for—to help you navigate these challenges. Also, I just sent you an invite to a private event on the 18th hosted by Quintin Hale. The Data Science Meetup on the 20th is another great opportunity to connect with professionals."

Cass's shoulders relaxed. "Thank you, Professor Avery. I'll be there for all of it," she said into the phone, offering a brief smile as she entered the information in her calendar.

"Good. And don't hesitate to reach out if you need anything before then."

The conversation ended with a quick goodbye. Setting her phone on top of a short stack of unfiled receipts, Cass adjusted the angle of the laptop screen. She rubbed her forearm, feeling a slight draft drift through the door. From somewhere in the front, a pan clattered, likely Booker finishing up in the kitchen.

Her phone buzzed again:

Ayesha: "Cass, did you get Prof. Avery's invite? I'm so excited!"

Isaiah: "Hey Cass! Just saw the invite. You going? This is huge!"

Cass typed quick replies, confirming her attendance. Then she turned back to the sales data, opening a new spreadsheet labeled Key Metrics.

Her fingers moved steadily over the keyboard as she ran basic stats—mean revenue per table, labor cost percentages, daily sales fluctuations. She wasn't looking for answers yet. Just patterns.

The steady drone of the refrigerator mingled with the distant clatter of pans.

*****

At eight thirty, Booker called it—closing early tonight.

The kitchen crew scraped grease from the oil trap, the dull scrape of metal against metal cutting through the quiet. Half-full trash bags landed with a heavy thud near the back door, the day's waste barely filling them. Stacks of fresh produce sat untouched—portions prepped for a dinner rush that never came.

Maya appeared in the back doorway in running clothes, her hair pulled back in a tight bun. She pulled out her AirPods, tucking them into a small pouch at her waist. Sweat glistened on her temples despite the cool evening air. She scanned the half-empty kitchen before stepping forward.

Booker looked up from the receipt book. "Didn't expect to see you tonight."

Maya exhaled, rolling her shoulders. Sweat had soaked through the back of her running shirt. "It's been a day. Needed to clear my head."

"After my clinic shift, I went home to check on the boys, then went for a run," she added. "Thought I'd help with closing, but looks like you're already there."

"Hey honey," she said, walking over to kiss Booker on the cheek. He nodded, flipping a page in the receipt book, his pencil hovering over columns of red figures.

Cass continued flipping chairs onto tables, her movements mechanical. Once, the place buzzed with busy energy at this hour—now, the kitchen stood too tidy and quiet. Empty tables that should have held dinner crowds were already wiped clean, hours before their usual closing time. Joey, the busboy, wiped counters with rags and tossed them into the laundry bin.

Booker remained at the cash register, finishing the day's receipts. "Another day done," he said, closing the logbook and setting his pen aside. His every movement was deliberate and slow.

Cass walked to the entrance and flipped the sign to Closed. Through the glass, the streetlights cast long shadows across the empty sidewalk.

"We need to talk," Booker said quietly to Maya. "But not here. Let's talk in the car."

Maya's eyes narrowed. "What now?" She studied him, searching his face. "You mentioned Hal earlier this afternoon. What did he want?"

Her jaw tightened, shoulders stiff.

Silence stretched between them before Booker turned toward the back door.

They stepped out into the cool night air. Maria and the other staff murmured their goodbyes before slipping off down the alley, their footsteps fading into the quiet.

Booker locked the doors, the metallic click echoing against the empty dumpsters and brick walls. Somewhere in the distance, a car horn blared, then silence.

They walked in silence to the car. Booker reached for the handle, but hesitated, his fingers tightening around the metal. He exhaled slowly, shifting his weight.

"Maya, I don't know what to do," he said, his voice tight. "Hal wants three months' rent in six weeks. We have to find a way."

He tried the ignition. The car wouldn't start at first, but after a moment, it roared to life. Maya let out a sigh. "Don't say we'll figure it out when I don't see how, Booker. You've already cut costs as much as you can. The restaurant can't handle more. But... if you say so."

Cass settled in the back seat, listening. Booker rested heavily against the driver's seat, starting the car at last.

"Dad," Cass began. "I found something in the data today that might help." Booker and Maya didn't speak, so she continued. "I've looked at our sales records. Some dishes sell well, others don't move at all. We could focus on the popular items, do promotions around them, maybe draw in more customers. Also, I noticed a group of students sitting at the corner booth—remember how often I studied there with friends? Maybe we can improve on that."

Maya glanced at Cass in the rearview mirror. Booker remained quiet. After a moment, Maya spoke. "That's a great idea, Cass." She turned at a traffic light and then added, "Maybe I can pick up more clinic shifts. We'd build savings for any needed renovations."

"WE HAVE A DEBT TO PAY!" Booker's voice cut through sharply. He paused, then addressed Cass. "I'm sorry. I didn't mean to snap at you."

Maya spoke up. "Hal's deadline might be a blessing in disguise, pushing us to face everything head-on."

Booker let out a short breath. "A blessing?" His grip tightened on the wheel. "Maya, we could lose everything. I just wanted the restaurant to work."

He drew a breath, steadied himself. "Maybe it's time to rethink this dream, or do something else. I got injured before, and it's been a struggle since."

The sharp ring of Maya's phone cut through the car. She sighed and glanced at the screen. "Yes, Mom?"

Grandma Evelyn's voice came through, firm and unyielding. "I've been thinking about what you said, Maya. It's time for Booker to step up for the family. You need to push him—"

Maya held the phone away slightly. "Mom, can we talk later? I'm driving."

But Grandma Evelyn kept going, explaining she hadn't visited the restaurant yet. Booker exhaled sharply and gripped the wheel, his knuckles pale against the leather. Cass, in the back, recognized the older woman's voice and manner.

Outside, a small storefront church had its doors wide open, the sound of a choir rehearsal spilling onto the sidewalk. A hand-painted sign near the entrance read, "All Are Welcome," though half the bulbs in the marquee had burned out.

The call ended, leaving an uneasy quiet in the car. Maya glanced at Cass in the mirror. Booker kept both hands on the wheel, focusing on the road.

City lights flickered through the windows, casting patterns across the dashboard. Two teenagers ran drills on a cracked basketball court, one in a faded Baron Davis "We Believe" jersey, the other in a classic Steph Curry #30 Warriors tee. The rim had no net, but they kept shooting anyway, their layups clean despite the broken court. They paused only when a group of toddlers waddled too close, then resumed—relentless.

No one spoke for the rest of the ride. Cass rested her folder beside her, eyes drifting to the streetlights as they passed. The engine's steady hum filled the silence.

MONDAY, JULY 1 | JOURNAL ENTRY

7: The times I wanted to message Logan but didn't. I don't know why. He'd probably say something nice, tell me to take a break, maybe even joke about taking me out. But I don't want to be another person's project. I don't want pity.

2: The number of times Isaiah hit me up today. Said he's "here if I need anything." I know he means well, but bruh, you finna pull up and bus tables? Code my stress into an app? Didn't think so.

6: Pages I read from Linda's old book before I tapped out. Smells like fryer oil and cinnamon, like the back kitchen at Booker's. She left. We still here, drowning. I should text her. Ask her if she saw this coming. But I already know the answer.

1: Tiny moment of hope. A regular said they glad we still open. That's it. That's the journal entry. I'm really out here tryna hold onto a two-second convo like it's rent money.

20: Dollars left in my account. That's a wrap. Every time I check my balance, it's lookin' at me like, Why you even here? Maybe I should start bringing my own snacks when I go out with my friends. Maybe I should stop going out at all.

TUESDAY, JULY 2

The doors of Prosperity CDFI opened onto a welcoming lobby alive with vibrant colors and community pride. A mural of Dr. Cecil L. Williams stretched across one wall, showing him surrounded by people engaged in acts of neighborhood rebuilding and collaboration. The words Hope Through Action arched above the image in bold, daring lettering. Above the image, the words Hope Through Action arched in bold lettering.

Booker led the way inside, Maya's hand resting lightly on his arm for support. Cass followed closely, clutching a folder filled with financial documents. Behind her, Archer and Carver veered off toward a cozy children's area, stocked with bright books and inviting beanbags. Their laughter rose briefly above the hum of conversation, drawing a few smiles from other visitors. Their laughter rose briefly above the lobby's low hum, prompting a few visitors to smile.

"Welcome to Prosperity CDFI, Mr. and Mrs. Freeman," the receptionist greeted warmly, her voice carrying the practiced ease of someone who truly enjoyed her work. A polished counter behind her displayed brochures on affordable housing, small-business funding, and educational grants. "Mr. Dawson will see you now. Please follow me." She guided them down a hallway lined with art celebrating community leaders.

In the office, Peter Dawson stood to greet them. Tall and lean, he offered a firm handshake, his shaved head reflecting a soft sheen under the lights. "It's a pleasure to meet you. Please, have a seat," he said, gesturing to a circle of chairs around a small table. Green plants softened the room's edges, and a bookshelf overflowed with guides on finance and community engagement.

Peter set a folder on the table, leaning forward slightly. "Before we begin, let me explain what we do here at Prosperity CDFI. We provide financial support to individuals and businesses that banks often overlook. We focus on helping communities thrive by finding creative solutions."

Cass sat straighter, her folder balanced on her lap. "So, you're not like a typical bank?"

"Not at all," Peter replied. "Banks aim to reduce risk for their investors. We focus on creating opportunities—everything from small-business loans to housing initiatives. We fill the gaps where traditional lenders step back."

Booker nodded, placing a hand on the table. "Good to hear. We're under pressure and need to figure out the next step." His thumb tapped against the wood briefly before stilling, his focus narrowing on the charts in front of him.

Peter opened another folder, spreading out the Freemans' documents. "Let's review your situation," he said, gesturing toward a chart outlining their current liabilities. Booker leaned in, his palm flattening against the table, while Maya adjusted her chair closer. She rested her hand lightly on the edge of the table, her fingers brushing it rhythmically as she studied the graphs. He pointed to charts and figures, and Booker's tapping on the table subsided. Maya leaned over a graph, her fingers brushing the edge of her sleeve, while Cass kept her folder in hand, shoulders held still.

"Your debt ratios are high," Peter said, tapping a chart. "Cash flow is tight, and liabilities are substantial. For example," he continued, pointing to a bar graph, "your current operating expenses exceed income by about 30%, which limits your flexibility. Debt restructuring might help, but it involves negotiating terms with creditors, and the results can be unpredictable."

Cass shifted her folder slightly, her hand brushing the edge. "Could we qualify for an emergency loan?" she asked, her voice steady.

Peter shook his head slightly. "Given your debt levels, that's unlikely. We can look into grants or funding programs, but those take time, and competition is stiff."

Maya glanced at the door, then back to Peter. "If we sold the business, would it cover what we owe?"

Peter hesitated. "Selling under pressure usually means selling at a loss. It might help but probably not enough to clear everything."

The room fell quiet. Booker's hand hovered above the table briefly before dropping flat, his focus staying on the numbers spread out before him. Maya leaned back in her chair, her arms crossed tightly, her eyes moving between Peter and the scattered papers on the table.

"What if none of these work?" Booker asked, his voice quiet but deliberate.

"Bankruptcy is an option," Peter said, his voice even. "It's not easy, but it can reset obligations and give you a chance to rebuild. There are challenges—credit impacts, potential asset losses—but it offers a path forward."

Booker exhaled, leaning back in his chair. Maya nodded faintly, her lips tightening before she spoke. "We'll think about it."

Peter gathered the papers into a neat stack. "I know this isn't what you wanted to hear, but we'll keep looking for ways to help. Call anytime with questions."

They stood to leave, the earlier laughter from the children's corner replaced by the quiet rustling of pages. Archer lounged on a beanbag, his face partially obscured by Stacey Abrams's Coded Justice, while Carver sat cross-legged, fully immersed in Kevin Hart's Marcus Makes a Movie. Booker stepped closer, his voice low but firm. "Time to go, kids."

Archer glanced up, blinking as though emerging from another world. "Already? We just got into these!"

Carver hugged his book close. "Do we have to leave right now? Can we come back?"

Peter stepped over, his tall frame filling the doorway. "You can bring them back when you're done," he said kindly.

Both boys turned to him, faces brightening. "Thanks, Mr. Dawson!" they chimed, clutching their new finds.

Carver looked at Cass as she knelt beside him. "Did you fix it?" he asked hopefully.

Cass straightened the book in his hands. "Not yet," she said in a measured tone. "But we're on it."

The family exited the building, walking under the mural of Dr. Cecil L. Williams. The words Hope Through Action seemed to follow them. Outside, Maya whispered something to Booker while buses rumbled past and footsteps echoed on the sidewalk. Cass gripped her folder, her focus set ahead.

*****

The late afternoon sun illuminated the pristine tables outside Gelato Dorato, their sleek surfaces gleaming under the golden light. Minimalist chairs and tables sat beneath modern awnings that cast soft, dappled shadows, swaying slightly with the nearby trees. A gentle breeze carried the faint sound of laughter from the park, mingling with the rich aroma of hand-churned gelato and the crisp, sweet scent of waffle cones. The cheerful jingle of the gelato parlor's glass door chimed softly each time a new customer stepped in or out, adding to the lively yet refined ambiance.

As the door to the gelato shop chimed behind them, Alex spoke up, pulling everyone's attention back. "It's a shame Lola's not here—I know she loves the blackberry gelato here."

Nia glanced at her phone. “She texted earlier and said she was busy.”

“I saw that. Busy doing what?” Cass asked, her tone light but her brow furrowed.

Nia shrugged. “Probably at a party in Berkeley. You know how she is—she doesn’t want us messing up her game.”

Cass frowned, pulling out her phone and typing a quick message. She hesitated for a moment before pressing call, but it rang straight to voicemail. Setting her phone back on the table, she shook her head slightly. “She’s not answering.”

Sophia leaned forward. “Don’t stress. Lola always does her own thing. She’ll turn up.”

Cass sighed, picking up her spoon and swirling the last bit of mango-coconut gelato in its gold-rimmed cup. The overhead speakers played H.E.R. & Daniel Caesar’s “Best Part”, its warm, honeyed melody blending seamlessly with the soft hum of conversation and the occasional clink of silverware against porcelain.

As she checked again for a message from Lola, a bank notification flashed on the screen: “Purchase: $17.90 – Gelato Dorato.” A moment later, another notification appeared: “Bank Alert: Your account balance is below $50.” Cass frowned slightly, her fingers lingering on the screen before swiping the alerts away. Her phone buzzed again—her mom: ‘$20 for gelato? I just put money in your account yesterday.’ Cass sighed, set the phone aside, and picked up her spoon, swirling the last bit of melted gelato as she rejoined the conversation.

Bright outfits and relaxed postures blended effortlessly with the parlor’s modern, minimalist décor. The soft chime of silverware against plates mixed with quiet laughter.

“This place is ridiculous,” Alex said, crossing her legs and adjusting her diamond studs. “They serve the gelato in these tiny handmade cups, but somehow I still feel fancy.”

“It’s the ambiance,” Nia mused, taking a slow bite of her espresso affogato. “The lighting, the marble counters, the overpriced artisanal flavors—it’s a whole aesthetic.”

Cass smirked, setting down her spoon. “So basically, we’re paying for the vibe?”

“Obviously,” Sophia said, tilting her phone just right to capture the soft glow of the neon sign behind them. “‘Gelato Dorato—where every bite tastes like luxury.’”

“You should copyright that,” Alex quipped.

Sophia laughed, but then turned toward Nia. "Where's our next stop?"

"The new Mexican place," Nia replied, scrolling through her phone. "You know, the one that serves Wagyu and Iberico pork tacos?"

Alex's eyes lit up. "Oh, yes. I saw that all over TikTok. We have to go."

Talk of summer travel soon began to drift around the table.

Sophia leaned in, nudging her chair closer. She glanced around the table before speaking. "I'm leaving for Taiwan after the Fourth, but we should do this again when I'm back."

Nia's grin widened as she turned to Sophia. "And you're definitely bringing us those special pineapple cakes, right?"

Sophia smirked. "Sunny Hills! Only if you're extra nice."

Alex shifted in her chair and sighed, crossing her arms lightly. "I didn't get to go anywhere this summer. But my parents are promising a long weekend in Mexico before school starts, so that's something."

She adjusted her diamond studs, catching the light and making Cass squint slightly. "Whoa, girl! Those earrings are fire! Isn't your birthday next month?" Cass asked.

Alex grinned. "Yes, but my dad said I deserved them."

Alex leaned back slightly, her tone nonchalant. "So, guess what? Dr. Stevens, my advisor, wants me to do Introduction to Surgery next summer. He said I showed real promise!"

"That's huge, Alex!" Sophia said, giving her a quick thumbs-up. "That camp must've been amazing."

Alex smiled slightly and chimed in, "Logan, you should've gone to the Johns Hopkins summer camp with me. It was incredible."

Logan tilted his head and replied, "I would've loved to, but I've been helping my parents at their practice all summer."

Sophia smirked. "We'll see. Depends on how nice you are to me. But I might sneak some extra boxes for Cass, too—she looks like she could use the energy."

Cass smiled slightly, setting her spoon down. "It's been a busy time at the restaurant. But I'll be at practice soon—I'm not missing another season."

"Oh, come on," Alex teased, nudging Cass lightly. "Come on, it's not like you're running the place solo. You just serve food and count-cash, right?"

Cass leaned back slightly, shaking her head. "Not really. It's more like solving puzzles every day—tracking inventory, troubleshooting mismatched orders, and understanding customer patterns."

"Businesswoman Cass, coming right up," Alex replied with a playful wink.

Logan leaned in. "Hey, Cass, how about you? You mentioned some interesting data projects you did at camp."

Cass set her cup aside. "We worked on a few. One project focused on disease outbreak predictions using social media. Another looked at traffic patterns in big cities."

Sophia said, "It looks like I need to bring a special box for Cass. She's juggling more than all of us!"

Logan nodded. "Cass, you make it sound way more interesting than I expected. Like, you're running a whole operation."

Jake studied Cass for a moment. "Isn't it a lot, handling both the restaurant and all this data stuff?"

Cass shrugged, tucking her phone away. "It keeps me busy, but I'm learning a lot."

Logan tapped the table lightly. "Let's plan another gelato meet-up for your next big milestone, Cass. We'll celebrate properly."

"Deal!" everyone said in unison.

Sophia pulled out her phone, angling it just right. "Let's take a picture—gelato and friends, the perfect combo! Everyone squeeze in."

"Alright," Nia announced, stretching her arms above her head. "Next stop, tacos. Logan, you coming."
"I'll meet you there," Logan said.

As the sky shifted to pink and blue hues, the group stepped outside, sharing a few final laughs. Alex, Nia, Jake, and Sophia headed off toward a new Mexican restaurant, leaving Cass and Logan to walk together.

"Want to stroll for a minute?" Logan asked, his hand brushing lightly against Cass's as he stepped toward the park entrance. The sounds of the bustling gelato shop softened behind them.

She nodded, and they made their way into the nearby park. "I've been thinking more about data science in healthcare," Logan said. "Could you explain it sometime?"

Cass glanced at her watch. "Sure. I saw some projects on disease prediction that were pretty impressive. But I've got to head back now or I'll be late to the restaurant."

Logan paused, then spoke quietly. "No problem. By the way, are you free next weekend?"

Cass glanced at him, her eyebrows lifting slightly. "Really?" she asked, her tone neutral but curious.

Logan smiled, shifting his weight. "Maybe we could have dinner or something. Just us."

Cass studied him for a brief moment. "That sounds nice. I'd like that."

"Great," Logan said. "I'll text you the details."

A vibration buzzed against the table. Cass glanced at her phone. A new email notification flashed across the screen: Your account is past due. Future orders and deliveries will be suspended until payment is received.

Her fingers tightened around the device. The easy rhythm of the conversation stalled. Across from her, Logan was still smiling, unaware.

She slipped her phone into her pocket and nodded. "Sounds good. Night, Logan," not waiting for his response.

*****

The desk lamp cast a gentle pool of light in Cass's bedroom. She sat at her laptop, its screen reflecting faintly on her reading glasses. On one side of her desk, Reaching for the Moon: The Autobiography of NASA Mathematician Katherine Johnson lay open beside a data notebook. On the other, a grease-stained printout of the restaurant's weekly sales data rested near the edge.

Color-coded columns filled the pages of her notebook, each row detailing various aspects of the restaurant's operations—sales, marketing, and costs. She flipped to a clean sheet and wrote in large letters: Sales, Marketing, Food Cost, Labor Cost. Beneath those headings, she jotted short notes: "Wednesday dessert anomaly? Check if data entry error," and "Confirm promo codes + social media posts." Her pen glided across the page as she wrote.

The rest of the room sat in near stillness. Her bed, with pillows and a folded quilt, formed a dim shape in the corner, while photos on the walls appeared and faded as moonlight shifted. A worn shelf stood nearby, lined with mended-spine books and math puzzle collections, plus a few restaurant inventory texts borrowed for cross-referencing recipes with actual sales data.

Cass opened a new spreadsheet on her laptop. She entered the day's sales figures from a photo Booker had sent—"salads: 15, burgers: 27, desserts: 9." After entering the data, she created a pivot table to analyze trends. Dessert sales showed an unusually high count compared to other weekdays, prompting her to recheck the sums. She exported the restaurant's order data as a CSV file and loaded it into Python for deeper analysis. When an error popped up about a missing column header, she opened the raw CSV file in a text editor and immediately spotted stray spaces in one of the column names. "Fix headers before running analysis," she jotted in her notebook, adding a note to check for staff data entry inconsistencies.

Noticing an odd discrepancy, she exported a CSV file of the orders Booker had shared. While reviewing the file in Python, a familiar error message popped up: "IndexError: list index out of range." She sighed and opened a Stack Overflow tab, searching for common CSV parsing issues. Threads mentioning improperly formatted headers caught her attention, prompting her to check for stray spaces or misplaced quotation marks in the data. As she scrolled, she jotted a reminder in her notebook: "Double-check exported CSV for header consistency."

Switching to GitHub, she reviewed an example workflow for handling messy data. She adapted the instructions to identify rows with missing revenue values and ensure consistency in the file's structure. After running the checks, she flagged several rows with missing revenue data and made a note to follow up with Booker about these gaps. Nearby, a printed sheet from her summer boot camp bore the phrase "Garbage in, garbage out," a reminder that accurate data entry was crucial." A printed sheet from her summer boot camp lay nearby, bearing the phrase "Garbage in, garbage out," a reminder of the importance of accuracy in data.

Time passed quietly, the laptop's fan blending with the distant chirping of crickets. The desk lamp cast a dim yellow glow over the room, highlighting the grease-stained sales data and a neatly organized notebook. Cass adjusted her glasses, scanning the revenue column—some cells were blank, others misaligned. She pulled up a bookmarked troubleshooting guide and began standardizing the values. Each adjustment brought more structure to the dataset.

She jotted in her notebook: "Ensure revenue column data type is consistent—review staff training for accuracy." A quick comparison with past reports showed similar issues recurring, particularly during peak hours. "Investigate system logging during rush periods," she added to her list before moving on.

Her phone buzzed at 11:45 PM, lighting up the corner of her desk. A message from her mother appeared:

Mom: "Don't forget to review your SAT prep materials tomorrow. You have months to prepare, but starting now will only help. Working on the restaurant data is not an excuse."

Cass looked at an untouched SAT study guide on the nightstand, then at a printed handout from camp repeating "Garbage in, garbage out." She wrote another note in her notebook: "SAT tomorrow—set study time. Verify dessert orders—Booker follow-up." She dismissed the phone notification and returned to her spreadsheet.

A new message arrived, prompting her to pick up her phone again:

Isaiah:

"Meeting you was the best part of camp. I really wanted to talk more—maybe we can video chat and plan something?"

She briefly looked between the phone screen and the rows of numbers on her laptop. After a pause, she typed:

Cass:

"Hey Isaiah, thanks for your messages. I appreciate your honesty, but I'm swamped with work right now. Can we talk later?"

She set her phone aside, directing her attention back to the data on dessert sales. She entered a note in her notebook: "Check local community calendar for Wed. events," referencing a camp reminder that correlation isn't causation. A quick bar chart showed a noticeable mid-week surge in desserts followed by a slump on Saturdays.

Further checks suggested a misdated batch of dessert orders. Cross-referencing timestamps with other receipts, Cass pinpointed discrepancies in #4532 and #4533, where the dates didn't align with typical order trends. She adjusted her workflow to flag inconsistent timeframes and circled the entries in her notebook. "Verify receipts #4532 and #4533—typo in date field? Confirm with Booker," she wrote, preparing to follow up during their upcoming Zoom call. She also added a reminder to explore whether these discrepancies were tied to newer staff members or recent system updates." She made a mental note to bring it up in their next scheduled Zoom call.""

The moonlight traced soft lines across the walls as the clock inched toward 2:10

AM. Cass saved her spreadsheet and leaned back, her hands resting on the desk's edge. The laptop's quiet fan and the occasional chirp of crickets filled the stillness. Her notebook lay open, pen resting across its pages. She lowered her head onto the desk, the lamp casting a warm circle of light over scattered notes and grease-stained data sheets as her breathing steadied.

WEDNESDAY, JULY 3

Cass woke at dawn, shifting in her chair as the first rays of sunlight fell across charts and graphs on her screen. The seat creaked as she straightened and gathered the printed data—figures on inefficiencies in inventory, underperforming menu items, and trends that might revive the family business. She closed her laptop and stacked her notes, pausing to glance at the SAT prep books lining a nearby shelf. A knock sounded at the door.

"Good morning," Maya said, stepping inside. Her nurse scrubs were crisp, and her hair was pulled back neatly. She surveyed the desk before focusing on Cass. "You look exhausted. Did you sleep at all?"

Cass gave a slight smile, pulling her sweatshirt around her shoulders. "I was just heading downstairs. I've made progress on the data—I think you and Dad will be interested."

Maya studied her. "Did you read my message last night?"

"I saw it," Cass said. "I've been working on the restaurant numbers. I really want to show you both."

Maya leaned against the doorframe, pressing a thumb to the edge of her scrub pocket. "I appreciate your dedication, but your SAT prep matters, too. Scholarships will keep your options open."

Cass glanced around the small space, books and mismatched furniture giving the room a cramped feel. "I'm balancing it," she replied.

Maya's tone softened. "Just be careful not to let one thing take over. And take care of yourself. Grab some coffee—we'll talk about your summer plans after breakfast."

Cass nodded. Before she could respond, footsteps pounded on the stairs as Archer and Carver appeared.

"Morning, Mom! Morning, Cass!" Carver called. "What's for breakfast? I'm starving."

Archer eyed Cass. "You look like you pulled an all-nighter."

Carver smirked. "She probably got run over by a truck full of books."

Cass rolled her eyes, a small smile appearing. "Funny. What do you two need?"

Archer dropped onto the edge of her bed. "So... that project you're doing with all the charts—what is it? Some school thing?"

Carver nodded. "Or maybe a math contest?"

“It’s for the restaurant,” Cass explained. “I’m helping Mom and Dad figure out which dishes aren’t selling and how to save on supplies.”

Archer’s brow furrowed. “You fix the restaurant using math?”

“Pretty much,” Cass said.

“That’s awesome,” Carver said. “But does it really work?”

Cass nodded. “It can, if we do it right. It’s like solving a puzzle.”

Archer shrugged. “Maybe you’ll save the place and be famous someday.”

Cass gave a short laugh. “Let’s just aim for saving the restaurant for now.”

Downstairs, Cass poured coffee while Archer and Carver argued over chairs. She carried her mug to the table, where Maya was seated.

“I’ve seen how hard you’re working,” Maya said. “But I’m worried you’re losing sight of other possibilities.”

“The restaurant is the main focus,” Cass answered, her voice turning sharp. “It’s our family legacy. I can make a difference.”

Maya let out a measured breath. “I know. But Grace at the clinic told me about internships in medical data—stable, respected paths you might want to consider.”

Cass gripped her mug, then set it down. “Mom, this data work makes sense to me. It’s not just numbers—it’s helping our community.”

Maya watched her for a moment. “I want what’s best for you, Cassie. Don’t let the restaurant pull you away from your future.”

Cass met her mother’s gaze. “What if my future isn’t somewhere else? What if the work I’m doing now is the real way I can make a difference?”

Maya sighed, shoulders dropping. “Just promise you’ll at least talk to Grace. Keep your options open.”

Cass gave a brief nod. “Okay.”

Maya pressed her fingertips to her temples before exhaling, tension tightening the corners of her mouth. “Promise me you’ll talk to Grace. Just... keep your options open.”

Cass nodded, unwilling to argue further.

*****

As Cass pushed open the front door, the familiar chime of the bell echoed through Booker's Pages and Plates, a place where history and flavor intertwined. Like on previous days, the brunch service was slow, leaving several empty tables among the tall, silent bookshelves. The usual aroma of beef patties and toasted buns was subdued, allowing the gentle scent of old books to fill the air. Over the speakers, "Groove Me" by Guy played softly, giving the restaurant a nostalgic mood.

Cass spotted her father at the host counter, where he was filing the reservation book and sorting through a short stack of invoices. "Dad?" she said. "Can I talk to you for a minute?"

Booker looked up, his expression shifting slightly. "Of course, kiddo," he replied, setting his pen down. "What's on your mind?"

Cass glanced at the paperwork. "About those improvements I mentioned in the car—I realize you and Mom were tired, and I might've pushed too hard. Sorry if I came on strong."

Booker shook his head. "What happened that night was on me. You did great, and I see how hard you've been working." He exhaled and spoke evenly. "I'm just not sure we should spend more money right now, not when we don't know if any changes will pay off."

"Dad, I've been analyzing our sales data day and night," Cass said, tapping the folder under her arm. "I think there are ways to improve efficiency and cut costs."

She began listing off the patterns she had found, pointing to numbers and suggesting new approaches. As her explanation continued, Booker's expression turned more serious, his eyes drifting toward the empty grill in the kitchen.

"That's good work, Cass," he said after a pause. "But we've got bigger issues. I had to cut Mike's hours today—he's only on for Fridays and Saturdays now."

Cass glanced at him, then at the kitchen door. "But he's one of our best. We can't lose him."

Booker folded the corner of a page in the reservation book. "We can't afford to keep everyone on the same schedule. I'm going to cover more shifts myself. It's been a minute since I worked the line, but we have to cut costs wherever we can."

"We already cut back labor, trimmed portions, even dropped online takeout services because the fees were eating into the profits. What else is left?"

Cass set her folder down, looking at the files as she spoke. "Mike's been here from the start. He's important to the restaurant."

Booker nodded briefly. "I know. He's brought in a lot, and I hate doing this. But we're at a point where we have no choice."

Cass rested a hand on the counter. "I'm sorry, Dad. I'll keep working on the data. We'll find a way to fix things."

Booker gave a small nod. "I appreciate that. But don't put all this on yourself. Your mom's been on me about making sure you study for your SAT prep. Don't stay here too late tonight. We can manage dinner service. Go home after sunset and focus on your studying."

Cass looked at the new messages piling up on her phone. She silenced it and gathered the rest of her notes. "Okay, Dad," she said quietly.

*****

At 11:50 PM, the house lay still as Cass descended the stairs for a glass of water, each step softened by the creak of old wooden treads. A slight chill pressed against her arms as she walked. A narrow beam of light stretched from the living room into the dark hall, drawing her attention. She paused at the doorway.

Maya sat beneath the dim light of a single lamp, her phone clutched in her hands. She breathed in sharply, releasing a hushed sob. Shadows deepened the lines of her face. She glanced up, startled by Cass's presence, then quickly wiped at her eyes, trying to regain composure.

"Oh, Cassie," Maya said, her voice catching. "I was waiting for your father. He hasn't answered my messages."

Cass settled into a chair beside her, resting a hand gently on Maya's arm. "He mentioned cutting Mike's hours. He's probably covering the shift himself and lost track of time."

Maya nodded, her fingers tapping lightly on the phone. She looked at it for a moment. "Booker and I used to dance together," she said quietly. "The floorboards would creak under us, and he'd spin me until I couldn't stop laughing." She paused. "We haven't danced in a long time."

She exhaled, gaze drifting to the muted TV in the corner, playing old reruns of Living Single. "Your Aunt Zora shares stories sometimes, and I realize how much I miss," she said, voice low. "I'm always running—work, the house, everything. There's never enough time."

The distant sound of cars passed outside, joined by the quiet ticking of a clock on the mantel. Cass switched on the TV, its flickering light casting shifting patterns across the living room. She watched it absently as she sat beside Maya. The minutes slipped by.

Close to midnight, headlights swept across the windows, followed by the low rumble of a car engine fading. Then came the jingle of keys at the front door. Cass and Maya rose from the sofa as Booker walked in, his backpack over one shoulder. The scent of oil and fresh herbs lingered on him, and the crisp night air clung to his clothes for a moment before vanishing into the house. His keys clattered onto the counter. He ran a hand over his face, offering a faint smile at the sight of them.

"Sorry it's so late," he said, his voice rough. "I stayed in the kitchen longer than I meant to."

Maya stepped forward and pulled him into a tight hug. Cass stood near the staircase, noticing the slight slump in his posture and how firmly Maya held him. She quietly adjusted a pillow on the sofa, then slipped upstairs, leaving them to that moment.

In her room, Cass perched on the edge of the bed, tracing the blanket's edge with her fingertips. The glow of her phone lit her face. She saw a missed message from Logan describing plans for their date. She quickly typed a reply:

Logan: "Hey Cass! I've been thinking about our date and am excited! How about we try that new Italian place downtown for dinner after going to Jack London Square? I heard they have amazing risotto. Could be fun to explore something new. What do you think?"

Cass: "Sorry I missed this! I love that idea. The Italian spot sounds great—I'm looking forward to it. Thanks for planning. See you soon!"

She tapped "send," then noticed a blinking notification at the top of her screen. Lola's name appeared, prompting a faint smile.

Lola: "Hey Cass! Are you asleep? Sorry I've been MIA and missed our last gelato run. How was it? And how are you?" Lola: "Also... tomorrow's July 4. Any plans? I'll stop by the restaurant in the morning. Don't kick me out, okay? 🙏"

Cass let out a short laugh at Lola's playful tone, then typed a response, her fingers moving quickly. She paused briefly, reread what she wrote, then hit send, still smiling.

WEDNESDAY, JULY 3 | JOURNAL ENTRY

3: The restless hours of sleep I managed last night.

7: The times I checked the restaurant's inventory data today, hoping for some good news. Instead, I just found more gaps. Missing numbers, mismatched orders, too many questions. We're running out of time, and I don't even know what we're running toward.

6: The hours I spent on SAT prep, flipping through practice questions but barely processing a word. Mom thinks I can just compartmentalize—study in the morning, save the restaurant in the afternoon, pretend everything's fine at night. My brain doesn't work like that.

4: The number of times my thoughts drifted to Linda—how much she loved this restaurant, and how she's gone now. Did she see this coming before we did? Did she leave because she knew?

1: The moment of relief when Mom apologized for missing my boot camp presentation. She looked so tired, waiting for Dad to come home. I wanted to tell her everything was gonna be okay, but I don't know if that's true.

12: The customers we had during lunch rush. Twelve. This time last summer, we'd have a line out the door. Now, it's barely enough to keep the lights on.

15: The seconds I stood in front of the mirror before heading to the restaurant, trying to hype myself up. Told myself today would be different. That I'd find something in the numbers, that I'd prove I wasn't just throwing ideas at a sinking ship.

10: The minutes Dad and I spent going back and forth about cutting costs. He doesn't wanna hear it. Doesn't wanna cut portion sizes, doesn't wanna do promo deals, doesn't wanna change anything. But if we don't change something, we won't have a restaurant to protect.

5: The times I almost told him about the missing money. But every time I opened my mouth, he just looked so tired. Like he already knew something was wrong but couldn't bring himself to say it.

8: The texts from Lola I left on read. She wants to hang out before the Fourth, but I don't have the energy to explain why I'm not in the mood for fireworks and barbecue.

30: The minutes I spent staring at my notes, re-running the numbers, trying to make sense of all the missing pieces. It feels like I'm looking at a puzzle, and someone threw half the pieces away.

11: The time on the clock when I caught Mom sitting in the dark, phone in her hand, waiting for Dad. She looked up when I walked in, wiped at her face like I didn't just see her crying.

100: The ways I wanted to ask her what's really going on. Where Dad's been. If we're already past saving this place. But I just sat next to her, let the silence fill the space.

∞: The fear that keeps me up at night. The realization that I might not be able to fix this. That I might be too late. That maybe, this story doesn't end with us winning.

Feature Selection

In a world of overwhelming information, not all data is created equal. Feature selection is the art of identifying the most important variables that influence outcomes. It requires focus and discernment, cutting through the noise to find what truly matters. The right features bring clarity, helping to simplify complex decisions and make sense of chaotic inputs. By prioritizing the key factors, feature selection creates a foundation for accurate predictions and well-informed decisions, shaping the paths ahead.

THURSDAY, JULY 4

The Fourth of July in Rockridge began with early-morning energy. The sun brightened the neighborhood as families left their homes, ready to celebrate. Yards and the local park quickly filled with activity. Strings of red, white, and blue lights hung over fences and bushes, and grills stood in place for the day's gatherings. The air carried the scent of freshly cut grass and the distant aroma of barbecue..

Cass passed the holiday preparations, noting local bands setting up gear for later performances around community spots. A flyer for First Fridays was taped to a street pole, its edges curling from the summer heat. Vendors arranged crates of handmade jewelry and artwork under pop-up tents, their tables stacked with Afrocentric prints and woven baskets.

She walked toward the restaurant, the sound of cheerful music fading as she reached the old book storage room that served as her temporary office.

Inside, morning light streamed through the open windows, stretching across stacks of paperwork and the laptop on a shaky table. Cass typed quickly once the spreadsheet loaded, reviewing rows of sales figures and inventory records. The keys clicked under her fingers as she worked to fix a half-completed chart, pausing to check an online tutorial whenever another formula refused to update. Laughter and the aroma of breakfast drifted faintly from the kitchen.

Lola appeared in the doorway with a tray of churros drizzled in chocolate sauce and a small bowl of vanilla ice cream. "Good morning! I brought you some study fuel," she said, placing the tray on the cluttered desk. Cass glanced at the pastries and ice cream, her stomach rumbling.

"Hi, Lola! I've missed you," Cass said, standing to hug her. Lola dragged an old chair from the corner and sat down, scanning the spreadsheets scattered around. "You're really buried in this," Lola said. "I've been so wrapped up in everything, I didn't realize how much you've been handling here. I'm sorry. I should have been here sooner."

Cass set her hands on her hips and turned the laptop screen toward Lola. "I've been trying for a week to match our new orders to the old system. Nothing's aligning." She tapped a column with her pen. "The dataset is a mess—missing values, formatting errors, inconsistent headers. I read articles about merge functions, but mismatch errors keep popping up." She exhaled. "I need to clean and preprocess it before I can even analyze trends. I'm stuck."

"Hey... I should be the one to say that," Cass added quietly. "We've both been busy. But thanks for coming now." She motioned to the tray. "And thanks for the churros."

Lola laughed and broke off a small piece of one churro, dipping it into the chocolate sauce. Cass did the same, swirling hers before taking a bite. A slight grin crossed her face at the crunch of the pastry against the cool ice cream.

“How was the last hangout? I heard it got dramatic. And Logan—didn’t you two seem like a good match? How’s that going?” Lola asked.

Cass’s cheeks grew warm at the mention of Logan. She closed one spreadsheet, opened another, and brushed aside a sticky note. “We’ve been texting. He asked me on a date,” she said, scrolling through numbers on the screen. “He also invited me to his party tonight. I wanted to go, but I’m behind on inventory analysis and can’t leave this unfinished.”

“Oh my gosh, Cass! A date? That’s amazing! When is it? Any plan? Are you definitely not coming tonight? If you need time for this, I get it, but it’d be fun if you went. You deserve a break. I’m excited for you!”

Cass smiled faintly, rubbing the back of her neck. “Thanks, Lola. I needed that encouragement.” She stacked a few printouts to clear space on the desk. “The date’s in two weeks. Tonight, I’m staying here. I don’t want to be at a party thinking about merge errors. But I’m going on the date for sure. Thanks for being so supportive. I’ll give you all the details afterward.”

Lola nodded. “I get it. If you want to go, though, you can talk to Logan about what’s going on. He might be more understanding than you think.”

Cass scrolled through another online forum. “It’s complicated. The restaurant’s in a tough spot, and I’m not sure how much I want to share with Logan. And Isaiah’s been texting, but he’s not going to the party. It’s a lot.”

“Isaiah?” Lola arched an eyebrow, smiling. “He’s still kind of cute.”

Cass raised one as well. “As a friend, sure. Not as a boyfriend.”

Lola checked her phone screen and stood. “It’s five. I need to get home and get ready for the party. I’ll see you later, okay?” She gave Cass a quick hug and picked up the tray, nodding at the few remaining pieces. “Enjoy the rest of those.”

Hours went by as Cass worked alone. The distant bursts of fireworks signaled the celebrations outside, but she stayed focused on her laptop. She hovered over a set of figures in the restaurant’s point-of-sale data, searching for a pattern that refused to emerge. Her phone buzzed with more notifications, and she pushed them aside to concentrate on the numbers. The savory smells of barbecued ribs and grilled seafood drifted in through the window, blending with the faint sense of summer rain against the pavement.

From the makeshift office, she heard a muffled hum of gatherings in the neighborhood. Earlier, a local band's upbeat music faded when a light drizzle passed through. Occasional clinks of glass and distant cheers from block parties contrasted with the quiet focus in her cramped space. She jotted a few notes on a yellow pad, then crossed them out moments later.

Her phone lit up with a message from Logan: Logan: "Happy 4th of July, Cass! Wish you were here." Cass: "Happy 4th, Logan. Maybe next year."

Almost at the same time, a group chat alert popped up from Isaiah and Ayesha: Isaiah: "Happy 4th, team! Hope you guys are enjoying the day." Ayesha: "Happy July 4, everyone! I hope this day brings liberation to all of us!" Cass: "Thanks, Isaiah, Ayesha. Happy 4th!"

Outside, the festivities continued, but Cass stayed intent on the inventory figures until Booker walked in. "Hey, Cass. How's it going?" He leaned against the doorframe and sorted through a short stack of receipts before setting them aside.

Cass looked up and offered a faint smile. "Hey, Dad."

"It's eight," Booker said. "Last order was an hour ago. Let's call it a night. Staff left a while ago, so it's just us. I could use your help cleaning up."

Cass closed her laptop and tidied her papers. "Sure," she replied, placing the reports into a folder. She joined Booker in the dining area, wiping tables and pushing chairs in while he counted earnings at the register. The fading noise of the holiday celebrations formed a subdued backdrop as they worked. When they finished, Cass locked the door and exhaled, folder still in hand. She flipped off the overhead light and followed Booker out. The data would remain for her to address the next day.

SATURDAY, JULY 4 | JOURNAL ENTRY

2: The hours I spent with Lola in the back office this morning. Felt normal for the first time in weeks—just talking, laughing, eating churros like we didn't have the weight of a whole restaurant on our backs. She said she should've been around more. I should've told her how much I needed her, but I just said, "You're here now."

1: The second I hesitated before telling her about Logan's invite. I don't even know why I was nervous—maybe because saying it out loud made it real. She went full hype mode, talking about outfits and how I should take a break. I told her I wasn't going to the party.

6: The times she tried to convince me to go anyway. "Cass, the numbers will still be here tomorrow." Yeah, and so will the unpaid bills, the low customer count, and the eviction notice sitting in Dad's office.

10: The customers we had today. That's it. A whole holiday, and we couldn't even pull in a dinner crowd.

3: The times Dad checked the front door, like he was waiting for more people to show up. They didn't.

12: The minutes I spent staring at the Fourth of July decorations still taped to the window. Faded, barely hanging on. Kind of like us.

4: The number of times I checked my phone for a message from Logan. He texted Happy 4th! but nothing else. Maybe he figured out I wasn't coming. Maybe I should've told him sooner.

8: The deep breaths I took before walking into the kitchen after closing. Dad was sitting at the counter, staring at a half-empty ledger like he was trying to rewrite the numbers with his mind.

30: The seconds I stood there before saying, "We should go home." He didn't argue. Just closed the book, sighed, and nodded.

5: The texts from my friends about fireworks, late-night food runs, bonfires. I could've gone. Could've pretended for one night that everything was normal. But I wasn't in the mood to lie.

11: The time I finally got upstairs. I could still hear distant fireworks, people laughing outside. The world kept moving like nothing was happening.

100: The thoughts racing through my head. About the numbers. About Logan. About what happens if we don't figure this out in six weeks.

∞: The sinking feeling in my chest. That this was supposed to be a day for celebrating. Instead, all I can think about is what happens when the lights finally go out.

FRIDAY, JULY 5

The stylish restaurant where Linda now worked stood only a few miles from Booker's Pages and Plates. Cass paused at the palm leaf–shaped door, noting its glossy finish and the lively chatter spilling onto the sidewalk. A warm breeze brushed her cheeks as she stepped inside, where string lights glowed against teal walls and hanging ferns. An upbeat, Latin-infused melody mingled with the sizzle of a stovetop flame, and the smoky aroma of grilled peppers drifted through the air.

She spotted Linda weaving through a crowded aisle, balancing plates of Wagyu and Iberico pork tacos. Linda moved with the same calm assurance she had shown at Booker's from day one, when she guided Cass on greeting and seating customers. As soon as Linda set her tray on a side station, she saw Cass near the entrance, offered a quick smile, and approached.

"Hey, Cass. It's really good to see you," Linda said, standing aside so a passing server could maneuver a tray of tall drinks.

"It's good to see you, too," Cass replied, gesturing at the colorful murals and sleek teak furnishings. "This place looks amazing."

Linda tied her apron strings tighter. "It's a steady job. Hurt to leave Booker's, though. I was there from the beginning, but Booker always preferred cooking over handling inventory. He wanted me somewhere with consistent hours."

Cass adjusted the tote bag on her shoulder. "We miss you. The restaurant isn't the same."

Linda guided Cass to a small table near the wall. The scent of freshly mixed cocktails drifted over as a bartender shook a metal tumbler at the bar. "I miss you all, too. Thanks for coming by. We can talk for a minute."

Pots clanged in the kitchen, and lively chatter rippled through the dining area. Cass leaned forward, hands resting on the table. "Something serious is happening at Booker's. We've found gaps in our finances and missing supplies. It might be overordering or stealing. Did you notice anything before you left?"

Linda glanced at a group of servers gathering extra cutlery. "I saw invoice totals rising, then supplies disappearing. It felt bigger than a simple ordering error."

Cass tapped the edge of the table, drawing a breath to respond—

"Linda! New party in Section Two needs menus!" the manager called.

Linda stood straighter and looked toward the station where menus were stacked. "Sorry, Cass. We'll pick this up again. Keep a close watch on your records."

“Thanks, Linda,” Cass said, stepping aside as a host guided a new group of diners. “We appreciate your help.”

Linda gave a quick smile before hurrying off. Cass stepped outside, where bursts of laughter and the aroma of sizzling meats trailed from the restaurant. Late-afternoon heat pressed against her skin as she walked two blocks to the bus stop.

At the bus stop, the AC Transit 51B pulled up. Cass scanned her pass and grabbed the metal railing as the bus lurched forward before she found a seat. A woman near the front nodded along to a song only she could hear, while a man two rows back tapped out a rhythm on the window with his knuckles. Someone in the back argued loudly over speakerphone, their voice rising over the hum of the engine.

She settled by the window, resting a hand on the bar as the city moved past. Passengers clutched shopping bags or tapped away on phones. A man across the aisle held a grease-stained paper bag, the smell of soy sauce and fried chicken cutting through the musty air.

Through the window, murals stretched along an alley wall, each a riot of bold colors and thick brushstrokes. Black Panthers, Oakland poets, and community activists stared back, their names scrawled in thick black ink beneath the images.

After a brief ride, Cass stepped off near Booker’s Pages and Plates. As she passed a barbershop, “Keep Ya Head Up” played from a speaker in the corner, blending with the low hum of clippers. Men inside debated the Warriors’ playoff chances, some still salty about the team’s move to San Francisco.

“They belong in Oakland, man. Chase Center ain’t got no soul,” one of the older guys said, shaking his head.

“That’s just ‘cause you ain’t been,” someone else shot back. “That place is the truth.”

A barber lined up a customer’s fade while a framed photo of Steph Curry hung near the register, next to a signed Raiders cap from the team’s last Oakland season.

The barber glanced up as Cass walked by. “Tell your dad it’s time for him to come in,” he called out. “I’m know he’s looking raggedy by now.”

Cass smirked. “Hey X, the restaurant has him buried. He’ll probably have to resort to his Warriors hat pretty soon.” Laughter rippled through the shop before the conversation shifted back to the game.

Cass crossed the small parking lot and slipped in through a side door. The afternoon sun streamed through a single office window, illuminating tidy rows of papers and a bright laptop screen. She set her tote on a spare chair and opened a spreadsheet.

"Linda mentioned overordering," she said, scrolling through purchase orders. A new file labeled "Discrepancies" contained every suspicious entry she had found.

The office door creaked open. Booker walked in, wearing a stained chef's apron and wiping sweat from his forehead with a dish towel. "Busy day?" he asked, setting the towel on a nearby shelf.

Cass angled the laptop so he could see the highlighted rows. "I talked to Linda. She noticed deliveries that never matched our invoices. Could be theft, or someone signing off on items we're not getting." She pointed at a highlighted cell. "These numbers stand out."

Booker leaned closer, his gaze narrowed. "If that's happening, we need to handle it right away."

Cass switched to another spreadsheet, reviewing stock data. "I still have more to check. I'm juggling a lot. I need at least an hour tonight for the SAT language section, plus I'm finishing a presentation for you and Mom. I want to show you what I've found so far."

Booker rested a hand on the desk. "That's fine. Take the time you need, but don't overdo it."

Cass opened another tab. "I'll do my best. Right now, I'm comparing orders to actual inventory. Once I've sorted the numbers, I'll share them with you."

Booker glanced toward the door, where distant clanging pots echoed. Cass returned her focus to the screen, adding more entries to the "Discrepancies" file. Rays of the setting sun inched across the floor as the dinner rush commenced in the next room. She typed a final note, then glanced at the schedule pinned to the wall. The next items listed were SAT study and a family presentation.

FRIDAY, JULY 5 | JOURNAL ENTRY

5: The hours I spent last night staring at the ceiling. My body was tired, but my brain wouldn't shut off. Every time I closed my eyes, I saw red ink on Dad's ledger, empty tables, and Hal standing in the restaurant saying, "It's just business."

1: The excuse I gave when Lola asked if I wanted to hang out. I told her I had too much to do at the restaurant, which wasn't a lie. But I also didn't feel like pretending I was okay.

6: The deep breaths I took before walking into work today. I told myself today would be better, but the second I stepped inside, I knew it wouldn't. The energy was off—tension thick in the air, like everyone was waiting for bad news.

10: The customers we had all morning. Barely enough to cover the cost of keeping the lights on. Dad won't admit it, but I can see it in the way he stares at the door, waiting for people who aren't coming.

4: The times I caught Maria and Sarah whispering. They stopped when I walked by. I don't know if it's about the money problems, the missing supplies, or something worse.

30: The minutes I spent in Dad's office after lunch, running numbers, checking invoices. More gaps. More things that don't add up. I don't know if it's bad math or something else.

2: The number of times I almost asked Dad if he noticed the missing money. I stopped myself both times. He already looks like he's carrying too much.

12: The texts I ignored. Friends talking about weekend plans, group chats lighting up with random memes. I can't even think about anything beyond this place, this problem.

8: The number of dishes left in the sink when I went to close up. Normally, we'd have triple that, the kitchen would be alive, the last-minute orders rolling in. Tonight, it was just me, Dad, and empty tables.

20: The minutes Dad and I sat in the car before leaving. Neither of us said much. Just sat there, letting the weight of the day settle in.

11: The time I finally got to my room. I should be sleeping, but my mind is still running. The numbers. The gaps. The fact that we're running out of time, and I don't know how to fix it.

100: The questions I have that no one's answering. What's Sarah hiding? Why did Linda really leave? Why won't Dad look at me when we talk about money?

∞: The feeling in my chest that this is slipping out of my hands. That I could find every missing dollar, every mistake in the books, and it still wouldn't be enough.

SATURDAY, JULY 6

Late in the evening, a soft overhead light illuminated the kitchen. Outside, the sky had shifted to a bluish gray, and faint laughter filtered down from Cass's younger brothers playing upstairs. The refrigerator hummed steadily, interrupted by occasional drips from the faucet.

Cass sat at the oak dining table, her laptop open and color-coded printouts arranged beside it. She tapped a pen against her notes until she heard footsteps.

"Mom. Dad," she said, taking note of their tired expressions. "Before we begin, I should say I took an SAT practice test last night. I got a 1290: 700 in math, 590 in reading."

Maya, scrolling through her phone, glanced up. The screen's glow cast faint shadows over her face. "Better," she said, setting the phone aside. "But you'll want at least a 1350 to stay competitive for a good school."

Booker joined them at the table, still dressed in his work clothes. He nodded for Cass to continue and pulled out a chair.

Cass brushed a finger over the top page of her printouts. "I've been going through the restaurant's data. I'd like to share some ideas I believe could help."

Maya stood with arms resting loosely, her gaze drifting momentarily to the dark window above the sink. Booker looked at Cass, his voice steady. "All right. Let's hear it."

Cass angled her laptop so both could see the screen, where several graphs were displayed. "We should remove low-margin dishes and those with ingredients we rarely use," she explained, tapping the chart with her pen. "Customers expect soul food classics, so maybe modernize our staples—pot roast, cornbread, okra, jambalaya—but keep them authentic."

She clicked to the next slide. "We also need more community outreach and better online presence. Plus, I've noticed oddities in our purchasing and maintenance records."

Booker leaned in slightly, while Maya stepped closer, her arms tightening. "Could that solve our main problems?" Booker asked.

Cass set the pen down, tension visible in her shoulders. "It's a start. People want that home-cooked appeal. Doing nothing could mean more losses."

Maya cast a quick look at the clock over the stove. "I've been picking up extra hospital shifts," she said quietly. "We need to be sure about our finances."

Cass brushed her notes flat. “Extra shifts alone may not cover everything. If we don’t adapt, we risk losing more than we can handle.”

A hush followed, broken by the drip of the faucet. Distant, muffled shouts from upstairs underscored the unease in the kitchen.

Maya exhaled. “Maybe it’s better to shut down than go broke,” she said, her voice subdued.

Booker shook his head, thumb tracing the table’s edge. “Cass has put serious effort into this. We have until August 10th—some time left. Let’s see what her data suggests.”

Maya’s arms remained folded. Cass clicked to a forecast on her screen, pointing at a rising line. “Cutting low-margin dishes, adjusting labor, and strengthening community ties can attract new customers. I plan to run anomaly detection in our purchasing logs to see what’s missing.”

Booker’s eyes scanned the colorful lines. “It’s our livelihood,” he said softly. “We need to be cautious.”

Maya offered a brief nod. “It’s good work, but there’s no guarantee.”

Cass met their eyes. “I know. Ignoring it won’t help.”

The overhead light glowed as another burst of laughter rose from upstairs. Finally, Booker straightened. “We can try a small-scale test.”

Maya shifted her stance. “And keep our current plan as a backup.”

Cass released a slow breath. “Deal. I’ll track everything carefully.”

Booker rested a hand on hers for a moment. “We’re proud of the work you’ve done. Just be careful.”

Cass picked up her papers and hesitated. “One more thing: could I involve my camp team? They’re skilled with spotting trends and anomalies. Might be what we need to solve our inventory issues quickly.”

Maya tapped her fingertips on the counter. “I’m not thrilled about outsiders in our business.”

Booker glanced her way. “If Cass thinks it helps, we shouldn’t let pride stop us.”

Maya paused, then gave a short nod. “All right. Keep it professional.”

Cass exhaled, relief flickering across her face. “Thank you. I’ll message them tonight." She closed her laptop and stood, gathering the printouts under one arm. ..

"Thanks," she added, voice quieter. The refrigerator's hum filled the moment, and the shouts from upstairs continued. Cass checked her phone, preparing a group message to her camp team.

Maya picked up her phone from the counter. Booker rose from his chair, looking between them. Worry lingered, but a touch of hope mingled with it in the warm lamplight. Cass typed the opening lines of her text, bracing herself for what lay ahead.

"We'll figure this out," she said. "Together."

*****

A dim glow from the streetlamp outside fell across Cass's bedroom. It was late on a Saturday night, and the quiet in the house was broken only by the low hum of her laptop fan. Cass sat at the edge of her bed, reorganizing spreadsheets and notes scattered on the comforter. After aligning the corners of a printout, she picked up her phone and dialed Lola.

"So, how did it go with your parents?" Lola asked when she answered. "You gave them that presentation, right?"

Cass set a half-open folder aside. "It went better than expected—probably because I did okay on my SAT. I got a 1290, which helped show them I'm serious about the restaurant. Now they're letting me reach out to the camp team for help."

"That's great news," Lola said. "I knew they'd come around."

Cass nudged a stray paper away. "Yeah, I wanted to update you before I message Ayesha. If Ayesha's in, maybe we can really turn things around."

"Perfect," Lola said. "Text her, and let me know. I've gotta run, so talk soon."

"Sure," Cass replied. "Bye, Lola."

She ended the call and typed a text on her phone.

Cass (to Ayesha): "Hey Ayesha, can we talk ASAP? I've got a situation with my parents' restaurant. Let me know if you're free!"

Cass set her phone down and smoothed a crease on a spreadsheet. Headlights from a passing car swept across the room briefly. Her phone vibrated with an incoming video call, and she propped her laptop on the desk, clicking "Accept." Ayesha's face appeared onscreen.

"Hey, Cass," Ayesha said, pushing a pen behind her ear. "Saw your text. What's up?"

Cass sifted through a few printouts. "Thanks for calling. I'm modernizing my parents' restaurant—menu updates, inventory tracking. They agreed to test some of my plan, but the data's messy."

Ayesha flipped open a small notebook. "I glanced at the files. Looks like issues in the sales logs. Maybe Isaiah can help. He's good at spotting patterns."

"That's a great idea," Cass said, highlighting something on her screen. "We're looking at sales trends, feedback—basically all the metrics. Could you review a few KPIs so we're on the same page?"

Ayesha jotted a note. "Sure. Professor Avery always says seeing the bigger picture is key. And I can't wait for details about the event on the 18th."

Cass nodded at her screen. "I'm planning to go if I can. Meanwhile, how about a meeting on Monday at three? I'll send a link to you and Isaiah."

"Sounds good," Ayesha said, closing her notebook. "Forward any new data, and I'll start looking at it tomorrow."

"Thanks again," Cass replied, attaching a file in an email. "Talk soon."

They ended the call. Cass sent the email, then organized a small stack of receipts on her desk. A faint rattle from a car passing outside came through the open window while she checked another set of numbers on her monitor.

About ten minutes later, her phone lit up.

Isaiah (to Cass): "Hey, heard you're setting up a project kickoff. Count me in?"

Cass paused her scrolling and typed back:

Cass (to Isaiah): "Yes—great to have the entire team working together again!"

She placed the phone aside, returning to the spreadsheet. Even with the late hour, she continued scanning line after line of numbers, preparing for the days ahead.

SATURDAY, JULY 6 | JOURNAL ENTRY

6: The deep breaths I took before I finally asked Dad about the missing money. He didn't look surprised. Didn't even ask how I knew. Just ran a hand over his face and said, "I'll handle it." But we both know that means nothing.

10: The customers we had during lunch rush. Another slow day. Another reminder that hope is not a business strategy.

4: The number of times I refreshed my bank app before finally closing it. Same balance. Same problem.

30: The minutes I spent in the back office running numbers before stopping. There's no point if Dad isn't ready to hear the truth.

5: The seconds of hesitation before I told Mom about Dad's reaction. She didn't say much. Just pressed her lips together and kept folding laundry. That silence? Louder than anything else.

8: The minutes I stood in the kitchen after closing, watching Dad sit at the counter, staring at the same receipts like they'd changed. He looks so tired.

20: The minutes Archer and Carver spent arguing about something dumb—who was better at Mario Kart or which Warriors era was the best. I let them go at it, let them fill the room with noise. It felt normal, even if just for a moment.

3: The unread messages from Isaiah. He keeps asking if I'm okay. I don't know how to answer that.

12: The times I thought about texting Lola. She'd listen. She'd tell me I'm overthinking. But I don't even know if I am.

100: The ways this could end, and I don't like any of them. I keep telling myself there's a solution I haven't found yet, but what if there isn't?

∞: The weight in my chest. That this place, this thing we built, is slipping. And no matter how hard I try to hold on, it feels like it's already gone.

SUNDAY, JULY 7

Early evening light glowed through the living room window, reflecting off the coffee table where Cass sat with her laptop. A steady hum came from the kitchen hood, mixing with the simmering of sausages, onions, and smoky spices on the stove. Maya's Gumbo filled the air with a warm aroma, bound for Grandpa's later.

Cass scrolled through a spreadsheet, tapping a highlighted row. Her stomach gave a soft growl, but she stayed focused on the screen.

"Mom. Dad. I need to stay home tonight and work," she said, lifting her eyes briefly. "I hope you understand."

Maya grasped the pot lid and wiped her brow with a dish towel. "Skipping family dinner won't solve anything, Cassie. A few hours with us won't ruin your progress," she said, setting the lid back in place. "We have to talk about priorities. Even with my schedule at the clinic, I find time to cook."

Cass stood and headed to the fridge. She poured a glass of ice water, a small smile on her lips. "What if I said I was studying for my SATs instead?"

Maya leaned one hand on her hip, mock-glaring. "You think that's funny? Don't test me. Aiming for 1350, remember?"

Cass shrugged, sipping from her glass. "I have a lot on my plate, Mom. Restaurant work and school."

Booker appeared from the hallway, the twins following him. They inhaled the Gumbo's scent, eyes bright with interest. "Your mother's been at this stew for hours," he said, resting a hand on Maya's shoulder. "Join us. Your grandparents will ask about you."

Carver hopped onto the sofa, trying to see Cass's laptop screen. "Why won't you come tonight, Cass?"

Maya shut off the exhaust fan, and the sudden quiet settled. "We're worried," she said, resting an oven mitt on the counter. "You've got the restaurant push and SATs—just don't overdo it."

Cass set her water down, her posture straightening. "I'm not obsessing. I'm trying to keep the place running and keep up with my studies." The stew's steam rolled from the pot, spreading heat under the light.

Booker slipped off his backpack and stood between Maya and Cass. "We won't force you," he said gently. "We see your dedication—thank you for that. Just remember to keep balance."

Cass gave a brief nod, her gaze flicking to the simmering stew. She closed her laptop, gathered her papers, and held them under her arm. The sun dipping lower cast longer shadows on the floor.

“All right,” she said quietly. “I’ll go upstairs and keep working.”

She stepped past the coffee table. The savory scent lingered in the living room, but she moved on, climbing each step with her notes tucked firmly in hand.

*****

As Cass continued working, a knock echoed through the house, shaking the stillness and making her pause. The persistent rapping grew louder, refusing to stop. A buzz on her phone followed, revealing a message from Lola: “I know you’re in there. Open up.”

With a resigned nod, Cass closed her laptop and headed downstairs. She paused at the bottom step, briefly straightening the mismatched cushions on her couch. The oscillating fans whirred in the background, stirring scattered papers but providing little relief from the summer heat.

At the front door, Cass drew a breath and cracked it open just enough to see outside. Lola stood on the porch, her arms filled with takeout bags, her gaze fixed on Cass with a mix of lighthearted insistence.

“Surprise, surprise!” Lola said, nudging the door open and stepping into the dim hallway. “Hope you’re ready for a feast.”

Cass glanced around at the clutter in the living room. “Lola, what’re you doing here?”

“We’re having dinner,” Lola declared, placing the food on the nearest free surface. One by one, she unpacked the containers. “Thai iced tea, spring rolls, pad ka pow, phad Thai, and mango sticky rice.”

Cass glanced at a stack of magazines and notebooks nearby. “You really didn’t have to come all the way. Mom dropped off some leftovers earlier.”

Lola set down the last container. “I’ve been worried about you, Cass. And tonight, I’m not giving you a choice. After years of waiting on the curb, I invited myself in.”

Cass hesitated, brushing a hand over her braided hair. “The house is a mess, and I’m swamped with work.”

Lola placed a hand on Cass's shoulder. "I'm here to see you, not the house," she said gently.

Cass let out a small exhale, then looked over the bags of food. "You really brought a lot. Feels like it could feed an army."

Lola let out a laugh. "Only if you'd refused to let me in. Since you didn't, let's eat."

Their laughter filled the room, easing the initial awkwardness. "I figured you'd skip a family dinner to bury yourself in spreadsheets. I'm your best friend, Cass, and I'm not letting you survive on charts alone."

Cass gave a faint chuckle. "Thanks, Lola. I guess I needed this more than I realized." She eyed the empty plates and utensils.

She paused, then spoke again. "I'm missing something in the data—it's all over the place. Dad used to record everything by hand, and now it's half on the computer, half missing... I've bitten off more than I can handle."

Lola slid a chair next to Cass and lightly patted her arm. "You're not failing. When did you last share a meal with someone, no screen in front of you?" She motioned at the spread of dishes. "Tonight, focus on dinner. We have plenty of food, so help me eat it. The data can wait."

Cass nodded, loosening her posture. She scooped up some pad ka pow and phad Thai, tasting the basil and lime. The flavors seemed to lift the tension from her shoulders. "You really didn't have to go to all this trouble."

Lola cut a spring roll in half, offering it to Cass. "Somebody has to keep you from forgetting to eat. You try to fix everything at once."

Cass paused after another bite. "Oh, by the way—there's a Zoom call on Monday at three. My camp friends will be on: Ayesha, Isaiah, everyone. Want to join?"

Lola winked. "Count me in. Wouldn't let you handle that alone anyway."

Cass shook her head, a slight smile appearing. "All right—don't say I didn't warn you."

Lola pushed a chair closer, arranging the takeout containers. "Let's eat before it gets cold."

Cass settled against the couch, eating in the warm glow of the overhead lamp.

SUNDAY, JULY 7 | JOURNAL ENTRY

2: The number of times I almost told Aunt Zora everything at Sunday dinner. She knew something was up—kept looking at me like she was waiting for me to just say it. But how do you say we're about to lose everything in between passing the greens and pouring sweet tea?

1: The second of hesitation before I finally asked Dad how we were gonna fix this. He didn't answer right away, just kept picking at his plate like the food was suddenly too complicated to eat. Then he hit me with "We're working on it." But who is we?

10: The minutes I spent helping Grandma Lillian clear the table, her hands moving slow like she had something to say but wasn't sure how to say it. She finally just squeezed my arm and said, "Your daddy's a fighter." I hope she's right.

4: The times I caught Mom watching Dad when he wasn't looking. Like she was trying to measure how much more he could take before he broke.

30: The seconds of silence in the car ride home. The boys were knocked out in the backseat, and me and Mom just sat there, letting the hum of the engine fill the space where a real conversation should've been.

8: The times I checked my phone, hoping for a text from Linda. Still nothing.

20: The deep sighs I let out while scrolling through my friends' group chat. Weekend trips, inside jokes, plans for next week. Feels like another world.

1: The time I finally flopped onto my bed, staring at my ceiling, trying to convince myself that tomorrow will be different. That I'll wake up and somehow things won't be crumbling.

3: The times Isaiah texted checking in. I finally hit him back with "Been busy. We'll talk soon." I don't know if that's true, but I didn't wanna lie either.

12: The number of half-finished thoughts sitting in my notes app. Ideas, strategies, ways to stretch the numbers, cut costs, bring customers back. But they all feel like throwing sandbags at a flood.

100: The what-ifs running through my head. What if this is it? What if I'm wasting my time trying to fix something that can't be saved? What if Dad's already decided, and he's just not telling us?

∞: The feeling that we're right at the edge. And once we go over, there's no coming back.

Decision Boundaries

Decision boundaries define the edges of choice, separating one outcome from another. They mark the transition between possibilities, clarifying distinctions and revealing hidden structures within the data. A boundary is not just a dividing line—it's the result of analysis and understanding, an insight into the forces at play. Decision boundaries are where chaos becomes order, where the uncertain takes shape, and where clarity emerges. They are the critical lines that shape the landscape of decisions.

MONDAY, JULY 8

It was a cool Monday morning, and a breeze drifted through the open windows of Booker's Pages and Plates. Booker had pushed two small tables together at the center of the dining area, calling his remaining staff to gather around. The air carried the scent of fried onions and spices from the night before.

He rested his palms on the makeshift table. "Thank you for coming in early," he said. "I wish I had better news. The restaurant... it's in trouble. We've been operating at a loss for months."

A subdued murmur passed through the group. Sarah, the waitress, folded her arms as she leaned back in her chair. Mike, the head chef, raised an eyebrow but stayed silent. Maria, the hostess, stood beside Joey, the busboy, who clutched his apron and wore a concerned expression.

"If we don't change things," Booker continued, "we might have to close. None of us wants that."

Sarah straightened slightly. "How bad is it really?" she asked. "We've heard warnings before, and the doors are still open."

Mike tapped his fingertips on the table. "If it's that bad, why haven't we cut extras like poetry nights or that fancy gelato? Feels like we're spending on things we don't need."

Maria glanced at Booker, concern in her eyes. "We've already cut staff. I don't get how it got worse so quickly."

Booker opened his mouth to respond, but Cass stepped forward, her laptop bag over her shoulder. "Hi, everyone," she said, keeping her tone level. "I've been looking at the financials, and it's more serious than it appears. We have unaccounted expenses and missing records. If we don't fix these issues, the restaurant won't survive."

Mike snorted softly, folding his arms. "Data camp," he muttered. "Must be nice to study in air-conditioned rooms while the rest of us sweat in real kitchens. Can I mention my missing overtime? I'm only working two days a week."

"Easy, Mike," Booker said, his voice firm.

Mike shifted his stance, his jaw set. "I just want to be paid for my time. I came in on my day off, and I'm only on the schedule twice a week."

Booker nodded quickly. "We'll figure out pay for this meeting. For now, we need to understand what's going wrong."

Sarah exhaled, shaking her head. “I have two kids younger than Cass. I’m working every shift to keep them safe at home, hopefully playing video games. When they go to the park for basketball, I worry. Now you’re telling me we might lose the restaurant? How does that happen?”

Booker sighed, his tone gentler. “I know. That’s why we’re trying to fix it.”

Cass spoke again, looking around the group. “Data doesn’t replace anyone’s hard work. It’s meant to find patterns, reduce waste, and help us be more efficient. If we work together, we can save this place.”

Mike kept his arms crossed. “And if the data says to cut staff, who goes first?”

“That’s not what this is about,” Cass said, meeting his gaze. “We’re trying to keep the restaurant open—and keep everyone’s jobs.”

Joey glanced at Maria. “What if waste isn’t the problem? What if the problem is people not coming in anymore?”

Cass adjusted her bag on her shoulder. “That’s part of it. But right now, we’re making decisions without data. We know ingredient costs have gone up, but menu prices haven’t changed. That means we’re absorbing the costs instead of passing them on, and it’s cutting into our margins.”

Maria frowned. “People are already complaining about prices. You think raising them will help?”

“Not across the board,” Cass said. “We can test small changes first. We run an A/B test—raise prices on a few select items for a week while keeping others the same. If sales hold steady, we know we can adjust without hurting business. If demand drops, we reassess before making permanent changes.”

Booker nodded. “So we see what works before committing to anything?”

Cass nodded back. “Restaurants do it all the time. We don’t have to guess—we can measure what works before making a final decision.”

Sarah ran a hand through her hair. “Okay, but what if it doesn’t work? What if people just stop coming?”

“Then we know instead of assuming,” Cass said. “Right now, we’re making decisions based on fear. Testing lets us respond with facts.”

Mike stood, pushing his chair away. “Right. So now we have to go to data camp? Trying to keep this restaurant going isn’t enough?”

No one answered. The weight of his words settled over the group.

One by one, the others dispersed, until only Cass and Booker remained in the quiet dining area. A faint breeze rustled the windows, and the lingering tension of the meeting settled into an uneasy calm.

As the staff left, muted conversations carried across the room—Sarah mentioning her kids, Maria murmuring something to Joey. Mike shook his head as he disappeared toward the kitchen, his footsteps heavy against the tile floor.

*****

"Hey, everyone," Cass said, her voice firm but slightly uneven. "I owe you all an apology. I should've reached out sooner." On-screen, Lola, Ayesha, and Isaiah listened closely, their concern visible in their expressions.

"I thought I could handle this by myself," she continued, her voice quiet as she spoke. "I didn't want to burden anyone. And honestly, I didn't want to reveal how bad things are. It's not easy telling friends that your family's business is on the brink of closing." Her grip tightened on the pen in her hand.

She glanced at the papers and open spreadsheets spread across her desk. The clutter was unusual for someone who typically thrived on order. Her posture shifted as she looked at the disorganized surface. "The restaurant's in serious trouble. We got an eviction notice, and I'm completely overwhelmed. I've been analyzing sales, inventory, and waste records, but nothing adds up. Missing items, unexplained waste—there are too many gaps. The deeper I look, the more it spirals. I just can't see a clear path."

Isaiah leaned closer to his camera, his tone calm. "Cass, challenges like this aren't meant to be tackled alone. That's why we're here—to help."

He paused, then added, "Oh—there's a data science meetup happening in Berkeley on Saturday, July 20. I wasn't sure I could attend, but I wanted you all to know. It might be a great opportunity to connect with people in our field."

Ayesha shook her head. "I can't go. I'm overloaded that weekend."

Cass hovered her pen above a notepad. "I'm not sure either. Things are hectic here."

Isaiah's tone stayed encouraging. "If you can make it, even briefly, you might pick up ideas for the restaurant's data issues." Then he repeated quietly, "Cass, challenges like this aren't meant to be tackled alone. We're in this with you."

Ayesha nodded. "Let's break down the biggest problem areas first. What's the top priority?"

"Food costs and waste," Cass said without hesitation. "Last week, we threw away nearly 20 pounds of vegetables that spoiled before we could use them. Waste logs show missing items, but the inventory isn't off in the same way. It seems like food is disappearing, and I can't figure out the cause. Labor costs are also high, and customer traffic has dropped. My parents are hesitant to do anything drastic. I don't know how to start."

"Let's apply Professor Avery's framework," Ayesha suggested. "Step one: define the problem. You've identified three key issues—food costs, labor inefficiencies, and declining sales."

Isaiah nodded. "Step two: gather and analyze data. What have you noticed so far?"

"I've flagged inconsistencies between waste logs and what the inventory says should be missing," Cass explained. "And for labor, I see employee hours spike on days when sales are really low—like we're overstaffing at the wrong times."

Isaiah focused on his screen. "Step three: propose solutions. For food costs, I can build a forecasting model—ARIMA or Prophet—to project inventory needs and detect weird spikes."

Lola's eyebrow shot up. "ARIMA? Prophet? You sure you're not making these up?"

Isaiah let out a short laugh. "Nope. Both are Python libraries. ARIMA examines patterns in historical data to predict future trends, and Prophet helps flag seasonal changes or sudden jumps."

Lola nodded slowly. "So fewer wasted veggies, or running out of chicken wings on a crazy Friday?"

"Exactly," Isaiah said with a grin.

Cass jotted it all down. "I'll handle the data prep—cleaning up timestamps, filling missing values. I've been practicing Python. Once the data is ready, we can feed it into the model."

"For labor," Ayesha continued, "we can try linear programming to align shifts with projected demand. We aim to minimize overtime but ensure enough staff for peak hours."

Cass tilted her head. "So we match staffing to sales forecasts without blowing the budget?"

"That's right," Ayesha said. "We'll watch KPIs like overtime levels and labor cost per shift."

Lola leaned forward, energy in her voice. "And for boosting sales, remember the restaurant's history and vibe—like the books and library concept. We can launch a loyalty program or special events. I'll work on visuals that connect all those ideas."

Cass nodded as she typed. "But first we've got to confirm the data's reliable. Some waste logs are incomplete, and inventory updates are late. If we match up timestamps and fill gaps with a pandas script, the results will be clearer."

Isaiah agreed. "Yes—and we'll define KPIs for each category: cost of goods sold for food, labor percentage for staffing, and maybe a retention metric for sales."

"We can build a central dashboard for ongoing monitoring," Ayesha added. "Tools like Tableau or Power BI can keep us informed in real time."

Isaiah nodded. "I'll handle the tech side so we can update metrics dynamically."

"How long will this data science approach take?" Lola asked, tapping a pen. "We don't have endless time."

Cass glanced at a note on her desk. "We've got until August 10th. If we stay organized, it's doable."

"That's where a project management tool helps," Ayesha said. "We can assign tasks, deadlines, and track everything."

Cass inhaled, voice warming with gratitude. "Thank you. I tried to fix it all alone, but I see now how much we can achieve as a team."

Isaiah smiled. "That's what data science is about—collaboration, not just coding."

Lola's face lit up. "I'll get started on the marketing plans. This place has so much character—it's perfect for a unique campaign. Maybe a small ad push on Yelp."

Cass nodded. "We have a lot of steps ahead."

Ayesha shut her notebook. "I'm ready."

They ended the call, the screen going quiet. Cass closed her laptop, still surrounded by notes. She looked at her written action items, the beginnings of a path through the chaos forming on the page.

*****

Outside, the sky deepened into shades of indigo and blue, with a silver moon casting pale light through the kitchen window. The last customers had just left, leaving tables scattered with the remnants of their meals. The bus boy arrived with a cart, wiping down tables and stacking dishes into the plastic bins.

Cass was focused on mopping up scattered crumbs and grease spots on the floor, then shifted to scrubbing the countertops and stacking dishes. The rhythmic clatter of pots and pans was the only sound in the almost-empty kitchen, accentuating the stillness of the space.

As Joey, the porter boy, pushed the swing kitchen door open with his cart, he approached the bin to discard the leftovers. Cass's gaze was drawn to the food waste logbook on the wall above the bin. Neither Dad, Mike, nor Joey used the log; the last entry was dated three months ago, signed hastily by Mike, with no added details.

"Dad?" Cass called out. "How often do we fill the waste logbook?"

Booker looked up from the stainless-steel bench, the pen in his hand hovering midair. "Umm... I'm not sure, dear. Mike was the only one who regularly signed the log. The other staff didn't always take the time to record the waste. Why do you ask?"

"I've learned that tracking food waste is important for restaurant management, Dad. If we keep a close eye on the waste records, we can figure out where things are going wrong and fix them. For example, we could see which items are getting thrown away a lot and then tweak our menu, inventory, and stock levels to match. It's a great way to save money and run things more smoothly. In some cases, the waste record can also help identify food stolen by staff."

Booker listened to Cass and nodded. "I see what you mean. I haven't been as diligent with keeping track as I should have been. I guess that's part of why we're in this situation now. If you think recording the waste is crucial, let's get on it. It's just you, me, and the porter boy handling the kitchen now, so it should be manageable."

"Thanks, Dad. I hope it's not too late for us to turn things around," Cass said.

Just then, her phone chimed with a new message. Cass finished up her task, wiped her hands on a towel, and slipped out of her apron.

Isaiah: "Hey, Cass! Good to see you brightened up this morning."

Isaiah: "I know you're busy, and I won't take too much of your time. I want to clarify something since we will work as a team."

Cass paused, considering how to reply. Another text was coming in.

Isaiah: "Cass, I reached out to connect on a personal level, and I want to say I'm sorry for making you feel uncomfortable the other day. It's clear you don't feel the same way."

Cass: "Actually, Isaiah, I'm unsure what I felt that day. There's just so much happening all at once."

She reread her message and realized she might have sounded a bit abrupt, so she added,

Cass: "Sorry if I came off as tense. It's just been a lot to process."

Isaiah: "I understand, Cass. I genuinely want to support you and this project, and I'm happy to be here for you in any way I can. I want to make sure you don't feel any pressure from me. First and foremost, we're friends, which matters most to me. I don't want to complicate things further. Just know that I'm here for you, no strings attached."

Cass: "Thank you, Isaiah. I truly appreciate it. Our friendship means a lot to me, and I want to ensure it stays genuine. I'm grateful to have you in my life and glad we can be there for each other."

Isaiah: "No problem at all. Just know I'm here for you, whether it's about the project or to talk… as a friend."

Cass: "That means a lot, Isaiah. I'm sorry for being so distant lately. I didn't mean to push you away."

Isaiah: "Anytime. Take care of yourself, Cass, and I'll see you at our Zoom meeting tomorrow." Outside, the sky stretched in deep indigo and blue, and a silver moon cast its glow through the kitchen window. The last customers had departed, leaving behind tables littered with used dishes. A porter named Joey arrived with his clearing cart, wiping down surfaces and stacking leftovers in a trolley.

Cass moved across the floor with a mop, collecting crumbs and clearing grease spots. She then scrubbed the countertops and stacked dishes to be washed. Pots and pans clattered in the mostly silent kitchen, emphasizing the night's quiet.

Joey pushed the swing door open and headed to the waste bin. Cass glanced at the food waste logbook on the wall above the bin. No one had used it for three months—Mike's signature was the last entry, scribbled without details.

"Dad?" Cass called. "How often do we fill the waste logbook?"

Booker looked up from a stainless-steel bench, a pen hovering in his hand. "Not sure. Mike was the only one who checked it. The others never recorded anything. Why?"

"I read that tracking food waste can help a restaurant manage costs and inventory," Cass explained. "It shows which items are being thrown out and whether we need to adjust orders or recipes. It can also reveal if staff are taking food."

Booker nodded. "Makes sense. I haven't kept up with it. If you think it's important, let's do it. With just us and Joey handling the kitchen, it's doable."

"Thanks, Dad," Cass said. "Hopefully we can still turn things around."

Her phone chimed with a new message. She finished wiping her hands, slipped out of her apron, and checked the screen.

Isaiah: "Hey, Cass! Good to see you brightened up this morning."

Isaiah: "I know you're busy, so I'll keep this quick. I just want to clarify something since we'll be working together."

Cass waited, watching for the next text.

Isaiah: "Cass, I reached out to connect personally, and I'm sorry if I made you uncomfortable the other day. It's clear you don't feel the same way."

Cass typed a brief reply:

Cass: "Actually, Isaiah, I'm unsure what I felt that day. There's just a lot happening at once."

She paused, then added a second note:

Cass: "Sorry if I sounded tense. It's been a lot to process."

His response arrived soon after:

Isaiah: "I understand. I genuinely want to support you and this project, and I'm happy to be here for you. I don't want you to feel pressured. First and foremost, we're friends—that's what matters. I don't want to complicate things further. Just know I'm here, no strings attached."

Cass: "Thank you, Isaiah. I appreciate it. Our friendship means a lot, and I'm glad we can be there for each other."

Isaiah: "No problem. Anytime you need me, I'm here—friend to friend."

Cass: "Thanks for understanding. Sorry I've been distant lately. I didn't mean to push you away."

Isaiah: "No worries. Take care of yourself, and I'll see you at our Zoom meeting tomorrow."

MONDAY, JULY 8 | JOURNAL ENTRY

2: The times I caught Dad rubbing his knee today. He does it when he's thinking too hard, when the stress is hitting him in a way he won't admit. I used to think it was just habit. Now I know it's pain.

1: The moment in the restaurant when I realized the playlist wasn't even on. The silence hit different. No old-school R&B, no faint hum of conversation, no steady rhythm of the kitchen. Just empty space where the heartbeat used to be.

6: The deep breaths I took before stepping into the back office. The air was thick in there. Like the bills stacked on the desk were pressing down on the room itself.

10: The times I told myself to just focus on the numbers. Don't think about what they mean. Don't think about how none of them add up the way they're supposed to.

4: The minutes I stood staring at Dad's ledger before closing it. He doesn't even bother hiding the red anymore.

30: The seconds of awkward tension when I asked Mom if she and Dad were okay. She gave me one of those tired smiles and said, "We're managing." Which is code for no, but I'm not about to tell you that.

5: The times Archer and Carver tried to talk to me about some show they're watching. I wasn't listening, but I nodded anyway. They don't need to carry this.

8: The times I checked my phone, still waiting for Linda to text back.

20: The number of discounts Dad applied today. He never used to do that. Used to say we weren't the kind of place that needed to do that. Guess we are now.

11: The time I finally sat down and forced myself to eat. I wasn't even hungry, but my hands were shaking from too much coffee and not enough food.

12: The different plans I ran in my head. Marketing strategies, cost-cutting ideas, ways to buy time. But none of them fix the real problem.

100: The amount of weight sitting on my chest every time I walk into this place, knowing we're running out of options.

∞: The fear that we've already passed the point of no return.

TUESDAY, JULY 9

From the dining area, Donny Hathaway's "A Song for You" filtered through the air, its gentle melody bringing both melancholy and hope. Cass sat behind her desk, surrounded by sheets of paper scattered across the surface. A light breeze slipped in from the open window, lifting the edges of the pages.

Although a bright, blue sky shone outdoors, it did little to brighten the old book room where she worked. The single white bulb Booker replaced earlier still flickered, sending a steady, blinking shadow across the wall. Cass glanced upward. She considered that it might not be the bulb—perhaps the mount, the switch, or some wiring issue. With a slight squint, she made a mental note to remind Booker about it again.

On her computer screen, Lola's voice resonated in her headset as she described part of a document. Cass listened, nodding occasionally. Suddenly, an email alert drew her attention to her inbox. Her heart rate seemed to quicken when she read the subject line: Invitation to the Tech Event by Quentin Hale 7/18. It came from Professor Avery, detailing an exclusive opportunity.

Ayesha, joining the Zoom call, noticed Cass's expression shift. "What's up, Cass? You look really excited."

Cass paused, then smiled. "Sorry for interrupting, Lola. Professor Avery just emailed—there's a major tech event on July 18 at Quentin Hale's place in Portola Valley, and we're invited! Quentin Hale himself will be there. My parents will be thrilled."

"Whoa, that's awesome!" Isaiah chimed in, leaning toward his screen. "Hale is that tech billionaire behind that huge location data company, right? And he's an alum of Standon University—where we did the summer data camp. He's also a major donor."

Ayesha clapped her hands lightly. "This is huge, Cass. A private event like this means only a select group is invited. It's a perfect chance to network with other data folks and maybe even get catering deals for your family's restaurant. We can't miss it."

Lola chuckled. "I'm proud of you all. Let me know if you need a stylist."

"Thanks, Lola," Cass replied. She turned to Ayesha and Isaiah. "You're right—this is a big moment. We can't miss it. Congrats, team!" She ran a hand over the old waste logbooks in front of her, flipping quickly through their pages. Her laptop, papers, and spreadsheets filled the narrow storeroom table, where she tapped in figures.

"Cass, about these sales and inventory discrepancies?" Isaiah asked, sounding more serious than usual as he shared his screen. "The numbers aren't matching up. We've got to find out why."

Cass looked at the highlighted rows. "Let's see what's causing this mismatch," she said, comparing the data on his screen with her notes.

Time passed as they worked. The sound of clanging pots and muffled conversation drifted in from the kitchen. Two hours later, the storeroom door creaked open. Booker stepped inside, pausing at the sight of cables on the floor and papers covering the desk.

"What's all this, Cass?" Booker asked, voice edged with impatience. "You've got wires and papers everywhere, and lunch service is about to start." He stood at the doorway, arms folded, scanning the tangle of equipment and open spreadsheets.

Cass slipped her headset down, glancing at the Zoom call still active on her screen. "Dad, I'm meeting with my team. We found some odd patterns in the inventory data that might help the restaurant. We were wrapping up before lunch."

Booker exhaled, eyeing the workspace. "I'm surprised you brought everyone on board so quickly," he said. His tone was measured. He turned toward the laptop. "Tell them I appreciate it—really."

A chime sounded from the front. Booker looked toward the dining area, where Maya appeared wearing hospital scrubs, accompanied by coworkers from the hospital. She smiled briefly at Booker.

"Maya?" Booker said, stepping out of the office. "Didn't expect you here now."

"Hey," Maya replied, still catching her breath. "We just finished a shift and wanted to grab lunch. Didn't realize there was a... big work session happening." She handed out menus to her colleagues and excused herself, walking toward Cass's space.

She tapped lightly on the storeroom's doorframe. "Cass, you seem busy. May I come in for a second?"

Booker glanced over at the hospital staff filling the dining hall. "Looks like you brought everyone," he said to Maya.

She let out a quick laugh. "Pretty much. We're all starving. That okay?"

"It's fine," Booker said, lowering his voice as he glanced at Cass's desk. "She's on a call with her friends about our restaurant data." His expression tightened, but his tone remained even.

Maya's eyes flicked over the setup. "I'm still not comfortable with all of this," she said quietly.

Cass swallowed, turning from the screen. "Mom—"

"We'll talk tonight," Maya interjected, holding up a hand. Her tone was calm but firm. Without waiting for a reply, she rejoined her coworkers at a nearby table, leaving Booker and Cass in the storeroom.

Booker relaxed his stance slightly. "You heard your mom," he said, nodding toward the still-active video call. "But let your friends know I do appreciate the help. Seriously." After another glance at the papers, he stepped out, returning to the dining area. Cass turned back to her meeting, preparing to wrap up the session.

*****

As evening fell, Cass paced near the front windows of the restaurant, carrying a stack of papers in one hand. She paused to finish wiping a countertop, then jotted a few final entries on the waste log hanging beside the freezer door. Outside, headlights appeared through the dim light, and she glanced up when Maya entered. Still in scrubs, Maya set her bag on a bench, rubbing the small of her back.

"You're early, Mom," Cass said. "Dad's in his office."

Maya looked over the cluttered work area. "Cass, what happened with you and your father today? Maria said you were both in the office during lunch service. She needed help out front."

Cass set the remaining papers aside. "I was on a call with some friends who are helping with the data for the restaurant. They volunteered—nobody forced them." She held up a small notepad. "I also have something to share with you and Dad."

Hearing voices, Booker stepped out of his office, arms folded. "What's going on?"

Cass stood a bit taller. "There's a private tech event coming up. Professor Avery, my mentor from the data science boot camp, invited me and my friends. It's at Quentin Hale's place in Portola Valley. It could be a big opportunity."

Booker's tone remained blunt. "We can't focus on that right now, Cass. This place needs us. We don't need fancy events distracting from what's important."

Maya folded her arms. "Is this one of those events where they showcase 'underprivileged kids' for show? I don't like it."

Cass set her notes on the counter. “Mom, it’s not like that. Meeting people in the industry could help me if I pursue data analysis, and any connections could also help the restaurant.”

Booker pressed a hand to his forehead. “Most of those influential people only care about big money, not a small family place that’s barely getting by. We’re already overwhelmed with our day-to-day problems.”

Maya shook her head. “We need practical fixes right now. I’m working extra hospital shifts just to cover bills. We let you try your data approach—focus on that first. Show real results, then maybe we’ll talk.”

Cass kept her voice level. “I’ve been checking which ingredients bring us the best margins. Dad, could you develop new dishes around those items? We might improve our profits if we highlight them.”

Booker shifted his attention to the notes on the counter. “You really think that’ll help?”

“I do,” Cass said. “The numbers show certain core ingredients earn us more than some of our current menu options.”

Booker gave a slow nod. “All right. If the data backs it up, I’ll see what I can create.”

Cass glanced between her parents. “Let me formally present what I’ve found—an overview of the records—and explain why this event matters. I’ll do it at family dinner on Sunday. Just give me a chance.”

After a moment, Booker nodded. “Fine, but make it convincing.”

“Thank you,” Cass said, setting the papers on her makeshift desk. Booker and Maya walked into the main dining area. Cass flipped off the overhead light and moved toward the restroom.

She turned on the faucet, allowing the water to wash over her hands. The soft sound of running water filled the small space as she rinsed away lingering grease. She dried her hands with a paper towel, then picked up her phone and glanced at the screen, which lit up with Logan’s name.

Logan: “Hey… how’s it going today? Busy day?”
Cass: “Yeah, quite a drama.”
Logan: “Want to talk about it over the phone?”
Cass: “Sure, I’m heading home now. Let’s chat a bit later.”

TUESDAY, JULY 9 | JOURNAL ENTRY

2: The number of shifts Dad covered today. He wasn't supposed to be on the line at all, but we're short-staffed, and we can't afford to bring anyone else in. He barely sat down, just kept moving like stopping wasn't an option.

1: The second I considered telling Mom what I found in the books. That money is missing. Not a lot at once, but enough over time to notice. Enough to make a difference. But I didn't say anything. Not yet.

14: The number of texts between logan and I tonight. I kept telling myself I didn't have time, but the truth? I didn't know how to let him in.

6: The deep breaths I took before trying to ask Maria about it instead. She acted like she didn't know what I was talking about, but she couldn't look me in the eye.

11: The time I finally left the restaurant, walking slower than usual. Like delaying going home would make any of this feel less real.

12: The moments I ran through every single piece of this puzzle in my head. Missing money. Linda leaving. The eviction notice. The slow days. The way Dad won't meet my eyes when I bring up the books.

100: The theories spinning in my brain, none of them good.

∞: The feeling that I just learned something important today. I just don't know what it is yet.

WEDNESDAY, JULY 10

Cass woke early, blinking at the morning light that slipped through thin curtains. She pushed herself out of bed and took a quick shower, then returned to her room—now a makeshift command center, with notebooks and printouts spread across the bed.

She entered food waste records into her laptop, comparing each entry to the inventory logs. As she worked, she paused at a finding: certain items vanished far too often, not just spoiling. Picking up her phone, she opened Zoom and sent a quick message to Ayesha and Isaiah.

Cass: "Morning, guys. I finished importing the waste records. Could you review the data? I need a second look to make sure I'm not missing anything."

After uploading the files to their shared drive, she accepted Ayesha's incoming video call. Ayesha's face filled the screen, her voice marked by concern.

"Hey, Cass. Good morning. How are you? You've been on my mind since yesterday."

Cass offered a faint, polite smile. "I'm okay, just dealing with a lot." She cleared her throat. "I don't have my parents' full support right now."

Ayesha frowned. "So, you're not going?"

Cass gave a small shrug. "I'm not sure. I'll figure it out somehow."

Isaiah joined the call. "Cass, maybe show your parents why this matters. Present your findings. We can help demonstrate the value."

Cass nodded. "That might help. For now, let's focus on the data. I want something concrete to show them."

While Ayesha and Isaiah examined the newest files, Cass opened another document with Lola's designs for a new menu template, loyalty cards, and a draft website outline. Lola's creative work looked polished, even though she wasn't on the call.

Ayesha's eyebrows arched as she clicked through Cass's folders. "Something isn't right. We saw issues before, but these updated numbers—waste logs, inventory, and the POS—show an ongoing problem."

Isaiah leaned closer, highlighting a table on his screen. "Yeah, it's clear. We need solid proof of what's really missing—supplies or money."

Cass's shoulders tightened at their conclusion. She glanced at the piles of notes on her desk, recalling the conversation with Booker and Maya the night before.

Straightening the top sheet, she glanced at the data again, then set her jaw and prepared for the next step.

*****

Cass arrived at the restaurant just as the sun reached its highest point. Her skin felt warm, carrying a faint trace of the summer air and blooming flowers. The streets seemed quieter than usual under the intense sunlight, and the sidewalks looked nearly empty.

Inside the kitchen, she called out for her father, who stood by the cooktop with sweat dripping from his forehead. Several customers waited by the cashier, forming a brief line.

"I know that look on your face," Booker called over the noise of the grill, "We'll talk soon, sweetheart! I'm still serving customers, and it'd be great if you could check with Maria—see what she needs."

Although the restaurant had seen better times, Cass thought it looked promising today. Even before lunchtime, over half the tables were filled with people seeking relief from the sweltering heat.

When the rush eased and the kitchen began to cool, Cass noticed her father removing his apron. She approached him right away. "That was quite a line-up, Dad. The heat must be drawing folks in," she said.

"Could be the sun, or maybe the new menu—it's likely both," Booker responded, glancing at the chalkboard with updated specials and smiling proudly. "Nice idea, Cass. I saw Maria updating the old chalkboard and listing appetizers, mains, and signature drinks. Figured it was your suggestion." He wiped sweat from his brow and gave Cass a pat on the back. "Let's see how people like these dishes and promos."

"Thanks for trying it," Cass said. "They're the same menu items, really—just more visible. I asked Maria to set them up so we can see if better exposure changes anything. Our menu is huge, and I think we need to pare it down. Some dishes might be causing us extra waste."

"And you're using the chalkboards to see which items customers focus on most," Booker said, nodding in agreement.

Cass looked relieved at his understanding. "Exactly. Also, Dad, I'm sorry about yelling at you yesterday. It's been tense."

She lowered her voice. “Dad, remember when I asked about the possibility of theft here? Ayesha and Isaiah helped me re-check the data, and we see real inconsistencies. It’s more than just spoilage.”

Booker’s jaw tensed as he adjusted his apron. “Cass, why would you think that? We handpicked everyone working here. They’re practically family. I can’t believe any of them would steal.”

Cass knew how personally he took each hiring decision, and that worried her most. “I get it, Dad, but please—just consider it. What would you do if someone was stealing? How should we handle it?”

Booker folded his arms, a vein visible in his neck. “We’d figure out the amount missing, how it happened, and who did it. Then, once we have proof, we’d fire that person and call the police and the state attorney. We’d also loop in our lawyer. If the employee was bonded—almost all of ours are—we might recover some of what we can prove was stolen.” He paused, shaking his head as if trying to convince himself. “Why the sudden concern, Cass?”

“I reviewed the numbers again this morning, and it’s worse than I thought,” Cass said. “Ayesha and Isaiah agree. We might be losing thousands. It points to theft.”

Booker’s expression stayed guarded, though his tone remained level. “Cass, maybe you’re reading too much into this. We should focus on bringing in more customers, like we did today. I don’t want you to get distracted by something that may be a misunderstanding.”

“But Dad, these numbers are off—seriously. We can’t just ignore it.”

Booker kept his voice low but firm. “I’m not stopping your work on the restaurant database. But I agree with Maya—your main priority should be your SAT prep. Don’t spend all your time playing detective.” He let out a weary breath, his tone somber. “We had a good crowd today, and that’s a positive step. Let’s not overshadow that with suspicion.”

“But Dad—”

“That’s enough, Cass. You have your answer.” Booker tightened his apron and walked back toward the kitchen.

WEDNESDAY, JULY 10 | JOURNAL ENTRY

2: The seconds it took for me to realize today felt different. Not normal, not fixed, but… something. There were actually people in the restaurant. Not just a handful—real customers.

1: The moment I caught Dad noticing too. He tried to play it cool, but I saw it. The way he stood a little straighter. The way he wiped his hands on his apron like he wasn't sure if this was real.

6: The deep breaths I took before checking the numbers in the back. I needed to know if this was just luck or if it meant something.

26: The customers who actually stayed to eat, not just browsed the books and left.

4: The seconds of hesitation before I showed Logan the numbers. I almost kept them to myself. But I didn't. And the first thing he said? "Cass, this is a start."

8: The texts from Isaiah and Ayesha today, already running numbers, testing theories, finding patterns. The team is locked in.

20: The minutes Dad and I spent cleaning up after closing, both of us pretending today was just another day. But it wasn't.

11: The number of times I looked at the register total. Still not where we need to be. But more than yesterday. More than last week.

12: The weight of all of this still sitting on my chest. But today, for the first time in a while, it wasn't just weight. It was momentum.

100: The ways this could still fall apart. But maybe—just maybe—we're finally moving in the right direction.

∞: The realization that today wasn't a miracle. It was work. And if we keep pushing? Maybe we can actually pull this off.

THURSDAY, JULY 11

Cass walked past the counter lined with framed black-and-white photos of Oakland's old trolley lines and market streets. The refrigerator hummed in the kitchen. A small corkboard near the hallway displayed shift schedules, handwritten notes, and her laminated infographic titled "Understanding Profit Margins in Restaurants"—detailing food costs and labor expenses for the staff.

The infographic's color-coded sections showed food cost percentages, labor costs, and weekly profit trends. At the bottom, a QR code linked to her online dashboard of live performance metrics for Booker's.

Inside the storeroom, a whiteboard leaned against one corner, covered with notes:

Optimize weekly inventory orders.

Analyze popular combos for pricing strategy.

Evaluate effect of specials on foot traffic.

Her laptop screen displayed the dashboard's bar charts and scatter plots showing the day's performance. A note about decreased drink sales sat next to her analysis of customer reviews—a sentiment-analysis tool she'd coded at boot camp. The tool sorted feedback into positive, neutral, or negative categories.

Late-afternoon light filtered through the small window, illuminating scattered notes and a half-empty coffee cup. Her phone pinged: Reminder: RSVP for Tech Meets Creativity Art Exhibit Tonight.

"Shoot," she said, clicking the notification.

A knock sounded. "Cass!" Lola's voice called from the hallway. She stuck her head in. "Knew you'd be hiding in here. This place gets smaller every time I see it."

"Hey, welcome to the cave," Cass said, shoving papers aside to clear a wooden chair. "Don't trip on the cords."

Lola squeezed in, her bracelets jingling. "Got some news. There's this sick art exhibit tonight at the community center. Tech meets creativity vibes. First Thai food, now art. We're getting cultured."

Cass's fingers tapped the keyboard. "Sounds dope, but I got this data stuff for Professor Avery tomorrow. Can't slack on that."

Lola reached across the table. "Yo, when's the last time we did anything fun? Something that wasn't about spreadsheets?" She pointed at the laptop. "One night off won't kill your data. Come on, please? I'm dying here. Need my bestie time."

"I dunno," Cass said. "Isaiah's about to drop this new inventory system, and the data's messy—"

"Cass." Lola drummed her fingers on the table. "The restaurant'll survive one night. I'm seriously about to lose it. Been feeling mad weird lately. Miss hanging with you."

"My bad," Cass said. "Been super wrapped up in all this."

"For real though. That's why this exhibit's perfect."

"Alright," Cass said, closing the laptop. "Let's do it."

"For real? Yes!" Lola bounced in her chair. "Wrap this up and let's bounce. Been too long since we just chilled."

"Facts," Cass said, stacking papers. "Thanks for the rescue."

They hugged, Lola's bracelets clattering against the desk.

"Six o'clock!" Lola called as she left. "Don't flake!"

Cass pulled out her phone, typing quickly:

Cass: Hey Mom & Dad - can I RSVP for the Hale event on the 18th? Need to tell Professor Avery something at tomorrow's mentoring session.

The phone buzzed almost immediately:

Maya: We'll discuss this at home.

Another buzz:

Booker: Let's talk about it tonight.

Cass tucked the phone away and gathered her papers. The refrigerator hummed steadily in the kitchen, mixing with the sound of dishes being stacked for the dinner rush.

*****

Banners announcing the exhibit fluttered in the breeze as Cass and Lola approached the Rockridge Community Center. The crowd's murmurs grew over the soft ambient music. The typically plain, utilitarian building was lit with digital art, its exterior shifting with color and motion. Strings of lights lined the perimeter, and animated projections danced across the walls in abstract patterns and playful scenes.

Inside, the transformation was just as striking. Formerly stark walls now showcased digital art and interactive installations glowing with vivid hues and neon accents against dark backdrops. After weeks of focusing on the monochrome world of spreadsheets, Cass's eyes reveled in the burst of creativity before her. She blinked, trying to absorb the sheer brilliance, feeling like she was entering a new realm filled with endless possibilities and inspiration.

They roamed the exhibit, stopping at each piece. Cass paused near a series of abstract paintings, each blending lines, strokes, and textures. One installation especially drew their attention: Tides of Change. A dimly lit room held a massive wall that shimmered with shifting colors and patterns. Sections of the display pulsed, the light intensities constantly changing.

"Whoa," Lola said quietly.

"Lola, look!" Cass stepped closer, her focus on the dynamic lights. "It's real-time data. The colors show water quality around San Francisco Bay."

Lola studied the display. "That's incredible."

Cass pointed to a spot where muted reds and bright greens moved together. "These patterns are pollution indicators. Areas with brighter colors mean cleaner water."

Lola noticed a nearby touch-activated screen. When she tapped it, the display shifted, and a recorded voice spoke with calm emphasis:

"Data is the mirror of our impact, reflecting the subtle shifts and stark revelations within our ecosystems..."

Cass repeated part of the narration, speaking softly. "In the ebb and flow of information, we find the power to transform both our intentions and our environment..." She turned to Lola. "This isn't just art—it's a call to action."

Lola nodded, her voice soft with understanding. "It's beautiful. And it's terrifying."

Cass glanced back at the glowing display, the vibrant patterns reflecting in her eyes. "Maybe it's the beauty that gets people to pay attention."

Lola stared at the glowing patterns of Tides of Change. "The colors shift and move, but they don't really go anywhere. Kind of like me," she said softly.

Cass nodded slightly, her eyes never leaving the display. "I get that," she said quietly.

The silence stretched between them. Cass leaned forward slightly, her fingers resting lightly on the table. When she spoke, her voice was calm, almost coaxing. "So," she began, meeting Lola's gaze directly, "what's going on? You said you were having a difficult time."

Lola laced her fingers together. "I... I don't know, Cass. That's the problem. Everything's supposed to be great, you know? I have freedom, my parents are supportive, and I'm doing well in school. But I feel... empty."

Lola took a deep breath, her gaze darting nervously around the vibrant space. Cass noticed her eyes glistening and placed a gentle hand on her shoulder. "Do you want to step outside for a bit?" she asked softly, her voice filled with empathy. The hum of the exhibit faded as they pushed open the doors. Outside, the cool night air enveloped them, a soothing contrast to the bright, overwhelming energy of the gallery.

Lola hesitated, then nodded. "Yeah... that might be good."

"You've had so much going on with the restaurant. You've discovered this incredible passion and found friends who share your dreams. And at this point, I'm just here. Existing. I have so many interests that I don't even know what passion feels like anymore.""

They left the building later, the night air carrying a faint jasmine scent. Crickets chirped in the bushes, and the streetlights cast long shadows on the sidewalk. Cass glanced at Lola, whose eyes glistened as she fought back tears.

"I'm so tired of talking myself out of these feelings," Lola said suddenly, her voice breaking and breath hitching. She stopped walking, her hands trembling as her shoulders rose and fell with uneven breaths. "I don't even know what excites me anymore."

Cass turned to face her, her voice steady. "Lola, you don't have to hold this in."

Lola wiped her face with the back of her hand. "Everyone thinks I have it all figured out, but I don't. Not even close. I feel like I'm floating, and I don't know where I'm supposed to land."

Cass reached for her friend's hands, holding them firmly. "You don't have to land anywhere right now. It's okay to just... float for a while."

Lola sniffled. "Maybe not," she conceded. "But at least you have options, both in boys and passions. Meanwhile, you've got two amazing guys practically falling at your feet." She let out a bitter laugh. "Honestly, I don't want to feel this way, but I can't ignore that I'm drifting without any real direction." Remember the night everyone went out for gelato? I wasn't busy. I just stayed home with my blankets over my head. I felt invisible, like I didn't belong anywhere. It was easier to shut everything out than to face a crowd of perfect skinny girls who all have it together with their perfectly planned lives and futures. I turned off my phone. I didn't want to be in a crowd of perfect skinny girls who all have it together with their perfectly planned lives and futures."

Cass's voice softened. "Lola, you're my best friend. You can always talk to me, no matter what's happening. And having a lot of interests isn't a bad thing—it means you're curious and open to new experiences."

Cass reached for her hand, holding it briefly. "We'll figure this out together. If you ever need to talk to someone professional, I'm here to help. If you just need a friend, I'm here too."

Lola hesitated, glancing away. "I don't want to be a cliché, Cass. Falling apart and needing help."

Cass gave her hand a gentle squeeze. "It's not a cliché to ask for help. It's brave."

They continued walking, their steps falling into an unhurried rhythm. The soft sound of shoes on pavement blended with the occasional hum of distant traffic. Soon, the park came into view, its empty playground silhouetted under the moonlight. Cass sat on a bench, resting her palms on the cool metal. Lola stood beside her, arms crossed lightly.

"All right," Lola said. "Let's break it down. What's going on with you, Logan, and Isaiah?"

Cass leaned back, looking up at the sky dotted with stars. "It's not just them. The restaurant's in trouble, and my parents argue a lot. I'm trying to be the hero for my family."

Lola gave her hand a brief squeeze. "You're allowed to have feelings, Cass. Caring about someone doesn't mean you're neglecting your family."

Cass's gaze dropped. "What if I hurt someone or mess up? What if I let my family down?"

They fell quiet for a moment before Lola spoke. "In art, we talk about negative space—the empty areas around the subject. People overlook it, but it's crucial to the composition."

Cass nodded thoughtfully. "That makes sense. I've been so focused on filling every space—fixing the restaurant, figuring out Logan and Isaiah—that I've forgotten about the space that's just me. Maybe I need to step back and see how it all fits together."

Cass paused, nodding slowly. "So I need to step back and see the entire picture?"

"You can't control everything," Lola said. "It's okay not to have a perfect answer yet. That goes for me, too." She gave Cass a quick smile.

Cass tapped her foot lightly. "I've spent so much energy looking for the perfect fix for the restaurant... maybe it doesn't exist."

"Welcome to being human," Lola said with a small laugh. "No matter what happens with the restaurant or with those guys, you've still got me."

Cass reached out, their arms briefly touching. "Right. And whenever you feel like you're drifting, talk to me. You're not alone in figuring things out."

Lola smiled as she linked her arm through Cass's. "Perspective. Sometimes you need to step back."

"Thanks, Lola. For tonight, for listening, and for being my best friend."

They walked on, their voices mingling with the soft cricket chorus under the dim glow of the streetlights.

spark a sense of renewed possibility.

One mixed-media piece—a collage of newspaper clippings, photos, and splashes of paint—caught Lola's attention. She studied it quietly. "It feels like life. Time moves on, and the present becomes history, even when it's messy and chaotic."

Cass observed Lola's expression. "You know you can talk to me anytime."

Lola blinked, steadying herself. "I know. It's just... people assume I have it all together, but I feel lost a lot."

Cass stepped closer and put an arm around Lola's shoulders. "You're not alone," she said quietly. "And you're more than a burst of color—you're the whole rainbow."

They left the building later, the night air carrying a faint jasmine scent. Crickets chirped in the bushes, and the streetlights cast long shadows on the sidewalk. Lola broke the silence. "So, are we going to talk about what happened, or are you going to keep staring at your shoes?"

Cass glanced up. "I'm juggling so much. I don't know where to start."

They stopped at a small park, where an empty playground stood under the moonlight. Cass sat on a bench, resting her palms on the cool metal. Lola stood beside her.

"All right," Lola said. "Let's break it down. What's going on with you, Logan, and Isaiah?"

Cass leaned back, looking up at the sky dotted with stars. "It's not just them. The restaurant's in trouble, and my parents argue a lot. I'm trying to be the hero for my family."

Lola eyed the horizon. "My parents don't fight—they just avoid each other. But I'm listening."

Cass exhaled. "I think Logan likes me... maybe Isaiah, too. But I haven't sorted out my own feelings. Everything's about the restaurant right now."

Lola watched her carefully. "So how do you feel?"

Cass traced a pattern on the bench. "I'm not sure. Logan's supportive, makes me laugh, and helps me see beyond the numbers. Isaiah and I connect over data and coding. We talk for hours about algorithms, and it's exciting. But with Logan, it's calmer, more grounded."

"Sounds like a head-versus-heart problem," Lola said, a slight smile on her face.

Cass shrugged. "Or head versus heart versus duty. I feel guilty even thinking about this when the restaurant needs help."

Lola gave her hand a brief squeeze. "You're allowed to have feelings, Cass. Caring about someone doesn't mean you're neglecting your family."

Cass's gaze dropped. "What if I hurt someone or mess up? What if I let my family down?"

They fell quiet for a moment before Lola spoke. "In art, we talk about negative space—the empty areas around the subject. People overlook it, but it's crucial to the composition."

Cass tilted her head. "I'm not totally following."

Lola met her eyes. "Maybe you're so focused on the main issues—Logan, Isaiah, and the restaurant—that you forget about the space that's just you. That space matters too."

Cass paused, nodding slowly. "So I need to step back and see the entire picture?"

"You can't control everything," Lola said. "It's okay not to have a perfect answer yet.

That goes for me, too." She gave Cass a quick smile.

Cass tapped her foot lightly. "I've spent so much energy looking for the perfect fix for the restaurant… maybe it doesn't exist."

"Welcome to being human," Lola said with a small laugh. "No matter what happens with the restaurant or with those guys, you've still got me."

Cass reached out, their arms briefly touching. "Right. And whenever you feel like you're drifting, talk to me. You're not alone in figuring things out."

Lola smiled as she linked her arm through Cass's. "Perspective. Sometimes you need to step back."

"Thanks, Lola. For tonight, for listening, and for being my best friend."

They walked on, their voices mingling with the soft cricket chorus under the dim glow of the streetlights.

*****

Porch lights cast long shadows across the driveway as Maya's car pulled up at 11:45 PM, the engine ticking softly in the cool night air. Her scrubs bore dark stains from a grueling twelve-hour hospital shift, and her work bag dragged against the concrete, leaving a faint, scratching sound.

The front door stood ajar behind Cass, spilling warm yellow light onto the porch where moths fluttered against the flickering bulb. The wooden boards creaked beneath her weight as she shifted on the porch. In the distance, a neighbor's dog barked, its sharp barks punctuating the quiet.

"Hey, Mom," Cass said, holding the screen door open as it whined on its hinges. "About the Hale event—"

Maya paused at the bottom step, her keys jangling. "Really? You stayed up to ask about this?" Her shoes scuffed against the wooden steps as she ascended. "I thought we agreed—better SAT scores before asking for anything else."

Cass tightened her grip on the doorframe. "The Hale Foundation invited us because of our final project. They're the ones who funded my camp scholarship. They even provided the laptop."

"And now you're bringing up more distractions," Maya said, her badge clinking against her keys as she reached the top step. Her bag slid off her shoulder, landing on the porch with a dull thud. "You're sixteen. Why would they even want you there?"

Cass squared her shoulders. “That’s not what this is. Professor Avery specifically selected our team to present.”

Maya sorted through her keys, her voice sharp. “Then what is it? Because from where I stand, it looks like you’re chasing after something that’s pulling you away from what matters.”

“Data science matters,” Cass said firmly, her grip tightening on the frame. “The restaurant’s numbers prove it.”

“The restaurant needs you here,” Maya said, slipping the key into the lock. “Not at some fancy party in Silicon Valley.” The key scraped loudly in the lock before it turned. “We’ll talk about this later. I need to shower and change.”

The door clicked shut behind her. Cass exhaled a long sigh, turning toward the staircase. Her footsteps were soft against the worn wood as she climbed. At the top step, the pipes groaned, and the steady rush of water told her that Maya had already started her shower. Passing by her brothers’ room, Cass caught sight of Carver and Archer through the open door. Both shook their heads in unison, exchanging a knowing glance before returning to their game console.

THURSDAY, JULY 11 | JOURNAL ENTRY

2: The number of outfit changes before I settled on something decent. It wasn't a date, but it also wasn't just a regular night. Lola would clown me if I looked like I just crawled out of the restaurant.

1: The second I hesitated before stepping into her car. Like my brain forgot how to just hang out. But then she hit play on some old school Bay Area mix, and it was like nothing had changed.

10: The minutes we spent talking about Logan. Well, Lola talking about Logan. Asking a million questions. I told her we were just working on the restaurant stuff, but she wasn't buying it.

4: The times she asked if I was actually excited for the date. I told her yes. She squinted at me like she didn't believe me.

30: The seconds of silence after she asked, "So when's the last time you just did something fun?"

5: The seconds it took for me to realize I didn't have an answer.

8: The times she caught me checking my phone. Not for restaurant stuff. Not for Logan. Just because. A habit now, like I was waiting for bad news.

20: The number of times she reminded me I was allowed to enjoy myself. "Cass, we are eating good food. We are cute. We are not talking about business tonight."

11: The amount of food we ordered. No regrets.

3: The times she brought up my birthday coming up soon. Talking about plans. Talking about how seventeen is gonna be a good year. I hope she's right.

12: The minutes we just sat there, people-watching, laughing, talking about nothing. I needed that more than I realized.

100: The reminders that I still have a life outside the restaurant. That I still have my people. That I don't have to carry everything alone.

∞: The feeling that maybe, just maybe, I'm allowed to be happy too.

FRIDAY, JULY 12

Cass logged into the Zoom session. She shifted her notes aside as the screen flickered to life, revealing Professor Avery's face.

"Good afternoon, Cass," Professor Avery said. "I hope you're doing well."

"Hi, Professor. I'm good and ready to learn," Cass replied, sitting up straighter.

"Excellent," Professor Avery said. "But before we dive in, I heard you've been applying your skills at your family's restaurant. Tell me about that."

Cass leaned closer to the camera. "Yes. I've been using the data analysis methods from camp—tracking sales patterns, inventory, stock-taking, and analyzing our purchases, reviews, and waste. We've made adjustments to the menu and updated inventory based on data mining. We're seeing more customers this week than last."

Professor Avery leaned forward, her expression warm but curious. "That's excellent progress, Cass. What kind of data mining techniques did you use?"

Cass adjusted her laptop slightly, pulling up a graph. "I started by analyzing sales data from the past six months. I noticed that certain dishes—like the fried catfish and the gumbo—sold consistently well on weekends but dipped during weekdays. Meanwhile, our desserts were over-prepped, especially during the lunch rush. By running clustering algorithms, I grouped items based on popularity and time of day."

Professor Avery nodded. "Good use of clustering. Did you incorporate any predictive models?"

"I did," Cass said, her voice picking up excitement. "I used ARIMA to forecast weekly demand and a simple regression model to identify how weather patterns affected sales. Rainy days actually boosted our takeout orders, especially for comfort food. That insight helped us adjust staffing and prep levels." She paused, a faint smile crossing her face. "I never thought I'd actually use ARIMA outside of camp. This... this feels incredible. Like everything we learned is finally clicking."

"Smart," Professor Avery said. "What about inventory?"

Cass pulled up another chart, her fingers hovering over the screen. "I flagged discrepancies between our waste logs and inventory counts. Certain items—like shrimp and sweet potatoes—keep disappearing. I used some of the anomaly detection methods we talked about in camp, but honestly, I feel like I missed something." She hesitated, then added, "I should've taken better notes back then."

Professor Avery's smile widened. "You're doing great, Cass. And don't worry—this is the perfect time to deepen your understanding. Given the inventory discrepancies you're noticing, you might look into isolation forests or z-score analysis for anomaly detection. Both could help pinpoint where things are going wrong."

Cass's fingers flew to her keyboard. "I'll look them up. I can't believe how much of this applies to real-world problems. It's like... everything we learned is coming to life in ways I never imagined." She glanced up at Professor Avery and grinned. "I'm not making that mistake again—I'm taking better notes this time."

"That's wonderful," Professor Avery said. "You're making an impact. What challenges have you faced?"

Cass spoke without hesitation. "Convincing my parents to trust the data was tough. They've managed the restaurant the same way for years, so going data-driven was a big change. I think they'll come around once they see better results."

Professor Avery nodded. "Tradition can be hard to shift, but you're on the right path. Keep tracking your progress—it'll be valuable."

Cass dipped her head slightly. "Thank you. Your guidance has helped a lot."

Professor Avery's tone stayed warm. "I'm glad to hear it. This experience—and the way you're handling conflicts—will serve you well in any data analyst role. Now, let's move on to today's topic: decision trees."

She shared her screen, revealing a decision-tree diagram. "A decision tree starts with a single node and branches out based on conditions. Each branch represents a choice leading to various outcomes."

Cass opened her notebook and began writing.

"Imagine standing at a crossroads," Professor Avery continued. "You can go left, right, or straight. Each path leads to different choices."

Cass kept her focus on the diagram, occasionally looking down to take notes.
"In many ways, life mirrors a decision tree," Professor Avery said. "Every choice leads to new possibilities. For instance, choosing to attend the camp gave you new skills and experiences."

Cass nodded. "Yes, it did."

“And now you’re applying those skills,” Professor Avery added. “Each decision builds on the last. Sometimes it’s complicated, but every path teaches us something.”

She paused briefly. “By predicting outcomes, a decision tree helps us navigate choices. Reflecting on our decisions helps us learn and grow.”

Cass kept writing. “Thank you, Professor Avery. This perspective helps a lot, especially with what we’re dealing with at the restaurant.”

Professor Avery’s expression stayed encouraging. “Keep exploring and trusting your ability to navigate life’s decision trees. These experiences shape us.”

She looked at the camera. “Everything okay, Cass?”

Cass turned. Maya stood in the doorway, arms crossed, expression firm.

“Hey, Mom. I’m on a Zoom call with Professor Avery, from the camp,” Cass said.

Maya stepped into view of the camera. “Professor Avery, thank you for helping Cassie, but I need to speak with you.”

Professor Avery nodded. “Of course, Mrs. Freeman.”

Maya’s voice was direct. “I appreciate what you’ve done for Cassie, but please don’t contact her anymore. She has another path, and she won’t attend the July 18 event. There’s no RSVP.”

Professor Avery spoke calmly. “Mrs. Freeman, Cass has shown exceptional potential. This event could be pivotal for her growth.”

Maya’s tone remained firm. “We’re aware of our daughter’s talents. Our decision is final. I ask that you stop communicating with her. Thank you.” She closed the laptop, leaving Cass to stare at the poster on her wall.

“Mom! Why?” Cass asked, raising her voice. “Professor Avery’s been a great mentor. You saw how hard I’ve worked at the restaurant with the data. Why end this?”

Maya’s posture stayed rigid. “Hard work? The restaurant needs your presence on the floor, not your ‘data science passion.’ If you want to help, greet customers and reduce labor costs—stop hiding behind a computer.”

Cass’s voice rose. “I’m not hiding. I’m analyzing numbers. I’ve already found ways to improve efficiency and reduce waste.”

Maya’s voice tightened. “While you’ve been analyzing, I’ve been hosting, washing dishes, and bussing tables. I also work full shifts at the clinic and volunteer on weekends. This isn’t about dreams, Cassie—it’s about survival.”

Cass pressed a hand to the desk. “What I’m doing does matter. Last week, I found a way to save five hundred dollars in staffing costs.”

Maya shook her head, her voice turning sharper. “Five hundred dollars doesn’t help much if the lights go out. Every day, I’m patching holes—covering extra hours because your father’s knee hurts. Where are you? Staring at charts instead of helping on the floor.”

“I’m not staring at charts,” Cass said, her tone clipped. “I’m fixing problems. Smiling at customers isn’t enough to save this place. We need a real plan.”

Maya’s laugh sounded bitter. “Do you think I don’t know that? I’ve cleaned floors past midnight and balanced books. It’s our livelihood, and we can’t wait for your plans to work.”

Cass stood straighter. “I’m not asking you to wait. I’m asking you to let me help with a strategy.”

Maya’s gaze stayed fixed. “Trust you? Cassie, I’m trying to keep this place from collapsing today. If you want to help, then do what needs doing—host, keep things moving, and lighten our load."

Cass spoke firmly. "I understand you're tired, Mom. But so am I. This is about more than one day's shift. I want to ensure we don't face the same issues a year from now."

Maya's stare remained unyielding. "What I see is you believing numbers on a screen will fix everything. Meanwhile, I'm dealing with customers and cleanup. We built this restaurant on sweat, not spreadsheets."

Cass's voice steadied. "Sweat alone won't keep it alive. We need more than hard work—we need strategy."

Maya's jaw set. "Strategy doesn't pay the bills when rent is due. We have no time for experiments. If you can't see that, then you don't understand what this family fights for."
Cass exhaled. "What are we fighting for, Mom? A business run the same way forever, even if it's failing?"

Maya's voice shot back. "We fight for dignity and respect. I don't want pity from anyone. I've worked too hard to avoid that, and your pipe dream could make us look worse."
Cass paused. "It's not a pipe dream. It's a better future. Why won't you believe in me?"
Maya crossed her arms. "Because this isn't about belief—it's about surviving. Until you learn that, there's nothing more to say."

She turned and walked out, her footsteps retreating. Cass remained by the desk, staring at the laptop with the dataset on the screen. The numbers stayed in front of her, and she gripped the desk edge, unmoving.

*****

Hours drifted past as morning faded into sunset. Cass sat on her bed, knees drawn close, eyes fixed on the blank wall opposite her. The slow turn of the ceiling fan and the muffled sounds of the street filtered through the quiet. On her desk, a stack of untouched notebooks and printouts lay scattered, exactly as they had been that morning.

Her phone buzzed on the nightstand, briefly illuminating the dim space. She glanced at the screen, pausing before reaching for it. The name "Logan" lit up, and after a moment, she picked up the phone.

Logan: "Hey, still awake?"

Cass looked at the message for a few seconds, then typed a quick reply.

Cass: "Yeah, why?"

She placed the phone down and glanced at it now and then, waiting. The screen lit up again moments later.

Logan: "Can I call?"

Cass's response was concise.

Cass: "Sure."

Her phone rang right away. She sat straighter, brushing her hair over one shoulder as she swiped to answer.

"Hi, Logan," she said softly.

"Hi, Cass," Logan replied. "Did I wake you?"

"No," she said, adjusting the blanket over her knees. "I was up. What's going on?"

He paused, then spoke in a lower tone. "I was thinking about our date tomorrow. I hope you're still free?"

"Yes, of course," she said. "We talked about that new Italian place for dinner. We could also check out the farmers' market at Jack London Square."

"That sounds good," Logan said. "How are you?"

Cass held the phone, her fingers lightly against its edge. "It's been... a lot. I had a fight with my mom."

Logan stayed quiet, and she explained the argument: her mother's view that Cass's data work was unnecessary, the mention of charity, and the insistence on focusing solely on hosting duties and school applications.

"Wow," Logan said, his voice subdued. "That's intense."

"She thinks using data isn't worth it," Cass said. "She wants me to stick to school stuff. Says the restaurant doesn't need spreadsheets, just someone to host and clear tables."

Logan exhaled. "That's not fair."

"She told me we're basically one step away from being a charity case," Cass continued. "That what I'm doing only shows we can't handle ourselves."

Logan's voice steadied. "That isn't true. You're doing amazing things. Anybody can see that."

Cass adjusted the blanket. "She said I'm wasting my time. That I don't belong in this data world."

"You do belong," Logan said firmly. "Everybody's contributing—the cooking, the extra shifts—and those are good. But your skills go beyond that. You're bringing something new and valuable, whether they realize it now or not."

Cass paused before replying. "Thanks, Logan. Sometimes it feels like no matter what I do, it's not enough."

"You're doing more than enough," he said. "I'm glad you told me about it. I can tell it's been hard."

Cass's voice grew quieter. "I don't share this stuff much. But talking to you is easier."

"I'm here," Logan said. "You don't have to handle everything alone."

"Thanks," she said. "For calling—and for listening."

"Always," Logan said. "Now try to get some rest. We have a big day tomorrow."

"Sure," Cass answered, a slight smile shaping her lips. "Good night."

"Good night, Cass."

After the call ended, the room fell silent again. Cass placed her phone on the nightstand and turned toward her desk. She gathered the scattered papers, stacking them carefully. The ceiling fan continued its soft hum, the city lights faintly illuminating her room. With a final look at her desk, she switched off the lamp and slipped into bed, leaving her phone within reach.

FRIDAY, JULY 12 | JOURNAL ENTRY

0: The number of words I could get out before Mom ended my Zoom call. One second, I was explaining my work to Professor Avery, the next? Laptop slammed shut. Just like that, my future—cut off.

1: The second I realized this wasn't just about today. Mom's been planning this. Blocking me from anything that doesn't fit her vision.

0: The deep breaths I took before yelling. Before asking why. Before she told me I was wasting my time and that the restaurant needed me to stop hiding behind a computer.

10: The hours I spent locked in my room afterward, staring at the same four walls, replaying her words, feeling them cut every time.

20: The minutes I spent staring at my laptop, knowing Professor Avery probably emailed me, wondering if I should even check.

5: The seconds of hesitation before I finally opened my inbox. There it was. Cass, I'm here if you need me. This doesn't change anything.

8: The texts from Logan asking if I was okay. I didn't answer. Not yet.

3: The number of times I told myself I wasn't gonna cry. Failed all three.

12: The moments I thought about leaving. Just getting out. But where? For what? Mom thinks this is about control, but it's about fear. She's scared I'll leave the restaurant behind. That I'll leave her behind.

30: The seconds I stood outside her door, debating if I should talk. But what would I even say? That she broke my heart today? That she made me feel like I didn't belong in the one thing that's ever made sense to me?

100: The thoughts in my head, none of them making sense, all of them screaming at once.

∞: The feeling that no matter what I do, it'll never be enough. Not for her. Not for the restaurant. Maybe not even for me.

Pruning

Pruning is the act of simplifying, removing unnecessary complexity to focus on what matters most. It's a deliberate process of cutting away branches that no longer serve the structure, reducing noise and improving efficiency. By eliminating distractions, pruning sharpens focus and strengthens outcomes. It's a reminder that not every path needs to be followed, and not every detail is essential. Simplicity is power, and pruning transforms a tangled structure into a clear and purposeful framework.

SATURDAY, JULY 13

Dappled sunlight filtered through the leafy canopy, throwing shifting patterns across the cobblestone paths as Cass and Logan walked through the farmers' market. A row of tents stretched down the street, their bright colors popping against the worn asphalt. Handmade candles, tie-dye hoodies, and stacks of vinyl records sat alongside crates of organic kale, sweet peaches, and baskets of lumpia. A vendor pressed a spatula against a sizzling plant-based patty, the sear crisping at the edges as smoke curled into the air.

A breeze from the Bay rustled the awnings above the vendor stalls. Cass tucked a loose strand of hair behind her ear. Kehlani's Honey spilled from a nearby café, mixing with the steady hum of the crowd. Across the street, a drummer tapped out a rhythm on a five-gallon bucket while a saxophonist played along.

Logan shifted his weight from one foot to the other. His hands went into his pockets, then back out. "You seem kinda chill today. And, uh—" He scratched the back of his neck. "You look nice. Like, really nice."

Cass glanced at him briefly, then looked away. "Oh. Uh, thanks. And for inviting me out." She nudged a pebble with her sneaker. "And for last night. I know I talked a lot."

A vendor nearby adjusted a rack of hoodies that read OAKLAND VS. THE WORLD in bold block letters. A row of fitted caps, each embroidered with The Town, lined the table's edge.

Logan exhaled, almost a laugh. "Nah, it's cool. Just wanted to make sure I was still on your schedule. But, uh..." He stuffed his hands back into his pockets. "I'm glad we got to talk."

Cass traced the edge of a wooden fruit crate with her fingertip, pressing against the grain. "I hate being that person—the one who just unloads on people." Her voice lowered slightly. "My mom would've been mortified. She's big on keeping things in the family."

Logan rubbed his thumb over his palm. "Yeah, see, my mom's the opposite. She tells her therapist everything." His mouth twitched. "Probably overshares, to be honest."

Cass pressed her nail into the crate, leaving a faint line. "You don't know her. She's all about appearances. Everything has to look a certain way. We have this great house in a nice neighborhood. You'd think we have it all together, but..." She shook her head. "I just wish the inside matched the outside."

Logan frowned slightly. "Like... what do you mean?"

Cass's shoulders tightened. "Don't even ask."

Logan started to say something but stopped. He adjusted his sleeve instead. "Alright." He nodded once, then exhaled. "But, uh… for real, I was happy to spend the time. Thanks for trusting me." He let out a quick breath. "I'm not that dude who runs his mouth. Whatever you tell me, it stays with me."

Cass looked at him for a long second. The crowd around them moved past, voices blending into the distant music.

Logan scratched the back of his head again. "That's, uh… how real connections work, I guess?" He exhaled sharply. "Never mind. You get it."

They drifted toward a quieter section of the market, where vendor stalls were spaced further apart. A table piled with jars of jam caught Cass's attention. Next to the jam, a woman in a Warriors beanie arranged bottles of hibiscus iced tea, each labeled Made in East Oakland in sharp, gold script. A hand-painted sign read: Cash, Venmo, or EBT—Support Local!

"Look at these!" Cass guided Logan closer. The sun reflected off the glass, illuminating neat rows of labels: Orange Marmalade, Fig Spread, Tamarillo, Beetroot Preserves. Logan picked up a jar of fig spread, turning it over in his hands.

"Man, my grandma used to make jam just like this every summer."

Cass leaned toward the vendor. "Excuse me, do you do bulk pricing? We're always looking for local products for the restaurant."

The elderly woman at the stall smiled. "Absolutely, baby. What's your spot?"

Cass nodded and tapped the lid of a jar. She described her father's restaurant, listing ingredients they sourced locally and pointing out dishes that used fresh preserves.

Logan stepped aside as another customer approached, but he didn't go far. His grip tightened slightly around the jar, thumb tracing the edge. His head tilted slightly as Cass spoke, eyes flicking between her and the vendor.

They moved away from the jam stall, finding themselves in a pocket of relative calm between two food trucks. The aroma of grilled seafood wafted around them as Logan touched Cass's arm. A blue-and-white AC Transit bus hissed to a stop nearby, its doors sliding open as passengers stepped onto the sidewalk. A man selling incense waved a bundle toward them.

"Black Love Special, two for five!" he called before stepping aside for a passing cyclist.

Logan slowed his steps. "Hey," he said. "I thought this was supposed to be a date—just us, having fun?"

Cass let out a short laugh. "Oh, Logan. My bad. I just can't help checking these things out whenever I see a chance."

Logan exhaled through his nose, the corner of his mouth pulling into a half-smile. "No worries. It's kinda impressive, actually. Just don't feel like you gotta work today."

Cass took his hand, squeezing lightly. "Okay, okay. No more business talk. I promise."

They found an empty bench near a flowering plum tree, away from the market's main thoroughfare. The drumming from the bookstore had faded to a distant rhythm, replaced by the gentle rustle of leaves overhead. A vendor adjusted a display of woven baskets, shifting them to keep the wind from knocking them over. One tipped sideways, rocking against another before settling back in place.

Logan flexed his fingers at his sides, his eyes shifting before settling back on Cass. A gust of wind stirred the vendor's awning, the fabric flaring before settling again. The crowd moved past them, voices overlapping with the faint rhythm of the street drummer in the distance.

"I started to notice you more toward the end of the school year," Logan said. "You don't try to fit in; you just do. You handle everything—getting into the program, the scholarship, working with your dad, taking care of your brothers—without slowing down. I just figured maybe you deserved someone in your corner too."

A vendor shifted a basket of peaches, nudging the ripest ones to the front before wiping their hands on a cloth and adjusting another crate. A child weaved through the stalls, laughter spilling behind him before he vanished into the crowd.

He let the words settle, watching her reaction. "Because whether you see it or not... someone's been thinking about you."

Cass turned the jar in her hands, her fingers running over the label before she set it back on the vendor's table. The glass clinked lightly against another jar. "I—" Her voice caught for half a second. "I didn't know you thought about me like that."

Logan gave a small shrug, shifting his weight. The awning swayed overhead, dappling light across his face as he glanced toward the vendor's table. "Yeah. I do."

A vendor at a nearby stall stacked fresh sourdough loaves into neat rows, their golden crusts catching the sunlight. A woman examined a bundle of fresh herbs, rolling a sprig of rosemary between her fingers before adding it to her bag.

Logan tilted his head. “Both of my parents are doctors. They have a private practice in Orinda, and they expect me to take over one day. They’ve already mapped out my med school, my residency, even where I should specialize. It’s all set, according to them.” He exhaled sharply. “But that’s their plan, not mine.”

Cass nodded, her fingers grazing the edge of the vendor’s table. “My parents say they don’t care, but that just sounds like code for the vision of a perfect daughter that they won’t tell me. They’ll only punish me if I don’t fulfill their dreams.” She let out a breath, shifting her weight. “I love soccer, but I never get to play. I enjoy data science, but it seems like the whole idea of using numbers is an offense to the old-school way.”

Logan tapped his fingers against his palm, glancing toward a vendor stirring a vat of steaming tamales. “I get that. My parents don’t say it outright, but they still make it clear that anything outside of medicine is a waste. It’s not just about me having a good life—it’s about making sure everything they built keeps going. If I walk away from their plan, it’s like I’m saying all their sacrifice wasn’t worth it.”

A burst of laughter rose from a group near the smoothie stand. The blender whirred loudly, momentarily drowning out the sound of passing footsteps.

Cass turned a jar of jam in her hands before setting it back on the table. “You feel like you owe them.”

Logan’s mouth pressed into a thin line. “I do. And I don’t. I mean, I get that they worked for everything they have. That’s real. But sometimes I wonder if they ever stop to think about what I want.” His foot nudged a stray pebble near the curb. “It’s like they already decided for me. Like I don’t get to want something different.”

They paused at a crosswalk, waiting for the light to change. The conversation shifted as they watched cars pass.

“Ever see Good Will Hunting?” Logan asked.

Cass shot him a look. “Do I look like someone who watches a bunch of movies about sad white guys?”

Logan pressed a hand to his chest in mock offense. “Okay, fair. But you might like this one. It’s about this janitor at MIT—except, turns out, he’s secretly a math genius.”

Cass raised an eyebrow. “And?”

“And he solves this impossible equation on a chalkboard when no one’s looking.

The professors lose their minds trying to figure out who did it." Logan nodded toward her phone. "That's basically what you're doing. Solving puzzles no one else can."

Cass smirked. "Except I'm not a janitor. And this isn't some elite university."

Logan grinned. "No, but it's kinda cooler. You're not solving problems for some rich professor—you're solving them for your family."

The crosswalk signal changed, and they joined the flow of pedestrians moving across the street. They emerged into a new section of the market, where the vendor stalls were arranged in a semicircle around a small plaza.

She let the silence stretch between them, watching Logan watch her. "Fine," she said at last. "I'll add it to my list." Then, after a beat: "But you know what movie you need to watch? House Party. Classic."

Logan's face lit up. "You won't regret it. But House Party? Didn't know you had taste."

Cass gave him a flat look. "Okay, you ever seen House Party?"

Logan shrugged. "That old-school one with the high-top fade dudes?"

Cass scoffed. "Yes. Kid 'n Play. Legendary. The dance-off alone is better than your whole movie."

Logan nodded, considering. "I mean... I do like a good dance battle." He smirked. "But only if I get to say How do you like them apples? at least once."

Cass narrowed her eyes. "If this is some rich boy inside joke, I'm walking away right now."

Logan chuckled. "Nah, just good taste. You'll see."

The plaza opened up before them, revealing a row of specialty food vendors. The late afternoon sun cast long shadows across the pavement as Logan's attention caught on a particular booth.

"Oh wow, this is my spot!" Logan grabbed Cass's wrist and pulled her toward a booth with a neon-bright banner.

Olipop – The Future of Soda

Ice-filled bins held colorful cans, condensation dripping down their sides. A chalkboard sign listed flavors: Classic Root Beer, Vintage Cola, Ginger Lemon, Orange Squeeze, and Strawberry Vanilla. A young Filipina woman stood behind the table, a Baybayin-script tattoo curling along her forearm. Her bright yellow Oakland Born, Olipop Made T-shirt clashed in the best way with her hot pink sneakers.

Logan reached for a can. “My parents banned pop a long time ago. This is the only thing they’ll let in the house.”

Cass folded her arms. “That explains why you talk about it like it raised you.”

The Olipop rep, Isla, grinned. “Then today’s the day, girl.” She tossed Cass a cold can. “We’re Oakland born, baby—straight outta Adams Point. First one’s on me.”

Logan cracked open his Classic Root Beer and took a sip. “Okay, so if soda is my personality trait, what does my flavor say about me?”

Cass tilted her head, considering. “Root beer? That’s like... safe. A little basic. But solid.”

Logan scoffed. “Basic? Nah, that’s classic. Timeless. Like Jordan 1s or a good leather jacket.”

Cass smirked. “More like New Balances and a Costco membership.”

Logan glanced down at his shoes. “Alright, that’s freaky. Your turn.”

Cass popped the tab on her Ginger Lemon and took a cautious sip, rolling the taste over her tongue. She side-eyed Logan before nodding. “Okay... this is good.”

Logan grinned. “Right? Now, let me guess—Ginger Lemon means you overthink everything, but deep down, you just wanna have a good time. Tell me I’m wrong.”

Cass swirled the can in her hand, watching the carbonation bubbles fizz against the sides. “I don’t think it could replace boba, but it definitely seems healthier.”

Logan nudged her shoulder. “Told you I got good taste. Now stop overthinking and let the fizz change your life.”

Cass smirked, tapping her can against his. “Fine. But this better be life-changing fizz.”

They drifted toward the edge of the plaza, where metal tables and chairs were arranged beneath string lights. The market’s energy had shifted as vendors began their end-of-day routines, the crowd thinning as the afternoon waned.

Logan slowed his pace. The sounds of the market hummed in the background—vendors calling out their final deals, the scent of grilled meats and sweet pastries mingling in the late-afternoon air.

Logan hesitated before speaking. “Hey,” he said, giving Cass a sideways glance. “Now that we’ve got our overpriced sodas, how about that early dinner—just us, no phones, no business talk? I know a place nearby with phenomenal sushi. But the real game-changer? Duck confit spring rolls. Crispy, savory, life-changing. You’re not ready.”

Cass laughed softly. “Duck confit spring roll? Logan, you have sophisticated tastes.”

Logan held his hands up in mock surrender. “Your dad’s the chef. I don’t want to disrespect your tastebuds.”

Cass tilted her head, considering it. “Alright,” she said, nudging him lightly. “But if this place has a dress code, I’m walking out.”

Logan chuckled. “Deal. No dress code.”

They left the plaza behind, moving through the last stretch of market stalls toward the main street. Their steps fell into sync, shoulders brushing occasionally. Logan glanced at her, his fingers shifting slightly against hers before his grip firmed. Cass responded in kind, her fingers curling against his as they passed the last few vendor stalls. The scent of sizzling skewers and honey-drizzled pastries lingered in the air, mixing with the hum of a street musician’s bassline.

As they crossed the street, Logan let their hands swing slightly. “You know,” he said, voice casual, “I’m glad we did this.”

Cass glanced up at him. “Yeah?”

“Yeah,” Logan said, squeezing her hand lightly. “I feel like we’re finally getting somewhere.”

Cass glanced down at their intertwined fingers, her grip shifting slightly before she met his eyes again.

Then, finally, she smiled. “Yeah...” She let their hands swing slightly. “Me too.”

The late-afternoon sun cast a golden glow over the sidewalks as they walked toward the restaurant, their steps unhurried, the day stretching out just a little bit longer.

SATURDAY, JULY 13 | JOURNAL ENTRY

85: The score I'd give myself for today's date with Logan. It felt easy. Natural. Like we weren't carrying a hundred different things in the back of our minds. But still, I have to stay casual. It was just one date, and emotions and atmosphere can cloud judgment.

10: The number of pages of charts, graphs, and notes I still have to prep for tomorrow's presentation. Logan made me forget about all of that for a few hours, but now it's waiting for me.

6: The number of people in my family who believe in me—Grandpa James, Grandma Lilian, Aunt Zora, Archer, Carver, and now Dad. Having his approval makes me feel like I can really do this. Like I'm not just playing around with numbers.

3: The number of hours of sleep I got last night. Or technically, this morning. I'll probably get even less tonight. Who knew summer could be more exhausting than a regular school day?

0: The chances I have of going to the Quentin Hale event. Mom made her decision loud and clear yesterday. Even Dad—who finally sees the value in what I do—couldn't change her mind. I wanted to scream. I still do.

1: The moment Logan grabbed my hand without thinking. It was small, barely a second, but I noticed. And I let it happen.

4: The times we made each other laugh so hard that people turned and stared. I don't remember the last time I laughed like that.

30: The seconds of silence after he asked if I was okay. I could've lied, said I was fine. Instead, I just let the silence sit between us, let him see me without forcing myself to fill the space.

5: The different ways I tried to downplay how much today meant. But the truth? It felt good to just be Cass for a little while. Not the problem-solver, not the fixer, just me.

8: The minutes we sat on the bench at the end of the date, neither of us rushing to leave. Like we wanted to stretch the moment out as long as possible.

20: The ideas spinning in my head about what happens next. With Logan. With the restaurant. With everything.

11: The number of times I caught myself smiling just thinking about the day.

100: The mix of emotions I'm carrying. Hope. Doubt. Excitement. Fear. It's a lot. But for the first time in a while, it doesn't feel heavy.

∞: The possibilities. Maybe this is just a good day in the middle of a storm. Or maybe, just maybe, things are actually starting to change.

SUNDAY, JULY 14

Logan's voice played through Cass's phone speaker. "Hey, I thought you could use some motivation. Here's a song that always gets me pumped up before a big event."

Cass clicked the link. The upbeat melody filled the car, bringing a lively energy to the drive. Her fingers adjusted the volume, letting the rhythm flow through the speakers.

"Is that Logan I saw?" Lola asked from the driver's seat, glancing at the softly glowing screen in Cass's lap.

Cass nodded, tapping her fingers on her knee in time with the music.

"Cass, are you in love?" Lola's quick grin caught the sunlight.

"Stop it, Lola." Cass laughed, turning toward the window.

Lola chuckled, her hands steady on the wheel. The smooth hum of the Tesla's engine blended with the music as they passed rows of tall trees, sunlight flickering through the leaves.

A neighbor's radio played KBLX, the smooth sound of Anita Baker floating through the evening air. From somewhere nearby, a deep voice called out, "Y'all still lighting fireworks?"

A second voice responded, "Always, bruh. This Oakland." A burst of laughter followed, then the pop of a distant firecracker.

A gentle knock on the car window drew Cass's attention. Grandma Lilian stood outside, smiling. "Ladies!" she called. "Come in!"

Cass opened the door and stepped out, smoothing her dress. Lola removed her sunglasses and tucked them into her purse as they walked toward the house.

Inside, the dining room glowed with candlelight and smelled of home-cooked food. Platters of Cajun potato salad, fried okra, chili con carne stew, grilled steak, and buttery corn-on-the-cob crowded the table.

Lola paused at the doorway. "Thank you for having me, Mr. and Mrs. Freeman," she said, addressing Grandpa James and Grandma Lilian with a polite nod.

Grandma Lilian stepped forward and wrapped Lola in a warm hug. "You can call me Grandma Lilian, and you're always welcome. Any friend of Cassie's is family."

Grandpa James gave a small chuckle. "Glad to finally meet you. Cass talks about you all the time."

Lola's voice came quiet but clear. "Thank you."

Everyone moved toward their seats, chairs scraping against the hardwood floor. Grandpa James adjusted his cufflinks and nodded toward the head of the table. "You saying grace or am I?" he asked Booker, who just waved a hand.

"It's yours, Pop."

The younger kids hushed as the prayer began, only the sound of the ceiling fan humming above them.

Once plates were passed and conversation resumed, Aunt Zora leaned forward, spooning chili onto her plate. "So, Lola, Cass tells me you're an artist? What's your medium?"

"Still dabbling. Painting, sketching and some graphic design." Lola passed the corn. "Though lately I've been staring at blank pages and canvases more than creating anything."

"Ah, the dreaded block." Aunt Zora nodded. "Started doing five-minute gesture drawings in the park last month. No pressure, just quick sketches. Broke right through it."

"You should see Aunt Zora's murals downtown," Cass said. "The one near the library with all the birds?"

"Are we gonna play spades tonight?" Carver's voice carried from the end of the table.

Archer leaned forward in his chair. "Yeah, Lola needs to learn."

Carver nodded. "We haven't played spades since Cass got back. You can't come to dinner and not play."

"True enough," Grandpa James said, reaching for the okra. "Can't be family without knowing spades."

"I've heard about Freeman family spades nights." Lola picked up her water glass. "Cass says they're brutal."

"Only if you renege," Aunt Zora said. "Or bid a bag you can't make."

"First lesson," Grandma Lilian pointed her fork toward Lola, "never cut your partner."

The conversation flowed as they settled around the table, passing plates and sharing stories. Lola sat quietly at first, watching the rapid-fire exchanges between family members. Her shoulders relaxed as Aunt Zora drew her into discussions about art, and soon her laugh joined the others. Silverware clinked against plates, voices overlapping in warm waves across the table. Once the meal ended, Cass stood, her hands resting on the table's edge.

"I have something I'd like to share with you all," she said. "Dad asked for your permission, Grandpa James?"

Grandpa James nodded and gestured for her to proceed. Lola helped connect Cass's laptop to the TV, making sure the cables worked. Booker dimmed the lights, and all eyes turned to the screen.

Cass stepped forward. "I've been analyzing data about our restaurant's operations, and I think these insights can guide us. Our sales figures have dropped below a critical threshold, and my analysis focuses on addressing that."

Bar charts showed declining sales. Scatter plots illustrated connections between menu prices and customer satisfaction, and a heatmap of peak hours appeared. Grandpa James leaned in, while others watched the screen.

Cass clicked to the next slide. "One major issue is excessive waste. Our spoilage records show losses above what's typical. Also, inventory discrepancies suggest possible theft."

Booker leaned back, his jaw tightening. "Cass, I said to drop that. Talk about loss, but no one is stealing."

Cass's tone remained even. "I'm not accusing anyone. The numbers just aren't adding up. Ignoring it may make things worse."

A brief silence settled. Then Grandpa James cleared his throat. "She's only showing what the data says, Booker. Doesn't hurt to look."

Booker exhaled and gave a small nod. "Fine. But let's focus on reducing loss, not blaming people."

Cass clicked to the next slide. "Agreed. To fix this, I propose tighter inventory controls, better staff training, and daily fryer cleanings to cut maintenance costs."

She moved to another slide. "On a positive note, the changes we've made have already let us pay down a month of rent. It'll squeeze some other expenses, but it shows good faith."

The room went quiet for a moment. Grandpa James spoke first. "Booker, you knew about this?"

Booker shifted in his seat. “Yeah, but I was waiting for the numbers to settle before saying anything.”

Grandpa James grinned. “It’s still progress.”

Lola cleared her throat, drawing attention. “I tested a small ad campaign on Yelp, and we saw an uptick in bookings. I’d like to try Instagram ads next, but I wanted Cass’s input first.”

Cass nodded with a brief smile. “That’s great, Lola. We’ll check the results and decide together.”

Aunt Zora gave Cass a thumbs-up, and Grandma Lilian patted Cass’s hand. Maya kept her arms crossed, though her expression eased slightly.

Cass turned to another slide. “To attract more customers, I’m proposing a rotating monthly artisan craft menu instead of a daily soup, live music events, a partnership with a local book club, and adding more books for younger crowds.”

She indicated a final chart. “By tackling these issues, we can boost efficiency by around thirty percent.”

The lights went up, and Grandpa James spoke first. “Impressive, Cass. That’s a lot of work.”

Aunt Zora nodded. “You’ve put real effort into this.”

Booker paused, then said, “We’ll try these ideas. But remember, I don’t believe anyone’s stealing.”

Maya’s voice softened. “Your whole family supports you, Cassie. Just promise this won’t hurt your studies. Ninety minutes a day for SAT prep.”

“I promise, Mom,” Cass said, her voice steady.

Grandma Lilian squeezed Cass’s hand, and Lola nodded. Archer spoke up from across the table. “Can you show us how that data stuff works? Seems cool.”

Cass laughed. “Sure. We can learn together.”

As conversation settled, Booker leaned back, his arms no longer crossed. “Alright,” he said. “I’ll call Hal on Monday about that payment. It’s not everything, but it shows we’re serious about turning things around.”

Grandpa James nodded. “Hal’s a fair man. He’ll respect the effort.”

Granny Lilian smiled. “It’s a step forward. Progress is what counts.”

Cass exhaled quietly and exchanged a glance with Lola, who gave an encouraging nod. Aunt Zora chimed in, “That’s how we do this—one step at a time.”

Booker glanced around, then looked at Cass. His expression shifted. “You did good work, Cass. Let’s keep building on it.”

After Booker’s nod of approval, Grandpa James pulled a deck of cards from the side table. The cards whispered against each other as he shuffled with practiced hands. “Time for spades,” he said. “Lola needs her first lesson.”

Lola perched on the edge of the couch next to Cass. Her eyes tracked each card as Grandpa James dealt them into four neat piles.

“The trick is to count everything,” Cass said, arranging her cards. “Just like the data analysis.”

“Watch out for Grandpa,” Archer called from across the room. “He sandbagged three hands last time.”

The first few rounds moved slowly. Lola studied each play, her cards held close. By the third hand, she slapped down a high spade, drawing whoops from around the table.

“Look who’s catching on,” Aunt Zora said, gathering the trick.

Cards tapped against the coffee table as the game continued. The steady rhythm of play mixed with bursts of laughter and commentary about missed bids. Carver kept score on a crumpled napkin, the numbers marching down the paper.

As the final hand ended, Grandpa James gathered the cards, tapping the deck against the table with a satisfied nod. “Not bad,” he said, his gaze sweeping over the group. “You’re getting sharper with every game. Keep at it.” He chuckled, shifting his attention to Cass. “You might have some competition.”

Dishes clinked in the kitchen. Maya’s voice drifted in—something about SAT prep schedules—but softer now. The sound of chairs scraping and containers snapping shut filled the room as the family moved through their familiar routines, each person falling into step with the others.

SUNDAY, JULY 14 | JOURNAL ENTRY

15: The minutes my presentation lasted. Weeks of research, hours of prep, and it all came down to those minutes. I wasn't nervous until I saw Mom's arms crossed, until I noticed Dad barely nodding along, until I realized I had to convince my own family that this could work.

2: The times I caught Mom's expression slipping, her eyes softening just a little. I know she doesn't want me wasting time on this, but for a second, I think she saw what I see.

1: The moment Dad finally said, "We'll try these ideas." No hesitation, no arguing. Just a real chance. For the first time, it felt like he believes in me.

6: The number of people in my family who have my back. Grandpa James, Grandma Lilian, Aunt Zora, Archer, Carver... and now Dad. Their support matters, but the way Dad looked at me today? That hit different.

4: The seconds of silence before Grandpa James was the first to speak. "Impressive, Cass." That was all I needed to hear.

30: The minutes after the meeting where we sat around like normal, like everything hadn't just shifted. The tension in the room finally lifted.

8: The number of books on the shelf that I suddenly wanted to share with Archer and Carver. If I can teach them, maybe they'll see what I see.

20: The number of times I glanced at Dad throughout the night. I don't think he even realized it, but I did. His posture was lighter. Like for the first time in a long time, he wasn't carrying everything alone.

11: The time we sat around playing spades, the sound of cards tapping the table, laughter filling the air. Like we weren't fighting for survival. Like we were just... family.

3: The times I caught Mom watching me. Not with anger, not with disappointment—just watching. Like she's trying to figure out who I'm becoming.

12: The amount of weight that lifted tonight. It's not fixed, not even close, but it's movement. And movement is hope.

100: The mix of emotions I'm feeling. Pride, relief, exhaustion, doubt. I should be celebrating, but my brain is already moving to the next step.

∞: The reality that we still have a long way to go. But for the first time, it feels like we're actually going somewhere.

MONDAY, JULY 15

It was Monday morning, and Cass shuffled into the hallway. As she approached the kitchen, her steps slowed. She could hear Booker's voice carrying softly from the living room. Pausing by the doorway, she leaned in just enough to catch the conversation.

"I've got this month's payment," Booker said, his tone steady but tinged with tension. "I'll send it over today."

A pause followed, and though Cass couldn't hear the voice on the other end, she could see Booker's grip tighten around the phone.

"Great," the voice finally said, sharp and businesslike. "Send it to me. I appreciate it. But let's not forget—this is what you owe me. And you still owe me. I'll meet with you on the 31st to see your plan for viability. Six weeks was gracious, and that ends on August 5th. When we first agreed to this deal, you told me your goal was to buy this from me. I've been waiting for years for you to put together your financing and take it off my hands. I need to see a plan, Booker."

Cass edged closer, her hand resting on the doorframe. Booker rubbed the back of his neck, his posture tightening as the voice on the other end continued.

"You can work as hard as you want, but I'm moving forward with my plans to sell the building. I've got one buyer in particular interested in converting the space into condos."

Booker's hand dropped to his side, but his voice remained calm. "I thought we had an agreement. You said you believed in this business."

"I did believe in you, Booker. But not anymore. I've lost faith. I don't believe in you." Hal's voice was cold, cutting through the room like a blade. "Get me the payment, but don't expect me to change my mind."

"Understood," Booker said quietly before ending the call. He stood for a moment, staring at the phone in his hand. Cass stepped into the room.

"Dad? Are you okay?"

Booker looked up, his face softening when he saw her. He slipped the phone into his pocket and offered a small smile. "It's okay, Cass. We just need to keep working hard. That's all we can do."

Cass stepped closer. The low whir of the refrigerator filled the pause that followed. Before she could say more, Sarah strolled into the kitchen, her tone light and breezy.

"Oh, I'm sure you'll figure it out," Sarah said, leaning casually against the counter as she reached for the coffee pot. "Honestly, it sounds like you're overreacting. You always make everything sound so dramatic."

Sarah's carefree shrug cut through the tension in the room. Booker placed a hand on Cass's shoulder. "Don't worry about it," he said quietly. "Let's focus on what we can control."

Sarah poured herself a cup of coffee, the faint clink of the ceramic mug against the counter punctuating her obliviousness. She left as quickly as she'd appeared. Cass turned back to Booker.

"We'll figure this out," she said firmly. Booker nodded. "I know we will."

The determination in his voice carried through the room. Cass gave his arm a squeeze before heading to the table. As she sat down, she opened her notebook, flipping it open with deliberate care. She pressed her pen to the page and began sketching out ideas.

*****

The hum of conversation mingled with Otis Redding's "(Sittin' On) The Dock of the Bay" playing softly in the background. Cass, her hair pulled back neatly, stood behind the register, taking orders from a line of lunchtime customers.

"I told you, Dad, we don't need to have everything on our menu," she said, passing an order receipt through the hatch on the wall.

Booker, wiping his brow, quickly plated dishes under the heat lamp. "You got this one right," he said, positioning a sprig of parsley on one plate. "Sometimes less is more. Table 14 is ready!" He stepped aside as Maria arrived, calling out the table number as she carried the plates away.

The door chime drew Cass's attention. She looked up, her face shifting when she spotted Isaiah entering with a woman at his side. Cass recognized the woman—her features resembled Isaiah's. He waved, and his energetic arrival stood out in the busy room.

"Cass!" Isaiah called over the chatter.

Cass thanked the last customer and moved around the counter, straightening her apron. "Isaiah! Good to see you." She glanced at the woman. "What brings you here?"

Isaiah rested an arm lightly on the woman's shoulder. "This is my mom, Mrs. Harris. We were in the area for her doctor's appointment, and I wanted to show her the restaurant I keep mentioning."

Cass offered her hand. "Hi, Mrs. Harris. I'm Cass. Isaiah and I worked together at the Summer Data Science Boot Camp."

Mrs. Harris took Cass's hand. "So nice to meet you, Cass. Isaiah told me wonderful things about you and your family's place."

"It's great you could stop by," Cass replied. "Let me find you a table. Lunchtime's been busier lately."

Mrs. Harris rested a hand on Cass's arm briefly. "We're excited to try the food. Isaiah's been talking about this place non-stop." Her eyes wandered around the restaurant. "I have to ask, how did you come up with such a special concept here? It's unlike anything I've seen."

Cass pointed to the shelves filled with books. "It used to be the Freedom Library, created by the Black community when public libraries weren't open to them. My dad wanted to honor that history, so he kept the bookshelves and much of the interior when he took over. We want to preserve that legacy."

Mrs. Harris looked toward the shelves lined with books, antiques, and photographs of notable figures. "That's remarkable, Cass. It's clear this place means a lot to you."

Cass led them to a booth near a window, where hanging potted plants cast light shadows on the table. "I'll make sure you get our best," she said, handing them menus. "Anything to drink?"

Once Cass jotted down their drink orders, she excused herself to the kitchen. From the service station, she glanced back occasionally, noticing Isaiah and his mom in animated conversation. Their lively exchange added a warm note to the busy scene.

A few minutes later, Cass returned with their drinks and a basket of cheese sticks and pumpkin seed cornbread. Booker followed behind her.

"Mrs. Harris, this is my dad, Booker, the owner," Cass said, before stepping away to pick up more orders in the kitchen.

Mrs. Harris's voice rose above the background music. "I haven't heard this song in ages. You have great taste in music."

Booker wiped his hands on his apron. “Thank you, Mrs. Harris. I’m Booker Freeman. Let me share a secret: I used to DJ back in the day.” He shaded the side of his face with a hand in mock secrecy. “Choosing the right music is as important as the food we serve.”

Mrs. Harris gave a quick laugh. “That explains it! This place has such a welcoming atmosphere. Please, call me Jamila.”

Booker nodded once. “We try to get every detail right.”

She glanced toward Cass, who was returning to the kitchen. “You’ve raised a wonderful young woman, Mr. Freeman. Isaiah said Cass is passionate about data. Have you talked about her college plans? She’d excel in a data program.”

Booker paused, adjusting his apron. “We’re still figuring it out. She’s good at this, but we want her to explore all her options.” He looked briefly at Cass. “Whatever she chooses, we’ll support her.”

Mrs. Harris nodded. “That’s good to hear. She’ll do amazing things.”

Cass stepped up to the table with a smile, shifting the conversation. “Isaiah, thanks again for installing the new inventory and waste record system. We’re aiming to cut our food waste by fifteen percent, and with your system, it’ll be a lot easier to track.”

Isaiah nodded. “Glad I could help.”

“And that seating algorithm you helped set up?” Cass continued. “It arranges tables based on party size, reservation times, and traffic flow. We’ve seen an eight percent rise in positive feedback—people say it feels more spacious.”

Mrs. Harris looked impressed, scanning the dining room. “That’s amazing. You’ve really found a calling, Cass.”

“Thanks, Mrs. Harris. But Isaiah did a lot, too,” Cass said. “It’s making a real difference.”

Mrs. Harris smiled at her son. “I’m proud of you, Isaiah.”

Isaiah smiled back. “Thanks, Mom. Cass is the one running the show. I’m just glad to assist.”

Maria arrived with their meals and set the plates down gently. “Enjoy!” she said.

Isaiah’s eyes flicked to the bright arrangement of food. “This looks great!”

Once they finished eating, Isaiah glanced at Cass. “Before we leave, could you show my mom the rest of the place? She’s interested in the whole setup.”

Cass nodded. “Of course.”

They stood from the table, and Cass led them through the restaurant, pointing out the historical items and rows of books left from the original library. Mrs. Harris paused near a display of old neighborhood photos. Her hand hovered over one showing a woman whose features bore a resemblance to Isaiah’s family.

A short distance later, they stopped by a sports history display. A black-and-white photo showed a high school girls’ basketball team holding up a championship trophy. Mrs. Harris leaned closer, her hand near the glass.

“This is the 1974 McClymonds High School girls’ basketball team,” she said quietly. “My mother was the point guard that year. They won state.”

Cass gave a brief nod. “That’s amazing! We keep these mementos to honor the resilience and history of this community.”

Isaiah moved in for a closer look. “Grandma on a basketball team—wow.”

Mrs. Harris stayed near the photo. “She often talked about how tough it was, but they pushed through every obstacle to win that championship.”

Booker approached, wiping his hands on his apron again. “The whole neighborhood was excited about that title. Your mom must’ve been a standout, Jamila.”

Mrs. Harris acknowledged him. “She was. Thank you for including this in your display.”

Cass adjusted the corner of the display table. “We want to keep these stories alive. They’re part of who we are here.”

Mrs. Harris looked at Cass. “I’m so grateful you have it here. My mother’s story means a lot to me.”

Cass gestured toward Booker. “We can make a copy of the photo if you’d like.”

Mrs. Harris brightened slightly. “That would be wonderful. Thank you, Cass.”

Isaiah watched them talk. “This place is more than I expected,” he said quietly.

Mrs. Harris looked around. “And all these books... do you sell them?”

Cass shook her head. “No, we lend them out. It’s part of keeping the Freedom Library’s spirit alive—people can borrow a book and bring it back once they’re done.”

Mrs. Harris ran a hand across a nearby shelf. “That’s such a meaningful idea.”

They circled back to the dining area. Mrs. Harris turned to Cass. “Thank you for the tour. It’s more than just a restaurant.”

Isaiah gave an approving nod. “It really is special, Cass. We’ll see you tonight online.”

Cass smiled. “Thanks for coming. It means a lot to show it to people who appreciate what we do here.”

Isaiah paused, meeting her eyes for a moment, then gave her a brief hug. “I’m glad I could visit.”

She returned the hug. “I’m happy you brought your mom.”

Just then, the door chimed, and Logan walked in, holding two cups of boba. He glanced in Cass and Isaiah’s direction, slowing momentarily before stepping forward.

“Hey, Logan,” Cass said, tucking a loose strand of hair behind her ear. “What brings you here?”

Logan’s gaze passed over Isaiah before returning to Cass. He shifted slightly, his grip firm on the cups. “Hey, Cass. Thought you might need a pick-me-up.” He looked at Isaiah. “Everything okay?”

“Oh!” Cass said, stepping aside. “Isaiah, this is Logan, a friend from school. Logan, this is Isaiah.”

Isaiah extended his hand. “Hi. I was just here with my mom for lunch.”

Logan shook his hand. “Nice to meet you. I brought boba for Cass—she’s been working hard.” He set one cup on a nearby table. “See you around, Isaiah.”

Isaiah nodded and waved. “Bye, man.” He turned to Cass. “I’ll catch you later. Thanks again.”

Isaiah and Mrs. Harris headed for the door. Booker appeared from the kitchen, wiping his hands once more.

“Cass,” he said, gesturing for her attention. “Could you introduce me?”

“Dad, this is Logan,” Cass said. “Logan, my dad, Booker Freeman.”

Booker crossed the room and shook Logan’s hand, holding it with a firm grip. “So you’re the boba delivery guy,” he joked.

Cass let out a short laugh. “Dad, he’s my friend from school.”

Logan stayed composed. “Nice to meet you, Mr. Freeman.”

Booker released his hand and looked at Cass. “I’ll be in the back if you need anything.” He turned and walked through the swinging doors.

Cass raised the boba cup. “Thanks for stopping by. You’re always looking out for me.”

Logan shrugged slightly. “Just wanted to check on you. You’ve been busy.”

Cass pointed to an empty table in a quieter corner. “Want to sit?”

They settled there. Cass sipped her drink, occasionally glancing at the doorway where Isaiah and Mrs. Harris had left. The scent of old books and the gentle clatter of dishes surrounded them.

Logan leaned forward. “Hey, are you free tomorrow? Alex and Tracy are organizing a soccer game in the morning. You want to join?”

Cass grinned. “A soccer game? Sounds fun. I’ll be there.”

Logan smiled. “Great. I’ll pick you up at nine.”

They chatted in low voices, the bustle of the restaurant continuing around them.

MONDAY, JULY 15 | JOURNAL ENTRY

8: The restaurant was nearly 75% full during lunch and dinner. I don't even know how we pulled it off, but it's working. The menu changes, the marketing, the small tweaks Logan and Isaiah suggested—it's all starting to click.

5: The number of dishes on the table during our small celebration tonight. It wasn't fancy, just a quiet moment with my family—Archer and Carver destroying their cookies, Dad enjoying his jambalaya rice ball bites, Mom sipping wine, and me with my lemon pepper wings. It's been forever since we sat together in the restaurant like this.

1: The hour Isaiah and his mom came by. Mrs. Harris was impressed—she saw what we were trying to do, what this place means. Isaiah seemed proud, like he was happy I let him see this side of my world.

3: The moments that felt off between Logan and Isaiah. Nothing bad, just... noticeable. Logan stayed through dinner, helped out, really got a feel for the restaurant. But there were these little pauses, like he was seeing all of it for the first time—the stress, the weight of it all.

4: The times I caught Logan glancing toward Isaiah, like he was trying to figure out something unspoken.

30: The seconds of silence after Logan invited me to the soccer game tomorrow. I didn't say yes right away. Not because I didn't want to go, but because I haven't let myself just go do something in a long time.

12: The minutes I spent overthinking it before I finally told him I'd be there.

100: The mix of thoughts in my head. The restaurant is thriving, but it's still on shaky ground. My family is closer, but Mom still doesn't fully see me. Logan and Isaiah are both here, but I don't know what that means yet.

∞: The feeling that I don't have to figure everything out tonight. For now, I'll just hold onto the small wins.

TUESDAY, JULY 16

Cass arrived at the community soccer field with Logan by her side. The early morning sun glinted through the dissipating fog, casting a golden glow over the damp grass. She adjusted the strap of her bag as her cleats pressed into the soft ground. The faint aroma of freshly brewed coffee drifted from a nearby café, mingling with the cool, earthy scent of dew.

Logan motioned toward the sidelines, where a man's voice was already booming across the field. "It's never just a friendly game if Tracy's dad is around," he said with a grin.

Cass followed his gaze to Tracy's father, who paced back and forth, cupping his hands around his mouth like an unassigned coach. Tracy was lacing up her cleats near the center circle. Cass tied her ponytail tighter and glanced toward the group gathering for warm-ups.

"Cass! You made it!" Alex called out, jogging over with a bright smile. Tracy looked up briefly, nodding at Cass before returning to her warm-up.

"It's been forever since you've been on the field," Alex said. "You ready?"

Cass adjusted her socks and smiled. "Guess we're about to find out."

The players greeted her with fist bumps and light banter as they divided into teams. Cass ended up opposite Tracy, who stretched her arms and offered a teasing smirk. "Let's see if you still got it."

The game began at an easy pace, with players calling out passes as they darted across the wet grass. The squeak of cleats mixed with laughter and the occasional cheer. Cass found her rhythm, weaving through defenders and making quick passes. Logan stood on the sidelines, clapping and shouting encouragement.

"Stay on her, Tracy!" her dad shouted. "Don't let her through!"

Cass dribbled past one defender, quickening her steps as she aimed for the goal. Tracy closed in, staying close. "Not bad," Tracy said, her tone light but competitive.

Cass feinted left, but Tracy anticipated the move and slid in, their legs tangling. Cass hit the ground with a thud. Tracy popped up quickly and extended a hand. "You good?" she asked.

Logan jogged toward them, his stride brisk. "Cass, you okay?" he asked, crouching beside her.

Alex's voice rang out from midfield, playful and loud. "All right, Logan, no need for an ambulance. She's fine!"

Cass laughed softly, taking Tracy's hand to stand. She brushed dirt from her knees and adjusted her shin guards. "I'm fine," she said. "Let's keep going."

Tracy nodded, giving her a light pat on the shoulder. "You're quick. Almost had me there."

They reset for the next play while Tracy's dad clapped from the sidelines. "That's how you play, Tracy! Stay tough!"

Cass threw herself back into the match, her movements sharp and focused. A few plays later, she intercepted a pass, dribbled past two defenders, and sent a crisp shot into the goal. Her teammates cheered, and Logan shouted from the sidelines, "That's my girl!"

By the final whistle, Cass's team was up 3-2. Players exchanged high-fives and friendly pats on the back as they gathered near the benches. Alex handed Cass a water bottle, grinning. "You played great today. That goal was solid."

"Thanks," Cass said, twisting off the cap. "Felt good to be back out here."

Tracy walked over, brushing stray grass off her shorts. "Hey, Cass. Sorry about earlier. Didn't mean to take you down like that."

Cass shrugged slightly, offering a small smile. "No worries. It's all part of the game."

Nia jogged over, holding her phone. "Boba run?" she asked, waving the screen. "Logan's treat, right?"

Logan laughed, shaking his head. "Looks like I'm buying. Meet back here after you all change."

Cass adjusted her bag and joined the others walking toward the changing area. The sun climbed higher, warming the field as voices and laughter echoed around them.

*****

Cass lay in bed beneath a teal-and-grey comforter, the edges tucked around her. She reached for her phone on the bedside table and opened Logan's profile, pausing briefly at his photo before typing a message:

Cass: "Hey Logan, still awake? Just wanted to share some good news. I secured better deals with our suppliers today! Our family's going to save a lot of money."

Logan's reply arrived almost instantly.

Logan: "That's incredible, Cass! I'm so happy for you. How are your elbows and knees?"

Cass: "They're a bit sore, but I can manage. Landing those deals gave me enough of a boost to ignore the pain for a while. How's everything on your end?"

Just as Cass set her phone aside, the door swung open. Archer and Carver stepped into the room, their steps louder than usual on the hardwood floor.

"Cass!" Archer called. "We need to talk. It's weird."

Cass sat up against the headboard, pulling the comforter closer. "What's going on?"

Archer dropped onto the bed, arms spread out, while Carver settled carefully on the edge. They glanced at each other, and Archer bumped Carver's elbow. "You tell her."

Carver frowned. "You're the one who insisted we tell her."

"Guys," Cass said, crossing her arms. "Just say what happened."

Archer shifted upright. "It's about the restaurant. We think we saw something off."

Carver nodded, clasping his hands together. "Mike was there the other night."

Cass paused. "Mike? What about him?"

"He showed up when he wasn't scheduled," Archer said. "I thought he only worked weekends now."

Cass tilted her head slightly. "What was he doing?"

Carver looked down at the hem of his shirt. "We saw him in the alley, talking to someone, but we couldn't see who."

"Talking about what?" Cass asked, her voice low.

Archer leaned forward. "We only caught a little. Something about the pantry and coming back to check it later."

Carver spoke quietly. "He kept glancing over his shoulder, like he didn't want anyone to see him."

Cass got up from the bed and paced the space between her desk and the door. "And you're certain it was Mike?"

“Definitely,” Archer said. “He wasn’t wearing his chef jacket, though.”

Cass stopped pacing, tapping her fingers on the desk. “Did he spot you?”

“No,” Carver answered quickly. “We stayed behind some furniture in the alley.”

“Good,” Cass said, turning to them. “Thanks for being careful. But why didn’t you tell me right away?”

Archer shrugged. “We weren’t sure it mattered, and we didn’t want to blow it out of proportion.”

“It matters,” Cass replied. “Mike isn’t supposed to be around on a non-work day. If he’s talking about the pantry on a delivery day, that’s suspicious.”

Carver leaned closer. “Do you think he’s stealing?”

Archer spoke up, keeping his voice steady. “I think he’s stealing.”

“I’m not sure,” Cass said, shaking her head. “But I’ll find out. Meanwhile, you two need to do something for me.”

“What’s that?” Archer asked.

“Don’t go back to the alley or the pantry alone,” Cass said firmly. “If you see anything else strange, come to me. No snooping by yourselves.”

Archer nodded right away. “We promise.”

Carver paused before nodding. “All right. We won’t go back.”

Cass allowed a small smile and ruffled Archer’s hair. “Thanks, guys. You did the right thing telling me.”

Archer grinned. “See? She’s going full detective on this.”

Carver rolled his eyes. “Only because you didn’t want to tell her first.”

Cass shook her head, amused. “Lucky for you both, I’m not sending you on any secret mission. Not yet. I’ll talk to Dad so we can tighten the delivery process. I’ll let you know if I need backup.”

“Secret agents,” Carver murmured, nudging Archer.

Cass returned to her desk as her phone buzzed with Logan’s new reply.

Logan: “Glad to hear you’re still feeling that boost. Keep me posted, okay?”

Cass glanced toward the window, where pale afternoon light filtered through the blinds. She typed a brief group message to Logan, Ayesha, Isaiah, and Lola:

Cass: “I know who’s stealing…”

TUESDAY, JULY 16 | JOURNAL ENTRY

2: The seconds of hesitation before I stepped onto the field. It had been too long. I felt it in my legs, in the way my heart pounded just standing there. But then I heard Logan's voice on the sideline, hyping me up, and I let myself breathe.

1: The moment Tracy's dad started acting like this was the World Cup. Pacing, shouting, directing plays like it was life or death. It was supposed to be a friendly match, but clearly, he missed the memo.

6: The deep breaths I took before sprinting down the field. The ball at my feet, defenders closing in—this was familiar. This was mine.

10: The minutes it took for me to find my rhythm. The way my body just remembered—the quick turns, the sharp passes, the instinct of knowing where to be.

4: The words Tracy said before knocking me down. "Not bad, Freeman." A challenge. A promise.

30: The seconds I laid on the grass, staring up at the sky after she tackled me. Logan was already running over, but before he could say anything, Alex was clowning him. "Relax, bro. She's fine."

5: The seconds it took for me to laugh, shake it off, and get back up. Because yeah, I was fine. And I wasn't losing.

8: The number of shots I took on goal. Only two made it in, but that second one? Perfect. I barely saw it before it hit the net, but I heard Logan on the sideline—"That's my girl!"

20: The minutes we all spent hanging out after the game, sweaty, tired, but happy. Tracy patted my shoulder, gave me that half-smirk. "Still got it."

11: The time I got home, still buzzing from the game. My legs were sore, my knees a little scraped, but I felt good. Better than I had in a long time.

3: The number of texts Logan sent before I even showered. "Proud of you." "You killed it out there." "Next time, I'm playing too."

12: The times I replayed his voice in my head. The way he said "That's my girl." I don't know what this thing between us is yet, but I know I like it.

100: The mix of feelings I'm carrying. About Logan. About soccer. About how today felt like a break from everything else waiting for me.

∞: The realization that maybe, just maybe, I need more of this. That I need to let myself have moments like this—just for me.

WEDNESDAY, JULY 17

Cass adjusted her laptop on the cluttered desk in her storage room office, the steady buzz of the fluorescent light overhead cutting through the quiet. She clicked into the Zoom call, her screen filling with the faces of Isaiah, Ayesha, and Lola. A colorful spreadsheet and a series of charts filled another window on the shared screen.

"All right, everyone," Cass said, leaning forward slightly, "let's start by reviewing the data from last week. Isaiah, can you walk us through the numbers for peak hours?"

"Got it," Isaiah said, clicking to highlight a bar graph. "So, based on last week's data, we saw a 15% increase in customer traffic during lunch, especially midweek. It looks like the adjusted seating algorithm is working."

"Great job, Isaiah," Cass said, nodding. "Ayesha, how are we looking on inventory?"

"Not bad," Ayesha replied, pulling up a separate chart. "But there's still some spoilage we need to address. I think tightening the delivery schedule and improving communication with suppliers will help."

Just then, the door creaked open, and Booker stepped into the room, glancing at the screen. "Morning, Cass. Are you in a meeting?"

Cass glanced back, smiling. "Morning, Dad. Yeah, we're reviewing some data. What's up?"

Booker stepped closer, his gaze shifting to the shared screen. "I've been thinking about your presentation at Grandma's. To be honest, I didn't get most of it then, but seeing this now..." He pointed to the bar graph. "It's got me curious. Can I join in?"

Cass gestured to the chair across from her desk. "Of course! Perfect timing."

Isaiah grinned. "Good morning, Mr. Freeman. Glad to have you."

Ayesha waved. "Good morning, sir."

Booker nodded. "Morning. Don't let me slow you down."

Cass adjusted her screen share. "This is perfect, actually. Isaiah and Ayesha can walk you through everything with me."

Isaiah clicked on another window. "Mr. Freeman, this graph shows how the seating algorithm optimizes table assignments based on party size, reservation times, and traffic flow. It's making the lunch rush more efficient."

Booker leaned closer, his elbows on the desk. "So this is why lunch feels smoother lately?"

"Exactly," Cass said. "It's all about reducing bottlenecks."

Ayesha pointed to another chart. "And here's what we're doing with inventory. We're tracking turnover more closely to minimize spoilage and maximize freshness."

Booker let out a low whistle. "This is impressive. It's like the data's telling me what my gut used to—but with way more precision."

Cass smiled. "That's the idea. It helps us spot trends you might not notice day-to-day. We're doing this on a small level, but just imagine what a one-percent improvement in efficiency does for companies like Amazon or Walmart. It's huge."

Booker nodded. "That's something I hadn't thought about before. Makes a lot of sense."

For nearly an hour, they discussed strategies and reviewed data, with Booker asking questions and jotting notes in a small pad. The hum of the light and the tapping of keyboards filled the room as they worked together.

As the call began to wrap up, Isaiah leaned toward the camera. "Mr. Freeman, Cass has an incredible vision for this place. It's been great helping her make it happen."

Booker smiled and nodded. "You guys are better than those corporate professionals. I appreciate all the help."

"Thank you, Mr. Freeman," Ayesha said. "It's been fun working on this."

Cass glanced at Booker, nodding slightly as she gestured toward the screen. "And this is just the beginning, Dad. There's so much more we can do."

He gave a slight nod in return. "You've got a great team, Cass. And now I can see why this work matters."

When the call ended, Cass turned to Booker, who remained seated, still looking at the charts on her laptop. "Thanks for taking the time to go through this, Dad. It means a lot."

Booker stood, patting her shoulder. "It's not just your work—it's the family's future. Let's keep moving forward together." He glanced at the charts one last time before heading toward the door. "This is good work, Cass. Let's pick this up later."

Cass nodded, watching him leave. She returned to her desk, organizing her notes as the fluorescent light hummed above. The buzz of collaboration lingered in the air, energizing the quiet space.

Later, as the kitchen filled with the hum of equipment preparing for dinner service, Booker said, "Isaiah seems like a nice guy."

Cass paused, a small smile appearing as she arranged plates on the counter. "Yeah, he really is," she replied. "But I think I like Logan. He's been supportive."

Booker nodded. "Well, I can see why. Logan is charming and considerate. If you're happy, that's what matters."

Cass glanced at him, her voice steady. "By the way, Dad... tomorrow is the tech event."

Booker's brows furrowed slightly. "Cass, I've been thinking about it all morning. I noticed you hadn't mentioned it, so I didn't bring it up. I'm really sorry you're going to miss the event." He stepped closer, resting a hand gently on her shoulder.

Cass shook her head, shrugging off his hand. "What's done is done. We need to focus on moving forward." She turned toward the new logging device on the wall, her tone firm. "Right now, that means sorting out our inventory and waste records and making sure this never happens again."

Booker leaned against the counter, his hands gripping the edge for a moment. He rubbed his brow and exhaled. "You're right. We'll get through this, Cass. And for what it's worth, I'm proud of how you've handled everything."

Cass turned back to him, her arms crossing tightly. "Why didn't you stand up for me with Mom? About the tech event and Professor Avery. You were the only person who could convince her."

Booker shifted his weight, his gaze flicking briefly toward the wall before dropping to the floor. His fingers tapped lightly against the counter. "I... I thought you mentioned the last day to RSVP was a few days ago, Cass. I haven't said anything more to your mother since then. I thought you'd... you'd accepted it."

Cass's fist came down hard against the steel bench, the sound reverberating through the kitchen. Booker glanced toward the doorway but quickly looked back at her.

"You knew how important it was to me. You saw how hard I worked all summer!"

"I did. And I'm sorry, Cass. I should have supported you more. It's just..."

"Just what, Dad? Just so I can keep working on your business?" She gestured toward the counter.

Booker rubbed the back of his neck, pausing. "I was scared, Cass. Scared of losing the restaurant, of letting everyone down. I thought focusing on the restaurant was the only way forward. I didn't realize..."

"Didn't realize what?" she asked, her tone sharp.

He looked up, meeting her gaze. "I didn't realize that I was asking you to sacrifice your dreams for mine. I see now that I've been unfair."

Cass stepped closer, her arms uncrossing. "Dad, I want to help. But I can't give up everything else—my future, my friends, my life outside this place. It's not fair to ask that of me."

Booker reached out, his hand brushing her arm gently. "You're right. It's not fair. And I promise you, Cass, I won't make that mistake again. Whatever happens with the restaurant, your dreams come first. Okay?"

"Okay." Cass nodded, her voice quieter. She placed a hand on his arm. "I just needed to hear that."

Booker pulled her into a hug, holding her briefly before stepping back. The faint clatter of utensils from the prep area and the distant murmur of voices from the dining room signaled the restaurant was beginning to stir.

Cass glanced at the clock on the wall. "Dinner service is starting soon. I need to get to the hostess desk."

The soft jingle of the front door bell echoed through the kitchen, followed by the hum of conversation as customers began to arrive. The bell rang once, then twice, and a third time as Cass made her way to the dining area. She paused briefly at a table near the photograph of Elaine Brown and Angela Davis, adjusting a menu and smoothing the tablecloth.

The murmur of conversation grew as more guests filtered in, their voices blending with the rhythmic clinking of glassware and silverware. The warm light from the dining room cast a cozy glow, and Cass straightened her apron before moving toward the hostess stand, ready to greet the next group.

*****

The grandfather clock in the corner of the living room chimed a deep, resonant echo. The bronze bird behind the glass chirped eleven times, marking the hour with its familiar cadence. Cass sprawled on the sofa, her SAT prep book and notes stacked neatly on the coffee table. She glanced at her phone, opening the test results page, where her latest practice test score—1310—was displayed in bold at the top.

A grin spread across her face as she stared at the number. She quickly took a screenshot and opened her family group chat.
Cass: "Just scored 1310 on my SAT practice test!"
She attached the screenshot and hit send.

Her phone buzzed almost immediately with replies.
Maya: "Cassie! That's fantastic! So proud of you. Keep it up!"
Booker: "Amazing work, Cass. I knew you could do it. Keep pushing!"

Cass smiled as she set the phone down beside her. Leaning back on the couch, she opened her social media feed and began scrolling. Lola's latest post appeared—a motivational quote alongside a selfie at Royal Park. Cass tapped the like button, then scrolled past Jake's soccer field photo with his dad and Alex's snapshot from a new taco restaurant.

Her phone buzzed again.
Logan: "Check outside your door ☺."

Cass tilted her head at the message, her eyebrows lifting. She set her phone aside and walked over to open the door. A bright bouquet rested on the porch, with a note tucked into the flowers: "Get well soon. ~Logan." Next to it sat a small basket holding patterned band-aids, fresh fruit, and an assortment of her favorite snacks.

Cass's grin widened as she picked up the gifts and carried them inside. She set them on her dressing table and adjusted the bouquet until it looked balanced. Switching on the LED lights strung across her wall, she stepped back, watching as the purplish hue bathed the room in a gentle warmth.

She grabbed her phone, snapped a picture of the bouquet and basket, and angled the camera to capture the lights. Then she opened her chat with Lola and uploaded the image.
Cass: "Look what Logan just dropped off!"

A response came almost at once.
Lola: "Okay, but where do I sign up for my personalized gift basket? This guy is a keeper!"

Cass laughed softly and typed back.
Cass: "Right? He even included my favorite snacks. And look at those band-aids—they're adorable."

Another message arrived from Logan.
Logan: “I’m glad you like it! I figured you could use a little break after all that studying.”
Cass: “I love it. Thank you for being so thoughtful. And guess what? I scored 1310 on my practice SAT today!”
Logan: “Cass, that’s awesome! I knew you could do it. Let me know when the real test is—I’ll bring you another bouquet when you ace that too.”

Cass chuckled as she typed.
Cass: “Deal. But you might need a bigger bouquet when I hit 1400.”
Logan: “Now that’s the confidence I like to see.”

Cass set her phone down and looked at her SAT book again. The LED lights cast a muted glow over her notes as she turned to the next page. She paused, tapping her pencil lightly on the margin, then leaned forward to study the practice questions.

WEDNESDAY, JULY 17 | JOURNAL ENTRY

10: The number of five-star reviews we received today across our online platforms. Customers are loving the new menu, the vibe, and the food. Seeing all those positive comments gave me a boost. It's proof that all the hard work Dad's been putting in—adjusting portions, improving recipes, and trusting the data—is starting to pay off.

3: The hours spent on Zoom with the team, running numbers, tweaking strategies, and double-checking inventory logs. Isaiah walked us through customer patterns and Ayesha pinpointed waste. We're locked in.

1: The moment Dad walked in mid-meeting, saw the charts, and actually listened. For the first time, he wasn't dismissing it as just numbers. He was curious.

6: The deep breaths I took before telling him straight-up—something's off in the books. The numbers don't lie, and now that I've looked closer, I think I know who's behind it.

10: The seconds Dad took before shaking his head. He doesn't want to believe it. He doesn't want to go there. But if I'm right, it's not just stealing—it's betrayal.

4: The texts from Isaiah after the meeting, telling me to keep pushing, to not let this go. He knows I'm onto something.

5: The messages from Lola hyping me up. She doesn't fully get it, but she knows I need someone in my corner.

8: The number of positive online reviews we got today. People are noticing the changes, and for the first time, it's not just hype.

20: The number of times I replayed my conversation with Dad. The way he said, "Cass, this could ruin someone's life." Like we're the ones making that choice. Like they didn't make it for themselves.

11: The practice SAT score I finally checked. 1310. Not bad. But also? Not the most important number in my life right now.

3: The seconds I let myself feel good about it before Mom came in, saw my screen, and started with the med school talk again.

12: The number of times I had to bite my tongue. She keeps acting like my future is a backup plan for when the restaurant fails. She doesn't get that I'm trying to save both.

100: The ways today felt like a turning point. The restaurant, my dad, the theft, the SAT, even Logan. Everything feels like it's leading up to something.

∞: The feeling that once we take the next step, there's no going back.

Entropy

Entropy measures uncertainty and disorder, capturing the unpredictability of information. High entropy reflects chaos, where outcomes are unclear and paths are uncertain. Reducing entropy means finding order, creating patterns, and making sense of the unknown. It's the pursuit of clarity in a complex world, where understanding replaces confusion. Entropy challenges us to embrace uncertainty as part of the process, recognizing that chaos often holds the seeds of discovery. It's where questions spark answers.

THURSDAY, JULY 18

A lone lamp dangled low from the ceiling, casting a dim glow against the cracked paint and yellowed ceiling. On the highest shelf, an old clock displayed 8:35 PM with faded red digits. Cass was seated on the bottom rung of a step stool, surrounded by storage racks lining three sides of the pantry. The musty scent of old inventory mingled with a faint metallic tang, lingering in the warm air.

Cass waited for this quiet moment of the day, when the customer flow was at its lowest, just before the dinner rush. Before entering the pantry, she had passed Booker in the kitchen, Maria sweeping up the porch, and Sarah arranging dishes and napkins on the dining tables in preparation for the evening service.

Her phone buzzed, pulling her attention from the shelves. She swiped it off the counter and glanced at the screen. Notifications from the "CDE (Chief Data Enthusiasts)" group chat filled her inbox. Tapping open the messages, photos and videos cascaded onto her screen.

The first image showed Ayesha and Isaiah standing against a hilly backdrop, arms raised in excitement. The caption read, "Wish you were here!" Cass studied the details—the name tags clipped to their jackets, the vivid green of the rolling hills, and the striking blue of the sky. Everything looked crisp and vibrant.

Swiping right, a video began to play. Ayesha's voice carried over the wind. "You wouldn't believe who just walked in—only the CEO of TechFuture Inc.!" The camera panned from Ayesha's animated face to Quentin Hale entering an elegant glass-and-steel building nestled among lush greenery. The video captured his confident stride as he disappeared into the building's sleek contours.

Cass flicked through more images and videos. One photo showed Ayesha in an emerald dress, the fabric shimmering under the lights, her smile bright and radiant. Beside her stood Isaiah, sharp in a black tuxedo with a satin lapel and a perfectly pressed shirtfront. Another photo focused on trays of tiny, elegant appetizers and glasses of sparkling punch held by younger attendees. Cass glanced down at her shoes, faintly stained with dried gravy from the lunch rush, before continuing to swipe through the updates.

Her fingers hovered over the keyboard.
Cass: "Thanks, everyone, for sending me all the photos and videos. I should've mentioned something about this yesterday at the restaurant. I haven't forgotten about it—not for a second. I guess this is just my way of coping."

The replies came quickly.
Ayesha: "It's okay, Cass. Honestly, I don't know how you're managing this so well. If

it were me, I'd be breaking something by now."
Isaiah: "Let us know if we can do anything to cheer you up. I don't mind playing the messenger if you want to contact Professor Avery or Quentin Hale."
Cass: "That's really kind of you, everyone. I might take you up on that offer, but please enjoy your time there. Don't feel like you have to play paparazzi for me, okay?"

The latest updates continued to stream in. She paused to watch another video, this time of the event's appetizers being served, and skimmed over more images of the venue, its glass walls reflecting the lush greenery outside. The faint buzz of the dusty air conditioner and the shuffle of cans in the pantry reminded her of where she was.

Another message popped up.
Ayesha: "Sorry, Cass, be back with more pictures and videos soon. The event is starting! Professor Avery is on stage to give an opening speech."
Isaiah: "We can't help but think of you the whole time, Cass. It would be a blast if you were here."

Cass stared at the screen for a long moment. Her fingers hovered over the keyboard, then paused. The soft ping of another notification broke the silence in the room. Cass locked her phone and set it aside. She reached for a bottle on the shelf but froze when Booker's voice broke through the quiet.

After the last of the customers left and Maria and Sarah were finishing their final tasks of the night, Booker came to speak to Cass.
"Cass?" His voice was low, his figure backlit by the dim light of the hallway. He stepped inside, his chef's whites rumpled and streaked with stains from the lunch service. His jaw was shadowed with stubble, and his expression was tired but focused.

Cass set the bottle down and stood, brushing off her hands as she walked toward him. Her sneakers squeaked softly against the freshly mopped floor, the sound echoing faintly in the quiet room. "What is it, Dad?" she asked, leaning against the doorframe, her arms crossing loosely.

Booker rubbed the back of his neck and twisted it a few times. "Let me in," he whispered. Cass stepped back to let him through. "I've been going over the numbers in the stock and inventory records since yesterday," he said, his voice low. "It's... it's worse than we thought. Someone's been doctoring the books for years. I should've seen it. I should've—"

"I've been telling you that something was off, Dad," Cass interrupted, her tone clipped. She tightened her grip on the edge of a nearby shelf. "If you'd just listened, if you'd taken the time to look at the data I showed you sooner—"

"I know. I know," Booker said quickly, his voice steady but low. His shoulders slumped, and he ran a hand over his face. "You don't need to remind me of my failures, Cass. I'm aware."

Cass's fingers flexed against the edge of the shelf. "Maybe if you'd listened sooner, we wouldn't be in this mess," she said, her voice strained.

Before Booker could respond, the storage room door handle turned. Both of them froze as Sarah and Mike stepped inside, their arms laden with bottles and bags. The sound of the bottles shifting in their grip was the only noise in the room, sharp and intrusive in the silence. Cass's eyes landed on the contents: premium liquor, bottles of wine, vacuum-sealed beef ribeye roasts, and cans of crab stacked at the top of the bags.

Cass stepped forward, her voice low and controlled. "So, you two are the one stealing our ingredients?"
Booker straightened, his voice cold and steady. "Mike, Sarah, what do you think you're doing?"

Sarah froze, her hands gripping the edge of a shelf as her face went pale. Mike set the bags down with a faint clatter, his shoulders tense as he stepped forward.
"Mr. Freeman," Sarah stammered, her voice barely audible. "We... we can explain."

Cass picked up a bottle of premium liquor she had set aside earlier, holding it in the air. "How could you?" she demanded, her voice steady but shaking slightly at the edges. "We've been struggling, and you're stealing from us?"

Mike sneered, stepping closer, his fists clenched at his sides. "Struggling? That's rich coming from you, Cass. You're off at your fancy camps while we barely scrape by. You keep cutting hours even though it's busy."

"You're not just clueless; you're selfish. You're a user," he said, his voice sharp and biting. "You've got a nice house in a nice neighborhood. You send your daughter to that fancy camp at that elite university. Got her on that special soccer team. Do you think we don't know who your friends are? They used to come here decked out in their luxury gear. You say the restaurant isn't doing well? Could've fooled us."

Booker's hands clenched into fists, his muscles tensing visibly. His voice came out low but firm. "You've been stealing from us for years?"

Mike shrugged, his tone cold. "Yeah, three years. And you didn't even have a clue. We've been selling your stuff all over town. Premium liquor, crab, steaks—all of it.

Too easy. You're too busy pretending you're some neighborhood hero."

Sarah stepped forward, her features tightening. "This place was circling the drain long before we took anything. We're just getting what's ours. Meanwhile, you're living large, pretending like everything's fine. You didn't notice because you didn't want to, Booker. This is on you. Besides, my kids are just as good as yours."

Before Booker could respond, Sarah grabbed a bottle of red wine from one of the bags and hurled it toward him. The bottle smashed against the shelf next to Booker, the glass shattering and spraying shards across the floor. Deep red wine splattered onto Booker's chef's whites as a jagged piece of glass sliced across his forearm.

Cass screamed, rushing toward him. "Dad!"
Booker staggered slightly, pressing a hand against the cut to slow the bleeding. His jaw tightened as he looked up at Sarah. "That's enough," he said, his voice cold and unyielding.

Sarah let out a short laugh, stepping closer. "You didn't care enough to notice, and now you're acting like the victim?"
Mike shifted, gripping another bottle tightly in his hand, his movements tense. "You're done, Booker. You don't have what it takes to run this place. You've been drowning for years."

The sound of sirens pierced the air, growing louder. Sarah glanced toward the door, panic flashing in her eyes. Mike froze, his shoulders slumping slightly, while his grip on the bottle loosened before he set it down.

"The police are on their way," Booker said, stepping forward to block their path. "Don't even think about running."
Sarah's lips twisted into a sneer as she looked between Booker and Cass. "You didn't notice for three years. That's on you."

The bell on the front door jingled as officers entered. Guns drawn, their commands were sharp as they cuffed Sarah and Mike. Booker leaned against a shelf, his hand pressing against his bleeding arm.

Cass stood frozen as the officers questioned her father. The bottles and bags Sarah and Mike had carried lay scattered on the floor, the contents shimmering under the flashing lights.

Maria appeared in the doorway, her handkerchief in hand. She rushed to Cass. "You alright, girl? You okay?" she asked, her voice trembling slightly.
Cass nodded, her hands trembling as Maria pulled her into a hug. "I was so scared, Cass. The moment I heard shouting from the pantry, I called 911. I'm just glad you

and your father are safe," Maria said, her voice soft but firm.

Cass wiped her face and turned to Booker, who was speaking to an officer nearby. His expression was calm but resolute as he nodded to their questions. Cass stepped forward as another officer approached her with a clipboard, ready to take her statement.

*****

Cass sat at the small, wobbly table outside the taco stand near the hospital. The neon sign overhead buzzed softly, casting a bluish glow across the table, while the scent of grilled meat and warm tortillas drifted through the open window. Behind the counter, the quiet fizz of a soda being poured blended into the hum of conversation and passing traffic.

She glanced at her phone, where her earlier message to Logan remained visible:

Cass: "Can I see you? I just need to get away."

He had arrived soon after, and now the two of them sat across from each other. "I'm so sorry, Logan, for involving you in all this," Cass said, her fingers resting on the edge of her cup.

"Don't mention it," Logan replied, keeping his tone calm. "I told you I'm here whenever you need help."

Cass managed a faint smile. "Even for an undercover mission like this?"

"It's pretty cool, actually," Logan said with a quick wink.

Cass stirred her horchata, watching specks of cinnamon swirl through the milky drink. "It's such a mess," she began. "Sarah and Mike... They've been with us since after the restaurant opened, and it turns out they've been stealing from us for years."

Logan leaned forward, setting his elbow on the table. "They've worked there forever. I thought they were basically family."

"So did we," Cass said, her tone edged with bitterness. She took a sip of her horchata. "They were taking premium liquor, ribeye roasts, canned crab—saying the food went bad or the supplier shorted us. I'm guessing they stole cash, too."

Logan set down his cup. "That's awful. How'd you figure it out?"

Cass's grip tightened slightly on her drink. "Isaiah helped set up a new inventory system. I noticed some discrepancies, and after digging deeper, it all pointed to them. My dad finally caught them in the act."

Logan placed a hand over hers. "That's impressive, Cass. You uncovered a real crime."

Cass glanced briefly at Logan's hand on hers before speaking again. "You should've seen my dad when Mike and Sarah admitted it. He stood there like he couldn't believe it. We were just getting back on track, and now this could ruin our reputation if it gets out."

Logan's thumb traced small circles on the back of her hand. "It's a lot, but you're handling it better than most people would. And think about it—this is real-world experience. 'Using Data Science to Save a Family Business' is going to sound pretty amazing on a college application."

Cass's expression shifted slightly, and she gave a small nod. "It does sound kind of impressive."

Logan grinned. "You're basically a legend already. Don't forget that."

Around them, the sounds of sizzling meat on the grill mixed with casual chatter, punctuated by the scrape of chairs against concrete. Cass glanced toward the hospital entrance in the distance. Maya was guiding Booker into their car, and he leaned on her for support. Cass's fingers curled around her cup as she watched.

Logan tilted his head. "Hey, you okay?"

"It's just... a lot," Cass said quietly. "My dad needs me at the restaurant, my mom wants me focused on academics, and I'm not sure what I want."

Logan gently lifted her chin so their eyes met in the neon light. "You're the smartest, most determined person I know. You'll figure it out, step by step."

Cass gave a small nod. "Step by step," she repeated.

A soft guitar strum flowed through the air, mingling with the ongoing clatter of plates. Logan smiled again, a playful spark returning. "If you need a taste-tester for new menu items, I volunteer. Especially if tacos are involved."

Cass let out a short laugh. "I'll remember that, but I'm not sure how much help you'll be, Mr. 'Ketchup-On-Everything.'"

Logan pretended to be offended, pressing a hand to his chest. "Ketchup is the food of champions, Cass. Don't knock it till you try it."

Their laughter eased the tension, allowing the day's weight to lift slightly. Cass stood, but Logan caught her hand.

"Hey, whatever happens, I've got your back. Data analyst, restaurant savior, future tech mogul—whatever you decide, I'm here."

Cass squeezed his hand once. "Thanks, Logan. Let's go."

JULY 18 | JOURNAL ENTRY

∞: The spite in Mike's and Sarah's eyes—how much hatred had they harbored toward us? All we ever showed them was kindness, treating them like family. Is this what happens when you treat staff like family? They eventually turn on you? I can't help but wonder how the rest of the staff feel about all of this.

3: The hours Dad spent at the hospital last night, getting his arm stitched up. Mom was with him, holding his hand the whole time. I sat outside the ER, staring at the glass on the floor, trying to hold it together. He's always been the strongest person I know, but seeing him bleeding and shaken… I've never felt so scared.

20: The number of things I should've said to him but didn't.

11: The time I texted Logan: "Can I see you? I just need to get away."

45: The minutes we sat at the taco stand, my hands wrapped around my cup, Logan just listening. Not trying to fix it. Not trying to tell me what to do. Just there.

3: The times he said, "You're handling this better than most people would." I didn't feel like I was handling anything. But hearing him say it made me feel a little less lost.

∞: The questions swirling in my head. How did we miss this for so long? How much damage did they really do? And most of all, how do we rebuild from this? Mike and Sarah didn't just take from us—they took from our community. The trust we had in them, the faith our staff had in us—it's all fractured now. And I don't know how to piece it back together.

∞: The regret for missing that tech event. Seeing Ayesha and Isaiah's pictures and hearing their stories is like salt in the wound. I should've been there, meeting people, learning, growing. Instead, I'm here, surrounded by broken glass and bitter truths. I know it's not fair to compare, but it's hard not to feel like I'm falling behind.

1: The napkin I secretly tucked into my bag to remember the night with Logan at the taco stand. It's silly, I know, but it felt like a small anchor in the middle of this storm. Sitting across from him, talking and laughing despite everything, was a moment I needed more than I realized. The cinnamon smudge from my horchata is still there, and every time I see it, I'll think of him telling me I'm stronger than I know.

Today was one of the hardest days I've ever had. Dad's quiet pain, the shattered trust, the weight of everything we've lost—it's overwhelming. But Logan's words keep replaying in my head: "Step by step." Maybe that's the only way forward.

One step at a time.

FRIDAY, JULY 19

The first light of dawn crept through Booker's Pages and Plates, casting a pale glow over the quiet, now eerily still restaurant. Cass moved through the space, her gaze inevitably drawn to the yellow police tape stretched across the door of the inventory room. The restaurant felt different now, tainted by the events of the night before. Police officers had gathered evidence, documenting everything from a shattered bottle to bloodstains and scattered footprints.

Cass paused at the corridor to the pantry and flicked the row of light switches. The restaurant came alight but still felt heavy. She caught her reflection in the window—dark circles under her weary eyes, her jaw tight. She looked exhausted, worn down—just like her dad.

Gripping the cool metal chairs, she dragged them across the wooden floor, the harsh screech cutting through the stillness. Her movements were quick and methodical as she arranged the chairs in a neat semicircle. She set up her laptop on the reclaimed library table, the gentle hum of its fan breaking the silence.

Linda walked through the front door with Maria by her side. Linda offered Cass a brief hug and a light pat on the arm. "I heard what happened last night," Linda said softly. "I wanted to be here with all of you this morning. This place is still like home for me."

Joey, the busboy, trailed behind them, eyes glued to the floor. He sank into a chair at the opposite end of Linda, nervously twisting his apron in his hands. The room filled slowly with staff members—Rick, Marcus, and others—each taking their seats with uneasy movements. The scraping of chairs and occasional coughs echoed louder than usual in the tense atmosphere.

The door hinges creaked as Booker entered, his steps deliberate and heavy. The bandage around his head and the red veins in his eyes drew immediate attention. Linda gasped, covering her mouth. She glanced at Cass, who stood at the threshold, waiting for Booker to step forward.

"Booker, are you okay?" Linda asked, her voice laced with concern. "What did the doctor say?"

Booker raised a hand in reassurance. "I'm fine," he said, though his voice was rough. "A couple of stitches and a mild concussion, but I'll be alright."

Maria frowned, leaning forward in her seat. "It's not just about you, Booker. You need to take care of yourself. What if something worse had happened?"

Booker gave a small nod, appreciating the concern but ready to move the meeting forward. He paused beside Cass, then squared his shoulders. He moved to the front of the room, his gaze sweeping across the staff.

"Thank you all for coming in early," he began, his voice hoarse but steady. "And thank you, Linda, for making the time to be here. I know last night's events have left us all shaken, but it's crucial that we address this together as a team."

As Booker explained the situation with Sarah and Mike, reactions rippled through the room. Linda shook her head in disbelief. "I can't believe it. Sarah's been here for years. How could she do this?"

Joey bounced his leg nervously, speaking up after a hesitant pause. "And Mike... he always seemed so laid back. Did they say why they did it?"

Booker sighed deeply, gripping the back of a chair for support. "They didn't say much, Joey. The police are still sorting through everything, but it seems like it started small—just taking little things—and then grew out of control." He paused, his gaze moving around the room. "But this didn't just happen overnight. Culture is what you allow or encourage, and I have to take responsibility for letting our culture drift. I was overwhelmed, trying to manage everything, and I let things slip through the cracks. That's on me."

Rick rubbed his chin thoughtfully. "Were there signs? I mean, should we have noticed something?"

Cass stepped in, her voice steady but firm. "There were patterns, but they were subtle. Sarah and Mike manipulated the manual data entries to make the shortages look normal. That's why it took digging into the numbers to uncover what was really going on."

The room shifted as understanding replaced skepticism. Marcus, who had been unusually quiet, finally spoke. "It's a good thing you caught it, Cass. But what happens now? Are we all going to be under scrutiny?"

Booker raised a hand. "This isn't about blaming anyone here. It's about making sure we're better protected going forward. And we have Cass to thank for getting us to this point."

Booker turned to Cass, pride shining in his eyes. "My daughter, Cass, uncovered what was happening. Her data analysis skills and dedication to this restaurant brought the truth to light."

All eyes turned to Cass. She clasped her hands together and nodded in acknowledgment, her gaze moving across the room. The mixture of curiosity, skepticism, and hope was palpable. Cass moved to stand beside her father, her voice calm and clear as she addressed the room.

"I know this is a lot to take in," Cass began. "First, I want to express my deep gratitude to Linda. For those of you who don't know, Linda brought these suspicions to my attention." She paused, then continued. "Now, I'd like to explain how we got here and where we go from here." Turning to her laptop, she projected a series of graphs and charts onto the screen behind her. "Over the past few weeks, I analyzed our sales data, inventory records, and financial statements. I found discrepancies that couldn't be explained by normal business fluctuations."

Cass guided them through the data, highlighting patterns that sparked her suspicions. She explained how she cross-referenced inventory levels with sales records and the waste logbook, uncovering instances where items left the restaurant without corresponding sales.

"It wasn't just about missing money or supplies," she said. "It was about recognizing patterns and anomalies that didn't align with how our restaurant operates. Sarah and Mike manipulated our manual data entries to show consistent inventory shortages."

The room grew quieter, the gravity of the situation sinking in. Maria's brow furrowed as she raised her hand. "How do we know it won't happen again?"

Cass nodded at the question, clicking to the next slide. "Moving forward, we're implementing new automation systems to prevent this from happening again. But more importantly, we're going to use data to improve every aspect of this restaurant—from inventory management to scheduling to customer experience."

She introduced plans for a new inventory system and emphasized the importance of routine waste logging. She outlined strategies for improving the menu and scheduling shifts based on predicted busy periods. As she spoke, excitement began to build among the staff.

Booker invited questions, and the room buzzed with voices. Joey raised his hand hesitantly. "But she's just a kid," he blurted, his voice uncertain. "No offense, Cass, but how can she run a restaurant?"

Before Cass could respond, Linda's voice rang out. "Joseph Ryan Miller, mind your words. That 'kid' has more sense in her little finger than someone twice her age. I've watched Cass grow up in this restaurant, and if anyone can make a difference, it's her."

Cass nodded, addressing Joey directly. "You're right, Joey. I am young, and my experiences are limited. But I've grown up in this restaurant, and I've gained new skills that can complement what we've built together. I'm not here to take over or make decisions alone. I'm here to work with all of you."

Her voice steadied as she continued. "I know change can be scary. But every decision we make will be backed by data and made with the best interests of the restaurant and its staff in mind."

Booker stepped forward again, his voice steady. "Now, I want to speak about commitment," he said, his eyes scanning the room. "You've heard our plans. If you're not ready to roll with us, there's the door. But know this—those of us who stay? We're building something better, together."

The room fell silent, tension thick in the air. Booker's words were clear but empathetic, acknowledging the gravity of the situation.

"If no one has anything further to share," Booker continued, "this meeting is dismissed. The law enforcement team has advised us to close the restaurant today, so you're free to go home. I'll see you tomorrow."

The staff broke into small groups, their conversations filled with questions, concerns, and tentative excitement. Joey approached Cass, twisting his apron nervously. "I'm sorry for what I said," he mumbled. "My mom's a single parent, and this job helps pay our rent. I was scared."

Cass offered a small smile. "I understand, Joey. I'm scared too. But we'll figure this out together." She gestured to his apron. "You're on the front lines every day—your insights could be invaluable. Let's set up a time to talk next week."

Joey's face lit up. "Really? I have some ideas that might help."

"That's exactly what we need," Cass replied.

As Joey walked away, Linda approached. "You handled that beautifully, Cass," she said. "You're going to do great things here."

"Thank you, Miss Linda. I couldn't do this without your support," Cass said. "My personal goal is to get the restaurant's performance so good that we can afford to bring you back."

Linda pulled Cass into a hug. "We're all in this together. You just keep leading the way."

Across the room, Booker gave Cass a nod and a smile. "You were amazing," he said as she approached. "I couldn't be prouder."

Cass replied, "Thanks, Dad. There's a lot to do, but my focus is on getting things back on track."

Booker adjusted the chair he was leaning on and nodded. "That's all we can do—stay focused and take it step by step. Together, we'll rebuild what this place stands for."

Cass glanced back toward the room as chairs scraped against the floor, signaling the staff's gradual dispersal. Quiet conversations filled the air as Joey lingered by the doorway, speaking softly with Maria, and Linda stood near the table, straightening papers.

Booker placed a hand on Cass's shoulder, his tone steady. "You've set something in motion here, Cass. This isn't just about fixing what's broken—it's about building something better, something stronger."

Cass nodded and gestured toward the departing staff. "It's a team effort. We'll move forward, step by step, and make it happen."

The room settled into a quiet hum as the last of the staff filtered out, leaving Cass and Booker standing near the table. Booker glanced toward the entrance, his voice quieter now. "This restaurant is everything to me, Cass. Thank you for giving it your all."

Cass adjusted the papers in her hand and turned to him. "It's everything to me too, Dad. And we'll keep fighting for it, together."

Cass typed a quick message to Lola: "Do you need a break as much as I do?"

Lola's response came right away: "I'm on my way. Too early for boba. Let's grab coffee instead."

Cass replied quickly, a faint smile forming: "Coffee works. We could check out some thrift stores after."

Lola's next text popped up almost immediately: "Deal. I'll pick you up. Telegraph here we come."

*****

The late afternoon sun cast a warm glow over the bustling Telegraph area of Berkeley. The hum of students and passersby surrounded Cass and Lola as they sat at a small outdoor table outside a busy coffee shop. The air was thick with the aroma of espresso, mingling with the tang of incense from nearby street vendors and the faint scent of sizzling food from food trucks parked nearby.

Cass cupped her hands around her warm coffee cup, her fingers tightening as if grounding herself. “Last night was a mess. Sarah and Mike—Dad called the police on them. They were stealing from the restaurant. It’s been going on for years, and Dad finally figured it out. Seeing them arrested was... a lot.” She paused briefly as a skateboarder zipped past their table, the clatter of wheels breaking the momentary silence. “Then this morning, Dad held a meeting with everyone about it. He was so serious—more than I’ve ever seen. He said it wasn’t my place to be there when the police came, but... I couldn’t just stand back. It’s hard, Lola. They weren’t just employees; they felt like family. Watching them like that, hands bound and expressions grim... I can’t forget it.””

Lola leaned forward, her elbows on the table. “They still played you, Cass. Played your dad, too. Everything your family built—gone like that. I know it sucks, but they made their moves.””

Cass hesitated, her fingers tracing the rim of her cup. “Did they really have choices, though? Mike’s rent kept climbing, and Sarah’s raising her little brothers. Maybe if we’d paid them more or tried something else—”

“Cass,” Lola cut in, her tone steady but sharp. “You can’t carry all that on your back. Your family did what they could to keep it running. Times were rough, sure, but stealing? That’s not it. They crossed a line.””

Cass nodded slowly, her gaze fixed on the table. “I know. But once they were cuffed, it stopped being just about theft. It became about who they are—two Black people arrested in a city where some folks already look for a reason to call us criminals. And the way Dad handled it... I know he was trying to protect me, but I feel like I should have done more.” She paused, her voice lowering. “Now people will say we should’ve known better, that it’s our fault for trusting them. Or worse, that Sarah and Mike getting arrested just confirms every stereotype people already have about us.”

Lola released a slow breath, her shoulders dropping. “I... I didn’t think about it like that.”

Cass straightened in her seat, her voice quieter but resolute. “I hate what they did, but I also hate what’s next for them. They’ll be another statistic, and nobody will care about their backstory. My dad’s right to press charges, but it feels like nobody comes out ahead.”

Lola reached across the table, resting her hand lightly over Cass’s. “You’ve already done so much for your family and the restaurant. You can feel all of this—anger, sadness, everything. But you can't fix it all."

Cass's jaw unclenched slightly, and she locked eyes with Lola. "Maybe. But I don't want strength forced on me. I want to be strong because I decide it."

Lola smiled faintly. "Then let's figure out how to make that choice together."

*****

After finishing their drinks, Cass and Lola wandered into a nearby thrift store, its racks spilling onto the sidewalk under the shade of colorful awnings. The mingling smells of old leather and fabric softener hit them as they stepped inside. A busker outside strummed an upbeat tune on his guitar, the melody trailing in behind them.

Lola stopped short, her eyes locking on the store's wild design. "Man, these stores all got their own thing going," she said, nodding at the mix of murals and vintage signs. She ran her fingers along a painted column covered in stickers and flyers. "It's like each shop is telling its own story."

She leaned over to a small business owner setting up some necklaces near the door. "Yo, your display's dope. You on social, or is it all word of mouth?"

The owner smiled warmly. "Mostly Instagram these days. It's great for reaching a younger crowd."

Lola nodded, her fingers grazing the necklaces. "Instagram's the move. Does it help you connect with people, or is it just to get them through the door?"

"A bit of both," the owner said. "We post regularly, and it definitely brings in curious shoppers. But conversations like these? They make the real connections."

Lola smiled and turned to Cass. "That's pretty inspiring. Now let's see if we can inspire Logan with your new look.""

Cass leaned on the edge of the counter, smirking. "Hey, look at who's working now."

Lola rolled her eyes playfully. "Networking is work, Cass. You could learn a thing or two."

"Smart," Lola added, nodding appreciatively before turning back to Cass. "Okay, now it's time to find you something fun to wear. Logan won't know what hit him."

Cass smirked, following her to the rack. The two moved through a jumble of vibrant fabrics and retro designs, their fingers brushing over corduroy and flannel. Cass's phone buzzed in her pocket, and she pulled it out to see a message from Logan: "What are you up to?" A pair of green Adidas Gazelles caught Lola's eye. She held them up with a grin. "This has Logan written all over it. Picture this at your next 'data hero saves the day' meeting."

Cass laughed, shaking her head. "Logan's not ready for anything this bold. But I'll humor you," Cass said, her thumbs hovering over her phone. She turned to Lola. "Did I tell you he came to visit me? Bought tacos while Dad was at the hospital."

Lola paused mid-rack sift, raising an eyebrow. "Wait, tacos? Like, he just showed up, played the hero, and got you tacos? That's some serious effort."

Cass shrugged, grinning. "Yeah, something like that. He's been... helping."

Lola smirked. "Helping. Right. And now you're thinking about sending him pictures? C'mon, let him wonder for once."

Lola raised her eyebrows and shook her head, grinning. "No way. You gotta surprise him. Let him see the whole look tomorrow. Isn't he going with you and your dad to that data science meetup? And now he's out here buying you tacos, too? Seriously, Cass, this boy's putting in work."

Cass plucked a yellow tank top and a soft denim jacket from the rack. She inspected the cuffs on the jacket and held the tank top up to her hoodie. Her phone buzzed again with Logan's follow-up text: "Hope you're not getting into trouble." Cass laughed quietly and pocketed her phone. "How about these? It's simple but works for everything."

"Now we're talking," Lola said, draping the jacket over Cass's arm. "Throw in these green Adidas Gazelles—it's perfect."

Cass caught a glimpse of herself in the small mirror by the rack. The yellow tank top popped against her neutral hoodie, the cropped jean jacket added just enough edge, and the green Adidas Gazelles added a bold, vintage touch. She adjusted the jacket over her shoulders, the outfit coming together with a mix of casual and bold elements. She gave a reluctant nod. "Fine. These will work."

As they walked toward the counter, Cass glanced at her phone one last time and grinned at Logan's final text: "Whatever you're up to, I can't wait to hear about it." She tucked the tank top and jacket into her bag, the faint smile still on her lips. The thrift store's bell jingled as the door closed behind them, the sounds of Telegraph humming in the background.

Lola clapped her hands together. "Perfect! I saw another store down the street I want to check out. Let's check out and keep it moving. Are we done here? There's more to see and do."

Cass raised an eyebrow. "Don't you ever get tired?"

Lola smirked. "Of shopping, or hanging with my bestie? No to both."

Cass stopped at the curb, adjusting her bag. "I gotta get back to the restaurant. Dad's probably waiting on me."

Lola groaned, rolling her eyes. "We just got started. There's so much more to check out."

Cass chuckled. "Rain check. Next time, I'll make it worth it."

Lola waved her off with a grin. "Deal. Go be responsible or whatever."

*****

When Cass returned to the restaurant after shopping with Lola, the atmosphere was subdued, almost eerie. The employees looked drained, like zombies shuffling through their tasks, their movements slow and mechanical. Maria's smile was tight, and her eyes darted nervously toward the kitchen every few moments. Rick, the sous chef, moved with tense efficiency, his jaw clenched as he called out orders. Even casual requests like drink refills were met with brief pauses, as though the staff were weighing each word before speaking. Maria walked past Cass with a tray in hand, offering a muted greeting before heading to the back, her usual lively demeanor replaced with cautious politeness.

In the kitchen, the usual energy was muted. The clang of pots and pans felt tentative, and the sizzling grills emitted only a low hiss. Rick, the sous chef, moved like he was running on fumes, his jaw tight as he worked. His eyes kept darting toward the swinging door leading to the storeroom, as if expecting something—or someone—to walk through at any moment. Staff whispers barely carried over the sound of running water, and their glances at one another were brief but telling.

Conversations among the staff carried on in lowered voices, their words punctuated by quick, nervous glances. At one table near the window, a customer leaned closer to the server, their tone hushed. "What happened to Sarah and Mike? Weren't they on the schedule this week?" Another guest nearby chimed in, glancing toward the kitchen. "They've been here for years. Did something happen?"

The server hesitated, her grip tightening slightly on the tray she held. “They’ve stepped away for a while,” she said, her voice steady but measured. Her eyes darted toward the kitchen as she quickly excused herself.

At another table near the center of the dining area, a couple spoke in equally low tones. “We heard the police were here last night,” the woman said, her voice carrying just enough to catch Maria’s attention as she passed by. “Do you think it’s connected?”

The man across from her shook his head, his eyes narrowing toward the staff. “Maybe. But something definitely feels off today. Everyone seems... on edge.” Maria quickened her pace toward the kitchen, her tray held a little tighter as she disappeared through the swinging door.

Later in the evening, as the dinner rush quieted down, Booker approached Cass as she walked through the dining area, his steps deliberate but his expression softer than usual. “Cass, you about ready to leave?” he asked, his voice quieter. “Tonight, I just want to be with the family. Your mom didn’t have to work late, so we can all have dinner together.”

Cass nodded, offering a faint smile. “Sounds good. I’ve got a meeting with the team, but I can do it from home. I’m feeling a bit tired anyway.”

“Sounds good,” Cass replied, offering a faint smile. “I’ve got a meeting with the team, but I can do it from home. I am feeling a bit tired anyway.”

Cass headed to her office. The restaurant’s muted hum followed her as she closed the door behind her. The faint scent of cleaning solution lingered in the air. She powered down her laptop, gathering her notes and slipping them into her bag before turning off the desk light and heading out.

At home, Cass powered up her laptop again at her desk. The soft chime of the Zoom call filled the quiet room as Ayesha and Isaiah’s faces appeared on the screen, Ayesha waving enthusiastically while Isaiah leaned closer to the camera, his energy barely contained.

“Cass! Finally,” Ayesha said, her grin wide. “We’ve got so much to catch you up on.”

Isaiah jumped in, his voice quick. “Cass, we missed you so much! this event was wild—it was at a quintin hale’s mansion, like some straight-up Silicon Valley dream. We had to go through layers of security just to get in—security gates, metal detectors, ID checks, all of it. Once we got inside, it was unreal—holographic displays you could swipe through, live AI demos, and robots doing stuff you wouldn’t believe. It felt like stepping into a whole other world.”

Cass leaned closer to the screen, tilting her head slightly. “Yeah? And you’re just now telling me this? Hit me with everything.” Her voice sounded engaged at first, but as the call went on, her responses became shorter, her energy fading.

Isaiah jumped in first. “Cass, the venue was incredible. Holographic displays, live AI demos, real-time data visualizations—it felt like the future.”

“And the people,” Ayesha added, her hands moving in quick gestures. “We met CEOs, data scientists, robotics engineers—even startup founders working on GPT agents and the next wave of robotics. Professor Avery introduced us to almost everyone. But, honestly? It was kind of disappointing, too.”

Isaiah nodded, leaning closer to the camera. “Yeah, for real. There weren’t enough women or people of color. These folks are out here building the future, but it’s all behind gates and closed doors. Most people don’t even get to see it, let alone have a say in it.”

Ayesha frowned, shaking her head. “It’s like they’re deciding how the world’s gonna look, and they’re not even letting everyone have a voice in it. It’s a huge missed opportunity.”

Cass leaned forward slightly, her voice quieter. “That’s a lot to take in. But at least you both got to see it. That means people like us can find a way in, right?”

Cass nodded. “That sounds wild. And Ms. Harper? Did you get to talk to her?”

“We did,” Isaiah said. “She asked about you. She even remembered your camp presentation. She said your ideas on data-driven environmental policies stuck with her.”

Ayesha chimed in. “She even asked why you weren’t there, but when we told her you were invited, she was cool about it. She said she trusted us to share what we learned with you—since, technically, you were part of it.”

“That’s good to hear,” Cass replied, tapping the edge of her notebook absentmindedly as she listened. Outside her office, the muffled sound of someone stacking chairs carried faintly through the walls. “I’m glad she noticed our team.”

The conversation turned to other highlights, with Ayesha and Isaiah recounting their experience in rapid bursts. “The NDA we signed was intense,” Ayesha said with a laugh. “But since you were technically invited, we figured it’s fair to share some things.” They spoke quickly, describing cutting-edge GPT agent prototypes that could hold full conversations and robotics demonstrations that felt like science fiction come to life. Cass nodded occasionally but was no longer offering detailed replies. She leaned back slightly in her chair, her eyelids drooping as her focus wavered. Cass nodded along, her focus sharp. Finally, she raised a hand, her voice cutting through their quick exchanges. Outside her window, the streetlights cast long shadows on the quiet sidewalk.

Ayesha's grin faded as she noticed Cass's head lower slightly, her shoulders seeming heavier. Ayesha leaned forward, squinting at the screen. "Cass, are you okay? You look kinda off—are you sick or something?"

"Wait, before we go any further, I need to tell you something," she said. Their expressions shifted as Cass explained the theft at the restaurant, the involvement of the police, and her dad's steps to address it.

Ayesha widened her eyes. "Cass, that's terrible. Are you okay?"

Isaiah leaned forward, frowning. "I can't believe that happened. That's a real breach of trust."

Cass nodded. "Yeah, it's been tough, but we're handling it. Sorry I didn't say anything before—I needed time."

"We understand," Ayesha said. "You don't have to go through it alone."

Isaiah spoke into his mic. "If there's anything we can do, just let us know."

"Thanks," Cass said. "Right now, we're focused on making sure it doesn't happen again." The sound of a chair scraping outside her office momentarily pulled her attention, but she shook it off and focused back on the screen.

Ayesha switched to a shared screen and indicated some figures. "Look here—these manual adjustments explain most of the discrepancies. About sixty percent of the losses come from that."

"That's huge," Cass said, setting her shoulders as she studied the data. "But at least now we know. We can start fixing it."

Isaiah nodded. "It's not just about catching the problem; it's a chance to come back stronger." His excitement barely registered with Cass, who had quietly rested her head on her hand, her eyes half-closed.

"Exactly," Cass agreed. "We're implementing new checks. My dad sees this as a wake-up call."

As the call wound down, Isaiah said, "We're with you, Cass. Whatever you need." He and Ayesha suddenly paused, noticing her silence. Cass's head was now fully down on the desk, her hair partially covering her face.

"Cass?" Ayesha asked, her tone shifting to concern. "You okay?"

Cass stirred slightly but didn't lift her head right away. "Sorry, just… it's been a long day," she muttered, her voice muffled.

Ayesha frowned. "You look wiped. Maybe you should call it a night."

Isaiah nodded. "Yeah, Cass, take a break. We can catch up more later."

Cass finally sat up, rubbing her temples. "Thanks, guys. I'll be fine. Just need some rest."

"Thanks, guys," Cass replied. "I appreciate it."

As the Zoom call ended, Cass moved from the desk to her bed, resting her head briefly against the cool wooden headboard. The room was still, the soft whir of her desk fan the only sound.

The muffled sound of laughter filtered up through the floorboards, mingling with the twins' playful shouts and the clink of dishes from the kitchen. Archer's voice rang out louder than the rest, followed by a peal of laughter that rose above the commotion. Cass sat on her bed, her laptop casting a blue glow in the dimness of her room. The screen showed a blank document, cursor blinking steadily. A dish shattered downstairs, followed by groans and more laughter.

A soft knock on her door broke the quiet. Three gentle taps—her father's signature. "Cass? Can I come in?"

"Yeah, sure," she replied, closing her laptop with a soft click.

Booker stepped into the room, the floorboard by the door creaking under his weight. His shoulder rested against the worn doorframe where height marks tracked years of growth. The desk lamp cast shadows across scattered notes and textbooks. A printout of Katherine Johnson's photo watched from the wall.

"You doing okay up here? Everyone's asking for you downstairs." The scent of her mother's pineapple upside-down cake drifted up the stairs behind him.

Cass shifted on the bed, tucking her legs beneath her. The mattress springs squeaked. "I'm fine. Just needed some quiet time."

Booker nodded, his keys jingling softly in his pocket as he moved. "I remembered you asked about a data meetup in Berkeley. Is that tomorrow?"

The desk fan whirred between them, stirring loose papers. Cass blinked, straightening. "Yeah, it is."

“Do you think you can still go? Did you have to RSVP?” Booker said.

“Is Mom okay with this? She told Professor Avery to stay away from me.” Cass’s voice was even.

Booker nodded. “She’s the one who mentioned it to me and suggested we go together.”

Cass blinked, her head tilting slightly. “Seriously?” she asked.

Booker nodded, his expression steady. “Seriously.”

Booker’s hand moved to the back of his neck, his shadow shifting slightly on the wall. “I just want to make sure you’re doing okay, kiddo. I think it could be good for you. And for me too.”

“You were just in the hospital last night, Dad. Are you sure you’re okay?” Cass asked, her voice steady but concerned.

Booker nodded lightly. “I’m fine. A couple of stitches and a mild concussion. Nothing I can’t handle. Don’t forget, I used to run into burning buildings to save strangers. I can handle this.”

Cass tilted her head, a faint smile forming as she crossed her arms. “Really, Dad? Logan?”

“Yes, really.” A smile tugged at his lips as he adjusted his stance, the floorboard groaning again. “He seems like a good kid, and I know you’ve been working hard. Having someone with you might make the trip more enjoyable.”

Cass hesitated, then offered a soft smile. “Thanks, Dad. I mean it.”

Another crash downstairs, followed by Archer’s voice: “It wasn’t me this time!” Laughter erupted, followed by Maya’s exasperated voice, “Boy, you better stop! Then who else, Archer? The ghost of the pantry?” Booker’s laugh rumbled in response, and Carver’s voice chimed in, “Definitely Archer!” as more laughter spilled through the house.

Booker’s laugh mixed with the chaos below. He stepped forward, the floor protesting each movement. His hand rested briefly on Cass’s shoulder. “You’ve earned it. Now come downstairs when you’re ready. Your mom’s already guessed the wrong ending—again—and she’s waiting for you to save her.”

After he left, the door clicked shut against its frame. Cass reached for her phone, its screen illuminating her face in the growing dusk. Her thumbs moved quickly: “Hey, are you free tomorrow? Thinking of heading to Berkeley for that meetup.”

Logan's reply lit up the room almost instantly: "I'm in. Can't wait to see you. I'm a bit nervous about spending time with your dad. He can be a little intimidating. He almost broke my hand the first time I met him with that handshake."

Cass replied quickly: "Everyone says that about him. Don't worry, it'll be great."

The phone settled onto her comforter with a soft thump. Cass adjusted her hoodie and tucked a loose strand of hair behind her ear. She paused at the top of the stairs, listening to the clatter of dishes and bursts of laughter below. Archer's voice rose, followed by a playful yelp from Carver. The faint scent of pineapple upside-down cake drifted through the air. She adjusted her hoodie, her steps unhurried as she made her way downstairs.

JULY 19 | JOURNAL ENTRY

6: The staff members who asked if Dad was doing okay after the meeting. Linda pulled me aside and said she's never seen him look so tired, and Marcus mentioned he seemed distracted during the prep shift. It's not just the betrayal; it's the fact that he feels like he failed all of us—his staff, his family, everyone who depends on this place.

15: The minutes I spent after the meeting trying to talk to him. I told him it's not his fault, that Sarah and Mike made their choices. But he just shook his head and said, "I should've seen it sooner." I didn't know what to say to that, because part of me thinks he's right. How did we not see it sooner?

5: The number of times my dad said, "No one's stealing, Cass. Stop worrying about it." He said it so often, like he was trying to convince both of us that everything was fine. But now, even he can't deny it. The truth is out, and the restaurant feels different—like some part of its heart has been torn out. It's been one day since we discovered the theft, and I'm still trying to process everything.

10: The number of hug GIFs Logan sent me today, along with encouraging stories about how people bounce back from setbacks. Even though he was busy working with his parents, he still made time to check in on me. It's like he knows exactly when I need that extra nudge to keep going. He even sent a story about a small bakery that came back stronger after a crisis. It made me smile, even if just for a minute.

SATURDAY, JULY 20

The lunch rush swirled around the hostess stand as Cass checked reservations. Forks clinked against plates, ice cubes rattled in glasses, and the sharp aroma of fried catfish mingled with fresh cornbread. Servers weaved between tables with practiced ease, their voices blending with the hum of casual conversations and the rhythmic creak of the front door opening and closing. Through the front windows, summer heat rippled off parked cars. The bell above the door chimed, sending a shaft of sunlight across worn floorboards. Logan stepped through, navigating between tables with practiced ease, a cup of boba tea in each hand.

At the hostess stand, he placed one drink near Cass's inventory sheet. Condensation beaded on the plastic, leaving a ring on the wooden surface. "Hey, Cass," he said, adjusting his collar. "I hope your dad likes me. I really want to make a good impression."

The kitchen doors swung open with a burst of steam and sizzling sounds. Booker emerged, his apron spattered with evidence of the day's specials - spots of red from marinara, streaks of golden curry sauce. A dish crashed somewhere in the kitchen, followed by a muffled apology.

"Good to see you again, Logan," Booker said, extending a hand. His wedding ring caught the light from overhead. "Oh, she's dragging you to the event too. I'm not sure if that means she likes you or wants to scare you off."

Logan chuckled, meeting Booker's grip. His pressed shirt contrasted with Booker's well-worn chef's whites. "It's good to see you again, sir. I'm excited to learn more. Are you doing better today?"

Booker shifted his weight, favoring his right leg. The movement was subtle but deliberate, a flicker of frustration crossing his face. "I'm fine," he said with a faint smile, "but it's my knee giving me trouble today."

Logan's eyes moved to the slight unevenness in Booker's stance. The ceiling fan whirred overhead, stirring paper menus.

Cass stepped in, her tone casual as she spoke over the dining room chatter. "Dad messed up his knee pretty bad as a firefighter, had to retire early. He actually found this place while walking around the neighborhood for rehab and decided it'd be his next chapter."

Maria appeared from behind a corner booth, order pad tucked in her apron pocket, plates balanced expertly on one arm. "Cass, aren't you going to introduce me to your friend?"

The introduction barely finished before Maria leaned against the stand, her elbow narrowly missing a stack of menus. “And what kind of friend is he, exactly?”

Logan’s response came with a quick wink, his confidence unshaken by the scrutiny. “I’m trying to work my way up the ranking.”

Cass offered him a brief smile, but her attention shifted as the door chimed again. A group of regulars entered, their usual table just being cleared. The rhythm of the restaurant continued - plates shuttling from kitchen to tables, voices rising and falling, ice clinking in glasses, and the steady pulse of another busy lunch service flowing around them.

*****

Afternoon sun slanted through the windows as the lunch rush faded. Bus tubs clattered in the kitchen while the remaining customers lingered over coffee. Booker gathered the staff near the antique card catalog, its brass handles gleaming in the light. Servers moved briskly, clearing tables and resetting silverware, their quiet efficiency blending seamlessly into the background. Cass stood beside him, laptop tucked under her arm, screen showing charts from the morning service.

“Listen up, everyone,” Booker said, adjusting his stance slightly as he clasped his hands together. His voice carried across the dining room, mixing with the hum of the dessert display case and the soft jazz from overhead speakers. The staff formed a loose circle - servers still in their aprons, kitchen crew in flour-dusted whites, hosts straightening their name tags.

“As you know, Cass and I will be attending a meetup in Berkeley today.” He paused as a bus boy stacked chairs nearby, metal scraping against wood. “I wanted to let you all know what to expect in our absence.”

His gaze moved across familiar faces, some who’d been there since opening day. “Maria, you’ll be in charge of the front of house. Rick, you’ll oversee the kitchen.” The industrial coffee maker hissed in the background, punctuating his words. “I trust you both to keep things running smoothly. If any issues arise, lean on each other like you’ve been doing—it’s been working.”

Maria shifted her weight, order pad still in hand. “We’ve got this, Booker,” she said, her voice steady but tinged with caution. Her fingers tapped lightly against the edge of the pad. “But what if something comes up that’s beyond us?” Booker gave her a reassuring nod, his gaze steady. “You’ve been handling everything like pros. I trust you to figure it out, and you know how to reach me if you need to.” Rick glanced at her and gave a small nod, silently echoing her concern.

The ceiling fan wobbled slightly overhead, casting moving shadows across the group. Booker gave a quick nod. “You’ve all shown tremendous flexibility these past few weeks. I trust you. And remember, Cass and I are just a phone call away.”

Cass stepped forward, her shoes squeaking slightly on the polished floor. “The data-driven approach we’ve been using has already brought good results. I’m confident we can keep the momentum going if we work together.”

A low murmur of agreement moved through the staff, mixing with the clink of dishes being sorted in the kitchen. The meeting dispersed just as Mr. Johnson approached from his corner booth, coffee cup in hand.

“I haven’t been here since the spring,” he said, gesturing with his cup, “but the service today was exceptional. The whole place seems more energetic.” He paused, his eyes sweeping the dining room. “It’s busier than I remember—and the portion sizes are a little smaller, but I’m guessing that’s intentional? Keeps things moving smoothly, I bet.”

Booker inclined his head, the movement causing his chef’s coat to catch the afternoon light. “Thank you, Mr. Johnson. You know how we do. We’ve made a few adjustments to manage the increased traffic while keeping things consistent. I appreciate your feedback.”

Cass exchanged a knowing look with Logan, who leaned against the hostess stand, shifting his weight as he glanced at her laptop. Her laptop screen showed the day’s numbers—green arrows pointing upward next to key metrics. “Green arrows mean good, right?” Logan teased, a grin playing on his face as he adjusted his stance. “Always,” Cass replied with a smirk. Behind them, the kitchen printer whirred to life, spitting out tickets for the early dinner prep as the hum of the restaurant carried on.

Booker clapped his hands lightly, drawing Cass and Logan’s attention. “Alright, let’s get moving. Berkeley’s not going to wait for us,” he said, gesturing toward the door. Cass closed her laptop, tucking it under her arm, and Logan straightened, following her toward the exit. The warm sunlight outside greeted them as Booker held the door open, the quiet hum of the restaurant fading behind them.

*****

Once they were settled in the car, Booker turned to Logan. “Why don’t you ride up front with me? Cass can take the back.”

Logan glanced at Cass, who gestured for him to go ahead. He climbed into the passenger seat, and Cass slid into the back, her laptop on her knees.

Booker pulled out of the parking lot and merged onto the highway. “So, Logan,” he said, watching the road. “Tell me about your family. What do they do?”

Logan shifted slightly. “Well, sir, my parents are both doctors. My dad’s a cardiologist, my mom’s a pediatrician.”

Booker raised an eyebrow. “A family of healers, huh?”

Logan nodded. “They’ve always helped people. Seeing that made me realize I want to do the same.”

Booker glanced his way. “That’s admirable, son. Have you introduced Cass to them yet?”

Logan shook his head. “Not yet, sir. She’s been busy with the restaurant and her data projects. We haven’t had the chance.”

Booker glanced at the rearview mirror, meeting Cass’s eyes briefly, then returned his attention to the road. Cass turned to the window, watching the scenery.

As they neared Berkeley, Logan looked back toward Cass. “I’m really impressed with everything you’ve been doing, Cass. Even though we knew each other before, seeing how you’ve pushed forward since the camp has been amazing.”

Cass leaned forward a bit. “I’m excited to see the pros in action today. Professor Avery’s been a strong supporter, and I’m thrilled she invited us.”

Logan nodded. “My parents always say that access and mentorship are big factors in success.”

Booker’s voice emerged again, even but firm. “That’s good for some, but not everyone gets those opportunities, Logan. Cass here wouldn’t have made it to the summer boot camp without a scholarship.”

He continued, his tone growing more direct. “Not everyone has two doctors for parents. There are folks who don’t have degrees and are focused on just keeping a roof over their heads and food on the table. Sometimes the future is something people can’t plan for because they’re busy dealing with the present.”

The car grew quiet. Logan looked toward Cass again, though she kept her gaze on the passing landmarks outside.

*****

"Professor Avery!" Cass called out as she entered the busy corridor outside the main hall. With Logan and Booker beside her, she navigated the clusters of people conversing and laughing. "I'm so glad we made it here. I'd like to introduce you to my father, Booker Freeman, and my friend, Logan."

Professor Avery offered a warm smile as she approached Booker. "Oh, hi! Yes, we met at the last book club event," she said. "I heard your talk and appreciated your points on strengthening the Oakland community and encouraging reading habits in younger generations. Wonderful!" She then turned to Logan, adding, "I believe we haven't met. I'm Professor Avery."

"I've heard so much about you from Cass," Logan said. "You're as humble and inspiring as she described."

Professor Avery waved a hand lightly. "I noticed her keen mind and wanted to encourage her. Maybe I see a bit of myself in her. But that's a story for another time. It's a pleasure to meet all of you," she said, shaking their hands. "Thank you for coming today."

"I'm sorry Maya couldn't join us," Booker said. "Feel free to stop by the restaurant anytime. We'd love to have you."

Professor Avery nodded. "I'll take you up on that offer, Mr. Freeman." She turned to Cass. "Do you have your laptop with you?"

Cass touched the bag at her side. "Of course! I'm ready."

Professor Avery smiled, signaled to someone nearby, and then handed Cass a small, neatly wrapped box.
"Professor Avery, what's that?" Cass asked, glancing at the box.

"This is for you," Avery replied, setting it in Cass's hands.

Cass untied the ribbon and removed the lid, revealing a glossy podcasting microphone. She held it up, examining its finish. "A microphone?"

"A podcasting microphone," Avery said. "I believe it's time you started sharing your perspective, Cass."

Cass glanced at the microphone. "My perspective?"

"Yes," Avery said. "You have a clear way of explaining data and encouraging curiosity. That has real value."

Cass ran a fingertip along the microphone's edge. "I'm not sure who would listen to me talk about data."

"Plenty of people," Avery said. "A lot of young folks see technology only as something to consume. You can show them it's something they can shape."

Cass nodded slowly. "But I'm no expert yet."

"That's exactly why your voice resonates," Avery said, her tone even. "You're relatable. You can make data science feel accessible."

Cass looked at the microphone again. "What if I make mistakes?"

Avery clasped her hands. "Everyone makes mistakes. What matters is that you keep going. You have so much to offer."

Cass lifted the microphone, checking its weight. Then she offered a brief smile. "Alright. I'll try."

"That's what I hoped to hear," Avery said quietly, placing a hand on Cass's shoulder. She nodded toward Logan and Booker, who both watched nearby. "The event is about to start. Please take your seats in the second row—I've reserved them for you."

At that moment, the event host called the meeting to order. "Let's give a warm welcome to Professor Avery, who has graciously joined us today."

Professor Avery stepped onto the stage. "Good afternoon, everyone," she began. "I'm pleased to be here to discuss how technology can serve the greater good."

Cass sat in the second row, her laptop resting on her legs.
"In this rapidly changing world, data science and artificial intelligence are central to driving positive change," Professor Avery continued. "We, as data professionals, hold a responsibility to use these tools to benefit our communities."

She paused, scanning the crowd. "On that note, I'd like to acknowledge Cass Freeman, a promising contributor to the field."

Cass stood and dipped her head in acknowledgment. Applause filled the room, and participants directed their attention toward her.

"Cass has applied what she learned at our university's summer camp to her family's restaurant, illustrating how data can shape real-world outcomes," Avery said. "Today, I've asked her to share some of her insights with you."

She motioned to Cass. "Cass, could you come forward? And bring your laptop."

Cass rose, carrying the laptop and the microphone she had just received. She climbed the steps to the stage and stopped at the podium, glancing briefly at

Logan, who raised a hand in encouragement.

Professor Avery rested a hand on Cass's shoulder. "I thought we could make this an impromptu hackathon," she said, addressing the audience. "All of you—professionals and students—are invited to learn from Cass's work and suggest ways to enhance her project."

Cass set her laptop on the podium and opened a folder of slides. A soft murmur went through the audience as she prepared to speak.
"Thank you, Professor Avery," she said. "And thank you all for attending."

She advanced to the first slide, displaying an image of Booker's Pages and Plates. "My family's restaurant has been a community gathering place for years, though we've had some difficulties along the way."

Cass outlined the restaurant's history, referencing her father's background and her grandfather James's connection to the Black Panther movement. She used charts and figures to illustrate the challenges the restaurant faced.

"By analyzing our sales and customer feedback, we identified areas needing attention," Cass explained. "If we treat this like a hackathon, we might quickly collect feedback and refine our approach in real time."

She glanced at Logan, who raised his phone to film. "We used predictive analytics to see how menu changes could affect satisfaction and revenue. Similarly, at a hackathon, a team could use those methods to anticipate participant engagement for certain sessions."

Cass clicked to the next slide, focusing on the menu. "We also leveraged customer preference analysis to optimize our offerings. At a hackathon, a similar approach would help shape session topics based on attendees' interests."

She went on, mentioning a loyalty program that rewarded consistent patrons. "At a hackathon, we might segment participants by engagement level and offer tailored rewards."

Finally, she mentioned events like book clubs and live music nights. "In a hackathon context, collaboration across diverse backgrounds fosters creativity—much like the sense of community we aim to build."

The room erupted in applause as she finished speaking.

Professor Avery took the stage again. "Thank you, Cass, for that enlightening presentation," she said. "Your work demonstrates true innovation."

*****

As the event stretched into the evening, the panel discussions explored the technical intricacies of data science and its practical applications. Cass and Booker sat on a round center stage with Professor Avery. The audience was arranged in a circular banquet setup, focused on the conversation unfolding from the platform. Booker shifted in his seat from time to time, occasionally jotting notes and scanning the room.

“Dad, are you okay?” Cass leaned over to him.

Booker gave a small smile, shaking his head. “I’m fine, sweetheart. It’s a lot to take in, but I want to listen.”

Leaning closer, Cass whispered brief explanations of a few technical terms into Booker’s ear, helping him keep up with the discussion.

A voice rose from the audience: “Mr. Freeman, you touched on something earlier about how tough it can be to navigate change, especially when you’ve used the same approach for a long time. Can you tell us why you hesitate to adopt technology in your restaurant? I think this insight could enrich our understanding of data science in the Hotel, Restaurant, and Café/Catering or HORECA industry, especially since Cass mentioned your deep connection to your customers and community.”

A low murmur ran through the room.

“I’ve poured my heart and soul into the restaurant, as you all know from how I came to own it,” Booker said, pulling the microphone closer. “Back then, data science was completely new to me. All I knew was the old belief that technology is cold, impersonal.” He paused, looking across the audience. “I worried that if we leaned too much on data, we’d lose what made our place special—the personal touch, the warmth that keeps our regulars coming back. But I realized that just keeping regulars isn’t enough. We need to keep growing, reaching a wider community, or we’ll stagnate.”

Another audience member raised a hand, and the committee member passed the microphone. “Now that you see why data technology is important in your industry, how do you plan to use it for future success? Restaurants in Walnut Creek and everywhere else are already using this technology.”

Booker answered each new question, and more inquiries followed, examining how data could enhance, not replace, the traditional approach of running a small business. Cass watched him respond as the discussion intensified.

"I'm going to be blunt: if you're not embracing data, you're setting yourself up for failure," someone called out from another side of the room. "You might as well hang a 'closed permanently' sign on your door."

Booker paused, and Cass glanced around, catching Logan's gaze.

Another speaker said, "Data isn't about chasing trends; it's about leveraging it for real growth. Without technology, businesses are on borrowed time." She continued, "But here's the thing: your menu sounds amazing. With a strong data strategy, focused marketing, and disciplined operations, you could have three locations instead of just one. Data can pinpoint how to scale and expand. You could open a dessert shop or run a food truck. The possibilities are endless. Data is just the tool to help you get there."

A hand shot up from the audience. A man around Booker's age stood, facing the panel. "Excuse me, sir. My name is David, and I run a flower shop."

Booker nodded. "Go on, David."

David cleared his throat. "I understand your concerns about preserving your business's identity. I felt the same way when I first explored data-driven strategies. I thought, 'It's just a flower shop; why bother with technology?' But then I discovered that data doesn't replace the human element—it enhances it. We've been able to provide more personalized and efficient service by using data to optimize our processes and learn what our customers want during certain seasons and occasions. That helped us adapt and grow without losing who we are."

Booker nodded slowly as David spoke.

Professor Avery smiled. "Thank you, David. Your perspective really demonstrates how data can align with a business's values and goals."

Booker turned to Cass and spoke quietly. "I think I'm starting to see it, Cass. The potential, the opportunity. It's not about replacing what we have, but building on it, strengthening it."

*****

As the panel discussion concluded, the atmosphere in the room relaxed, with light bites circulated around the tables and glasses of water being refilled. The air hummed with excitement and competitive energy, lively murmurs, and chatter buzzing about the upcoming session.

“And now, ladies and gentlemen, the real work begins! It’s time for our hackathon!” Professor Avery exclaimed, raising her hand as she returned to the center platform. The room erupted into applause as participants prepared to display their skills and ideas.

“In teams of four, your challenge is to create data-driven solutions that enhance our case study of the evening, Booker’s family restaurant. Consider optimizing operations, engaging the community, and crafting a more personalized customer experience.”

Cass moved quickly to join the activity as teams began to form, her energy matching the bustling environment around her. Ideas darted across the room, and whiteboards screeched as diagrams and flowcharts were sketched and filled in, each bursting with potential. She worked alongside different groups, answering questions and contributing to discussions with precise and practical insights.

One team, which Logan had joined, focused on creating a digital community board, a platform where customers could share their experiences, give feedback, and connect with the restaurant on a deeper level. Meanwhile, another group addressed the supply chain, brainstorming strategies to optimize inventory management and minimize waste while preserving the unique blend of modern soul food and old library charm that defines Booker’s Pages and Plates.

The energy in the room only grew as the hours ticked by. Booker observed how Cass navigated the flurry of activity, her expertise evident in every interaction. Professor Avery eventually took a seat next to him, and he turned to her with a thoughtful expression.

“I have to admit, I’m a bit overwhelmed,” Booker said. “The last ninety minutes felt like a whirlwind. Is it always this intense?”

Professor Avery chuckled, her eyes crinkling at the corners. “Welcome to the tech world, Booker. Speed, experimentation, and collaboration are the heartbeat here.”

Booker released a long sigh, glancing over to where Cass stood, deep in an animated discussion with a group of participants. “She’s something, isn’t she?” he said, his voice soft with pride.

Professor Avery followed his gaze. “Cass is exceptional, Booker. Her passion, drive, and ability to bridge the gap between data and real-world impact at her age… it’s a gift.”

"I really shouldn't be surprised. She's been fascinated with counting numbers since she was a little girl. But this world is so different from what I know. I just want to make sure she's making the right choices and not losing herself in the process."

"Booker, I understand your concerns. But trust me when I say that Cass is on the right path. She has a sharp vision and a strong moral compass. She's not just chasing numbers; she's using data to make a real difference."

Booker nodded and scanned the room before lowering his voice. "But... how many people here actually look like us, Avery? I mean, truly look like us? Does Cass belong in all of this?"

Professor Avery paused, considering his words. "It's a fair question, Booker. And it's one I've grappled with myself. But let me ask you this: how many of us are actively working to change that? How many of us are stepping up and claiming our place? There are tech communities of color committed to creating pathways and onramps for what I like to call 'emerging figures.' Brilliance and innovation know no color or gender."

"But the road ahead won't be easy, will it?"

Professor Avery shook her head with a knowing smile. "No, it won't. But that's why it's so important. That's why we need people like Cass, like you, to keep pushing forward, to keep demanding change." She looked him in the eye, her voice unwavering. "We're not just fighting for ourselves, Booker. We're fighting for the generations to come. We're fighting for a future where talent and hard work are the only things that matter."

*****

The evening air in the kitchen carried the low churn of the dishwasher and the lingering aroma of dinner, a quiet backdrop to the dim overhead glow. Maya stood at the counter, phone in hand, glancing at the clock on the wall. Booker leaned against the doorway, arms folded, while Cass sat at the table, scrolling through notes from the hackathon earlier in the day.

Maya adjusted her grip on the phone and looked toward Booker. She rubbed her hands together briefly, then said, "I think it's a good time to call Professor Avery. I need to apologize. What do you think?"

Cass glanced up, setting her notes aside. "It's not too late, but she might still be up. I say go for it."

Taking a deep breath, Maya nodded and dialed. She put the call on speaker, the ringing seeming to stretch on before a familiar voice answered.

"Hello, this is Professor Avery," came the voice on the other end.

"Good evening, Professor Avery. This is Maya Freeman, Cass's mother," Maya began, her tone measured. She looked at Booker, who gave a slight nod.

"Mrs. Freeman, good evening. How can I help you?" Professor Avery replied, her tone professional.

Maya tightened her grip on the phone and took another breath. "I wanted to apologize for my behavior during the mentoring call last week," she said, her voice carrying a careful tone. "I realize now that I was out of line. The camp meant a great deal to Cass, and the positive impact it's had on her is clear."

Booker shifted slightly, glancing at Cass, while Maya continued. "I appreciate your call, Mrs. Freeman," Professor Avery said after a moment. "It's evident how much you care about Cass, and I'm glad the camp had such a meaningful influence on her."

Maya nodded as she exhaled softly. "Thank you. I also wanted to share some good news. The changes we've made at the restaurant, inspired by Cass's data-driven ideas, have already started to make a difference. Sales are up, and customer feedback has been overwhelmingly positive. It's all thanks to the tools and insights Cass gained from the program."

"That's wonderful to hear," Professor Avery said, her tone lifting slightly. "Cass has so much potential, and it's exciting to see how she's applying what she's learned. I'd be happy to continue mentoring her if she's interested."

"That would mean so much to us," Maya replied. "And, Professor, I hope there are no hard feelings about how I acted. I truly respect your work and expertise, and I'm sorry for any disrespect I showed."

"No hard feelings at all, Mrs. Freeman," Professor Avery assured her. "I appreciate your honesty. And I'd love to visit your restaurant sometime soon."

"You're welcome anytime," Maya said, her smile widening. "We'd love to have you."

For a moment, the kitchen was quiet except for the hum of the dishwasher and the faint ticking of the clock. Maya turned to face Cass and Booker. Cass pushed back her chair, standing as though to absorb her mother's words. Her grin spread wide, and her eyes lit up.

"Mom, that was...amazing," Cass said. "I can't believe you just did that. You were so cool."

Maya gave a soft chuckle. "Well, it was time to make things right. And now that we're all on the same page, you need to keep pushing forward. But don't forget, your SAT prep still needs attention."

Cass laughed lightly, nodding. "I know, I know. But seriously, thanks, Mom. That meant a lot."

Booker stepped forward, wrapping an arm around Maya's shoulders. "You handled that well, Maya. I think Professor Avery was genuinely impressed."

Maya smiled, leaning into Booker's side. "Let's hope so. And Cass, we're proud of you. Keep showing us what you're capable of."

Cass glanced back at her notes from the hackathon, her expression sharpening with focus. "Okay, time to keep this momentum going," she said with a grin.

The kitchen felt warmer now, a place that seemed energized by fresh possibilities and steady support.

JOURNAL ENTRY

5: The number of mistakes I made while talking to the pros at the hackathon. Honestly, I was so nervous that I tripped over my words more times than I care to admit. But they were patient, and their advice was solid. Mistakes or not, I'm learning—and that's what matters.

2: The number of times I hugged Professor Avery. I hope she didn't think it was too much, but when she gave me that podcasting microphone and told me my voice mattered, I couldn't help myself. She believes in me more than I believe in myself sometimes, and that kind of support feels rare.

80%: The table occupancy rate during tonight's dinner service. Even after all the drama with the theft and the news coverage, the restaurant was packed. It's wild to think that something so terrible might've brought us new customers. Now, we have to keep them coming back—and that means growing our team and staying ahead.

45: The minutes I spent leaning over Dad's shoulder, explaining terms at the hackathon. Watching him take it all in, jotting down notes, and asking thoughtful questions, made me so proud. He's stepping out of his comfort zone for the sake of the restaurant and for me. It reminds me that we're in this together.

10: The conversations I had during the hackathon where I felt like I actually belonged. Sure, there were moments of doubt, but then there were times when I realized I could keep up, that I could contribute something meaningful. It's amazing how a day like this can shift your perspective.

∞: The gratitude I feel for people like Professor Avery and my family. From Logan cheering me on from the audience to Mom making things right with Avery, it feels like the people around me are rooting for me in ways I didn't even know I needed. It's humbling and motivating all at once.

Today was a mix of challenges, growth, and surprises. The hackathon pushed me out of my comfort zone, but it also showed me how far I've come. There's still so much to do—more work, more learning—but for the first time in a while, it feels possible. And that's enough for now.

SUNDAY, JULY 21

The living room was quiet except for the hum of the refrigerator in the adjoining kitchen. Cass sat cross-legged on the couch, her phone balanced on her knee. The clock on the screen read 10:20 PM. Her chat app was open, showing Ayesha's profile image. Earlier, Cass had tried calling Ayesha, and the call had gone unanswered. Ayesha had not replied to Cass's text from the previous night, either.

Cass typed a quick message:

Cass: "Hey Ayesha, free to chat?"

She pressed send. Ayesha's status briefly flickered green before returning to red. Cass set her phone on the coffee table. Moments later, it vibrated with an incoming call.

"Hey, Cass," Ayesha's voice greeted her.

"Hey, Ayesha. Sorry to call so late," Cass said, leaning forward on the couch. "I just wanted to check in. You didn't reply to my text yesterday, and I left you a missed call this afternoon. How are you?"

"Yeah, I'm good. Sorry about that," Ayesha replied. "I was at work when you called. What's up?"

Cass cleared her throat, keeping her gaze on the dark TV screen. "I wanted to apologize for how I acted yesterday. I know you and Isaiah only meant well by sending those live event updates. I just couldn't stop thinking about how much I missed out."

"Cass, I get why you were upset about not going. I didn't take it personally," Ayesha said. "By the way, I wanted to let you know—I got an internship offer from the Hale Group on their advanced analytics team. Isaiah's still a junior, so he didn't get an offer, but they were really impressed with him and want to stay in touch. They said our presentation at camp stood out, especially how we connected classroom projects to real-world work. The restaurant project showed our curiosity, passion, and the impact we could make."

Cass turned the phone in her hand, tracing its edges with her thumb. "Wow, Ayesha. Congratulations. You deserve this. You've always put in the extra hours with data science."

"You're not angry, Cass? Are we still okay?" Ayesha asked.

Cass tapped her foot lightly against the carpet. A dog barked outside, its voice echoing between fences. "Of course, Ayesha. I'm sorry I sounded surprised. I really am happy for you both. Last year, you didn't get the chance, but this year you did. I still have time—maybe next year. You'll be my inspiration."

Cass brushed her sleeve over her cheek, then spoke again. "And if you need more time for your internship, don't worry about the restaurant project. It's going well, and Dad's excited about the new spicy shrimp dish. He's still learning all this tech stuff, so I can handle more tasks."

"Thanks, Cass. Isaiah and I were worried about telling you, especially with everything you mentioned about the police and the attack. It just seemed like bad timing," Ayesha said.

"Thanks for caring," Cass said, glancing briefly at her pinkie finger. "But don't tiptoe around me next time, okay?"

"Promise," Ayesha replied.

They ended the call, and the living room settled back into its quiet. Cass placed the phone on the coffee table and leaned into the cushions. She scrolled through a list of movies on the TV, her attention drifting over several titles. Outside, a breeze shifted the curtains, and moonlight traced faint patterns against the floor. Finally, she chose a film, its shifting light flickering across the room. Twenty minutes passed, the scenes unfolding at a steady pace, blending with the stillness of the house.

*****

Cass sat curled on the couch, the TV's flicker lighting the room. She held the remote loosely in one hand, paused on a frame from CODA. The clock on the wall ticked softly. From the kitchen, the refrigerator hummed at steady intervals. Beyond the window, a streetlight blinked, and the moon cast a cool glow over the curtains.

A soft creak on the stairs drew her attention. Her mother, Maya, stepped into view, a bonnet snug around her hair, the hem of her robe brushing lightly against her slippers. She paused, offering Cass a faint smile.

"Cassie, you're still up?" Maya asked, lowering her voice.

"Couldn't sleep," Cass said, placing the remote on the coffee table. "I needed some time to relax. This movie is about a girl in a deaf family who loves music. She's torn between staying home to help them or following her dream of singing."

Maya eased into the armchair across from her. “That sounds beautiful. Is it good?”

“It’s pretty amazing,” Cass replied, resting against the cushions.

Maya’s eyes moved to the muted TV screen, though her hands fidgeted slightly with the edge of her robe. “I came down to check on you. Things have been tense.”

She folded her hands in her lap. “I wanted to say I’m sorry. And I want to listen more than I talk this time.”

Cass sat up straighter. “You know how much I wanted to go to that event, Mom. Because I missed it, Ayesha and Isaiah both got internships, and I’m left behind. I’m happy for them, but it still hurts.”

Maya’s hands tightened around the armrest. “You’re right. You deserved to go. Booker and I should have supported you.”

A moment passed, the paused movie reflecting faintly in the TV’s black edges. Maya spoke again, her voice lower. “Remember at dinner, we talked about Grandma Lillian and her usher stories?”

Cass’s posture eased slightly. “Yeah. The first time she was called Mother Freeman, and she had no clue she’d ‘graduated’ into that role.”

Maya let out a small laugh. “She was something else. But it reminded me of my own mother—Grandma Evelyn. We didn’t visit her much, and she never really trusted me. I’m scared you might feel that way about me someday.”

Maya turned to the window, her gaze following the moonlit sky. “On the night I graduated high school, the moon looked like this. I had my heart set on becoming an artist and designer. When I told her, she threw my certificates to the ground and pushed me to be more ‘practical.’ She wanted me to be more successful than she was. She believed art would always be there once I had a stable path. But the world changed, and I lost the chance.”

Maya pressed her lips together, then looked back at Cass. “I see so much of my younger self in you—your energy, the way you chase your passions. I stayed quiet because I was afraid you’d lose that spark, like I did. But you need to know: you don’t have to pick one path over the other. I’ll be here, no matter what you decide. I love you, Cass.”

Cass turned fully toward her mother, standing in front of the TV. She watched Maya closely, her own expression shifting. “I don’t want that to happen, either.”

Maya moved closer, stopping a short distance away. She gently placed a hand on Cass’s shoulder. “You can follow your passion and still be practical. You’re strong enough to do both, and I'll be cheering you on."

Cass's lips curved into a faint smile. "Thanks, Mom."

Maya gave her shoulder a gentle squeeze. "I love you, Cassie. Now finish your movie. I'll see you in the morning."

She turned and headed upstairs, her slippers brushing softly over each step. Cass stood still for a moment, her gaze on the empty staircase. Then she picked up the remote again. The voices from the paused movie waited silently on the screen, and she pressed play, letting their dialogue fill the room as the clock edged closer to midnight.

SUNDAY, JULY 21 | JOURNAL ENTRY

1: The number of times I apologized today. First to Ayesha, then to Mom. Friendship takes work, and so does family. Apologizing isn't easy, but it feels good to clear the air. I need to figure out how to stop being so caught up in my feelings all the time.

3: The days it's been since Dad's injury. His cut is healing, and thank God it wasn't worse. Watching him power through makes me realize how much he holds together for all of us, even when he's hurting.

2: The brothers I'm worried about. Carver and Archer are still struggling after what happened with Mike. They thought he was the coolest, and now they don't even know how to process what he did. I hate seeing them confused and hurt—it feels like their world got flipped upside down.

5: The times I thought about the staff today. Everyone's walking on eggshells, trying to rebuild trust after everything that happened. I just hope we can come together again. This place only works if we're a team, and that's something we're all still figuring out.

0: The number of books Aunt Z's date has read since COVID. She had us cracking up at dinner, telling us about him and how she could never take someone seriously if they weren't committed to growing and learning. I love her honesty—it's like she knows exactly what she wants and doesn't settle for less.

45: The minutes Logan and I spent on the phone tonight. We didn't talk about anything major—just little things like his day working with his parents and random stories that made me laugh. It was the most relaxed I've felt in days. He has this way of making everything feel a little lighter, even when the world feels heavy.

4: The predictive models I tested today to forecast weekend demand. Each one gave me slightly different results, which makes me wonder—how do you know when your model is "good enough"? It's frustrating, but also exciting. This is the kind of challenge that keeps me going.

2: The ideas Lola pitched for using social media analytics to drive more traffic. One was tracking which posts get the most engagement and correlating them with sales spikes. The other was running A/B tests on ad campaigns to see which messages resonate most. She's just starting to explore data, but her creativity is inspiring.

12: The variables I included in my customer loyalty model. It's a work in progress, but the early results suggest we should focus on incentivizing frequent takeout orders. I need to dig deeper to figure out what motivates those customers and how we can encourage even more repeat visits.

∞: The gratitude I feel for the tools we have now. Every time I find a new insight in the data, I think about Grandpa James's story of his grandfather teaching himself to read by candlelight. It makes me appreciate the privilege of being able to access and use technology to solve problems.

Today was heavy, but it was also a reminder that relationships—whether with friends, family, or the people we work with—take effort. Apologies, patience, and forgiveness don't always come easy, but they're worth it. And tomorrow, we try again.

MONDAY, JULY 22

Cass climbed out of the car and waved as Aunt Zora drove away, her brothers hopping out behind her. The sun was dipping low in the sky, casting a warm glow across the front of their house. She stepped forward, adjusting her backpack. Archer and Carver scrambled past her, their voices overlapping as they raced inside.

"You all better not leave your shoes everywhere!" Cass called after them, stepping in and setting her backpack on the floor. She heard their laughter echo from the living room.

Aunt Zora's car disappeared down the street, and the house was quiet. Cass slipped off her sneakers and walked over to her brothers, who were sprawled on the couch, flipping through channels.

"Hey, Cass," Carver said, turning to her with a grin, "you are actually saving the restaurant. That is pretty cool."

Archer nodded eagerly. "Yeah, we heard Dad talking about how you are using all that math stuff to figure things out. Is it true?"

Cass smiled and shook her head. "I mean, I am helping out, but it is not like I have all the answers."

"Still," Carver said, tossing a cushion at Archer, "you are good at this. Really good. Math is hard, but you make it look easy."

Carver fiddled with a loose thread on his shorts. He lowered his voice. "You know," he said quietly, "you remind me of Grandpa James when you talk about technology and helping people."

Cass felt warmth spread through her chest at the comparison. Their grandfather had always talked about using their skills to lift up their community.

"Look, it is not easy," Cass said, leaning forward. "I just put in the work. You know, one thing I realized at camp? A lot of the kids there had been coding and doing all this tech stuff for years. Their parents work at big tech companies, so they have got a head start."

"So we have to start now?" Archer asked, sitting up straighter.

Cass nodded. " Exactly. If we want to create technology that matters, we need to start now. Coding, robotics, whatever has got your attention. It is not just about getting jobs at big companies. It is about building things that solve problems, whether that is helping small businesses like ours or creating something entirely new. The tech world needs all kinds of thinkers and builders."

Carver's brow furrowed. "But what if we are not naturally good?"

Cass shook her head, a small grin crossing her lips. "It is not about being naturally good at something. It is about having what people call a growth mindset. Believing you can learn and get better. When I started, I was not excelling at math, but I kept telling myself I could improve. And I did. Your brain is like a muscle. The more you work it, the stronger it gets. You can get better at anything if you just do not quit and believe in your ability to grow."

Archer leaned forward. "Okay, but what if we do not have a lot of money to buy all this stuff?"

Cass picked up an old remote from the coffee table, turning it in her hands. "I do not really work with hardware like that, but you do not need to spend a lot to start. Equipment like Arduino or Raspberry Pi is good if you can get it, but even if you cannot, you can find things around the house to work with."

Carver glanced at Archer. "But what if we cannot get even that?"

Cass looked around the room and spotted an old toy truck sitting in the corner. She picked it up and held it out to Archer and Carver. "Let us say you start with something like this," she said. "This could be the base for a robot or some kind of moving gadget. All you need to do is figure out what parts still work and what you can repurpose."

Archer leaned closer. "But how do we even know where to start?"

Cass turned the truck over and pointed to the bottom. "Start by taking it apart. Figure out what is inside. Like here, this little motor," she said, indicating a small metal cylinder. "It probably still works, and you could use it to make something spin or move. If you are not sure what something does, look it up. There are guides online that break it all down."

Carver adjusted his seat on the couch. "What about power? Do we not need batteries or something?"

Cass set the truck down. "Probably, but you do not need anything fancy. Look around the house. Old chargers, leftover batteries, stuff you already have lying around. The point is to get creative with what is here. Even broken stuff can have parts you can use."

Archer folded his arms. "So we are basically raiding the house for junk?"

"Not junk, but potential," Cass said. "But yes, do not break anything that is still working, or we will all get in trouble. It is not just about building cool stuff," she added. "It is about solving real problems. Start small, but think big. The bigger the problem, the bigger the impact. Maybe you will create something that not only helps people in our neighborhood, but neighborhoods in Mexico City, or Delhi, or Nairobi."

Carver straightened up. "What about that old RC car in the closet? Could we use that?"

Cass nodded. "Definitely. It probably has wheels, a motor, maybe even a controller you can take apart. Start with that and see what works."

She leaned back on the couch, pulling her SAT book closer. "I would help more, but I have got SAT prep and the restaurant to deal with. You two can handle this, though. Just start working with stuff and see what you can figure out. If you hit a wall, I can look at it when I have time."

Archer stood and glanced at Carver. "So you want us to figure it out on our own?"

"Exactly," Cass said, picking up her phone. She tapped a few links and handed it to Archer. "Here are some free guides and tutorials. If you are stuck, check these out. But the real learning comes from just trying things. Take things apart. See how they work. Do not be afraid to fail."

Carver stood and motioned toward the hallway. "Okay, we will start with the RC car."

Cass flipped open her SAT book and turned to the next section. The muffled sound of her brothers moving through the house carried into the living room, followed by the faint clatter of something dropping onto the floor.

MONDAY, JULY 22 | JOURNAL ENTRY

1: The number of things we actually got done on the call tonight. Honestly, it was mostly just fun to talk. Lola said she's working on some new ad ideas, which sounds exciting, but the highlight was hearing Ayesha talk about her internship. She's killing it, and every story she tells makes me want to push myself harder.

5: The number of corny data jokes Isaiah made during the call. "Why was the equal sign so humble? Because it knew it wasn't less than or greater than." Seriously, they were awful, but the way he cracked himself up made it hard not to laugh. I don't think I've ever seen him so relaxed.

20: The minutes I spent on the phone with Aunt Zora, talking about last week's theft. She called it "trauma with a capital T," and she's not wrong. Every time I think about Mike and Sarah, I feel this mix of anger and sadness. Aunt Z said it's okay to feel both, that it's part of processing what happened. I know she's right, but it still feels heavy.

2: The times Carver and Archer reminded me why I love being their sister. When we got home, they were full of questions about math, tech, and what they need to do to get ahead. It felt good to share what I've learned and to see them getting excited about the possibilities. They might not realize it yet, but they've got so much potential.

∞: The gratitude I feel for the people around me. Even on nights when we don't get much work done, I'm reminded how lucky I am to have friends like Lola, Isaiah, and Ayesha, family like Aunt Zora, and my brothers who look up to me. They make all the chaos feel worth it.

Tonight wasn't super productive, but it felt like a reset. Sometimes, just talking and laughing is enough to remind you why you're pushing so hard. Tomorrow, I'll get back to work, but for now, I'm holding onto this moment of connection.

TUESDAY, JULY 23

Cass walked past the counter lined with framed black-and-white photos of Oakland's old trolley lines and market streets. The refrigerator hummed in the kitchen. A small corkboard near the hallway displayed shift schedules, handwritten notes, and her laminated infographic titled "Understanding Profit Margins in Restaurants"—detailing food costs and labor expenses for the staff.

The infographic's color-coded sections showed food cost percentages, labor costs, and weekly profit trends. At the bottom, a QR code linked to her online dashboard of live performance metrics for Booker's.

Inside the storeroom, a whiteboard leaned against one corner, covered with notes: Optimize weekly inventory orders. Analyze popular combos for pricing strategy. Evaluate effect of specials on foot traffic.

The morning prep sounds had given way to the lunch service clatter. Her laptop screen displayed the dashboard's bar charts and scatter plots showing the day's performance. A note about decreased drink sales sat next to her analysis of customer reviews—a sentiment-analysis tool she had coded at boot camp. The tool sorted feedback into positive, neutral, or negative categories.

Maria stepped into the storeroom, her order pad stuffed in her apron pocket. "Cass, I hate to pull you from the numbers, but we're getting slammed up front. These new menu combos you created are bringing in crowds. I've been running food and managing the door for the past hour, and I could really use your help with the flow."

"On my way," Cass said, closing her laptop.

The clinking of glasses filled the air as she stepped out of the storeroom into the bustling restaurant. The hum of conversation and sizzle from the open kitchen mingled with the rich aroma of spices and freshly baked bread. At the hostess stand, Cass greeted customers with a smile as they entered, her voice cutting through the steady clamor of orders being shouted from the kitchen.

She motioned to a family waiting nearby, pointing them toward an open table as the flow of guests continued without pause. Sunlight streamed through the windows, catching the steam rising from plates as servers weaved between crowded tables, narrowly avoiding each other in the bustling space.

Booker approached, wiping his hands on a towel, his eyes scanning the packed dining room like a captain assessing a ship in choppy waters. "We're neck-deep out here. I think your mom just got off her shift. Call her and ask if she can come by and bring the boys. We need all hands on deck."

Cass nodded, already reaching for her phone. “What about Linda? Think she’s free?”

“Good idea,” Booker replied, sidestepping a passing tray. He turned toward Maria at the takeout counter. “Maria, see if Linda’s working at the other place. If she’s not, tell her to hustle over here.”

Maria gave a quick thumbs-up, already dialing. Meanwhile, Cass called Maya. “Hey, Mom. Can you and the boys come help out? It’s packed here. Booker’s asking.”

On the other end, Maya’s voice was steady but quick. “We’ll head over now. Give us ten minutes.”

“Thanks, Mom,” Cass said before hanging up. She tucked her phone into her pocket and surveyed the dining room. Steam fogged the windows, and the line at the takeout counter snaked to the door. Trays of food passed constantly from the kitchen, adding to the steady rhythm of movement. Joey darted between the kitchen and counter, juggling steaming bags for delivery drivers, nearly losing his grip before recovering with a quick shift of his hands.

Outside, a growing crowd gathered near the entrance. Some guests peered in through the windows, their expressions equal parts curious and impatient. A staff member stationed near the door managed the queue, announcing a 45-minute wait time. The unusual rush for a Tuesday evening was palpable, with guests chatting and taking selfies against the restaurant’s exterior.

Inside, guests wandered among the bookshelves and photo displays, marveling at the collection of memorabilia. A couple stopped to inspect an old photograph of Oakland’s trolley lines, while another guest snapped a picture of a book titled Hidden Gems of the Bay Area. “I didn’t know this place was part museum,” one woman remarked as she browsed.

“What’s going on today?” Joey muttered, his brows furrowed as he darted past with another set of takeout bags. “Did we make the news or something?”

Maria, balancing a tray of drinks, called back, “Feels like a Friday night, not a Tuesday!”

Within minutes, Maya walked through the door, her scrubs slightly wrinkled but her stride purposeful. Carver and Archer followed close behind, already tying on aprons. At thirteen, the twins moved with a blend of eagerness and awkwardness, nearly bumping into each other as they scrambled to grab trays.

“You’re late,” Cass teased as they reached her.

"We're here now," Carver shot back, almost tripping over a chair but laughing it off as he grabbed a tray from the stand.

"Table seven needs clearing," Maya said, hefting a full tray of dishes. "Archer, you take that. Carver, start on table three."

"On it," they replied in unison, darting into the busy dining room. Carver rushed toward a table, knocking over a nearly empty glass of water but quickly apologizing as he wiped it up with a napkin. Archer expertly balanced a tray loaded with drinks, weaving through the crowd without breaking his stride.

Cass handed menus to a waiting group and answered questions about the specials. Nearby, Maya balanced drinks in one hand and greeted customers with the other, her movements smooth and practiced as she blended seamlessly into the restaurant's flow. Booker waved her over from the counter, where he was speaking to a guest about catering options.

As Cass moved to assist, the pace seemed to intensify. A tray of glasses clinked as a server squeezed past, narrowly avoiding a collision with Joey. Every table was filled, the takeout line stretched to the door, and catering requests kept coming. Maria hung up her call and signaled to Booker, confirming that Linda would be arriving soon.

The familiar jingle of the doorbell announced Linda's arrival, her hair tied back and sleeves rolled up. She stepped in with a grin. "Heard you needed backup."

"You have no idea," Booker replied, pointing toward the kitchen. "Start with table five, then we'll see how much more chaos we can throw your way."

Linda tied on an apron with practiced ease and grabbed a tray. "Got it," she said, slipping into the flow with the confidence of someone who had done this a hundred times before. She greeted regulars as she moved, cracking a quick joke with one and nodding to another.

Guests throughout the dining room snapped photos of their food, angling their phones for the perfect shot of steaming gumbo and tagging the restaurant in posts. The clatter of dishes and hum of conversation mingled with the flashes of cameras. "Did you see the post?" one guest asked loudly, showing a glowing review to their tablemates.

Cass overheard as she passed. "Excuse me," she said, her tone polite but curious. "What are you talking about?"

The guest tilted their phone toward her. "This. Someone posted about the food here, and it's blowing up. People are saying it's a must-visit."

A text order came through, pulling her attention back to the moment. She pulled out her phone, but instead of answering, quickly shot off a message to Lola: What did you do?

Moments later, her phone buzzed, and Lola's name lit up the screen. Cass picked up and quickly ducked into her office, shutting the door against the bustling chaos of the dining room.

Lola's laughter crackled through the phone. "Hey! Just checking in. Are you seeing more traffic?"

Through the office window, the hum of activity in the crowded restaurant was evident. "Swamped. Absolutely swamped. What did you do?"

"Oh, just launched a few ads," Lola said casually. "I got us on Oaklandish, a couple food blogs, and Instagram. Just wanted to open up the floodgates for one day to see what happened."

Her voice remained steady as she responded. "Well, it worked. Can you turn it off now? Next time you do this, we need to be better prepared."

Lola laughed again. "Got it. Consider this a test run. I'll dial it back."

Cass ended the call and slipped her phone into her pocket as she reentered the dining room. The restaurant hummed with energy—from the packed tables to the steady shuffle of takeout bags. Her family hustled around her: Maya balancing plates with ease, Archer darting between tables, and Carver chatting with a group of guests as he cleared their dishes. Every corner of the room seemed alive with movement, the buzz of conversation blending with the clatter of dishes, the rhythmic calls from the kitchen, and the occasional flash of a camera. Regulars waved at Booker as they passed. "Full house today, huh?" one man said. Booker laughed, wiping his brow. "You have no idea."

Cass stepped toward the kitchen, giving Joey a quick nod as he darted by with another set of bags, then gestured for Carver to grab an extra tray from the counter. Her quiet directives kept the hive running smoothly as the staff moved with practiced coordination, each action purposeful. The team wasn't just handling the surge—they were thriving. They weren't just handling the surge—they were thriving.

*****

The restaurant had finally settled into silence. The last chairs were flipped onto tables, the floors mopped, and the lights dimmed to a gentle haze. Everyone gathered around a large table near the back, their exhaustion softened by the lingering buzz of a busy night. Booker leaned back in his chair, a towel draped over his shoulder, and let out a long sigh.

"What the heck just happened?" he asked, shaking his head. "Linda even came in for the last hour to help after leaving her other job. And on a Tuesday!"

Maya leaned forward, her elbows on the table as she sipped from a glass of water. "I don't think I've ever seen the place this packed. We had lines out the door and takeout orders nonstop."

Cass chuckled, glancing at her phone where a few late texts from Lola blinked on the screen. "That's because Lola decided to run a little experiment."

"An experiment?" Booker asked, narrowing his eyes. "What kind of experiment?"

"She launched some ads," Cass explained. "We're on Oaklandish now, a couple of food blogs, and Instagram. She said she just wanted to 'open the floodgates for one day to see what happened.'"

Booker's jaw dropped slightly. "She opened the floodgates? That's one way to put it."

"Well, it worked," Maya said with a slight smile. "Too well, maybe. If today's any indication, people love this place. It's incredible."

Carver, sitting cross-legged in his chair, perked up. "Wait, does this mean we're going to be on the schedule now?"

Archer, slouched next to him, nodded. "Yeah, we were awesome today. Everyone loved how fast we cleared tables. We should get official shifts."

Booker looked between the two boys and let out a short laugh. "Oh, you think you're ready for the big leagues now, huh?"

"Why not?" Carver said, grinning. "You're always saying how the restaurant's a family thing."

Maya smirked. "Well, I think you both proved yourselves today. But don't get used to Linda saving the day. That woman already has two jobs."

Cass leaned back in her chair, rubbing her temples. "We need to be better prepared next time. When Lola runs another ad campaign, we need to know ahead of time so we can have more staff on hand."

“I’ll talk to her tomorrow,” Booker said. “But seriously, on a Tuesday? This is incredible. Makes me wonder what Friday night’s gonna look like.”

The room fell quiet for a moment as they looked around the table, taking in the aftermath of the day. They exchanged small nods and brief smiles, seeming to reflect on how they had managed the sudden rush.

Archer broke the silence. “So, do we get paid for today or what?”

Everyone burst out laughing, the sound carrying through the empty restaurant. They had tackled an unexpected challenge, and relief tinged their laughter.

As the laughter settled, Booker turned to Linda, who remained at the table, sipping from a mug of tea. “Linda,” he said, his tone steady, “if the business keeps going like this, I’d love to bring you back full-time. You’re family, and there’s no one else I’d trust more.”

Linda set her mug down, her eyes glistening under the dimmed lights. “I’d love to come back, Booker. There’s no place like home.”

Booker nodded, his shoulders easing as he sat back in his chair. The group lingered around the table for a few more moments, the evening’s exhaustion mingling with a sense of possibility in the quiet, softly lit restaurant.

*****

The Zoom call window filled the screen of Cass’s laptop, perched on the edge of her bedroom desk. Behind her, the faint glow of her bedside lamp cast a warm hue over the room, highlighting the stack of worn books on her nightstand and the patterned quilt neatly folded at the foot of her bed. Lola adjusted her camera, and Isaiah leaned back in his chair, earbuds in. Ayesha’s box was dimly lit, her face partially shadowed. She gave a small wave.

“Thanks for making time, everyone,” Cass said, settling into her chair. “Ayesha, if you need to head out early, we understand. Big internship day tomorrow, right?”

Ayesha smiled faintly. “Yeah, but I wanted to hear how everything turned out. This sounded wild.”

Just then, Maya peeked her head into the frame, her scrubs slightly wrinkled and her hair loosely tied back. “Booker crashed,” she said with a small laugh, “but I wanted to peek in and say hello and thank you. I never knew a restaurant in Oakland could have a viral moment like this. You all really pulled something off today."

Lola waved, grinning. "Thanks, Mrs. Freeman. I'm looking at things now, and I think I could do this again. Maybe even better next time."

Maya nodded. "Just don't make it a habit of breaking the pantry in one day. Goodnight, everyone." She waved and slipped back out of view.

Ayesha, here are the highlights, then you should log off and get some sleep." Cass adjusted her notebook. "Lola, your ads really made an impact. To-go orders were off the charts, and we saw a big spike in beer, wine, and cocktail sales. The average order was 40% higher than normal."

Ayesha yawned, covering her mouth. "It sounds like you have a lot more to unpack, but I'm going to crash. Internship starts at 7 a.m., and they don't mess around."

Cass smiled warmly. "Go get some rest, Ayesha. Thanks for joining us."

"Goodnight, everyone," Ayesha said before logging off.

Maya peeked her head back into the frame briefly. "I'm heading to bed too. You all keep up the great work, but don't forget to rest yourselves. Goodnight!"

She waved, disappearing once more.

"Lola, you were running around Telegraph like a detective on a shopping spree," Cass said, grinning.

"Well, my 'detective work' worked," Lola said, laughing. "I noticed how local businesses use authenticity and pride to connect with people. For Booker's, I highlighted the trolley photos, the vintage library shelves, and the family-run story. It all resonated."

Lola shrugged, smiling. "I don't have a fancy slide deck, but I can show some screenshots and charts from the sites I used to pull the data." I'm all about social media, so I tried a few things I've seen in some online tutorials. I used A/B testing to experiment with different ad placements and target demographics. I focused on Bay Area foodies, Oakland Black history enthusiasts, and people interested in Bay Area soul food. I didn't think it would cause such a rush."

"Incredible job, Lola," Isaiah said, leaning closer. "Seriously, you've outdone yourself." "Where did you get these metrics?"

Lola tapped her keyboard, bringing up a chart to share. "I pieced them together from free analytics sites. One of them offered a simple machine learning template. I analyzed your daily sales info alongside user engagement, comparing which demographics responded best to the ads. That gave me a few key time slots to post ads."

A bar chart appeared, showing traffic spikes. "Instagram led the charge, with over 50% of the clicks coming from there during lunch hours. Oaklandish brought in a steady stream of visitors, especially in the afternoon when locals were browsing. And the food blogs? They really came through during dinner, driving a last-minute rush."

"Instagram makes sense," Isaiah said. "Incredible job again, Lola. Honestly, it's amazing how much traction you created. People were tagging their food everywhere. I saw three separate stories from friends. It felt like everyone was talking about Booker's tonight."

Cass tapped her pen against the desk. "So this wasn't just ads doing the work—it was the feedback loop. The more people tagged us, the more others joined in."

"Exactly," Lola said, smiling. "But we have to be strategic moving forward. This kind of buzz doesn't last forever unless we keep feeding it."

"So, what's next?" Isaiah asked, leaning closer to his camera. "You're amazing, Lola. I mean, everything about this campaign was incredible. What are the plans for doing this again, or was this just a one-time thing?"

"That's what we need to figure out," Cass replied. "If we're going to make this sustainable, we'll need to plan better. We barely kept up today." She looked at Lola. "Can you focus your next campaign on one item? Something high-margin, like the rockfish bites?"

"Already on it," Lola said. "And I'll work in some teasers about Booker's history. The stuff people love—the trolley photos, the library shelves—it sets the place apart."

"I'm usually about art and other creative work," Lola added with a shrug, "but I read about these tools and gave them a spin. Turns out people really connect with those Instagram stories."

"Perfect," Cass said, scribbling notes. "Let's regroup next week to see what's feasible. And Lola—great job. Seriously."

"Thanks," Lola said with a grin. "And tell your dad thanks for letting me run wild with this one."

"I will," Cass said. "He was impressed—once he stopped drowning in rockfish."

Laughter filled the call before Isaiah leaned back, stretching. "Alright, I'm out too. But before I go, Lola—seriously, incredible job tonight. You're amazing. You really pulled off something special. This was fun, though. You all did amazing."

The laughter on the call faded as Cass clicked out of Zoom, the screen shifting to a test prep window.

She glanced at her desk—an SAT prep book lay open beside scattered notes and a highlighter. She exhaled, rolling her shoulders, then picked up her pencil, tapping it once against the page before flipping to the next section.

On her screen, two windows sat side by side—SAT prep questions on one, restaurant sales data on the other. A timer ticked down in the corner.

She flipped through a reading comprehension passage, scanning the multiple-choice options. Her gaze lingered, unfocused. She blinked hard, then pressed her fingers against her temples. The room was quiet except for the soft hum of the oscillating fan.

Her phone buzzed. A message appeared on the screen:

Isaiah: Still grinding? Get some sleep, Cass.

She read it, tapped the screen once, then sent back a simple ☺ before setting the phone face down.

The highlighter in her hand moved quickly across the page. She reached for her water bottle, took a sip, then turned to the next question.

Outside, a car passed, headlights sweeping briefly across the window. The faint sound of Archer and Carver's voices drifted from their room, but the house remained still.

Cass tapped her pencil against the desk once, then refocused, eyes locked on the next problem.

TUESDAY, JULY 23 | JOURNAL ENTRY

5: The number of times today I thought, "Lola, how did you pull this off?" She's always been good at her own social media—posting cute pics, funny captions, the works—but now she's diving into ads like she's been doing it for years. She said she just wanted to try it out, and suddenly we're on Oaklandish and food blogs, with a dining room so full it felt like a festival. It's wild.

5: The number of times Isaiah said, "Good job," to Lola during our call today. And then there were the three times he added, "You're amazing." I don't know what's going on there, but something tells me I'm going to be hearing about it soon. I don't have the energy to deal with her love life right now, though. I'm still recovering from the chaos her ads unleashed.

6: The texts Logan sent me today. They were simple—little updates about working with his parents and asking how things were going at the restaurant. I missed having him around, but it was nice knowing he was still thinking about me. I wonder what he would've said if he'd seen how packed the place was.

3: The times I felt completely overwhelmed today. Lola's ad campaign brought in so many people, we could barely keep up. The dining room was packed, the takeout line was out the door, and catering inquiries kept rolling in. It was chaos, but for once, it felt like the kind of chaos we could celebrate. Like we were finally getting somewhere.

∞: The gratitude I feel for my family tonight. Mom coming straight from the clinic to help. Dad juggling the kitchen and takeout like a pro. Even Carver and Archer stepping up, clearing tables like they'd been doing it for years. Watching us all pull together reminded me why this place matters so much. It's not just about the food—it's about us.

SUNDAY, JULY 28

At 7:30 AM, sunlight spilled through half-open curtains onto Cass, who sat cross-legged on her bed in a thin tank top and cotton shorts. The phone on her nightstand displayed the time in green blocky digits. The house remained largely silent, broken only by the distant snores of sleeping family members and the occasional creak of settling wood.

She lifted her laptop onto her lap and opened the College Board portal, which loaded in calming blues and whites. The reading section appeared. Twenty minutes later, her posture stiffened at a dense passage. She glanced from the screen to a loose page of notes balanced on her pillow. Her forehead creased as she ran her finger along a line of text, then she selected an answer, pushing out a small breath.

At 8:45, she flipped back through the final reading questions, giving them one last scan. Then, with a quick shift of her legs, she moved on to the writing section. She leaned in closer and tapped the keyboard, eyes narrowing at a question about misplaced modifiers. Next came math. She paused at a multi-step word problem, pencil scratching with a determined rhythm as she worked through each step. Occasionally, she adjusted the angle of her laptop or took a quick sip from a water bottle on her nightstand. Upon reaching a graph question, she scrolled up twice to confirm the axis labels before entering her solution.

Meanwhile, the aroma of brewing coffee drifted from the kitchen. Water pipes rattled as someone else in the house started a shower, and the low murmur, the twins' voices, floated up the stairs. Occasionally, the volume spiked as they swapped heated remarks over a TV remote. A neighbor's dog barked once outside, then fell silent.

By 10:45, Cass reached the final screen. She hovered the cursor over the "Submit" button, shifting her weight as if steeling herself for the outcome. A faint click later, the page refreshed to reveal, in bold text: "Congratulations! Your test has been submitted." Not long after, a new notification arrived: "Your SAT Results Are Ready." The site reloaded and displayed her score: 1380.

She let out a short gasp and did a subtle victory dance, shuffling her shoulders and swaying side to side, before typing into her group chat:

Cass: Just got my practice SAT score. 1380!

Ayesha: GIRL YOU CRUSHED IT! 🔥 I KNEW all those late-night question drills would pay off!!! Isaiah: Excellent work. Data doesn't lie. Practice leads to better outcomes. Logan: Yoooo nice one! Colleges better make room! Lola: You're unstoppable, Cass! Scholarships are definitely in your future!

Cass: Haven't told them yet. Waiting for family dinner tonight.

Aunt Zora's name appeared next:

Aunt Zora: Still on for hair tonight after dinner?

Cass: Yes, see you then!

From the hallway, the twins' argument about channel choices rose in volume. Cass shut her laptop, rolled off the bed, and grabbed a towel from a nearby hook. She stepped out of her room, pulled the bathroom door closed behind her, and twisted the shower faucet on. Steam soon spread across the mirror, and the steady patter of water echoed against the tile, a brief retreat from the day's noise.

*****

A gentle candlelight glowed in the dining room of the Freeman house, multiple candles casting soft, golden light across worn oak. Steam rose from the pot roast, mingling with collard greens and fresh cornbread. Cass sat near the table's far end, five flickering candlesticks set between Aunt Zora and Archer. The polished table surface reflected decades of family meals, its wood smooth from countless plates passed.

Heads bowed as Grandpa James said grace, his deep voice filling the room with words of gratitude. As the family settled into their seats, the soft clink of silverware began.

"Before we start," Cass said, her phone screen illuminating her face, "I want to share something." Forks paused mid-air, water glasses settling on the table. She held up the screen. "I just took another practice SAT. 1380."

Booker's fork clattered against his plate. "1380? Baby girl!" His chair scraped back as he stood.

Maya pressed a hand to her chest. "That's thirty points above what we talked about, Cassie."

Archer elbowed Carver. "Harvard better watch out."

"Yale too," Carver added, reaching for a biscuit. "All those late nights paid off."

Booker lifted his glass, ice cubes clinking. His proud smile widened as he raised his glass higher. "To Cass—carrying forward the Freeman name with hard work and excellence," he said, his voice too loud and filled with excitement.

Glasses rose around the table, candlelight dancing off crystal rims. The scent of pot roast grew stronger as steam escaped from beneath the serving dish lid.

"It's just practice," Cass said, adjusting her napkin. "I'm scheduled to take the real test in October."

"Girl, please." Aunt Zora reached over to pat her hand. "We're celebrating now and later. And speaking of passing things with flying colors - have you thought about where you want to apply?"

Cass adjusted her napkin. "Stanford's data science program is amazing."

"Stanford's great," Aunt Zora said, spooning greens onto her plate, "but don't sleep on Howard or Spelman. Those HBCU connections run deep. My roommate from Spelman? She's a VP at UPS now. People there really invest in your success."

Maya set down her fork. "I don't care where she goes, as long as it's a full ride. We can't be taking on loans with the restaurant situation."

"There's the Hale Foundation scholarship," Cass said, her voice careful. "The same one that paid for the summer program."

Booker set his glass down, his expression growing serious. "You know, watching you work so hard, it reminds me of everything I didn't do. I wasted my high school years, thought I had all the time in the world. Then senior year hit and all my friends were talking about college tours and applications. I ended up at community college, then the fire department." He shook his head. "Not that there's anything wrong with that path, but I didn't even give myself other options."

"But look at you now," Aunt Zora added. "Running your own business."

"A business I started after getting injured," Booker said. "I want better planning for my kids. Georgia Tech has a strong program, and don't forget about UCLA and USC. They're not too far from home, and both have excellent programs. With your scores and grades, I'm sure you could get a lot of scholarship dollars. Some schools even offer full tuition for National Merit Scholars."

"Berkeley's right here," Carver piped up. "You could still help with the restaurant."

Archer snorted. "Please. She's going somewhere fancy. MIT or nothing."

"Wherever you go," Maya said, passing the cornbread, "just make sure the money makes sense. These schools love to talk about diversity until it's time to pay for it."

“That’s why those HBCU connections matter,” Aunt Zora said. “They look out for their own. Plus, the recruiting teams actually look like you.”

The candles flickered as serving dishes continued circulating. College names floated across the table—Stanford, Howard, MIT, Berkeley—while steam rose from the pot roast.

Grandma Lillian set down her fork. “Cass, you come from a long line of determined folks. It’s not just about the school name; it’s about what you make of it.” She passed the cornbread to Archer. “Now eat something while we’re all dreaming big.”

Grandpa James cleared his throat from the head of the table, and the family turned toward him. He reached into his pocket and drew out a small, worn rectangle of paper. “I want to show you something that came in the mail yesterday,” he said, raising the card so everyone could see its faded ink and frayed edges. “My first library card.” He rotated it in his hands. “My brother found it while cleaning the old house and sent it over.”

All eyes settled on the card, its humble presence drawing the family closer around the table.

“I remember the day I got this,” James went on, his voice gravelly. “It was 1958, right after they desegregated the public library. I was one of the first Black kids to get a card.” A slight shine appeared in his eyes as he passed the card to Booker, who studied it and then carefully handed it to Maya. She turned it over, her fingertips tracing the lettering.

Cass eventually held the card and could make out her grandfather’s younger face in the small photo. His expression appeared stern, with bright eyes full of possibility.

“Cass,” James said, meeting her gaze, “I’m proud of your passion for learning. This data science you’ve taken up, it’s a whole new world, isn’t it? The way of the future.”

Cass nodded. “Yes, Grandpa. There’s so much to explore in data, and it has real potential to make a difference.”

James rested against the back of his chair, watching her. “There was a time when folks like us risked their lives just to learn,” he said. The table grew still, plates and utensils momentarily forgotten. “Knowledge was hard to come by,” he continued, his voice dropping. “My daddy told me about his grandfather, a slave on a Georgia plantation. He learned to read in secret, crouched by candlelight, using scraps of newspaper.”

His tone remained steady as he recounted the story: “One night, the overseer caught him, dragged him out to the yard, and beat him. Then they severed the first joint of every finger so he couldn't hold a pen."

A weighted silence settled in the room. James paused, then continued, "But that man—your great-great-great-grandfather—never stopped. He figured out how to write with those damaged hands and passed on what he knew through quiet lessons and hidden gatherings."

He shook his head, looking around the table. "Our ancestors couldn't afford books like encyclopedias, and even if they could, they often weren't allowed in libraries. These days, everything's at our fingertips. Sometimes, I wonder if that makes it less valued."

James shifted his focus from Booker to Aunt Zora, then to Cass and the twins. "Your dad and my daughter don't recall 'Colored Only' signs or riding in the back of the bus," he said. "But I remember. I remember the look in my mama's eyes when I asked why we couldn't go to the 'good' library downtown."

His gaze swept the room. "Generations of our people suffered under slavery. They held onto a dream that one day their children could learn freely. It's painful to see anyone throw away that chance."

James paused, then looked at Cass again. "He only had a seventh-grade education, but he taught me to value learning. That's why I named your father Booker—after Booker T. Washington."

He turned to the youngest grandchildren. "Archer Freeman. Carver Freeman," he said, motioning for them to step closer. They both approached. "Do you know what it means to be a Freeman?"

James glanced at each of them. "Our name, Freeman, isn't just some label. It's a declaration—an announcement to the world that our ancestors claimed their own freedom. When they were finally free, many took the name Freeman to show who they were."

He placed a hand on each boy's shoulder. "Every time you sign your name or hear it called, you carry the courage of the people who came before you."

He straightened a little, addressing them both. "But being a Freeman isn't only about history. It's also about what comes next—using the freedom our ancestors won to do good in the world. Whether you end up becoming doctors like your mom, running a business like your dad, going into data science like your sister, or finding another path entirely, remember the legacy of your name."

James leaned in slightly, lowering his voice. "Teach your own children what it means to be a Freeman. Respect education, stand up for justice, and don't take freedom for granted. Can you do that?"

Archer's jaw set as he nodded. Carver's eyes flickered as he gave a firm nod, his hand brushing the hem of his shirt.

Booker lifted his glass. "I want to propose a toast—to our family, our past, and our future. Together, we can accomplish anything."

Glasses rose and clinked softly, the candlelight reflecting off their rims. The flame from each taper cast a gentle glow on the family's faces. They returned to their meal, the table regaining its casual conversation. Yet the recollection of James's words stayed with them, intertwined with the evening's warmth and the echoes of every Freeman who had come before.

*****

Cass sat cross-legged on the stool while Aunt Zora's hands moved steadily through her thick curls. The scent of coconut oil blended with the lingering aroma of cinnamon in the kitchen. Dinner at her grandparents' had ended. LL Cool J's voice rumbled through the speakers of her aunt's Clawson loft, the steady beat of a 90s rap mix easing into the evening.

Zora's hands moved with practiced ease, parting and twisting Cass's hair into neat braids. They had followed this routine since Cass was young. "You know," Zora began, her voice quiet, "your daddy never could sit still long enough for me to braid his hair when we were younger. Always wriggling and complaining, but once I started, he'd settle right down, like he knew I had him."

Cass offered a small smile and leaned forward. The crackle of popcorn from the stove filled the kitchen, blending with the scents of coconut oil and butter. "Yeah, sounds like him," she said. "I've missed this. Feels like everything's been moving too fast."

Aunt Zora chuckled, her hands still weaving. "Girl, you got a lot going on! Data bootcamp, trying to drag your parents into the 21st century—yes, I heard about the meetup in Berkeley and the white dude that's been following you around. I can't keep up!" She laughed again, though her gaze rested on Cass with a measured intensity.

As she finished another braid, Zora's voice lowered. "And I also know it's not looking good for the restaurant. Are you okay?" she asked gently. Cass paused, her eyes lingering on a knot in the wood of the kitchen table. "I'm still processing everything, and I still believe that it will work out somehow," she responded. Zora sighed, tying off the braid. “You’ve got the faith of Deacon James, ’cause I just don’t see it.”

Zora’s fingers paused briefly before picking up another section of hair. “Life will do that if you let it. But you’ve got people who’ll help you slow down when you need it.” Her voice shifted, a hint of curiosity in the question that followed. “Speaking of people… you’ve been seein’ that boy Logan a lot lately, huh?”

Cass uncrossed her legs and shifted on the stool, her fingers brushing against her shorts. “Yeah,” she said, her gaze drifting briefly to the floor. “We’ve been hanging out. It’s just… fun to get to know him better.”

Zora’s hands kept working, but her tone took on a thoughtful edge. “Logan’s a nice boy, I’m sure. But I gotta ask… you ever wonder what he’s really lookin’ for, Cass? I mean, he’s white. Some boys like to experiment, if you know what I mean.”

Cass’s fingertips tapped lightly against her thigh. She glanced toward the window, where evening light was fading, then settled her attention back on the braids. “I don’t think it’s like that, Aunt Zora,” she said quietly. “Race hasn’t really come up. We’re just… hanging out. You’re being a little old school.”

Zora let out a quiet chuckle. “Old school, huh? Maybe. But sometimes, old school ways keep you from making old school mistakes. I just want you to be sure he’s interested in you for the right reasons, not because he’s curious.”

Cass shifted again, her hand brushing the fabric of her shorts. The smell of freshly popped popcorn drifted over from the stove. “I get that,” she said with a soft exhale. “But honestly, Aunt Zora, it’s not that deep. We’re just spending time together. It’s nice to have someone around who doesn’t expect anything from me.”

Zora’s hands slowed as she finished another braid. “I hear you, baby. I do. But these things can get complicated real quick, especially when race gets involved.”

Cass was silent for a moment, LL Cool J’s voice filling the pause. She cleared her throat, and her posture tightened slightly. “Maybe you’re right,” she said. “But right now, it’s just fun. And I like getting to know him.”

Zora moved on to the final section of hair, her grip steady. “As long as you know what you’re doing,” she said gently. “But just remember, you deserve someone who sees all of you. Not just what’s convenient or interesting to them.”

Cass nodded once, lifting a hand to the newly braided rows. The last of the popcorn popped on the stove. She let her fingers skim the neat style. “I’ll keep that in mind.”

Zora tied off the final braid and stepped back to look at her work. “There. You look beautiful, as always.”

Cass's phone buzzed on the kitchen counter. She glanced at the screen: a text from Logan about meeting up at the cafe tomorrow.

"That's probably him right now," Zora said, her voice neutral.

"I'll talk to him later," Cass said, leaving the phone face down. She ran her fingers over the smooth rows, nodding in acknowledgment. "Thanks, Aunt Zora. For everything."

"You're welcome, baby." Zora moved to the stove. "Now, how about some popcorn before we start the movie?"

The smell of butter and popping kernels soon filled the kitchen. Zora pulled up a stool beside Cass, resting a hand on her knee. "Just remember, you've got family who'll always have your back—Logan or no Logan."

Cass smiled slightly, her shoulders settling as they moved into the living room. The opening scenes of The Wiz played on the TV. She grabbed the bowl of popcorn and sat beside Zora on the couch.

Moments later, Aunt Em's voice filled the room as she sang.

Cass watched the screen as The Feeling That We Had played softly in the background.

SUNDAY, JULY 28 | JOURNAL ENTRY

∞: The amount of pride I feel carrying my family's legacy. Grandpa said he named Dad after Booker T. Washington because education and progress were the keys to freedom. And now, I'm using data—something my ancestors couldn't even dream of—to fight for our future. It's like everything I've been doing is part of the same story, just written with different tools.

3: The number of times Aunt Zora made me rethink everything tonight. She always has a way of weaving in wisdom with a side of popcorn and laughter. I love her for it, even when her questions about Logan make me second-guess myself. I don't think he's the type of guy to 'experiment,' but I never thought I'd see myself with a white guy either. And now, I'm wondering how he's going to react to my new braids.

10: The hour we drove home from Grandpa's. The car ride was quiet, but you could feel something different in the air. Grandpa's words hit all of us, even Dad, who started rambling about expanding the restaurant like we didn't have Hal breathing down our necks. Mom quickly grounded him, but for a moment, it felt like he believed in something bigger than the deadline.

10: The questions Aunt Zora would probably ask him. "What are your intentions with my niece?" "Do you know who Bayard Rustin is?" I can already hear her, and I can already see Logan trying to answer, looking at me for backup. But if he could handle that—and I think he could—then maybe he really is someone I can let in.

Tonight, sitting at that table with all the noise and the stories and the food, I couldn't stop thinking about how much Logan doesn't know about me yet. About us. About where I come from. If he's going to be in my life, he has to understand all of this—the good, the messy, the complicated. But maybe, just maybe, he could.

Leaf Node

The leaf node is the endpoint of a journey, where decisions are finalized, and outcomes are determined. It's the culmination of the pathways and choices that led to this point, the result of countless splits and conditions. Each leaf represents a resolved question, a moment where uncertainty transforms into clarity. The leaf node reminds us that every journey has a destination, but the path taken is what gives it meaning. It's the end that defines the process.

MONDAY, JULY 29

At exactly 10 a.m. on Monday, as "U.N.I.T.Y." by Queen Latifah played softly over the restaurant's speakers, the bell above the front door jingled. Cass stood at the hostess stand, arranging menus. The sharp scent of cleaning solution lingered in the air, mixing faintly with the last traces of breakfast. She glanced up, her brow furrowing when she saw Hal walk in, followed by a sharply dressed man holding a clipboard. His gaze swept across the dining room, lingering on the worn hardwood floors and the faded light fixtures.

"Good morning, Mr. Rodríguez," Cass said, her tone measured. "Can I get you a seat? Was my dad supposed to meet you?"

Hal gave her a faint smile and said, "No, just looking around."

Cass set the menus down, her fingers hovering briefly before catching sight of a folder the man was carrying. In bold, elegant lettering, it read, "The Gentry." Her hand stilled on the counter as she stepped closer. "Excuse me," she said, nodding toward the folder. "What's 'The Gentry'?"

The man, David Chin, smiled politely, holding the folder slightly higher. "Oh, that's the new name for the luxury condos I'm planning to build here," he said in a matter-of-fact tone.

Cass stiffened, her jaw tightening briefly. Without a word, she turned and walked briskly toward the kitchen. Pushing the door open, she caught Booker's attention as he was plating an order. "Dad," she said, her voice clipped. "He's calling it 'The Gentry.' Condos. He's planning to build condos."

Booker wiped his hands on a dish towel, his jaw tightening. "Stay here," he said firmly before stepping out of the kitchen.

Cass lingered by the door, listening to fragments of David's conversation with Hal. "We'll have to demolish most of the interior," David was saying, his voice calm and businesslike. "But the structural integrity is solid. It shouldn't be too difficult to get permits. I'd like to move fast on this—my investors are ready, and I don't want to keep them waiting."

Hal nodded, his hands in his pockets. "We'll make it happen," he replied. "I'll handle the logistics."

Cass stepped back into the kitchen, gripping the edge of the counter as she glanced through the small window in the door. Booker's steps were deliberate as he approached the men, his posture stiff. The faint buzz of the overhead lights blended with the scratch of David's pen on the clipboard, and a hush settled over the dining room. The staff exchanged quick glances but remained quiet, their movements slowed.

Joey, the busboy, entered the kitchen carrying a tray stacked with glasses, his steps quick and uneven. He set the tray down near the sink and turned to Cass, wiping his hands on his apron. “What’s going on out there?” he asked, his voice hushed as he nodded toward the door.

Cass didn’t look away from the window. “Mr. Rodriguez brought someone in,” she said, her words clipped. “They’re talking about condos.”

“Condos?” Joey’s brow furrowed as he leaned slightly closer. “Like... replacing the restaurant?”

Cass gave a small nod, her grip tightening on the counter. Joey’s mouth opened as if to say more, but he closed it quickly, his gaze darting toward the window. The faint murmur of voices filtered through the door, David’s calm and measured tone carrying above Hal’s occasional replies.

Joey shifted on his feet. “Does Booker know?”

“He knows,” Cass replied, her tone flat. “He’s handling it.”

The clink of glassware echoed faintly as Joey picked up a few stray cups from the counter and added them to the tray. He hesitated, his hands hovering over the pile. “Do you think they’ll go through with it?”

Cass didn’t answer immediately. Her eyes stayed on the dining room as Booker slowed his pace, his hands at his sides. She finally spoke, her voice low but firm. “They will if we don’t stop them.”

Joey stood silently for a moment, watching her before nodding and stepping back toward the sink. The hum of the overhead lights seemed louder now, filling the quiet kitchen as Cass’s gaze followed Booker across the dining room.

Booker cleared his throat as he reached Hal. “Hal, can I speak with you for a moment?”

Hal turned and nodded. “Of course.” He motioned for David to wait, then followed Booker to a quieter corner near the bar.

“Hal, what’s going on here?” Booker asked, his voice low but firm. “You bring someone in here without telling me?”

“Booker, this is happening,” Hal said flatly. “You have not fully paid me everything that you owe. You are in violation of our agreement.”

Booker's fingers curled briefly around the edge of the bar, but his voice remained steady. "We're working on it. You know we're doing everything we can to get back on track."

Hal crossed his arms, speaking in a firm tone. "It's too late for that. I've given you more chances than I should have. David is interested in converting this space into condos, and I need to move forward."

Booker opened his mouth to respond but paused, glancing back at the staff, who were still watching from a distance. A server peered out from the kitchen door, retreating when she caught Booker's eye. Hal followed his gaze and sighed. "Look, I'll give you until the end of the month to settle everything. After that, it's out of my hands."

Booker nodded slowly, his face set. "Thanks for the time, Hal," he said, his voice tight. He turned and walked back toward the kitchen, his grip tightening on the dish towel in his hand. A hush lingered in the dining room long after David and Hal resumed their conversation, their voices low and steady, as if nothing had just been disrupted.

*****

After Hal and David left, Booker retreated to his office, the tension in his shoulders unmistakable. The overhead lights cast a steady glow, the silence broken only by the soft creak of his chair as he leaned back. Cass followed shortly after, her notebook tucked under her arm. She knocked gently on the open door, catching his attention.

"Dad, can we go over the numbers?" she asked, stepping inside. Booker gestured for her to sit, his expression weary but attentive.

Cass opened her laptop and brought up the latest metrics, turning the screen toward Booker. "It looks like we've managed to scrape together enough for another month and a half's payment," she said, her voice steady despite the weight of the news. "Our labor costs have also gone down by 8%, and we've seen an increase in repeat customers. But it's not the full amount."

Cass hesitated for a moment before meeting his eyes. "Do you think Hal will accept that?" she asked, her voice steady but tinged with uncertainty."

Booker glanced at the desk calendar. "Hal agreed to a meeting on the 31st to make a determination on the viability of the restaurant going forward," he said, his voice tinged with resignation. "We'll need to make a strong case."

Booker rubbed his temples, letting out a long breath. "We've worked so hard, and it still doesn't feel like enough," he muttered, his fingers resting on the edge of his desk. "But Cass, this presentation is incredible. The progress we've made—it's because of you." "Do you think Hal will accept that?"

Cass hesitated, then shook her head. "I don't know. But it's better than nothing. We should try."

Before Booker could respond, Maria appeared in the doorway, clutching her apron tightly. Her fingers twisted the fabric nervously as she stepped inside. "Sir, do you want me to gather the staff now? Are we going to tell them about... everything?" she asked, her voice cautious but filled with concern.

Booker looked up at her, his face lined with exhaustion. He glanced at Cass before nodding slowly. "Yes. They deserve to know the truth," he said. "Even though business has been better than ever—labor costs down, waste reduced, customer satisfaction climbing—it might not be enough.""

Maria nodded and excused herself to gather the staff, her footsteps fading down the hallway. Cass leaned forward, her notebook open to a presentation draft. "Dad, let's focus on what we've accomplished," she said, rotating the notebook to face him. "This presentation can emphasize the progress we've made—labor costs down, waste reduced, higher customer satisfaction. We'll make sure Hal sees that.""

Booker gave a faint smile, his expression softening. "You're right," he said softly, "and thank you for putting this together. You've done an amazing job." "We've come this far—let's keep going for as long as we can."

"I understand, Sir. Although not everyone knows about it—especially with more crowds coming in, most assume that everything's fine," Maria whispered.

Booker considered her words and nodded. "Maybe it's best to let them think that for now." But before Maria could answer, he shook his head. "No, we can't. It's not right. I need to tell them. Otherwise, when Hal kicks us out, it'll be a shock. What do you think, Cass?"

Cass set the cash tray aside and walked over, her eyes meeting her father's. "I agree with you, Dad. If I were in their position, I'd want to know beforehand."

Booker nodded. "Okay, Maria, can you please gather the staff in my office? It's still early, and we have some time before the first customers arrive."

“I will, Sir,” Maria said, excusing herself.

Cass placed a reassuring hand on Booker’s arm as they walked toward his office. “We’ve tried so hard, Dad. Let’s hope Hal sees that when we talk to him.”

Booker gave a small nod, his shoulders slumping slightly. “We’ll see, sweetheart. We’ll see.”

TUESDAY, JULY 30 | JOURNAL ENTRY

4: The number of times I've played Logan's playlist today. It was sweet of him to send it, but seriously—"Eye of the Tiger"? It's like he's trying to turn this into some 80s training montage. Don't get me wrong, the thought counts, but maybe next time, no cliché pump-up songs. Still, the gesture made me smile when I needed it most.**

3: The times I've thought about Mike and Sarah and their families today. Are they really going to jail? I know what they did hurt us, but jail? That's their whole lives, their families' lives, turned upside down. I wonder if they're sitting somewhere, thinking about the choices they made and wishing for a way to undo them. I'm trying not to feel sorry for them, but it's hard not to.

5: The moments I caught Mom surprising me with her support. For so long, it felt like she was ready to walk away from the restaurant, like she'd already accepted defeat. But today, when we were going over the numbers and the presentation, she leaned in—really leaned in. She even had ideas for the community engagement slide. Seeing her fight for this place alongside Dad and me made me realize how much she still cares.

2: The times I caught myself wondering if there's someone else we can call for help. Hal seems so determined to sell this place and turn it into some cookie-cutter condos. The Gentry. Even the name sounds sterile, like something ripped out of a real estate brochure. I can't believe he's willing to destroy all of this just to line his pockets. But who else can we call? Who else would care enough to step in?

∞: The frustration I feel knowing how far we've come and still wondering if it'll be enough. We've reduced labor costs, cut waste, brought in more customers—and Hal still acts like it's not good enough. It's like no matter what we do, he's already made up his mind. But how can he look at everything we've accomplished and not see the potential here?

4: The number of suspicious texts from Lola about Isaiah. I don't have the energy to deal with her love life right now. Whatever's going on with Isaiah, I hope she figures it out soon, because I can barely handle my own problems, let alone hers.

6: The times I've run through tomorrow's presentation in my head, tweaking every slide, every line, every graph. Dad keeps saying it's amazing, that I've done more than anyone could've asked for. But I can't help feeling like it's not enough. What if Hal doesn't care about the progress we've made? What if he just sees dollar signs and ignores everything else?

Today has been a rollercoaster of emotions—hope, frustration, fear, and everything in between. We're fighting so hard for this place, and I just wish someone would fight for us the way we're fighting for the restaurant. Grandpa James keeps saying to keep the faith, and I'm trying. But faith feels so fragile right now. Still, we've come this far. We can't stop now.

WEDNESDAY, JULY 31

There was a sudden shift in the atmosphere when the bell above the door jingled twice from across the room. The first chime rang out when the door opened, and the second followed with a trailing creak as it closed and the lock clicked into place. The rusted edges of the door's hinges and the old closer at the top groaned under the strain as the door swung closed. Cass held the pages tightly in her hands, glancing at Booker as he paused mid-sentence, straightening his posture before walking over to the man by the door.

"Good afternoon, Sir. Welcome. Mr. Booker and the family are expecting you," Cass said, her voice polite but strained as she gestured toward the sharp-eyed man standing at the entrance.

Booker quickly followed, stepping forward to welcome Hal. "Thanks for coming, Hal. We really appreciate your time." He led him to the largest table where Cass had set up her laptop and papers. Hal, at one end, the Freeman family arrayed around him. "Please, have a seat."

Hal gave a curt nod, his thin eyes surveying the room behind a pair of glasses before he settled into the chair. The silence in the room was heavy, the family's tension palpable. Cass caught Booker's gaze briefly, her own unease reflected in his eyes.

"Booker, Maya, I see the whole family's here for this. Shall we get started?" Hal asked, pulling a ballpoint pen from his breast pocket. The intensity in his voice surged across the room as if an invisible wire were binding them all together.

Booker stepped forward, trying to mask his demeanor despite the tension. "Hal, thank you for coming. We appreciate the chance to show you what we've been working on."

Hal nodded, narrowing his eyes slightly. "Well, since we all know each other, let's cut to the chase. Show me what you've got."

Booker cleared his throat, reaching into his pocket. "First, Hal, we want to demonstrate our commitment." He slid an envelope across the table. "This is a check for two and a half months' rent. We know it's not the full amount, but we ask for your patience as we implement our new strategies."

Hal's eyebrows rose as he opened the envelope; his poker face gave way. He looked up, his gaze moving from Booker to Cass. "Alright, I see you've got some setup here. What are these new strategies?"

Cass took a few steps forward and clicked on the laptop's keyboard to start her presentation. Her voice remained steady, though her fingers hovered over the edge of the laptop, her nails digging slightly into the plastic. Just as she had rehearsed, she guided Hal through their implemented changes: the data-driven food pricing adjustments, regular and special menu modifications, systemized inventory and waste management, an improved brand identity, and innovative marketing initiatives. A series of vibrant charts and graphs displayed positive trends, boasting of their progress and the arduous work they had put in.

“As you can see,” Cass concluded, pointing to a projection graph, “based on these trends, we’re not just on track to break even. We’re projected to start turning a profit within the next quarter.”

Hal spread out the spreadsheets and graphs on the desk, pressing the corners flat with his palm. Cass stood near the edge of the table, and the rest of the family gathered behind her. The overhead lights cast a muted glow on the pages as Hal scanned row after row of numbers. After a few moments, he leaned back in his chair, his expression thoughtful.

“I have to say, I’m impressed, Booker. I never thought that you could pull out something like this. Your daughter here must have put a lot of work into this.”

Booker nodded and rested a hand on the back of Cass’s chair. “She poured a lot into it, Mr. Rodríguez. We’ve all been behind her ideas, and we’re seeing results.”

Cass shifted her weight slightly, her voice steady. “Absolutely, Mr. Rodríguez. If you happened to pass by during lunch or dinner, you must have seen the crowds.”

“I’ve witnessed many businesses rise and fall over the years,” Hal began, lightness in his voice despite the impending revelation. “When faced with hard times, most either throw in the towel or stubbornly cling to the same approaches, hoping for different outcomes.” He paused, letting his gaze drift from Booker to Maya and Cass. “But you all have done something different. You’ve adapted and innovated. The results are clear. I do believe in the data you’ve presented here; they make sense. However—”

Hal removed his glasses and shook his head. “I have to take my own advice. I cannot just keep doing what I have been doing, holding onto properties in a changing market, hoping things will work out. This neighborhood is transforming, and as a businessman, I need to adapt too.” He gestured at Cass’s presentation. “Your data shows you understand this principle. Change or die, right? Well, I am changing too.”

He leaned forward slightly. “I’m here to make business decisions, not personal ones. This is about results, not promises. Booker, Maya, I have a line of buyers with their paperwork ready. One developer, in particular, has been persistent about getting an inspection scheduled. The market is shifting, and I need to shift with it. I cannot afford to wait any longer. I'm sorry."

"But Mr. Rodríguez," Cass interceded, "you've seen our improvements. Can we negotiate? Give us one week to bring you the full payment—by August 7th. If we can't, we'll vacate the premises."

Hal's expression remained neutral. "The market is what it is. These developers are planning mixed-use developments, luxury condos. That's where the neighborhood is headed." He spread his hands. "Your family is adapting to survive. Well, this is my adaptation." His voice hardened slightly. "If I miss this opportunity, if these buyers walk, will you cover my losses? Will you guarantee my mortgage payments?" He shook his head. "It's simple economics."

"Simple economics?" Cass stepped forward, her voice rising slightly. "You talk about adaptation, but you're just following the money. This restaurant has been here for nearly a decade. We're part of this community. You can't just—"

"Cass." Booker's voice was sharp, cutting her off.

Hal's expression hardened. "Part of the community? Tell that to my mortgage company, Miss Freeman." He gathered his papers. "I appreciate your passion, but this isn't a debate."

He glanced at Booker and Maya, who gingerly pushed their chairs back, their movements deliberate and silent as they avoided looking directly at each other. "I will send you a follow-up email regarding your evacuation and the new buyer's inspection schedule." Hal extended his hand, but Booker remained unmoving, his eyes fixed on the table as if rooted to the spot. After a moment of tense silence, he extended his hand mechanically, his movements stiff and detached. "It's okay, Mr. Freeman. I understand you're upset," Hal said, his tone devoid of sympathy as he shook Booker's hand briefly.

Booker tightened his lips, his fingers pressing harder against the edge of the table. His shoulders sagged slightly as if the tension was finally weighing him down. Hal adjusted his glasses and strode toward the door without a second glance. His footsteps echoed against the tiled floor, sharp and deliberate.

The bell jingled twice again, the sound reverberating in the tense stillness left behind, marking his departure with a finality that no one dared to break.

"Dad?" Carver asked, his voice breaking the weighted silence in the room.

Booker remained in his seat for a moment, his hand still resting on the table where Hal had been moments before. He exhaled shakily and whispered, "I never thought it would end like this." Slowly, he stood, his movements heavy and deliberate, before walking toward his office. A few moments later, the muffled sound of crying seeped through the closed door, breaking the silence. Cass and Maya exchanged glances, both wiping at their eyes quietly. Carver fidgeted with the hem of his shirt, his fingers tugging at the fabric, while Archer sat motionless, his gaze fixed on the floor, his shoulders slumped.

The door closed softly behind him, but the silence that followed was deafening. A few scattered pages drifted to the floor as the family stood frozen, their eyes darting toward the office door.

Maya's hands trembled slightly as she clutched her apron, her gaze fixed on the closed door. She held her lips in a firm line, her eyes glistening.

No one spoke.

WEDNESDAY, JULY 31 | JOURNAL ENTRY

1: The number of times I wanted to scream at Hal today. All the effort, all the progress we've made, and he just brushes it off like it's nothing. Why is he so bent on selling this place and destroying everything we've worked for? We've never been in a better position—better than we've been in years. How can he not see that?

3: The times Grandpa James told me to "keep the faith." He said he's praying for us, that miracles happen when you least expect them. I know he means well, but it's hard to hold onto faith when someone like Hal can just sweep in and decide the fate of everything we've poured our lives into. Still, Grandpa's steady belief makes me feel a little less like I'm shouting into the void.

2: The moments of unexpected support from Mom today. There was a time when I thought she wanted to let the restaurant go too, like she was ready to move on. But seeing her today, backing Dad up, fighting for this place—it reminded me how much it means to her too. She's not giving up, and neither am I.

7: The charts and graphs I showed Hal during the meeting. I poured everything into that presentation—hours of analyzing data, finding trends, and creating projections that prove we're turning things around. He even said he was impressed, but then he called himself "just a simple businessman" like that excuses everything. It was like he heard us, but he wasn't really listening.

5: The minutes of silence after Hal left. No one said anything, but the air in the room felt heavy, like we were all carrying the weight of his decision. Dad's face was blank, but I could see how much it hurt. When he finally went to his office and closed the door, I knew he was breaking down. Hearing him cry through the door was like a punch to the gut. I've never felt so helpless.

∞: The feeling of injustice I can't shake. Hal looked at our work, saw the progress we've made, and still decided to walk away. It wasn't about the money—we know we can pay him if he gives us the time. It's like he's choosing to destroy something just because he can. How is that fair? How can someone care so little about what this place means to us and to the community?

This day was a rollercoaster of hope and heartbreak. We were so close, but now it feels like we're further than ever. Still, Grandpa's words keep echoing in my head—"Keep the faith." I don't know if I believe in miracles, but I do know this: I'm not giving up. Not yet.

Forest Growth

A forest of trees provides depth, diversity, and resilience. While one tree may offer insight, a collection of trees offers a fuller understanding, combining perspectives for stronger outcomes. Forest growth represents collaboration—multiple paths and perspectives coming together to solve complex challenges. Each tree is unique, yet together they create a unified system, stronger than the sum of its parts. It's a reminder that growth comes not just from individual effort, but from collective knowledge and shared strength.

SATURDAY, AUGUST 3

The restaurant was bustling, a steady hum of conversations and clinking silverware filling the air. Customers lined up near the hostess stand, some asking Cass if the news about the restaurant closing was really true. She nodded politely, offering smiles and brief answers, though each question briefly slowed her responses. The rows of shelves filled with books, once the heart of the old library, stood quietly against the walls, a backdrop to the vibrant energy of the day. Her fingertips brushed against the edge of the hostess stand, the grooves worn smooth from years of use, and she paused there for a moment. Her phone buzzed in her pocket, momentarily drawing her away from the flow of voices and movement.

She pulled it out, the screen lighting up with Ayesha's name and a photo of the two of them from a late-night computer lab session, surrounded by textbooks and empty coffee cups. Cass hesitated for a moment before answering, her expression briefly tense as she pressed the green button.

"Hey," Cass said, speaking in a subdued tone.

"Hey, Cass," Ayesha's voice had a soft note as she asked, "I was thinking about you. How are you holding up?"

Cass exhaled slowly, stepping out from behind the hostess stand and walking toward the center of the dining area. "I don't know. It feels... weird. Like I'm walking away from something important."

Ayesha hummed softly, her pause indicating she was choosing her words. "It's not walking away, Cass. It's carrying it with you. You've done everything you could, and sometimes letting go is the hardest part—especially when it's something your family built."

Cass walked through the restaurant, her footsteps echoing softly in the quieter corners of the space. The rows of shelves filled with books, once the heart of the old library, now shared their place with polished wooden tables and carefully arranged chairs. The faint hum of the refrigerator in the kitchen added a low undertone to the lively murmur of the crowd. The smell of aged paper mingled faintly with the lingering aroma of food, evoking a comforting blend of old and new.

Near the front, a Polaroid of her father as a young man rested against the counter, his arm around a firefighter's helmet. Beside it, a worn photograph captured her grandparents outside their first home, the address barely visible on the faded curb. Tucked nearby, an old newspaper clipping chronicled the restaurant's grand opening. The edges had yellowed, but the headline remained clear: 'A New Chapter for a Historic Space.'

"It's not just the restaurant," Cass said as she traced a finger along the edge of a table, the wood smooth and familiar. "It's everything. The memories, the people. It feels like I'm losing more than just a building."

"I know," Ayesha said gently. "But those memories? They don't disappear because the doors close. They're still yours. You'll always have them, Cass. And knowing you, you'll find a way to carry them into whatever's next."

There was a brief pause before Ayesha spoke again at a lower volume. "You know, my grandmother passed during COVID. We couldn't even have a real funeral. She was the heart of our family—hosting dinners, telling stories, keeping us together. I thought losing her meant losing all of that. But I still have her stories, her recipes, the things she taught us. She isn't here, but what she gave us didn't disappear. It's with me every day, shaping the way I move through the world."

Cass's eyes drifted over the walls adorned with photographs: her father cutting the ribbon on opening day, a packed dining room during a community event, Booker laughing with a group of regulars. She stopped at one photo of her family standing together in front of the restaurant, their smiles wide under the freshly painted sign. Her fingers brushed the edge of the frame, pausing there.

"That's how I see this restaurant," Ayesha continued. "It's more than a place. It's the stories, the people, the way you and your family made everyone feel welcome. That doesn't disappear, Cass. It's part of you, and it's part of everyone who's ever been here."

Cass moved toward the far corner of the restaurant, stopping near a booth where she had sat countless times with her parents. She was silent for a moment, her posture shifting. "You always know what to say."

"It's part of my charm," Ayesha quipped, her tone light. "Seriously, though, I mean it. And I need to thank you, Cass. For trusting me with something so personal, so important. This was more than a project for me—it's the most meaningful thing I've ever worked on. When I started, I thought it was just a step to make some money. But now? I get it. I see the real value in what you and your family built."

Cass blinked, her hand resting on the back of the booth. "Ayesha... you didn't have to say that."

"I did," Ayesha said firmly. "Because it's true. You taught me so much, and I'll always carry that with me."

Cass's lips curved into a small smile. "You really are full of surprises, you know that?"

“Always,” Ayesha said, speaking firmly. “And Cass? Whatever happens next, you’re not doing it alone.”

“Thanks, Ayesha,” Cass said, her voice soft. “For everything.”

“Anytime,” Ayesha replied.

The line went quiet after they said goodbye. Cass slipped her phone back into her pocket, her fingers trailing along the edge of the booth, pausing briefly. She stood near the booth for a moment longer, running her fingers along its edge, before slowly making her way back toward the hostess stand. The voices around her ebbed and flowed, vibrant and alive, as Mr. Johnson approached her with a kind smile, moving calmly amid the bustle of the restaurant.

“Cass, I just wanted to say how much this place has meant to me and my family over the years,” he said, his tone measured but warm. He leaned in, pulling her into a gentle hug. “You’ve built something special here, and I know whatever comes next for you will be just as remarkable.”

He pulled back and scribbled something on a small piece of paper, pressing it into her hand. “Call me when you open your next spot,” he said with a wink. “I’ll bring my whole family—we’ll be your first customers.”

Cass looked down at the number in her hand, her smile growing as she nodded. “Thank you, Mr. Johnson. That means a lot.”

As he walked away, Cass slipped the paper into her pocket. She returned to the hostess stand, her hand brushing over its familiar grooves as the energy of the restaurant buzzed around her.

*****

The feedback jar at the front desk overflowed with comment cards, a testament to the community’s appreciation for the restaurant. As the last few guests made their way out, servers moved with brisk efficiency, clearing remaining dishes and carefully taking down the evening’s decorations. In the kitchen, the clatter of plates, the rush of steam, and the hum of the dishwasher signaled the final stage of the night’s work.

Cass stood near the counter, wiping down a tray. She glanced over at her father, Booker, who stood quietly at the center of the room with his hands resting on the countertop. His shoulders sagged slightly, and when he spoke, his tone was clear.

"I want to take a moment to acknowledge not just tonight, but how all of you have responded since learning that the restaurant would be closing," he said, directing his gaze around the kitchen. "We've known for some time that we were fighting uphill, on borrowed time. But the way you've faced it—with heart, resilience, and dedication—has been nothing short of extraordinary. You've been the soul of this place, the reason so many people kept coming back. As the famous coach said, 'We didn't lose, we ran out of time.' That's what this feels like—not a loss, but the end of the time we were given to fight."

Maria stood at the back with a tray of utensils, nodding with a small smile. Around her, the other servers exchanged glances. Their shoulders eased, the tension of the evening fading.

"To the front-of-house team under Maria—you set the tone. You welcomed every guest like they were family. I heard you received a significant amount in tips tonight. You deserve every cent of it," Booker said, speaking with an appreciative note.

Maria's smile widened, and she gave a small, teasing shrug. "We learned from the best," she quipped, earning a few chuckles.

Turning to the kitchen crew, Booker's expression softened. "To the kitchen team—you were outstanding tonight. We cooked beautifully, and the customers loved our food. You turned out plate after plate with precision and care, even when things got hectic."

Marcus, the head chef, lifted his chin, a grin curving at one corner of his mouth. "You keep giving speeches like that, Booker, and we might let you back on the line," he joked, prompting laughter from the kitchen staff.

The light mood settled as Booker exhaled, gripping the counter's edge. "But I need to say something else. I need to apologize. This isn't just about tonight. Over the years, I let you down in ways I'm still coming to terms with. I should have listened more. I should have seen what was happening right under my nose. And for that, I am deeply sorry."

Cass paused in her wiping, holding the tray against her side as she watched her father. He stood with shoulders slightly hunched, yet his words carried steadily through the room.

"We've learned a lot over these past few weeks," Booker continued. "Hard lessons, sure. But the biggest one? It's never too late to learn. Almost anyone can be a teacher if the student is humble enough to listen. And I've had some incredible teachers in this room."

Joey, the youngest on the team, shifted on his feet, returning Booker's glance with a quick, shy smile.

"You've taught me resilience, teamwork, and what it means to truly care about something bigger than yourself," Booker said, his voice wavering briefly. "We were able to return some of the items we recovered to our suppliers, but there's still fresh food here that can't wait. I want each of you to take as much as you need—vegetables, meat, dairy—whatever helps your families. Anything left will be donated to the shelter. This restaurant has always been about more than just serving meals; it's about taking care of people. Donating to the shelter is one last way we can give back."

He paused and looked down at a few papers in his hand. "We're still working through the finances. Once all the debts are settled, I'll calculate what's left and distribute it fairly among you. I know this hasn't been fair, and I want to do what I can to make it right."

Maria nodded, stepping forward. "We'll make sure everyone takes something home tonight," she said firmly.

"And you've been staying late, cleaning this place more than I could have asked for. But the final cleanup before the movers come? That'll be on me," Booker said, his voice resolute. "I'll be the one scrubbing the grease traps and mopping these floors one last time. It's my responsibility to close this chapter properly."

Maria laughed softly. "Even the storeroom, Booker?"

A ripple of laughter passed through the group as Booker nodded. "Yes, Maria, even the storeroom."

He stepped back, letting his hands fall to his sides. "What I hope you carry with you isn't the mistakes or the struggles—it's the good we created here. The connections we made, the meals we shared, the lives we touched. This restaurant was more than a business. It was a place where people felt seen, heard, and cared for."

Cass remained near the counter, tray in hand, her gaze trained on her father. Booker scanned the room. "Thank you for everything. I respect you, I value you, and yes—I love you. Love is a strong word, but it's the only one that fits. You've made this place what it is, and I will never forget that."

The room broke into applause, the sound echoing against the walls. Cass clapped along with the others, her smile unwavering as she watched Booker stand amidst the warm reception.

"Thank you, Booker," Maria said, raising her voice above the clapping. "For believing in us. For creating this place. We won't forget it either."

Marcus discreetly wiped at his eyes with the corner of his apron, and Joey offered Booker a hearty thumbs-up.

As the applause subsided, Booker caught Cass's eye. She nodded at him, meeting his gaze. He returned the nod, and they shared a brief exchange of relief.

The team began gathering their belongings, discussing how to divide the leftover produce. Booker stayed still for a few beats, observing, then turned to Cass.

"You okay, kid?" he asked quietly.

Cass stepped closer. "I'm more than okay, Dad. That was... incredible."

He set a hand on her shoulder. "We'll get through this, Cass. Together."

Cass nodded, placing the tray on the countertop. "Absolutely," she said, her voice steady. They stood side by side, watching the final moments of the restaurant's closing shift play out, prepared to face what lay beyond together.

SATURDAY, AUGUST 3 | JOURNAL ENTRY

1: The number of times I caught myself wanting to freeze time today. Everything felt so vivid, like the restaurant was alive in a way I hadn't seen in years. The hum of conversations, the clinking of silverware, the smell of food mingling with the scent of old books—it felt like the heart of this place was beating louder than ever.

22: The messages I got asking about the restaurant. Some were from friends, others from regulars who've been part of this place for as long as I can remember. It's overwhelming to hear how much the restaurant means to people, and it reminds me this isn't just about us—it's about a whole community that feels tied to these walls.

3: The times Ayesha stopped me in my tracks with her words today. "You're not walking away, Cass. You're carrying it with you." I don't even know how she does it—always knowing the right thing to say. And when she shared that story about her grandmother, I realized she was right. This place isn't going away; it's becoming part of me, part of all of us who've been here.

4: The photos I stopped to look at on the walls. There's one of Dad cutting the ribbon on opening day, and another of a packed room during a community event. But the one that hit me the hardest was our family, standing in front of the sign on opening day. We were all smiling, full of hope. It's hard to believe that moment was the beginning of a journey that's now coming to an end.

1: The note Mr. Johnson gave me today. "Call me when you open your next spot," he said, slipping me his number like it was no big deal. But it was a big deal. It felt like hope, like he believed in us enough to know there's something after this. I tucked that piece of paper into my pocket like it was a lifeline.

6: The hugs shared in the restaurant tonight. Maria and Linda hugged Dad like they were holding onto a piece of their own history. Customers hugged me, sharing their memories of meals and moments here. Even Ayesha squeezed me through the phone somehow with her words. I didn't realize how much I needed that until now.

5: The trays of leftover food Dad insisted on giving to the staff and donating to the shelter. "This place has always been about taking care of people," he said, and I felt it in my chest. It's not just about the food or the books or the walls. It's about the way this place has always made people feel seen and cared for.

This isn't just a goodbye—it's a reminder of what we've built here. Ayesha said the memories don't disappear when the doors close, and she's right. This restaurant will always be part of me. And no matter what happens next, I know we'll carry it forward.

MONDAY, AUGUST 5

The soft strains of "It's So Hard to Say Goodbye to Yesterday" drifted through the restaurant, a gentle counterpoint to the faint squeak of Booker's cloth against the counter. Chairs were stacked on tables, the chalkboard menu leaned awkwardly against the wall, and the faint scent of lemon cleaner lingered in the air. Yet the aroma built up from years of meals, laughter, and late nights still clung in place, unmoving.

Booker's hands moved in slow circles over the countertop, his shoulders slumped. His eyes lingered on the register, the same one he had taught Cass to use when she was just tall enough to reach the buttons. He opened his mouth as if to speak but paused, the cloth stalling mid-swipe.

Maya bustled by the bookshelves, her clipboard clutched tightly. Her pen tapped in rapid bursts against the board. "Cass, if you're just going to stand there, you might as well go home," she said sharply. Her tone cracked slightly, and she turned away, focusing on her list.

Cass stood still by the chalkboard, her hand brushing its smudged letters. "I am working," she said quietly. "I just... I don't know what to leave behind."

Maya sighed heavily, her pen coming to a stop. "We have a system. Keep for home. Keep for storage. Sell or donate. Throw away. Focus, Cass."

"No one's throwing anything away," Booker muttered. He moved toward the window, fiddling with the blinds despite their perfect alignment.

Cass's gaze shifted to a shelf of memorabilia. Her fingers grazed an old photo of her dad spinning vinyl at an event. The edges were curling, the image faded. "We can't just sell this," she murmured.

"Key personal items, Cass," Maya replied, her tone softening. "The rest has to go."

Booker sighed, leaning against the counter. His voice was quieter this time. "Gerald called earlier. Left me a message."

Maya froze, tension in her shoulders becoming more pronounced. "Gerald? The previous owner?"

Booker nodded, running a hand through his graying hair. "Yeah. He said he heard about the restaurant and wanted to reach out. He was... kind about it. Said something like, 'Business fails sometimes, but that doesn't erase what you built.'" Booker's voice cracked slightly, and he cleared his throat. "He said I have a lot to be proud of. That he knows how hard this is."

Maya's pen hovered above her clipboard, her expression relaxing. "That was nice of him," she said quietly.

Booker gave a small, dry laugh. "He also offered to reach out to some of his connections. Said he'd make sure we don't throw away any books. I told him we've got a system, but..." He trailed off, shaking his head. "I'll call him back later tonight. Maybe he can help us figure out what to do with the ones we can't keep."

Cass, standing near the bookshelf, turned to face them. "We can't just get rid of them, Dad," she said, her voice trembling. "These books aren't just decoration. They're part of what makes this place special."

Maya set her clipboard down, her hands smoothing the edges of her sweater. "Cass, we're not getting rid of them. Gerald's connections might find homes for them. They're not going in a dumpster. But we can't keep everything. You know that."

Cass's fingers brushed over the spines of the well-worn books, her gaze lingering on each title. "It's not fair," she whispered. "This place isn't just a restaurant. It's a part of us."

Booker stepped closer, resting a hand on her shoulder. "It is. And it always will be. But Gerald's right—it's not about the walls or the tables or even the books. It's about what we did here, the people we served. And that doesn't go away, Cass. Not ever."

Her phone buzzed in her pocket, and she glanced down at a string of texts from Logan, Isaiah, and Ayesha, each offering concern and help: Logan: "Thinking about you. Call if you need anything." Isaiah: "Don't forget, you're not alone in this. We're here." Ayesha: "This sucks. I hate that you're going through this, but you're strong. Don't forget that. ♡" A second buzz followed. Lola's name flashed on the screen.

Cass swiped to answer, her words halting slightly. "Lola, I can't talk right now."

"Cass, do you need anything? We can—"

"No," Cass interrupted. "Please let everyone know I'm fine. I'm just... probably not being a good friend right now. I need to spend time with my family."

Lola went quiet for a moment. "Okay. But if you change your mind..."

"Thanks, Lola," Cass said softly, ending the call.

She slipped her phone into her pocket and excused herself, retreating to the storage room she had turned into her makeshift office. Data notebooks and spreadsheets filled the desk, a clear reminder of her efforts. She sank into the chair, her head dropping into her hands as tears ran down her cheeks.

The door creaked open a few minutes later. Booker and Maya stepped in, their features drawn. Booker crouched beside her, placing a hand on her shoulder, while Maya knelt on her other side.

“Cass,” Booker began, his voice low. “You don’t have to carry all of this. This isn’t your fault or your responsibility.”

Maya’s voice lost its earlier edge, replaced by a calm resolve. “We’re proud of you, honey. You’ve done more than we ever could’ve asked for. You have the skills now to tackle so much more. There’s a bigger world out there—things that can really make an impact.”

Cass lifted her tear-streaked face, her words tumbling out. “But I don’t want anything else! I want this. I want to save this place. If I’d learned about data and technology sooner, maybe I could’ve helped more.”

Maya crouched beside her, keeping her gaze fixed on Cass. “No, you don’t. It might feel like you want this forever, but it’s not your dream, Cass. It’s ours. And it’s okay to let it go.”

Cass blinked, pausing as Booker settled his other hand on her shoulder. His tone was gentle but firm. “You’ve helped in ways we never imagined. But this isn’t the end. Professor Avery says the world’s changing, and it needs folks like you. People who can use technology to make things better for everyone.”

Maya leaned closer, her posture more open. “We’ve all noticed how you focus when you talk about new ideas. The things you did weren’t just for the restaurant—they were for you. You’ve always counted things, always excelled at math. Maybe this summer showed you a path you were always meant to take.”

Cass sniffled, her lips trembling as she looked from one parent to the other.

“A few weeks ago,” Maya went on, “you stood here and demanded that we follow the data and the truth. That’s who you are. And I think there are people out there who need to hear that same truth—from a brilliant, determined, Black young woman from Oakland like you.”

Booker smiled faintly, brushing away a tear. “You’ll carry this place with you, wherever you go. What you’ve learned here—it’s already shaping who you are.”

Maya reached for Cass’s hand, squeezing it tightly. “You’ll do great things, baby. This is just the start.”

Cass nodded slowly, her breathing now steady. She kept her gaze on the floor for a moment before exhaling.

The room grew quiet, broken only by the low hum of the refrigerator in the corner. Shadows stretched across the tables, and the stillness seemed to linger in the space.

The bell above the front door jingled softly, a gentle chime that often welcomed friends and familiar faces.

Booker, Cass, and Maya stopped talking, pausing to listen. The faint sound of voices carried through the hushed restaurant.

“Maria? Linda?” Booker called, his voice lifting slightly.

Cass and Maya exchanged glances before the three of them walked out from the back, nearly in step.

Maria and Linda stood near the entrance, their faces holding soft smiles. Maria’s fingers trembled around the bouquet she carried. Linda rested a hand on the door frame, as if steadying herself.

“We know you told us not to come, Booker,” Maria began, her voice shaking. “But we just couldn’t stay away. This place... it’s been like a second home. We had to see it again.”

Her eyes swept the room, shining with unshed tears.

Linda nodded, her voice hardly above a whisper. “I didn’t think it would be this difficult. But being here... it’s like saying goodbye to a piece of myself.”

Booker turned to face them, cloth still in hand. He stared for a moment, then cleared his throat, his voice catching briefly. “You didn’t have to come. I didn’t want it to be harder for anyone.”

Maria stepped forward, placing the bouquet on the counter. “For the restaurant,” she said softly. “For all the memories.”

Booker stepped closer, his face shifting as he opened his arms. “Come here, both of you.”

Maria went right into his embrace, her shoulders shaking as she leaned against him. “I don’t know how to say goodbye to this place,” she murmured.

Cass stood behind them, her posture rigid. She had grown up with Maria and Linda always around, their shared stories woven into the restaurant’s history. Seeing them now, eyes wet with emotion, made the moment even heavier.

Linda finally stepped further in, her gaze traveling over the chalkboard menu and the lines of books. "It doesn't feel real," she said, her voice breaking. "So many people loved this place."

Maria turned to Booker. "You've accomplished something amazing here. Never forget that."

Booker's jaw tensed. He gave a slow nod, his voice rough when it emerged. "Thank you. For everything."

The bell above the door sounded again, its ring cutting through the hush. Hal walked in.

Booker reached for the stereo, moving slowly as he turned off the music mid-lyric. The abrupt silence fell over the group.

"I thought I'd find you here," Hal said quietly, stepping into the room with a folder under his arm. His suit jacket was unbuttoned, tie slightly loosened - signs of a long day of meetings.

The kitchen crew paused their prep work, and Maya set down her clipboard. The sound of chopping ceased as everyone turned to watch Hal approach Booker.

"The buyer withdrew their offer," Hal announced, his voice carrying a mix of resignation and frustration. He pulled a chair from a nearby table and sat down heavily, placing the folder in front of him.

The words settled in the air, met by silence. Nobody responded at first, and Cass blinked, her posture tensing as Hal continued.

"Before anyone says anything, let me explain." He opened the folder, revealing documents with the city's letterhead. "The buyer discovered a lingering historic designation process from ten years ago. Gerald started it right before I bought the building, but it got hung up in the system somehow. Never approved, never denied - just sitting there." Hal's jaw tightened. "I've already started working to get it denied, but the Planning Commission has ninety days to respond. Until then, I'm legally required to disclose the pending designation to any potential buyer."

He ran a hand over his hair, exhaling sharply. "Do you understand what position this puts me in? If the designation goes through, renovation costs could double. No modern HVAC, no structural changes without special approval." He tapped the documents with his index finger. "I had plans for this capital. Now I'm stuck with a property I can't easily sell, and my money is tied up here while the bureaucrats take their time. Any serious buyer is going to walk away or demand a steep discount until this gets resolved."

Cass's hands curled on the back of the chair. Her voice wavered. "Mr. Rodríguez, I'm sorry about what I said before. Please—"

Hal raised a hand, cutting her off. "Hold that apology. Sometimes the market has other plans." His mouth twisted slightly. "The deal is off, and for now, you can stay."

Booker straightened in his chair, his gaze steady. "Hal, now that the restaurant's improving, we might qualify for financing. If you'll consider it, I'd like to revisit our original arrangement."

Hal tilted his head, studying Booker with renewed interest. He closed the folder slowly. "That's an interesting proposition." His tone remained businesslike. "Find your own lender and bring me a solid offer. Then we'll talk. But don't expect me to wait forever if another buyer comes along who can handle the historic designation."

Cass glanced at Booker and squared her shoulders. She took in Hal's skeptical look, but she turned toward her father, as if silently voicing support for his idea.

Cass nodded, her words careful. "Thank you, Mr. Rodríguez. We won't waste this chance."

Hal's expression shifted slightly, though he remained brisk. "See that you don't." He stood, tucking the folder under his arm. His chair scraped against the floor as he pushed it back. The door swung shut behind him with a soft click.

The echo of Hal's departure lingered, and nobody spoke at first. The kitchen crew gradually resumed their work, the quiet sounds of preparation filling the silence. Booker let out a breath. He rubbed a hand over his face, his features shifting from tightness toward a more relaxed look.

"Well," he said, breaking the silence, "you might have heard him differently, but I heard him say, 'the place is ours.' He just doesn't know it yet!"

Maya raised an eyebrow, clipboard still in hand. "What do you mean, Booker?"

Without answering, Booker walked to the stereo. His movements were calm and deliberate as he turned the volume dial and pressed play. The familiar opening bars of "Ain't No Stoppin' Us Now" by McFadden & Whitehead flooded the room. A new energy seemed to ripple through the space.

Maya blinked, her lips twitching in a nearly concealed smile. "Booker Freeman, what are you doing?"

"What does it look like?" he replied, stepping closer with a playful light in his eyes. "I'm celebrating. Come on, Maya. We could all use a little joy."

Before she could object, he grasped her hand and led her toward the open floor near the tables. Cass paused for a moment, watching as her parents began to sway together in time with the music. Booker spun Maya once, then again, and she laughed—a bright sound that carried across the room.

"Dad!" Cass called out, a smile spreading across her face.

"Don't just stand there, babygirl," Booker said, his voice spirited. "Join us!"

Cass lingered briefly, then laughed as Maria grabbed her hand. "Come on, Cass," Maria urged, pulling her onto the makeshift dance floor. Linda followed, flashing an easy grin as she clapped in rhythm.

The restaurant, once tense with worry, was suddenly buoyed by lively motion. Cass moved in a hesitant twirl, but the encouraging beat around her led her into easier steps. Maya slipped an arm around Cass, guiding her in a loose spin.

Cass watched Booker dip Maya dramatically, drawing more laughter. She stood still for an instant, focusing on the sight of them dancing with complete abandon.

"You okay?" Maria asked, stepping beside her.

Cass nodded, her tone soft. "Yeah. I think I am."

Maria nudged her gently. "Good. Because this? This is everything."

Cass looked around, taking in Booker and Maya dancing, Linda sharing a joke with Mike, and Joey pulling exaggerated moves that had everyone clapping. The restaurant buzzed with a momentary brightness. Cass kept her eyes on the swirl of motion, staying in that hopeful space a little longer.

As the song ended, Booker raised his hands with flourish. "One more!" he called out, a broad grin lighting his features.

MONDAY, AUGUST 5 | JOURNAL ENTRY

1: The number of miracles I witnessed today. I can't believe I'm even writing that word, but that's what it feels like—a miracle. Grandpa said he and Grandma had been praying for this, that they always knew it would work out. I don't know if I believed him until now, but maybe they were right. Maybe this really was divine timing or something close to it.

3: The number of times I caught myself crying today. Not the sad kind of crying, but the overwhelmed, "how did this even happen" kind. This morning felt like the end of everything. We were packing up, saying goodbye, and now, here we are, unpacking and putting things back like we never left. It's surreal.

2: The number of people I saw glowing with happiness—my parents. I've never seen them like this, not even on their best days. Mom had this energy that made me feel like everything was finally going to be okay, and Dad? He smiled so much today I didn't even recognize him at first. It's like a weight they've been carrying for years just vanished.

8: The shocked faces of Logan, Lola, and Ayesha when I told them the news. Lola's jaw literally dropped, and Ayesha kept saying, "Wait, what? Are you serious?!" over and over. Logan just smiled in that quiet way he does and said, "I knew you'd figure it out." Hearing that from him made me feel… I don't even know. Seen, maybe? Loved, for sure.

4: The hours Maria and Linda stayed tonight, helping us unpack everything we'd boxed up. They didn't even ask—they just started pulling things out and putting them back in place, like they wanted to make sure the restaurant felt like itself again. Maria even rearranged the bookshelves with me, and we ended up talking about some of her favorite novels. It was the most normal moment in a day that felt anything but.

FRIDAY, AUGUST 9

The sun sank low, casting the sky in soft hues of orange and pink, which shimmered on the rippling surface of the Oakland Estuary. Cass kept her eyes on the path, the crunch of pebbles underfoot blending with the soft lap of water against the rocks. Her fingers fidgeted with the seam of her jeans, and her steps occasionally faltered as she matched Logan's pace.

The salty tang of the bay filled the air, mixing with the sweet scent of blooming jasmine from a nearby garden. A lone sailboat drifted across the water, its white sail catching the fading sunlight. In the distance, the hum of a boat engine merged with the rustling leaves on the breeze, underscoring the twilight scene they shared.

They walked in a companionable quiet, their hands brushing, sometimes folding together for a moment before letting go. Their steps kept time with the gravel's crunch, and distant seagulls cried overhead, adding gentle echoes to the evening calm. Cass slowed whenever Logan's hand lingered in hers, glancing at the path, the water, and the breeze that lifted her hair. Each occasional touch of his fingers gave her pause, as though wordless signals passed between them.

"Cass, can I ask you something?" Logan's voice broke the silence.

Cass looked up, letting out a small laugh. "Of course, Logan. Anything. But other than my mom and my granny," she added, punctuating the moment with a playful chuckle.

She drew in a sharp breath when Logan stopped, turning fully to face her. The fading sunlight painted his features in a soft, golden glow. His voice was low under the wind and waves.
"I've been thinking a lot about... us," he began, "about what happened at the farmers market, how we've been connecting lately, and... the last soccer game." He paused, his expression intent. Cass stood still and listened, her posture rigid as he spoke.

"I really like you, Cass. Like, really like you," he went on. "And I know things aren't settled right now—with the restaurant, school, and everything—but I wanted to be honest with you." He paused, his gaze steady. "I don't want to be with anyone else. I want to be with you."

Cass was silent for a moment before finally saying, "Logan, I—" The words caught in her throat as a small, nervous smile curved her lips.

"Logan..." she began again, her voice unsteady. She took a deep breath. "I like you too. A lot. And I want to thank you. For everything. Thank you for your patience and support and for understanding what I've been juggling with the restaurant. It's given me a new respect and admiration for you."

Logan beamed and gently cupped her cheek, his eyes bright in the gilded light. "Can I kiss you?" he asked. A wave broke against the pebbles nearby, and the wind whipped around them, carrying off the soft "yes" Cass breathed as she nodded.

Logan leaned in, closing the short distance. Their lips met in a gentle, tentative kiss that gradually deepened. The sound of the surging water accompanied them, the evening air wrapping around the pair as they shared that moment by the shore.

They eased apart, and Cass's cheeks showed a faint flush as her breath came in short bursts. She looked up at Logan, standing close at the water's edge.
They stayed in place, fingers intertwined.
"I've wanted to do that for so long," he murmured.
"Me too," she answered, a shy smile appearing. She tilted her head toward the sky, where the first stars blinked against a darkening blue. Nearby, two birds settled on the branch of a tree.

Cass inhaled the salt air. "So, what does this mean for us, Logan?"
He glanced at her. "I believe we can be together if that's what you want too, Cass."
She nodded, shifting her gaze from Logan to the birds perched side by side. "I want to be with you, but there's a lot going on in my life right now. I don't want to pull you into that chaos."
Logan shook his head, his hand settling over hers. "You're not dragging me into anything. I want to be part of it, both the good and the bad. We'll figure it out. But I need to know—do you want me or Isaiah?"

Cass studied Logan's face.
"Logan, I've always liked you. And you know Isaiah is into Lola, right?"
"Yeah, I know," Logan said. "But sometimes, watching how you two talk, I wonder if there's... something else there."
Cass chuckled, shaking her head as the breeze tousled her hair. Logan reached over and gently tucked a loose strand behind her ear.
"You, Logan," she said, her voice unwavering. "I want you."

Logan's face lit up, catching the last rays of sun. "You have no idea how glad that makes me," he said, drawing her into a firm embrace.
She turned slightly and glanced toward the distant lights by the water. Then she looked up at him again. "I'm trying to balance the restaurant, figure out data science for my future, and keep everything under control," she said quietly, "but I want you beside me while I figure it out."

Cass rested her head against Logan's arm as they strolled along the estuary. They traded stories of summer camp adventures, funny school memories, and future aspirations. The path curved near a secluded bench overlooking the water, and Logan gestured toward it. They settled onto the weathered seat, which gave a gentle creak. The sky had deepened into a rich blue, and stars shone above like tiny beacons.

They sat without speaking for a while, watching the starlight shimmer on the water. A cool breeze carried the distant hum of conversation and faint music from nearby cafés. Logan slipped an arm around Cass's shoulders, pulling her closer so she could rest her head on his shoulder.

"This feels nice," Cass whispered, her gaze fixed on the glittering horizon. "Promise me this isn't just a fling or experiment."
"I promise," Logan said, pressing a light kiss to her hair.

They lingered together for a while, leaning into each other. As they neared Cass's house, Logan slowed his steps, looking toward the illuminated windows. A small figure—Carver—peered out, eyes wide. Cass laughed, waving for him to move along. Someone inside pulled him away from the window.

Their shared laughter faded into the evening air. "I think the boys are going to roast me once I get inside," Cass joked.
She turned back to Logan, noticing a subtle change in his expression. The smile stayed, but his tone shifted. "Cass, there's something I've been meaning to ask you."
"What is it, Logan?"
"Are you ready to make this official?"
"I'm ready."
"Then let's capture our first kiss and share it with the world!" he said, grinning mischievously.

Cass let out a bubbly laugh, clapping her hands once. "Let's do it!"
They stood side by side as Logan lifted his phone, adjusting the angle until both faces filled the frame. He leaned in for another kiss, and the camera's click cut through the night, preserving that instant against the backdrop of the softly lit street.

FRIDAY, AUGUST 9 | JOURNAL ENTRY

1: The number of times I've said it to myself tonight—I have a boyfriend. OMG, I have a boyfriend. I don't even know how to process that yet, but it feels so surreal and amazing at the same time.

5: The days we spent prepping for the fall menu launch. Every single second of the chaos was worth it. Seeing the restaurant alive tonight, full of laughter and clinking glasses, felt like watching a dream come to life. Mom was in her creative zone, pulling everything together with this energy I haven't seen in years. It reminded me of how much this place means to her, to all of us.

8: The number of looks Logan and I got tonight. I know what they're thinking—he's white, I'm Black. I could practically hear the questions behind those stares. But honestly? I don't care. Logan makes me feel seen in a way I didn't know I needed. Let them look. We've got nothing to prove to anyone but each other.

2: The times Logan brought me boba this week. He's definitely taken over Lola's role as my official supplier, and honestly, I'm not mad about it. He even remembered my weirdly specific order—half sweetness, extra tapioca. It's the little things like that, you know?

3: The number of dishes Dad let Logan taste tonight. Watching them connect was so cool—like, I've never seen Dad so chill around a guy I'm into. Logan was all polite and asking about the spices like he was trying out for MasterChef. And when Dad laughed at one of his jokes? That sealed it. Logan fits in, even when everything feels like a whirlwind.

6: The times I've replayed our walk by the estuary in my head. The way the sunset hit the water, the way he looked at me when he said he wanted to be with me—it's like every rom-com I've ever watched suddenly made sense. And that first kiss… I don't even have words. Just thinking about it makes my stomach do these weird flip things.

7: The conversations we had on that bench, about everything from summer camp to what we want to do in the future. He doesn't just listen—he actually hears me. It's wild to think that if I hadn't gone to camp, if I hadn't learned all this data stuff, none of this would've happened. The restaurant might not have survived, and I might not have met Logan the way I did. It's like every decision I made led me to this moment.

1: The promise he made to me tonight. "This isn't a fling, Cass. I'm in this for real." Hearing him say that? It was like someone put all my doubts in a box and locked it up. For the first time in a long time, I feel like I'm not just balancing the chaos—I'm building something strong, something worth holding on to.

I don't know what's ahead for us or for the restaurant, but tonight feels like the beginning of something bigger. And I'm ready for it.

SATURDAY, AUGUST 10

The restaurant glowed under strings of fairy lights, the air filled with movement and conversation. Light patterns shifted across the ceiling, reflecting off the polished wooden floors. The tables, tucked against the walls, opened the space for dancing and mingling. The scent of freshly baked bread and spiced cider blended with cinnamon and floral arrangements, filling the room.

Laughter and the clinking of glasses added texture to the evening, creating a symphony of celebration. Guests arrived for the fall menu preview, the culmination of weeks of preparation. Cass and Lola had worked together to invite all their friends, filling the space with familiar faces and warm laughter. As the crowd streamed in, Lola leaned close to Cass and whispered, “This turnout is amazing.”

Cass grinned, nodding toward the growing crowd. “I know. It’s like everyone really wanted to be here tonight.” Their shared excitement sparked as they exchanged high-fives before splitting up to greet more friends.

Cass positioned herself at the entrance, welcoming guests with a smile, a quick handshake, or a brief hug. Nearby, her parents, Maya and Booker, mingled with ease, shaking hands and exchanging warm words with familiar faces. Maya’s laughter rose above the hum of conversation as she reconnected with an old friend, while Booker clapped a guest on the back, his steady presence anchoring the room’s energy.

Cass crouched to chat with a young child holding a balloon, her laughter ringing out as she pointed him toward the dessert table. With each new face that arrived, she exchanged warm greetings, ensuring everyone felt welcomed into the bustling celebration. Adjusting her dress absently, she continued to circulate, her energy mirroring the vibrant atmosphere of the room.

“Cass!” Ayesha’s voice rang out above the hum of chatter. She burst through the doors, her parents trailing behind, their eyes widening as they took in the neatly lined shelves and gleaming wood accents of the old library. The colors shimmered under the lights as she pulled Cass into a tight, exuberant hug. “You’ve told me about the history, but seeing it in person? This is unreal!”

Cass replied, “Thanks, but it was mostly my mom’s vision. And Lola helped a ton—she’s been orchestrating everything like a maestro all day.”

Ayesha grinned knowingly. “Your mom is incredible, and this place is just breathtaking,” she said, her gaze sweeping across the room. “Where’s Isaiah? Not here yet?”

“I need to soak all of this in,” Ayesha said, spinning slowly as the lights shimmered against the polished wood. “It feels like stepping into a different world.”

“But don’t forget about the food,” Cass said with a playful nudge, her smile widening.

“Never,” Ayesha said, flashing a grin as she turned back to take another look at the room.

The hum of chatter and laughter blended seamlessly with the low bassline of “Candy Rain” by Soul for Real playing softly in the background. Guests swayed slightly to the rhythm, their conversations punctuated by subtle head bobs and knowing smiles exchanged over the familiar track.

Cass’s grin widened as she noticed Logan slipping through the door, a bouquet of roses in his hand. “You made it!” she exclaimed.

“Wouldn’t miss it,” Logan replied warmly, handing her the flowers. “Thought these might add to the magic tonight.”

Nearby, Sophia and Alex entered with their parents following behind, their smiles wide as they took in the festive scene. Moments later, Isaiah walked through the doors with his mother by his side. Cass’s face lit up with recognition, recalling their last visit when Mrs. Harris had shared stories about Isaiah’s childhood. For Lola, however, it was the first time meeting her. Mrs. Harris carried herself with the same warm yet confident demeanor, her smile inviting as she stepped into the lively scene.

Lola, standing nearby, seemed to straighten her posture and step forward, her voice cheerful as she greeted them. “Hi, Mrs. Harris! I’m Lola,” she added eagerly, extending her hand. “I helped Cass with the decorations tonight.”

Isaiah’s mother smiled graciously and shook Lola’s hand. “Thank you, dear. It’s wonderful to be here. This place looks absolutely beautiful. And yes, I also heard Isaiah mention you bought him his very first boba!” Lola grinned at Isaiah, her enthusiasm evident as she said, “He wouldn’t stop talking about it—it’s such a sweet memory!”

Cass nodded toward Mrs. Harris with a warm smile. “We’re so glad you could make it. It means a lot to have you here tonight. Now please get in there and try some of the hors d’oeuvres! Make sure to grab the Cajun Style Fried Deviled Eggs—they’re something special.”

Not far behind, Ayesha and Isaiah’s mothers arrived, exchanging warm greetings with Booker and Maya. Logan’s parents followed shortly after, their expressions a mix of curiosity and delight as Booker introduced them to Maya.

"It's so wonderful to finally meet you," Logan's mother said warmly.

Maya extended her hand with a welcoming smile. "Likewise. I've heard so much about you both." Cass stepped in to greet Logan's parents, who turned to her with warm expressions.

"We're so proud Logan has met someone like you," his mother said, her tone sincere. "You're welcome at our house any time." Cass nodded, her gratitude conveyed through her smile. Cass stepped away quietly as the conversation shifted toward medicine and healthcare. A little later, she found her mom near the dessert table, straightening a floral arrangement.

"Mom, everything looks perfect," Cass said, stepping closer.

Maya turned, her face lighting up. "Thanks, sweetheart. You know, just decorating the place with Lola was so much fun. It reminded me of how much I've missed doing this kind of thing."

"You mean, like, parties and decorating?" Cass asked, tilting her head.

"Not just decorating," Maya said, gesturing around the room. "Creating something beautiful, bringing people together. I've already got ideas for a holiday theme. Imagine snowflakes, warm lights, maybe even a cocoa bar."

Cass smiled. "That sounds amazing. You should go for it, Mom."

Maya placed a hand on Cass's shoulder. "I think I will. It's time to start re-embracing my passions."

Cass nodded, her hands brushing over the edge of the tablecloth as she leaned closer to Maya, the soft hum of conversations filling the space between them. "Let me know how I can help. I'm all in." A little later, she found her mom near the dessert table, straightening a floral arrangement.

Warm greetings and familiar voices surrounded her, each exchange adding energy to the evening. She paused briefly near the dessert table as Isaiah cracked a joke, drawing a burst of laughter from nearby guests. Cass smiled, watching as guests leaned toward one another, their animated conversations punctuated by bursts of laughter that rippled through the room. Nearby, Maria approached Cass and Booker, her expression serious but hopeful. "I just heard," Maria said softly, leaning closer. "Mike and Sarah were given a suspended sentence."

Booker nodded, his expression thoughtful. "Yeah, I heard too. Their lawyers also called about setting up some restitution."

Maria's eyebrows lifted slightly. "That's good to hear," she said, glancing around at the festive crowd. "At least there's some accountability."

Cass exchanged a look with Booker before Maria excused herself, heading back toward the kitchen. Maria's words prompted Cass and Booker to exchange a glance. Booker straightened his tie, then rubbed the back of his neck, exhaling deeply before nodding. Cass adjusted her dress and gestured toward the dessert table, motioning to a group of guests as the sound of laughter and conversation swirled around them, blending seamlessly with the celebratory energy. Grace's warm thanks to Maya drifted toward her. Nearby, Cass overheard Linda speaking animatedly to a group of guests. "I'm so happy to be back," Linda said, her voice bright with enthusiasm, her hands gesturing expressively. The group nodded warmly, offering encouraging words as they clinked glasses in celebration of her return. Nearby, laughter from her old soccer teammates bubbled up, carrying shared memories of seasons past. Across the room, Grandpa James was deep in conversation with Mr. Johnson, a long-time customer, discussing the Port of Oakland and its impact on the community. At the dessert table, someone exclaimed over a dish from the new fall menu, telling Booker, "This sweet potato risotto is absolutely divine—I've never tasted anything like it." When Booker turned to nod toward her, Cass adjusted the strap of her bag and continued circulating through the room. She noticed Lola standing off to the side, her shoulders slightly slumped. Cass followed her gaze to the door, where it was clear her parents hadn't arrived. Later, Cass saw Lola chatting animatedly with Grandma Lillian, her spirits clearly lifted.

Grace Chen, the administrator of the clinic where Maya volunteered, entered with her characteristic warm smile and a kind word for everyone she passed. She paused to speak with Cass, lightly touching her arm. "Cass, I heard from your mom about everything you've been doing here. She also told me about your project on asthma rates. I would love to hear more about it sometime. She's so proud of you, and honestly, I can see why. The combination of your leadership and creativity sounds is remarkable." As she approached Maya, her tone softened. "Maya, it's so good to see you here. Are you ready to come back to volunteering at the clinic? We miss having you around."

Moments later, Professor Avery arrived, her commanding presence instantly captivating the room. Dressed elegantly yet understatedly, she made her way to Maya first, pulling her into a warm hug. Cass caught a snippet of Professor Avery's later conversation with Dawson about data and financial literacy, their words weaving a thread of optimism for future projects.

"Thank you so much for the invitation, Maya. It means the world to be here tonight," Avery said sincerely. After exchanging smiles, she moved to shake hands with

Booker before turning to Cass.

“Cass,” she began, her voice resonant with pride. “Tonight is not just about the restaurant. It’s about resilience, growth, and the data-driven journey that got us here. Your ability to analyze trends, identify opportunities, and rally the team has been remarkable. The results speak for themselves—not just in numbers, but in the atmosphere tonight. I couldn’t be prouder.”

Professor Avery glanced at Peter Dawson nearby and added, “In fact, I’d love to profile this project in the department newsletter. It’s a perfect example of how data science and community collaboration can create lasting change.”

Cass straightened and said, “Thank you, Professor. That means so much.”

The energy shifted as Peter Dawson, a familiar face from the CDFI, arrived. His firm handshake for Booker and steady presence brought an air of reassurance. “This is what community looks like,” he said warmly. “You’ve built something special here, and it’s only the beginning.”

After a moment, Dawson added thoughtfully, “Booker, Maya, if it’s okay with you, I’d love to discuss the possibility of leveraging some of Cass’s strategies for other local businesses. What she’s done here is remarkable, and it could be a real game-changer for others in the community.”

Cass’s former soccer coaches entered next, their boisterous laughter filling the room. One joked, “She’s still dodging cleanup duties, I bet!” Cass adjusted the strap of her bag and joined in the lighthearted laughter.

Booker invited everyone to take their seats as the meal was about to begin. Cass moved quickly through the room, ensuring everything was in order, her energy vibrant as she greeted guests and coordinated final touches. Logan’s mother caught her attention, waving gently. “Cass, we saved a seat for you,” she called warmly, gesturing to a spot at their table. Cass hesitated for a moment, scanning the room to ensure all was running smoothly, before making her way over with a grateful smile.

Guests marveled at the beautifully arranged dishes as servers moved gracefully through the room, trays balanced with precision. Plates of sweet potato risotto, slow-roasted beef brisket, and shrimp with fried corn fritters were garnished with delicate microgreens, showcasing artistry that married comfort with elegance. The aroma of the sweet potato risotto and other fall menu highlights filled the air, creating a quiet buzz of excitement as servers described the dishes in soft, practiced tones.

The sweet potato risotto, topped with fried sage leaves crackling under a drizzle of brown butter, filled the air with a nutty warmth. Plates of slow-roasted brisket shimmered with a glossy ancho-chili glaze, garnished with ribbons of pickled red onions. Shrimp rested atop golden fried corn fritters, paired with a vibrant herb aioli that popped with citrus. A signature fall drink—spiced apple cider with a twist of candied ginger—was served by the servers in glass mugs that fogged slightly from the warmth.

Ayesha leaned toward Professor Avery with a playful grin. "Keep this between us," she whispered conspiratorially, "but this new menu is already 20% more profitable than the last one. Cass's strategies really hit the mark."

Professor Avery's brows lifted with admiration. "Impressive," she replied softly. "She's just getting started." Her eyes twinkled with pride as she nodded, keeping Ayesha's secret safe.

Around the room, audible gasps of appreciation mixed with murmurs of approval as guests took their first bites. "This risotto is unbelievable—I've never had anything like it!" one guest exclaimed, their voice cutting through the hum of conversation. Another leaned closer to their tablemates, nodding enthusiastically over the tender brisket, their fork raised mid-air.

Phones flashed as a few food bloggers captured the artistry of the dishes, their quiet commentary adding to the vibrant energy of the room. The buzz of approval swirled around the tables, amplifying the sense that Cass's work was not only strategic but truly transformative.

"This isn't just food—it's a story on a plate," one of the bloggers said softly as they adjusted their angle for another shot. Another added, "This is going to blow up online. Elevated soul food with heart? People will love it."

Cass glanced toward the servers weaving through the tables with smooth efficiency, catching snippets of guests' delighted reactions as plates were passed. She exhaled with a quiet sense of satisfaction, her focus already shifting to ensure the next course was ready.

After the meal booker cleared his throat, Booker spoke with steady conviction, his hand lightly brushing the microphone as he glanced at Maya standing beside him. Her admiring gaze locked on him, her pride unmistakable as she stood tall, her hand resting gently on his back.

"Tonight, we're not just celebrating survival—we're celebrating progress, we're celebrating ownership!" Booker's voice rang out, commanding the room's attention.

“Alright, son!” Grandpa James called out, his voice booming with pride as he raised his glass. He gave Booker a firm nod, the gesture brimming with quiet approval.

Booker stood tall, his voice resonating with pride and gratitude. “Through a partnership with Peter Dawson and the City of Oakland, I’m thrilled to announce that we’ve secured financing for the building. And Hal has officially accepted our offer to purchase it.”

He paused, a smile spreading across his face. “I can’t tell you how happy it makes me to know we’ve been able to buy this property—not just to own it, but to ensure its future as a cornerstone of this community.”

The crowd erupted in cheers, glasses raised high in celebration. Hal, seated nearby, lifted his glass with a warm, approving smile. “To Hal and Booker!” a guest called out, prompting a spontaneous toast. Hal nodded graciously, his smile widening as he exchanged a look of quiet satisfaction with Booker.

Beside Booker, Maya leaned in, her voice just audible above the applause. “You’ve always been the heart of this, Booker. They can see it now.”

Her words brought a soft laugh from him, a flicker of gratitude crossing his face as he glanced her way. He raised his own glass in acknowledgment, his gaze sweeping the room.

Gasps of surprise quickly turned into enthusiastic applause, the room alive with energy. Booker raised a hand to gently quiet the crowd, his voice steady with emotion as he continued, “This restaurant has always been more than just a business. It’s a home where we’ve shared meals, laughter, and life itself. And while these past few months have been challenging, tonight is about resilience and hope. Because of all of you, we’re still here, and now, we’re here to stay.”

Booker turned slightly, his voice softening as he added, “I also want to take a moment to thank Maya—my partner in every sense of the word. Maya, your vision for this place has always been the light guiding us forward. Thank you for keeping us grounded and pushing us to dream bigger.”

Maya, standing beside him, gently squeezed his arm, her pride evident in her smile as Booker’s words resonated through the room.

He paused again, scanning the crowd with warmth in his eyes, his expression softening as he began to acknowledge the people who made the night possible. “None of this would be possible without Cass, Ayesha, Isaiah, and Lola. Their determination and creativity have kept this place alive. And what made all the difference was the data. By identifying where we were losing money, streamlining our operations, and optimizing our supply chain, the team transformed what seemed impossible into reality."

Booker's voice grew stronger as he continued, "I also want to give a special thanks to Professor Avery for challenging my perspective on the role of technology in the community. Her insights pushed us to embrace innovation in a way that serves everyone. Let's give them the round of applause they deserve."

The crowd erupted into applause once again, the infectious energy building as guests clinked their glasses and embraced the celebratory moment. Cass caught her mom's eye across the room, and Maya raised her glass slightly in a silent gesture of pride, her smile unwavering as the fairy lights cast a gentle shimmer across her face.

Nearby, Grandpa James and Aunt Zora shared a laugh, reminiscing about family gatherings. Their quiet words of encouragement blended into the celebratory hum of the room, grounding the evening in a shared sense of history and hope for the future.

Booker steadied his voice, his conviction unshaken as he brought the moment to a close. "This restaurant has always been more than just a business. It's a home—a place where we've shared laughter, meals, and life itself. And while these past few months have tested us, tonight is a reminder of what's possible when we come together. Because of all of you, we're still here, and now, we're here to stay."

Another wave of cheers and applause broke out, filling the space with renewed energy. Cass exchanged a knowing smile with her mom, their connection mirrored in their matching expressions of pride and joy. Across the room, Booker's parents and Aunt Zora laughed together, their voices rising briefly above the din as they reminisced about family traditions and offered quiet encouragement for the future.

The evening crescendoed as Booker turned up the stereo, the opening chords of Yeah! by Usher, Lil Jon & Ludacris filling the room.

A collective "OHHHHH!" rang out, followed by laughter and claps.

Maya arched an eyebrow, hands on her hips as she turned to Booker. "Really?"

Booker just grinned, pulling her toward the center of the floor. "Come on now, you know this is a classic."

Maya shook her head but couldn't fight her smile as they started to move, her body falling into rhythm against his. Their movements grew bolder with every beat, Booker adding an extra spin that made Maya laugh out loud.

Guests twirled and swayed around them, their laughter blending with the music. Across the room, Isaiah grabbed Lola's hand and pulled her toward the floor. "C'mon, no sitting this one out."

Lola giggled, rolling her eyes but following his lead, letting him twirl her under his arm before they both bounced to the beat.

Cass spotted her brothers, Carver and Archer, near the edge of the dance floor. Carver nudged Archer, a grin spreading across his face. "Bet you can't keep up."

"Oh, bet," Archer shot back.

Without hesitation, they jumped in, their moves sharp and full of energy. Archer stomped, and Carver slid effortlessly beside him. They fed off the cheers, spinning and hitting every beat like they'd been waiting for this moment.

"Alright, Carver and Archer!" someone called out, and a ripple of applause followed.

Meanwhile, a group of food bloggers in the corner lifted their phones, recording live. Their excited whispers mixed with the beat. Even Professor Avery clapped to the rhythm, her usual composed demeanor giving way to genuine enjoyment.

Logan leaned toward Cass, grinning like he'd been waiting for this all night. "It's our turn, girl. We're not sitting this one out."

Cass let out a short laugh, shaking her head, but Logan was already leading her to the floor.

To her surprise, his moves were smooth, confident, making the small crowd around them cheer as they fell into sync.

Cass matched him easily, letting herself enjoy the moment as their steps blended seamlessly with the music.

Then, just as Ludacris' verse hit, Cass broke away, rushing toward the stereo.

The music cut out for half a second—a brief moment of confusion, anticipation crackling through the air.

Logan looked at her, breathless. "What are you doing?"

Cass's fingers moved with precision, scrolling through the playlist before smirking.

"Hold up," she called out. "Y'all forget about the Electric Slide!"

A few cheers erupted, but Cass wasn't done.

“We’re doing the Brookfield and the Smeeze tonight!”

The speakers kicked back to life, and over the sound system came a commanding:

“GIVE ME A BEAT!”

A new bassline dropped, LaRussell’s GIVE ME A BEAT! hitting the room like a shockwave.

The crowd roared.

Carver and Archer immediately hit the Brookfield, their arms swinging with effortless style as their feet bounced to the rhythm.

Isaiah and Ayesha slid back into the Smeeze, their moves so clean and fluid that guests stopped dancing just to watch.

Lola grabbed Cass’s wrist, pulling her forward. “Nah, girl, you started this. Show ‘em what you got.”

Cass bit her lip, hesitating for half a second—then hopped straight into the Smeeze, her rhythm perfect.

“OH, SHE REALLY DO THIS,” Ayesha hollered, hyped beyond belief.

Even Logan—who had NO idea what was happening—watched, grinning like he just discovered something new about her.

Across the floor, Isaiah spun Lola dramatically, then transitioned into a slow, exaggerated Thizz Dance, his head bobbing with playful exaggeration.

Carver and Archer joined in, their arms locked as they perfected a synchronized Oakland Boogie.

More guests jumped in, mimicking the moves as best they could. A few struggled with the Smeeze, but that didn’t stop them from trying

Maya, breathless from laughter, turned to Booker. “We are never getting these kids off the floor now.”

Booker chuckled, shaking his head, but his expression was nothing but pride.

The floor wasn’t just full—it was alive.

The music, the laughter, the movement—it all swelled into something bigger than a party.

This was culture. This was community. This was a win.

Cass wiped her forehead, breathless but buzzing with joy.

She turned to Logan, who was still watching her, an amused smirk on his lips.

"So," she panted. "You still think I don't know how to celebrate?"

Logan laughed, shaking his head. "You win, Freeman."

Cass grinned.

Just then, the speakers crackled again.

E-40's unmistakable voice hit the room, deep and smooth, riding over a bassline that rattled the floor.

Cass raised an eyebrow at Logan. "Now, this is how we do it."

And with that, she stepped back into the music, the room pulsing with life, rhythm, and the unstoppable energy of a city that knew how to celebrate.

SATURDAY, AUGUST 10 | JOURNAL ENTRY

1: The number of people I counted on my side when this day began—and it was just me. But by the end of tonight? I've lost track. Maybe that's what real community feels like—like people pulling you in when you least expect it.

2: Logan's parents were so nice. I was nervous, like sweaty-palms-awkward laugh nervous, but they just smiled like they'd known me forever. When his mom said, "We're proud Logan met someone like you," I didn't even know how to answer. Do you just say "thanks"? Because I felt like I needed to say more, like, "I'm trying, but I don't always feel like I'm enough." But then Logan grinned at me, and all that insecurity kinda melted away. Meeting them made me realize how much this connection means—not just to me, but to the people who care about him too.

3: The times I wanted to cry when I saw the restaurant glowing tonight. There was this moment, when I was standing by the entrance, watching guests pour in, and it hit me: this wouldn't have happened if I hadn't gone to that camp. If I hadn't learned how to make sense of all those confusing spreadsheets or figure out where the money was leaking, we'd probably be closing our doors instead of hosting a celebration. That camp wasn't just about data—it was about finding a part of myself I didn't even know existed. Who knew Excel could feel this powerful?

4: The conversations with Hal that made me rethink everything. I used to think he was just this gruff guy who didn't care about the restaurant's future. But seeing him tonight, raising his glass and smiling like he was proud of us, made me realize I've been too quick to judge. He didn't just take the money and walk away—he trusted us to carry this place forward. Maybe he's not so bad after all.

5: The number of dances I didn't sit out tonight. Logan pulled me onto the floor, and somehow, his confidence made it impossible not to move. Even when I felt silly, he just laughed and kept going, like none of it mattered except the two of us having fun. And when I queued up the Electric Slide? Forget it—everyone joined in, even Professor Avery. Watching the crowd try the Brookfield and the Smeeze was pure chaos, but in the best way.

6: The plates of sweet potato risotto I saw wiped clean. That's how you know you've got a hit. Ayesha leaned over to whisper that the new menu is already outperforming the old one. It's wild to think about how something so simple—analyzing the numbers, optimizing the recipes—could make this big of a difference. But it's not just about the food. It's about what it represents: survival, progress, hope.

7: The people I hugged tonight. Ayesha, of course, with her energy lighting up the room. Mom, who's already planning a holiday theme with snowflakes and cocoa bars. Booker, who gave a speech that had everyone clapping like crazy. And Grandpa James, who looked at me with this quiet pride that made me want to tear up again. It wasn't just a celebration—it felt like the beginning of something stronger, like we've finally found our footing again.

8: The times I caught myself smiling just thinking about the future. I didn't think I'd get to this point, where I could stand in the middle of the restaurant and feel… whole. Like all the struggles, all the nights I stayed up staring at spreadsheets or doubting myself, were worth it. And now? Now it feels like the only way is forward.

Tonight wasn't just about the restaurant or the food or even the celebration. It was about knowing we're not just surviving—we're thriving. And maybe for the first time, I believe we're here to stay.

FRIDAY, AUGUST 16

The high school parking lot thrummed with first-day excitement—cars weaving through crowded lanes, clusters of students shouting greetings, and bursts of laughter rising above the low rumble of engines. Cass stepped out of Logan's car, slinging her backpack over one shoulder. A few heads turned, taking note. She and Logan had gone Instagram official just a week earlier, and this was the first time many of their peers were seeing them together. Logan came around the car and slipped an arm over her shoulders.

"You ready for this chaos?" he asked with a grin.

Cass smirked. "Always. But don't think you're hiding in the back with your boys. You're sitting up front with me."

"Alright, alright." Logan held up his hands in mock surrender. "Anything for you, Freeman."

As they walked toward the main entrance, one of Logan's football teammates jogged up and slapped his shoulder. "Yo, Logan, you better not start skipping practice for her," Lincoln said, his grin stretching wide as he gave Cass a playful once-over. "She must be somethin' special. You serious about this guy?"

Cass tilted her head, smirking. "Yep. You got a problem with that?"

"Nah," the teammate said, grinning. "Just don't distract him too much."

Logan shook his head with a laugh. "I'll see you at practice, man."

Logan's arm stayed around her shoulders as they stepped inside. The familiar halls hummed with first-day bustle—the faint smell of freshly waxed floors mingling with the shouts of reunions and the sharp clatter of lockers slamming shut.

Near the main staircase, Alex and Sophia waved them over. Sophia held up a bright yellow box. "Sunny Hills pineapple cakes from Taiwan! First-day treat. Trust me, they're fire." Sophia grinned, bouncing on her toes as Alex let out an exaggerated laugh. She handed the box to Cass with a broad smile.

"Thanks! These are legit amazing," Cass said. "You didn't have to do this."

Sophia shrugged. "My aunt hooks us up every time she visits. She's obsessed with these. Plus, it's a thank-you for that night at the restaurant. My parents can't stop talking about it. My mom's still embarrassed about that video of her and my dad dancing."

"We gotta do brunch there next time," Alex chimed in. "That spot is unforgettable."

"Brunch sounds perfect," Cass said, glancing at Logan, who nodded. "Let's make it happen."

The group lingered, chatting until the bell rang. As Alex and Sophia headed to their first class, Logan nudged Cass gently. "See? Not so bad."

Lola bounded toward them, curls bouncing with every step. "There you are! First day and already stuck together. Selfie time!" She held up her phone and snapped a picture before typing furiously on her screen.

Cass raised an eyebrow. "Who are you sending that to?"

"Isaiah," Lola said, flashing a sly grin. "Gotta show him I'm out here thriving."

"What!" Cass gawked. "You've been dodging my calls, and I saw you dancing with him in the kids' book section of the restaurant. Keep it classy, Lola!" She grinned. "So, is the good ship LoSaiah is officially sailing now?"

"Not official yet," Lola said with a smirk, "but soon."

"Just make sure you don't crash it," Cass quipped.

Alex chimed in, "Lola, if you land him, there's no way he's getting away. Dude's probably already hooked."

After snapping a few more photos, Lola inspected her phone and smirked. "You're lucky I didn't post these with some corny caption."

"Let me see," Cass said, reaching for the phone.

"Nope." Lola held it just out of reach. "I already sent it, and you're not reading my texts."

Cass laughed. "Fine. Then send me one."

"Done," Lola said, hitting send. Her expression softened. "Too bad he's not here. I keep thinking how wild it'd be if he went to school with us."

"Total chaos," Cass teased. "But the good kind."

"Exactly," Lola said, her cheeks flushing. "For now, I'll keep him on his toes."

"Smart move," Logan said, chuckling. "Gotta keep him guessing."

With a dramatic flourish, Lola tucked her phone away. "Enough about me. Let's make junior year legendary."

Cass smiled, standing amid the easy rhythm of her friends' banter. "If this year's anything like the summer, it's gonna be unforgettable.

*****

Cass stepped into Ms. Jennings' office, the heavy oak door clicking softly shut and muffling the sounds from the hallway. The soft trickle of a desktop fountain and the faint scent of jasmine drifted through the space.

Ms. Jennings glanced up from her desk, surrounded by neatly arranged papers, books, and trinkets. "Just a moment, Cass," she said, slipping a document into an envelope with practiced ease. "Please, have a seat."

Cass lowered herself into the chair across from the desk, setting her bag carefully on the carpet. "I wasn't expecting to get called in, especially with school just starting," she said, her fingers twisting the strap of her bag.

"Don't worry, you're not in trouble," Ms. Jennings said, smiling. "I wanted to follow up on some feedback I've received about you. Professor Avery has been talking about how impressed she was with your performance at the data science camp and your contributions to the analytics meetup. She's really excited about the idea of a student-led data science group here at school. She was particularly impressed with your project on predictive analytics for urban transportation and how you led a technical discussion with professionals."

Cass shifted slightly in her seat. "Thanks! The camp was such a great experience, and working with those professionals was really eye-opening. It showed me how data science can solve real problems. And thanks again for writing the recommendation."

"You're welcome," Ms. Jennings replied. "It's a joy to help students like you get into these important programs."

"And your enthusiasm was clear," Ms. Jennings said, standing to retrieve a folder from her bookshelf. "Have you ever thought about starting a data science club here at school?"

"Starting something new can feel overwhelming," Ms. Jennings said. "But you're uniquely suited for this. Imagine teaching other students Python, R, and applied statistics, practical skills that could really help small businesses or nonprofits in our community."

Cass adjusted the strap of her bag, her gaze fixed on Ms. Jennings as she waited for her to continue.

“When I was your age,” Ms. Jennings continued, pulling a framed photo from her shelf, “I started our school’s first computer science club. I was nervous, but starting that club changed everything. It gave me confidence and opened doors I never expected.” The photo showed a younger Ms. Jennings standing beside a science fair project. “You don’t need to have all the answers. What matters is taking the first step.”

Cass looked at the picture as Ms. Jennings brought over a small robot figure from another shelf. Wires jutted out at odd angles, and a lopsided smile was drawn on its face. “My first attempt at robotics,” Ms. Jennings said, laughing. “Not state-of-the-art, but it taught me more than any textbook ever could.”

“So, what do I do first?” she asked.

Ms. Jennings handed her a yellowed checklist. “This guide has helped many students launch clubs over the years. Start with an informational meeting to gauge interest. I’ll help you organize it, and I might even get Professor Avery to join via video call.”

Cass took the checklist and nodded firmly. “Thank you, Ms. Jennings. I’ll do it.”

Ms. Jennings smiled wider. “Excellent. I know you’ll make a difference here.”

As Cass stood, the oak tree outside the window rose, its branches stretching under the afternoon sky.

“Count me in,” she said, her voice steady as she held the checklist tightly.

*****

The gentle glow of Cass’s desk lamp cast a warm circle of light across her cluttered desk. Her bedroom was dim, lit only by the lamp and the faint gleam of stars through the window. The soft murmur of voices drifted up from downstairs, mingling with bursts of laughter from the twins.

A soft ping broke the stillness, and Cass turned again toward her laptop. An email notification flashed on the screen. Then, Cass clicked it open. As her eyes scanned the message, she immediately reached for her phone and dialed Logan. The line barely rang before he picked up.

“Hey, Cass, what’s up?” Logan answered, his voice relaxed.

"I just got an email from the community soccer league," she began, her words rushing forth at once. "You won't believe this. They are using an algorithm to reassign players and teams."

"Wait, what? An algorithm for soccer team assignments?" Logan asked, his words punctuated by a laugh. "How does it even work? It's cool that a league is trying something so innovative."

Cass leaned forward, her posture shifting. "It's brilliant! They are analyzing performance stats from previous seasons, including goals, assists, and speed, to balance out the teams. No one will have an unfair advantage, and it's supposed to make the games more competitive next year." No one will have an unfair advantage, and it's supposed to make the games much more competitive next year.

"They're even holding a draft night to unveil the team assignments," she added. "I wonder how Alex will take it. Or Tracy and her dad."

"Or how Tracy and her dad will react," Logan said with a chuckle.

"True," Logan replied, his voice quiet. "That sounds pretty awesome. So... does that mean you're playing again?"

Cass reached under her desk and picked up the cleats, brushing off a fine layer of dust that had settled over months.

"It might be fun to play again," she admitted, glancing at the cleats under her desk. "Now that Dad has a handle on the restaurant..."

Logan spoke, voice upbeat. "We should go for it. You are always juggling so many things, but maybe this could be your break, something just for yourself."

Cass picked up the cleats tucked under her desk, brushing off a fine layer of dust before setting them carefully on the desk.

"You know what? Maybe I will," she said, her voice unwavering and sure. "I think I need this."

"Well, whatever happens, you've got my vote for MVP," Logan said.

"Thanks, Logan," she replied, her voice lifting slightly. "We'll see how it goes."

They both laughed. Cass set the cleats on her desk, faint starlight tracing patterns across the room as laughter from downstairs filled the quiet. Tomorrow, she'd lace them up and step onto the field, the official schedule already set.

She stood up, cleats in hand, and stepped into the hallway.

The End...

Acknowledgements

First, to God who gave me this incredible idea and who wakes me up every morning.

***

There is not enough ink, paper, or time to properly thank everyone who has contributed to this book and to my life.

To those whose names may not be listed here but whose presence has touched my journey in ways both big and small - thank you. I carry with me the memories of our shared experiences and the lessons learned from each of you. Your influence has woven itself into the very fabric of this story, and I will never forget how you've shaped both me and this book.

To my wife, Connie, my children, and my extended family - thank you for enduring and supporting this project with love, patience, and unwavering faith. Your belief in me, especially when the hours grew long and the path seemed uncertain, has been my greatest source of strength. This book would not exist without your sacrifices, your understanding, and your constant encouragement. You have been the foundation upon which this story was built, and for that, I am forever grateful.

To my brother, Matthew - thank you for being a steadfast sounding board, offering wisdom and perspective when I needed it most. Your support means more than words can convey.

To my parents - thank you for the early investment in technology that helped chart the course of my life. Your foresight and commitment gave me the tools to pursue my passions and shaped my understanding of the world.

To the coaches, mentors, managers, pastors, and teachers who invested so deeply in my life - thank you. Your guidance, your belief in me, and the lessons you imparted continue to resonate with me every day. I am who I am because of the impact you've had on me.

To my guys - Thank you for the encouragement, accountability, and support. For the check-ins, the challenges, and the moments of clarity when I needed them most. For pushing me to keep going, for keeping me grounded, and for reminding me why this work matters. Your friendship and brotherhood mean more than I can express, and I'm grateful to have you in my corner.

To my team - thank you for being a group whose talent, passion, and dedication inspire me every day. Your hard work and creativity are reflected in everything I do, and this project is no exception.

To Rhonda Glover Reese and Elva Hicks Glover - thank you for your unwavering support, your belief in this project, and for always being there to lend a hand when needed. Your encouragement has meant the world to me, and I deeply appreciate all that you've done.

To the editors and early readers of this work - thank you for your patience, your insightful feedback, and your vision. Your efforts were integral in bringing this book to life, and I am deeply grateful for your time and dedication.

I have been the beneficiary of great relationships, opportunities and sincerely appreciate the kindness, generosity, and wisdom of so many people who have shaped my journey. From casual conversations that sparked new ideas to deep, meaningful discussions that challenged me to grow, each interaction has left an imprint on my life and on the pages of this book.

To my colleagues and friends in the tech industry, education, and publishing-thank you for sharing your expertise, your encouragement, and your belief in the power of stories to inspire change. Your contributions, whether through mentorship, collaboration, or simply cheering me on, have been invaluable.

Lastly, to every reader who picks up this book-thank you. Thank you for allowing me to share this journey with you, for embracing these characters, and for joining me in exploring the limitless possibilities that exist in STEM, in storytelling, and in life itself.

This book is the result of a community, a collective effort of love, wisdom, and encouragement. I am honored and humbled to have had so many incredible people walk alongside me on this journey.

With deep gratitude,
Bryan H. Kelly

About The Author

From devouring books in rainy Seattle to leading tech teams in South Korea, Bryan Kelly's journey has always been fueled by a love of great stories and the thrill of solving puzzles. His path in technology took him from Bradley University to a 25-year career in some of the world's biggest tech companies, where he led global engineering teams and transformation initiatives. Along the way, he earned an Executive Leadership Certificate from Seattle University—but more importantly, he discovered his greatest joy in sharing stories that make complex ideas feel simple.

The idea for Cass Freeman sparked one afternoon as Bryan scrolled through summer programs in data science for his kids. He realized how few stories existed where young people—especially those from backgrounds where opportunities in tech can feel out of reach—could see themselves in the field. That moment lit a fire: what if he could combine his passion for storytelling with his tech expertise to create a world where curiosity, resilience, and problem-solving take center stage?

Beyond telling a compelling story, Bryan was committed to depicting technology with honesty and accuracy, ensuring that Cass Freeman authentically reflects the real-world challenges, innovations, and opportunities in STEM. He wanted young readers to see not just that they belong in tech, but that there's a real path forward for them.

Today, Bryan lives in the Bay Area with his wife of 26 years, Connie, their children, and their ever-curious tortoise, Tank. Whether he's writing, traveling, or getting lost in a great book, he's always drawn to big ideas—and through Cass Freeman, he invites young readers to see technology not just as a career field, but as a place where they belong.

Author's Note

Some histories don't make it into textbooks, but they shape the world around us in ways we can still feel today. *Cass Freeman: Decision Trees* blends fact and fiction, weaving real struggles and triumphs into Cass's journey.

A Freeway Through the Heart of Oakland

The construction of Interstate 880, like many freeway projects across the United States, wasn't just about roads—it was about power, displacement, and who was considered expendable. In the 1950s and 1960s, federal and state officials approved the construction of multiple highways that cut through Black and working-class neighborhoods under the banner of "urban renewal." In Oakland, West Oakland bore the brunt of this policy. Once a thriving Black community, home to the jazz clubs of 7th Street, the Pullman porters who helped fuel the Civil Rights Movement, and generations of families who built businesses and legacies, it was gutted by the construction of I-880, I-580, and the Cypress Freeway.

Highway planners routed freeways through communities that had little political power to resist them, displacing thousands of families, destroying homes, and severing businesses from their customers. What followed was a cycle of economic decline, forced migration, and environmental harm. Today, the legacy of those decisions is visible in the air itself.

Oakland is home to two major freeways—Interstate 880, which cuts through historically Black and Latino neighborhoods, and Interstate 580, which runs through wealthier and predominantly white areas of the city. But there's a stark difference between them: heavy trucks are banned from I-580 but allowed on I-880. This means that diesel pollution, which is linked to asthma, heart disease, and shortened life expectancy, is concentrated in West and East Oakland, affecting the people who live there. In these areas, children are far more likely to develop asthma and other respiratory illnesses, and residents experience significantly higher rates of premature death due to air pollution (Environmental Defense Fund, 2021).

For decades, Black and Latino communities have fought for environmental justice, pushing for cleaner air and health protections, but the inequalities remain stark. While these systemic injustices aren't the central focus of Cass Freeman: Decision Trees, they form the world Cass is growing up in. Like so many before her, she is learning to ask why things are the way they are—and what she can do to change them.

Growing up, I didn't think much about freeways beyond the traffic they caused. But as I learned more about the history of city planning and displacement, I started seeing the roads differently—not just as infrastructure, but as a map of past decisions that shaped entire communities. That's the kind of awareness I wanted Cass to have in this story.

The Fight for Libraries and Access to Knowledge

Another real-world inspiration in this book comes from the history of private libraries and Black-led reading spaces. Before public libraries were truly accessible to all, many communities relied on subscription-based libraries, which required fees or memberships, effectively barring Black readers from access to books.

But Black communities built their own. In 1833, the Library Company of Colored People was founded in Philadelphia as one of the first lending libraries for Black Americans. During Reconstruction, Freedmen's Bureau schools (1865-1872) established reading rooms to help newly freed Black citizens access education. In the 1960s, at the height of the Civil Rights Movement, activists created Freedom Libraries, temporary reading spaces set up in the Deep South to counter segregation and expand literacy. These weren't just places to check out books—they were sites of resistance and empowerment (JSTOR Daily, 2021).

Even in cities with public libraries, racist policies often limited access. In Oakland, Carnegie-funded libraries opened in the early 1900s, but Black and Chinese patrons faced discrimination in borrowing books and using reading rooms. The legacy of exclusion meant that Black-owned bookstores and independent reading spaces became lifelines for knowledge.

Booker's Pages and Plates in Cass Freeman: Decision Trees carries that spirit, standing as a testament to what's possible when people fight to make learning and community accessible. Like Cass, every generation must decide: Will we keep the doors open for the next?

The Power of Patterns—In Data and in History

Cass's journey is about more than data—it's about recognizing the patterns of the past, questioning them, and shaping something new. The freeway through West Oakland wasn't an accident. The libraries that denied Black readers weren't a mistake. These were choices.

And just like Cass, we all face choices about how we engage with the world around us. Cass is learning to see the world through patterns—of data, of history, of power. My hope is that young readers do the same. Because the patterns of the past don't have to shape the future. That choice belongs to us.

— Bryan H. Kelly

Further Reading & Sources

For those interested in the historical and environmental issues mentioned in this book, here are a few sources worth exploring:

Oakland's Freeway & Air Pollution

- Environmental Defense Fund. A Tale of Two Freeways: Air Pollution in Oakland. Available at www.edf.org/airqualitymaps/oakland/tale-two-freeways.
- KQED. Trucks Are Banned on Oakland's I-580—Why? Available at www.kqed.org/news/11879641.
- Environmental Defense Fund. Health Disparities in Oakland's Air Quality. Available at www.edf.org/airqualitymaps/oakland/health-disparities.
- Oaklandside. How Freeways Changed West Oakland Forever. Available at www.oaklandside.org.

Black-Led Libraries & Access to Knowledge

- JSTOR Daily. Freedom Libraries and the Fight for Library Equity. Available at www.jstor.org/daily.
- Selby, Mike. Freedom Libraries: The Untold Story of Libraries for African Americans in the South. Rowman & Littlefield Publishers, 2019. **ISBN: 978-1538182444.**

Glossary

UNDERSTANDING DATA

A/B Testing: A/B testing is an experiment where two versions of something, like a website or an ad, are shown to different groups to see which one performs better. One version is the original (A), and the other has a change (B). The results help businesses make data-driven improvements.
Why it matters: Companies use A/B testing to optimize marketing, improve user experience, and increase sales by figuring out what works best.

Algorithms: An algorithm is a set of step-by-step instructions a computer follows to solve a problem or perform a task. Algorithms power everything from search engines to social media feeds. They can be simple, like sorting numbers, or complex, like recommending movies.
Why it matters: Algorithms help process huge amounts of data quickly, making decisions in everything from healthcare to finance.

Clustering Algorithms: Clustering algorithms group similar data points together based on their characteristics. They help businesses segment customers, detect patterns, and organize large datasets. Popular clustering methods include K-Means and Hierarchical Clustering.
Why it matters: Clustering helps businesses personalize marketing, detect fraud, and improve recommendations.

Confidence Intervals: A confidence interval is a range of values that estimates an unknown number, like the average height of all students in a school. It shows how certain a result is, usually with a percentage like 95%. The wider the interval, the less precise the estimate.
Why it matters: Confidence intervals help businesses and scientists measure uncertainty and make more reliable predictions.

CSV (Comma-Separated Values): A CSV file stores data in a simple format where values are separated by commas. It is commonly used to share and store structured data, like spreadsheets. Almost any data analysis tool can open CSV files.
Why it matters: CSV files make it easy to transfer and analyze data between different programs.

Data Science: Data science is the process of collecting, analyzing, and interpreting data to find patterns and make decisions. It combines math, statistics, and programming to uncover insights. Businesses use it to predict trends and solve problems.
Why it matters: Data science powers recommendations on Netflix, fraud detection in banking, and even sports analytics.

Data-Driven Decision Making: Data-driven decision making (DDDM) means using facts and numbers instead of guesswork to make business choices. Companies analyze past trends to predict future success. This approach reduces risks and improves accuracy.
Why it matters: It helps companies avoid costly mistakes and make informed choices that lead to better results.

MAKING PREDICTIONS

Anomaly Detection: Anomaly detection identifies unusual data points that don't fit expected patterns. It helps detect fraud, system failures, or even diseases by spotting outliers. Methods include Isolation Forests and Z-Score Analysis.
Why it matters: It helps companies catch problems early, whether it's a hacker attacking a system or a factory machine failing.

ARIMA (Autoregressive Integrated Moving Average): ARIMA is a statistical model used to analyze and forecast time series data. It helps predict future trends by identifying patterns in past data. Businesses use ARIMA to forecast sales, stock prices, and economic trends.
Why it matters: ARIMA improves decision-making by predicting future outcomes based on historical data.

Decision Tree: A decision tree is a flowchart-like model that helps make decisions by following different paths based on conditions. It breaks down complex problems into smaller, simpler steps. Businesses use decision trees for customer service automation, fraud detection, and financial planning.
Why it matters: Decision trees make it easier to analyze complicated decisions and predict possible outcomes.

Feature Selection: Feature selection is the process of choosing the most important data points (features) to use in a predictive model. By removing unnecessary information, models become faster and more accurate. It improves efficiency in machine learning and data analysis.
Why it matters: Choosing the right features makes machine learning models more effective and prevents unnecessary computation.

Hyperparameters: Hyperparameters are settings in machine learning models that control how the model learns from data. They affect accuracy, speed, and performance but must be tuned manually. Examples include learning rates, the number of decision tree splits, and the size of neural networks.

Why it matters: Properly tuned hyperparameters improve model performance and accuracy in real-world applications. **Logistic Regression:** Logistic regression is a type of statistical analysis used to predict binary outcomes, like whether a customer will buy a product (yes/no). It helps businesses understand how different factors influence decisions. Logistic regression is commonly used in medical research, finance, and marketing.
Why it matters: It helps companies and researchers predict outcomes and make data-driven decisions.

Predictive Analytics: Predictive analytics uses past data to predict what might happen in the future. Businesses use it to forecast sales, hospitals use it to predict patient needs, and sports teams use it to analyze performance. It relies on statistics, machine learning, and historical trends.
Why it matters: It helps organizations make better decisions and prepare for the future instead of reacting to problems too late.

Prophet: Prophet is a forecasting tool created by Facebook that helps analyze and predict trends in time series data. It is designed to handle seasonality, holidays, and other patterns that affect predictions. Businesses use it to forecast sales, website traffic, and financial performance.
Why it matters: Prophet makes forecasting easier and more accurate, helping businesses plan for the future.

Random Forest Model: A random forest is a machine learning model that combines multiple decision trees to improve accuracy. It reduces errors and prevents overfitting by averaging the predictions of different trees. Random forests are commonly used in fraud detection, medical diagnoses, and recommendation systems.
Why it matters: Random forests make reliable predictions and handle large datasets effectively, making them useful in many industries.

Regression Analysis: Regression analysis is a way to find relationships between variables, like how studying more hours might lead to better test scores. It helps predict future outcomes by understanding past data. Different types, like linear and logistic regression, are used in data science.
Why it matters: Businesses and researchers use regression to make forecasts and understand important trends.

Seasonality Analysis: Seasonality analysis identifies repeating patterns in data that happen at regular intervals, like daily, weekly, or yearly trends. Examples include holiday shopping spikes, flu seasons, or energy consumption trends. Businesses use it to plan for predictable changes in demand.
Why it matters: Recognizing seasonal patterns helps companies prepare and optimize strategies based on expected trends.

Sentiment Analysis: Sentiment analysis is the process of using AI to determine whether a piece of text expresses positive, negative, or neutral emotions. Businesses use it to analyze customer reviews, social media posts, and surveys. It helps companies understand public perception of their brand.
Why it matters: Sentiment analysis helps companies improve customer satisfaction by responding to concerns in real time.

Time Series Analysis: Time series analysis looks at data collected over time to identify trends, patterns, or seasonality. Examples include stock prices, weather patterns, and sales data. Special models like ARIMA and Prophet are used for forecasting. Why it matters: Visualizing time-based data makes it easier to spot trends and patterns over time, helping businesses, economists, and scientists make better predictions.
Why it matters: It helps businesses predict sales, governments plan resources, and scientists study climate change.

Z-Score Analysis: Z-Score analysis is a statistical method that measures how far a data point is from the average. It helps identify unusual values or outliers in a dataset. Businesses use Z-Score analysis to detect fraud, track financial performance, and analyze quality control.
Why it matters: Z-Score analysis helps identify anomalies that could indicate risks, errors, or new opportunities.

TOOLS FOR ANALYSIS

ETL (Extract, Transform, Load): ETL is a process used to move data from one system to another. "Extract" pulls data from sources, "Transform" cleans and organizes it, and "Load" stores it in a database. This process ensures data is ready for analysis.
Why it matters: ETL helps businesses integrate and manage large amounts of data efficiently.

Geocoding: Geocoding is the process of converting addresses or place names into geographic coordinates (latitude and longitude). Businesses use geocoding to analyze location-based data, such as customer distribution and delivery routes. It is also used in mapping services like Google Maps.
Why it matters: Geocoding helps businesses make location-based decisions, such as optimizing delivery routes and targeting local customers.

GitHub: GitHub is an online platform where programmers store, share, and collaborate on code. It tracks changes using version control, allowing teams to work together without overwriting each other's work. Many open-source projects and companies use GitHub for software development.
Why it matters: GitHub makes teamwork easier and helps developers keep track of code changes over time.

GPT Agent: A GPT Agent is an AI-powered system that can generate human-like text, answer questions, and automate tasks. It is based on large language models like OpenAI's GPT. Businesses use GPT Agents for customer support, content creation, and data analysis.
Why it matters: GPT Agents help automate repetitive tasks and improve efficiency in industries like marketing, customer service, and education.

Heat Maps: Heat maps are visual tools that show data intensity using colors. They are commonly used in website analytics to see where users click the most, in sales reports to highlight high-revenue areas, and in sports to track player movements.
Why it matters: Heat maps make complex data easy to understand, helping businesses identify trends and improve user experience.

Isolation Forests: Isolation forests are a machine learning method for detecting anomalies in large datasets. They work by identifying data points that don't follow normal patterns. They are often used in fraud detection and cybersecurity.
Why it matters: Isolation forests help businesses detect fraudulent activities, system failures, and security threats quickly.

JIT (Just-In-Time): Just-In-Time (JIT) is a system where businesses produce or order goods only when they are needed, reducing waste and storage costs. It is commonly used in manufacturing and retail. JIT helps businesses stay efficient and avoid overproduction.
Why it matters: JIT saves money by reducing inventory costs and ensuring products are available when needed.

Kaggle: Kaggle is a website where data scientists and machine learning enthusiasts compete, share code, and collaborate on projects. It provides datasets and challenges that help people practice their skills. Many companies use Kaggle competitions to solve complex data problems.
Why it matters: Kaggle is a great place to learn data science, test skills, and connect with experts.

Linear Programming: Linear programming is a mathematical method used to find the best possible outcome in a given situation. It is often used in business and engineering to optimize resources like time, money, or materials. Examples include minimizing costs or maximizing profits.
Why it matters: Linear programming helps businesses make the most efficient use of their resources.

Merge Functions: Merge functions are used to combine data from multiple sources into a single dataset. In tools like SQL and Pandas, merging helps organize and analyze data efficiently. It is commonly used in data science and business reporting.
Why it matters: Merging data helps businesses and researchers organize information and gain better insights.

Pandas: Pandas is a Python library that helps organize, clean, and analyze data in tables. It is widely used in data science for handling spreadsheets and databases. Pandas makes working with large datasets much easier.
Why it matters: It's a key tool for data scientists to process and analyze information quickly.

Pandas Script: A Pandas script is a Python program that uses the Pandas library to process and analyze data. It can filter, sort, and manipulate large datasets quickly. Many data scientists use Pandas to clean and explore information.
Why it matters: Pandas scripts make working with data easier and more efficient in research and business applications.

Power BI: Power BI is a tool that helps businesses turn raw data into easy-to-read charts and reports. It connects to different data sources and provides real-time insights. Companies use it to track performance and find trends.
Why it matters: Power BI makes complex data understandable and helps businesses make informed decisions.

Python: Python is a programming language used for data science, AI, and web development. It is easy to learn and has powerful tools for handling data. Many data scientists use Python to write scripts that analyze large amounts of information.
Why it matters: Python makes it possible to automate tasks, build AI models, and analyze big data easily.

SQL (Structured Query Language): SQL is a language used to store, retrieve, and manage data in databases. Businesses use it to quickly find and analyze large amounts of information. It is essential for anyone working with data.
Why it matters: SQL powers search engines, apps, and financial reports, making it a must-know for data professionals.

Tableau: Tableau is a software that helps people visualize data in graphs, charts, and dashboards. It makes complex data easier to understand. Businesses use it to track performance and make decisions.
Why it matters: Visualizing data helps people spot patterns and trends that aren't obvious in raw numbers.

Telemetry: Telemetry is the automatic collection of data from remote locations, often used in vehicles, smart devices, and online applications. It helps businesses monitor performance and make real-time adjustments. Telemetry data can improve efficiency and safety.
Why it matters: Companies use telemetry to track and improve the performance of everything from self-driving cars to mobile apps.

Version Control: Version control is a system that tracks changes to files over time. It allows teams to collaborate without losing progress. Popular tools like Git help programmers work together efficiently.
Why it matters: It prevents data loss and makes teamwork easier when multiple people edit the same project.

BUSINESS INSIGHTS

Cash Flow: Cash flow is the movement of money in and out of a business. It helps businesses track if they are making a profit or losing money. Positive cash flow means a company has more money coming in than going out.
Why it matters: Monitoring cash flow helps businesses stay financially healthy and avoid running out of money.

Churn Analysis: Churn analysis examines why customers stop using a product or service. It identifies patterns that help businesses reduce customer loss. Companies use it to improve customer satisfaction and retention.
Why it matters: Reducing churn saves money and helps businesses grow by keeping more customers.

Churn Rate: Churn rate measures how many customers stop using a product or service over a certain period. A high churn rate can mean customers are unhappy. Companies work to lower churn by improving products and customer service.
Why it matters: Keeping customers is often cheaper than finding new ones, so businesses track churn closely.

Conversion Rates: Conversion rate is the percentage of people who take a desired action, such as making a purchase or signing up for a newsletter. It helps businesses measure the effectiveness of marketing and website design. A higher conversion rate means more customers are engaging with the business.
Why it matters: Tracking conversion rates helps businesses improve their strategies to attract and retain customers.

Customer Lifetime Value (CLV): CLV estimates how much money a customer will spend at a business over their lifetime. Companies use this to decide how much to invest in keeping customers happy. A high CLV means a customer is valuable to the company.
Why it matters: Understanding CLV helps businesses focus on long-term success instead of short-term sales.

Customer Segmentation: Customer segmentation is the practice of dividing customers into groups based on characteristics like age, location, or spending habits. Businesses use these segments to tailor marketing strategies. It helps companies understand customer needs better.
Why it matters: Personalized marketing increases sales and improves customer relationships.

Debt Restructuring: Debt restructuring is when a company changes the terms of its debt to make payments more manageable. This can involve lowering interest rates, extending due dates, or negotiating new terms. Businesses use it to avoid bankruptcy and improve financial stability.
Why it matters: Debt restructuring helps companies stay afloat during financial difficulties.

Financial Modeling: Financial modeling is the process of creating a mathematical representation of a business's financial situation. It helps companies forecast revenue, expenses, and risks. Investors and executives use financial models to make strategic decisions.
Why it matters: Financial modeling helps businesses prepare for the future and manage risks effectively.

KPI (Key Performance Indicator): KPIs are measurable goals that track how well a business is doing. Examples include sales growth, customer retention, or social media engagement. Good KPIs help businesses stay focused on success.
Why it matters: Without KPIs, companies wouldn't know if they're improving or failing.

Operational Efficiency: Operational efficiency measures how well a business uses its resources to maximize output. It involves reducing waste, improving processes, and increasing productivity. Companies strive for efficiency to lower costs and increase profits.
Why it matters: More efficient operations mean lower costs and higher profits for businesses.

POS (Point of Sale): A POS system is the technology businesses use to process sales, track inventory, and manage customer transactions. It includes cash registers, card readers, and software that records sales data. Many businesses use POS systems to streamline operations.
Why it matters: POS systems make selling products easier and help businesses track their financial performance.

POS Reconciliation: POS reconciliation is the process of matching sales records from the POS system with actual cash and credit card transactions. It ensures that all money is accounted for and detects errors or fraud. Businesses perform this daily to prevent financial mistakes.
Why it matters: Accurate reconciliation prevents financial losses and keeps business accounts balanced.

ROI (Return on Investment): ROI measures how much profit a business makes compared to what it spends. A high ROI means the investment was worth it, while a low ROI suggests it wasn't. It's used to evaluate marketing campaigns, projects, and company performance.
Why it matters: Businesses use ROI to decide where to spend money for the best results.

DATA QUALITY & MANAGEMENT

Data Cleaning: Data cleaning is the process of fixing or removing incorrect, incomplete, or duplicate data. It ensures that the data being used is accurate and reliable. If the data is messy, any analysis or predictions based on it could be wrong.
Why it matters: Clean data prevents bad decisions and helps businesses and scientists get reliable results.

Data Integrity: Data integrity means ensuring that data is accurate, consistent, and secure throughout its lifecycle. This involves preventing mistakes, unauthorized changes, or corruption of data. Reliable data is essential for making good decisions.
Why it matters: Without data integrity, businesses could lose money, and scientists could make incorrect conclusions.

Data Pipeline: A data pipeline is a system that moves data from one place to another for processing and analysis. It involves collecting, cleaning, transforming, and storing data before it is used. Pipelines help automate workflows and ensure data is always up to date.
Why it matters: Data pipelines allow businesses to analyze real-time data efficiently, supporting better decision-making and automation.

Data Validation: Data validation checks that data is correct, complete, and in the right format before using it. This helps prevent errors by catching issues early. Validation can include checking if dates are formatted correctly or ensuring values are within a reasonable range.
Why it matters: It helps prevent mistakes in reports, predictions, and customer interactions by making sure data is trustworthy.

GIGO (Garbage In, Garbage Out): GIGO means that bad data leads to bad results. If incorrect or low-quality data is used in analysis, the conclusions will also be flawed. This applies to everything from business reports to artificial intelligence.
Why it matters: Ensuring high-quality data helps businesses and researchers make accurate and reliable decisions.

Merge Functions: Merge functions are used to combine data from multiple sources into a single dataset. In tools like SQL and Pandas, merging helps organize and analyze data efficiently. It is commonly used in data science and business reporting.
Why it matters: Merging data helps businesses and researchers organize information and gain better insights.

Missing Data Imputation: Missing data imputation is a technique for filling in gaps in a dataset using estimates based on existing information. For example, if a customer didn't fill in their age, an algorithm might guess based on similar people. It prevents gaps from causing errors in analysis.
Why it matters: Missing data can lead to incorrect results, so filling in the blanks smartly helps keep predictions accurate.

Version Control: Version control is a system that tracks changes to files over time. It allows teams to collaborate without losing progress. Popular tools like Git help programmers work together efficiently.
Why it matters: It prevents data loss and makes teamwork easier when multiple people edit the same project.

VISUALIZATION & REPORTING

Bar Charts: Bar charts are visual representations of data using rectangular bars to show comparisons between categories. They are commonly used in business reports and research to compare values. The height of each bar represents the amount of data in that category.
Why it matters: Bar charts make it easier to compare different groups and understand trends at a glance.

Dashboard: A dashboard is a visual interface that displays key business data in an easy-to-read format. It combines graphs, charts, and summaries to provide real-time insights. Businesses use dashboards to track performance, sales, and operational efficiency.
Why it matters: Dashboards help businesses monitor progress and make data-driven decisions quickly.

Heat Maps: Heat maps are visual tools that show data intensity using colors. They are commonly used in website analytics to see where users click the most, in sales reports to highlight high-revenue areas, and in sports to track player movements.
Why it matters: Heat maps make complex data easy to understand, helping businesses identify trends and improve user experience.

Power BI: Power BI is a tool that helps businesses turn raw data into easy-to-read charts and reports. It connects to different data sources and provides real-time insights. Companies use it to track performance and find trends.
Why it matters: Power BI makes complex data understandable and helps businesses make informed decisions.

Scatter Plots: Scatter plots are graphs that show the relationship between two variables by plotting dots on a grid. They help identify trends, correlations, and outliers. Scientists, economists, and businesses use scatter plots to analyze relationships between factors.
Why it matters: Scatter plots reveal connections between variables, helping businesses and researchers make better decisions.

SQL (Structured Query Language): SQL is a language used to store, retrieve, and manage data in databases. Businesses use it to quickly find and analyze large amounts of information. It is essential for anyone working with data.
Why it matters: SQL powers search engines, apps, and financial reports, making it a must-know for data professionals.

Tableau: Tableau is a software that helps people visualize data in graphs, charts, and dashboards. It makes complex data easier to understand. Businesses use it to track performance and make decisions.
Why it matters: Visualizing data helps people spot patterns and trends that aren't obvious in raw numbers.

Time Series Plots: A time series plot is a type of graph that shows how data changes over time. It helps identify trends, cycles, and patterns. Businesses use time series plots to analyze stock prices, sales performance, and website traffic. *Why it matters: Visualizing time-based data makes it easier to spot trends and make better decisions.*

Made in the USA
Columbia, SC
22 April 2025

03ce7af3-e4a7-4b8f-95f0-e190a537ff65R02